Ga

At the gate th... ...ked back at the gard... ...us, here. I first saw it in summer, and now I've seen it in all the seasons but spring."

"You'll like it then," Amelia said. Her resolve not to cry weakened, and her eyes filled with tears. "The mimosa and azaleas bloom then. That's its prettiest season."

"You're more beautiful than all of them," he said, pulling her into the security of his embrace. "I like to think of you like this garden—changing, yet never changing. Everlasting. I wish this could be our whole world."

"I'll bring all of your letters here to read them," she promised, as her unchecked tears stained her cheeks and dampened the lapel of his wedding suit. "It will be as if you're here beside me. And whenever I write you I'll send you a leaf or a pressed flower so you'll always have the garden with you, too."

"Do that, Amelia," he said softly. "You do that."

She found there was too much she wanted to say, so she said nothing at all.

Everlasting

LYNDA TRENT

HarperPaperbacks
A Division of HarperCollinsPublishers

This is a work of fiction. The characters, incidents, and dialogues are products of the author's imagination and are not to be construed as real. Any resemblance to actual events or persons, living or dead, is entirely coincidental.

HarperPaperbacks *A Division of* HarperCollins*Publishers*
10 East 53rd Street, New York, N.Y. 10022

Cover illustration by Peter Fiore

First printing: March 1991

Printed in the United States of America

HarperPaperbacks and colophon are trademarks of HarperCollins*Publishers*

10 9 8 7 6 5 4 3 2 1

To Erin Elaine Trent and new beginnings.

Even the seasons form
a great circle in their changing,
and always come back again to where
they were. The life of a man is a circle from
childhood to childhood, and so it is in
everything where power moves.

—*Black Elk*

PROLOGUE
JANUARY, 1986

THE PONDEROUS GRANDFATHER CLOCK TICKED away the quiet minutes in the hall as Amelia Radcliff made her way to the front window. Her movements were slower these days, especially with the gusty winter wind aggravating her rheumatism. A twinge of pain drew her attention to her blue-veined hand as she brushed aside the lace curtain, but she reflexively dismissed the discomfort and peered across the lawn to the circular driveway. The sound she had heard was the arrival of a long black limousine, and even as she watched, her sister's legs swung out of the dim interior. Leave it to Electra to arrive in style.

Amelia waited until Electra paid the driver, then let the curtain fall back. Thank goodness Electra was alone this time, she thought as she smoothed the lace folds into place. At least age had some advantages.

Although she heard Electra mounting the steps and crossing the wide porch, Amelia waited. The bell chimed deep in the shadowy recesses of the house. Amelia paused a few more seconds, then crossed the marbled foyer to the front door.

"For heaven's sake, Amelia. It's cold out here. Didn't you hear me drive up?" Electra bustled into the house in a cloud of furs and Chanel. "Where's Jansen? She's supposed to open the door."

"If you mean Helga, she's in the kitchen, I expect. Her hearing isn't what it once was." Amelia carefully closed the door against the blustery Virginia day. The heavy bolt clicked automatically into place. "I don't know why you've taken to ringing the bell as if you're company, anyway."

Electra ignored her. "Good heavens, but it's hot in here! Why do you have the thermostat set so high?"

Amelia cast a disgruntled look at her sister. "It feels quite comfortable to me. Take off your coat and you'll be cooler."

Electra slipped the silver fox from her shoulders and carelessly draped it on the hall tree. Her dress, an impeccably cut rich navy, shaped her still-remarkable figure, encasing her in an aura of elegant sophistication—as did all Electra's clothes. She firmly believed she was one of her best showcases for the fashions she designed. She glanced at Amelia's good but serviceable dress and made a visible effort not to grimace.

As they passed through the wide oak doors into the front parlor, a mantel clock, ticking in silvery notes, chimed a quick tune signaling the half hour. Amelia settled into a wing chair near the fireplace. "I expected you earlier."

"My plane was late leaving New York—an abominable snowstorm. The pilot said it would be snowing here by tomorrow."

"I hope not. It's so hard to go outside in the snow." The longing on Amelia's face as she looked toward the wide windows was tinged with disappointment. "I'm always afraid I'll fall. And my legs and back ache when it's cold."

"Well, you don't have to worry about being cold in here." Electra went to the thermostat on the wall and turned it down several degrees. "It's like an oven in this room."

Amelia drew a steadying breath. This was no ordinary visit. This was the beginning of a new cycle in her life, one she had dreaded for months. "So you've come home to stay," she stated, rather than asked.

"Yes." Electra walked over to the end table and picked up one of the fragile porcelain figurines. "I've come home at last." With a brittle laugh she added, "I'm eighty now. It's time I retired."

"Eighty," Amelia mused as if the age surprised her. "Then I'm seventy-eight."

"You don't remember?"

Amelia shrugged. "There are so many more important things for me to keep up with. My age seems trivial."

Electra sighed as she replaced the figurine at a slightly different angle. "How I envy you. All these years and you've never had to leave Willowbrook."

Amelia made no response.

"At last I'm home to stay." Electra strolled over to the fireplace and let the crackling flames warm her legs. "We'll be just as we once were. The Radcliff sisters at home."

"That was a long time ago. Most of our friends are dead. And many of the ones who aren't have been put away in old folks' homes."

"Nursing homes," Electra corrected as she resumed her pacing.

"Whatever you call them, the result is the same."

"Then we'll make new friends," Electra said with a flare of exuberance. "Younger ones, who will enjoy dancing and music and excitement."

"In Catawba Mills?"

"We'll import them if necessary!" With a dramatic flair, she swept open the curtains. The pale sunlight streaming onto the Aubusson rug brightened its age-mellowed floral design. "No more melancholy! Willowbrook will be full of laughter again!"

Amelia gripped the arms of her chair more firmly than necessary and boosted herself up. Wordlessly she went to the figurine Electra had moved and put it back in its former position. Then she walked to the thermostat and returned it to the setting she preferred. "Close the curtain, Electra, or you'll fade the rug."

Her sister frowned. "You act as if you're a hundred years old."

"Well, I'm getting there. Where is your luggage?"

"It's to be sent from the airport. I was in such a hurry to get home to Willowbrook, I didn't want to wait for it."

Amelia nodded. "Sam Tucker's boy works there. He'll see to it."

"Sam Tucker?"

"His grandfather owned the dry goods store downtown."

"Oh, *those* Tuckers. I haven't thought of them in years." Electra wandered back to the fireplace and stroked the mantel's dust-free satin finish. She hadn't expected the place still to be kept so spotless.

Darkness returned to the room as Amelia drew the curtains back into place. Electra turned to her with a scowl of disapproval. "This place is like a museum. I'm half afraid to talk out loud in here."

"Papa bought this carpet at the turn of the century, and I've taken care of it all these years. I'm not going to let it fade now." Amelia sat back down and regarded her sister. "Are you sure you've made the right choice? Willowbrook will be awfully slow after New York City."

"I know." Electra wrapped her arms around her slim body in a hug. "I've dreamed of this day since I left here that first time. Do you remember, Amelia?"

"I remember."

"It was in the late spring, and I was sure I would make my fortune and be home again in a year, maybe two." Her smile wavered. "That was nearly sixty years ago."

"Over sixty," Amelia corrected as she straightened the tatted lace armrest cover. "Sixty-one years this coming spring," she repeated.

"Well, I'm home at last. Just as I said I would be."

"And now it's my time," Amelia mused. "My time to get out there and see the world."

Electra was quick to point out the obvious. "You're a little old to strike out on a jaunt around the world, don't you think?"

Amelia held out her thin, knotted hands and studied the years she saw sculpted there. With mild reproach, she said, "I was about to say that."

"For goodness' sake, don't start in on me the minute I walk in the door!" Electra sat on the velvet couch and crossed her legs. "That's not my fault. One of us had to do something."

"Yes. One of us had to do *something*," Amelia echoed

with accusatory emphasis on the last word.

Electra looked away, not wanting Amelia to see the crimson that she knew must be coloring her pale cheeks. "Don't start in on that, either. How was I to know?"

Amelia studied her sister. Electra looked much younger than her years; she could easily have passed for a woman of seventy. Ruefully, Amelia had to admit the same was not true of herself. Her appearance, like her age, was usually a trivial matter to her, but today, right now, she cared that her older sister looked younger. "Maybe I will travel," she said to goad Electra. "I could take Helga as my companion. We could see the world."

"Helga can barely see across the room, and she can't hear a doorbell."

"Then I'll be her companion. That would be an amusing switch."

"You never did seem to understand that our servants are not our equals."

The barb hit home, and Amelia responded with a scathing glare. "That was a long time ago," she said, her voice trembling with suppressed emotion. "A long, long time ago."

Electra regretted the pain her caustic comment had inflicted and wanted to apologize, but experience had taught her it was better simply to drop the matter. After all, Amelia was not likely to apologize, either. Feeling edgy, Electra fished in her handbag for a cigarette, and as she lit it, she noticed Amelia was glaring at her through the haze of white smoke.

"You shouldn't smoke, you know."

"At my age? I do as I please."

"What you do to your body is up to you. I meant it's

not good for the furnishings. After you leave I always have to air out the whole house."

"I won't be leaving. Remember?"

Amelia looked briefly confused, then snapped, "Of course I remember."

Electra drew the smoke deep into her lungs, then exhaled it upward toward the chandelier. She felt terribly uneasy, not so much because they were squabbling, but because Amelia had aged so in the past year. Amelia was, after all, her younger sister, and Electra didn't like to be reminded of the passage of time. She feared growing old, and had fought it since she discovered her first wrinkle. Her only comfort was that she looked younger than Amelia. Although both had gray hair, Amelia's was the shade of old ivory while her own was pure silver—thanks to her hair stylist. Her face was much smoother, too, as a result of cosmetic surgery. But when it came to a comparison of their eyes, Amelia won out. Hers were still a pale silver and looked surprisingly young in her crepe-skinned face. Electra's gray eyes, however, appeared much older, having seen more and experienced more, having lost their innocence early.

Electra tapped the ashes from her cigarette into a crystal ashtray. She knew she shouldn't have assailed Amelia for her lack of respect for social boundaries. Amelia had long ago proved that class distinctions meant nothing to her. Even then, that incident had come to nothing, really. After all, who was she to be making judgments about anyone else's behavior, given the colorful life she'd led. She smiled.

Amelia paused in the doorway. "I'll tell Helga you'll be here for dinner."

Electra's smile faded with her concern. "Surely she knows that. Didn't you tell the staff I would arrive today?"

For a moment Amelia looked as if she was trying to remember. "Of course I did." She turned and tottered out of the room.

Electra snubbed out her cigarette and blew the smoke out the side of her mouth. Amelia was even more absent-minded today than when Electra had last visited. Perhaps she had returned at a propitious time. If Amelia was becoming senile, as Electra suspected, she would need someone to look after her. Or to otherwise provide for her.

Electra stood up and gazed appreciatively at the exquisite room with its velvet fabrics, its oil paintings of the Muses, and its oak-paneled walls and ceiling. She was home at last. Home to stay! The words sounded like a litany in her heart as she felt the security and serenity of Willowbrook enfold her. The house was quiet now. As quiet as a sepulcher. But it had not always been that way. As Electra breathed deeply of the scents of lemon oil and lavender and roses, she was filled with the sense of nostalgia she had long denied. From her handbag she took out her father's pocket watch, and as she wound it with the crown that had long ago been worn smooth from use, she admired its beautiful gold-filigreed face. Holding the watch to her ear, she tilted her head fully from one side to the other as her father had taught her to do as a child, listening through the familiar ticking for the distinctive, though faint, single-note chime he had said was the hallmark of a fine Elgin watch. On the first try, she heard nothing but the ticking; then, moving her head more rapidly, she was rewarded as the watch once again shared its secret with her—a secret that had come directly from her father, a secret that was so special she had never told another soul. It was her only direct link with the innocence of her childhood.

SPRING, 1925

Sweet spring, full of sweet days and roses,
A box where sweets compacted lie.

George Herbert

CHAPTER 1

WILLOWBROOK SAT ON ITS GRACEFULLY ROLL-
ing lawns like a genteel lady come to tea. Birds sang in the
domed greenery of the large oaks, and the distant Appalachian Mountains were forever hidden by the tall evergreen
forests surrounding the estate and its neighboring town of
Catawba Mills, Virginia. Charlottesville was the closest
town of any size, and if the family in residence at Willowbrook had been asked, they would have claimed that city
as their place of origin.

The Radcliff fortune had begun in Charlottesville, and
William Radcliff had chosen his bride Leila Stewart from
among the prettiest and wealthiest debutantes that city had
to offer. That had been two decades before when Willowbrook celebrated its fiftieth year and the century was new.

The marriage had been reasonably happy, William felt,
and while he had wanted a son, he was pleased with his
two daughters. He had been as faithful to Leila as most
men were to their wives, and if she had known of his
occasional licentious episodes, she had never dropped so
much as a hint of it.

However, the felicitous sense of well-being that pervaded life at Willowbrook had been disturbed for a time by recent catastrophes: a war that spanned continents and was said to be the war to end all wars, and the unexpected death of Leila.

Although his beloved Leila had been quiet and retiring—in great contrast to him—she had kept Willowbrook running with skillful efficiency, and had so well trained their daughters in the proper management of Willowbrook's staff that after her death the precision of the household operations had never faltered. Even though she had been gone almost two years, at times William still felt as if she were there, only in another room.

A peal of laughter from outdoors drew William's attention to the window, and as he looked out across the grounds, his younger daughter Amelia raced past on her white hunter, a group of her friends fast upon her heels. He would never have to worry about Amelia, he surmised. She was much like him—happy and outgoing and eager for life. Three of the young men in her entourage were serious suitors, and any of the three would make an illustrious match.

Amelia was as beautiful as she was popular. Her hair was a thick, rich auburn, and her eyes were clear silver, a hallmark of the Radcliff family. All she need do was give her dimpled smile and she would be engaged before dinnertime. Although William was reasonably certain all three of her suitors had proposed, he was dismayed that not one of them had yet solicited his permission for her hand. With a heavy sigh, he regretfully acquiesced to the fact that many of the time-honored customs and proprieties seemed to have vanished after the war. Times were changing, and he would have to adjust.

Turning back to his desk, William began to sort through the most recent mail from his textile factories in Charlottesville. He had a secretary to take care of correspondence, but in the past year the girls' social invitations and parties were enough to keep the secretary fully employed, and thus he had seen fit to handle the business correspondence himself. At least that was the reason William gave himself that no eyes but his own saw the mail from the factories these days.

At a rap at the door, William looked up to see his elder daughter Electra. Like her sister, Electra had quicksilver eyes, framed by long, dark lashes, but whereas Amelia's were bright and laughing, Electra's were like placid pools of pure sterling. Her hair was as black as her mother's had been and as smooth and straight as if she'd ironed it. However, since her debut she had worn it up, of course, layering it atop her head in perfect order. Everything about Electra was calm and orderly, William thought. She was a near perfect reflection of her mother.

"May I come in?" she asked, her voice low and lilting.

"Of course, of course." William closed his ledger and put his fountain pen back in its marble inkwell. "I was just thinking how much like your mother you are."

Electra gave him one of her rare sweet smiles. "Thank you, Papa. I try to be."

A frown creased William's brow, and he laced his fingers over the swell of his vest. "Sometimes that isn't always best. Your mother often took life much too seriously. You're young. You ought to be out having fun. I just saw Amelia ride past leading the pack. Why aren't you with them?"

"You know I don't enjoy riding as much as Amelia does."

"Take the Duesenberg, then. Gather up some of your friends and go for a spin over to Charlottesville."

"Perhaps later." She reached in the pocket of her jersey skirt and drew out a folded paper. "This is the guest list for the party next weekend." Electra's voice had become tight, as if she was battling to keep her emotions in check.

William nodded, fixing his gaze on the paper she had handed him, intentionally avoiding eye contact with her. He disliked confrontation and had anticipated Electra's objection to what he'd done. "Amelia and I presented it to Mrs. Adams this morning," he said, hoping Electra would let the matter pass.

"Papa?" Electra burst forth in exasperation. "Why wasn't I consulted? You have Wally Harrison's name here."

"Yes, I know. The Harrison boy is a fine lad. I've known his people for years."

"Wally Harrison is a bore! He follows me about like a puppy dog. If I turn suddenly, I run right into him."

"The lad adores you. You ought to give him some encouragement."

"Never. Not if he were my last hope on earth. I tell you he's *boring*."

William's countenance stiffened as it always did when he was forced to yield his rational viewpoint to the emotion-based pleading of his daughters. "All right, then. The invitations haven't gone out yet. We'll strike his name and add young Beaufort."

"*Frank* Beaufort?" she asked as if she knew dozens by that last name. "Not Frank. He's worse than Wally."

"Now see here, Electra. You're too blasted particular." William pushed up from his desk and strode over to the window. "There's not a thing wrong with either of these boys. You're just too particular for your own good."

"I have to be, Papa. How can I decide which beau will be the best husband for me if I blind myself to their faults?"

"Discernment is fine. I encourage it. Lord knows I don't want to see either of you girls settled in an unhappy marriage. But blast it, Electra, all men have some faults."

She shook her head stubbornly. "I won't settle for second best."

"Second best! The Harrison family is among the finest in Charlottesville, and the Beauforts' ancestors came over on the *Mayflower!* Both boys have impeccable character and could support you in splendid style." He gazed speculatively at her for a moment, then decided to play his trump card. "You're the elder, you know. Since I have no son, Willowbrook will be yours someday."

"I always assumed that, Papa."

"But I'm determined to see it remain in our family. If you don't marry, how will you be able to pass it on?"

"Of course I'll marry," she said with a laugh. "What an idea!"

"You're going to be twenty years old this August. Almost two full years older than your sister, and you still aren't engaged."

"Papa," she said with a teasing smile, "it's only March. I have months yet before I'm an old maid."

Frustrated, William Radcliff studied his daughter. Even when she smiled, her reserve was apparent. She almost never laughed in a spontaneous burst of delight the way Amelia did. Although William had never admitted it to anyone, he wished Amelia had been the elder and thus his heir. "It's just that I feel sure Amelia will have offspring to inherit Willowbrook."

"So will I. What a morbid conversation. You'd think we both had one foot in the grave."

William didn't answer.

"Papa, I'm going to mark Wally off the list and add Jonathan Cooper instead of Frank."

"No, you won't. Young Cooper is sweet on Amelia."

"We have to have another man to make an even number at the table."

"Amelia has Reggie Smyth-Downs and Carleton Edgeworth coming. She only has two sides, you know."

"We can seat Jonathan across from her. Don't you think that would be interesting?"

"Electra, you know that wouldn't be right at all. No, you must invite one of your own beaux to the party."

In Electra's frown William saw a hint of his own stubbornness. "If I do, whichever one I choose will take the invitation as encouragement, and I have no intention of doing that."

"Look," William said with strained patience. "You have a responsibility to Amelia, you know. As the younger sister, she can't become engaged until you do. It wouldn't be proper."

"Has she finally decided on someone?"

"No, of course not. She won't feel free to do that until you've made your choice."

Electra shrugged. "I'll decide in time." After a moment's thought, she continued, "I'll tell you what. Let's give a big party on the evening before my twentieth birthday, and I'll announce my intended then."

Her father eyed her with skepticism. "You will?"

"I promise. That gives me several months to decide, and I'll be firmly married by this time next year. Does that make you happy? After all, I don't want to be an old maid any more than you want me to." With another of her small, closed smiles, Electra tucked the guest list back into her pocket and left the room.

William continued to stare at the open doorway for a long while after she'd gone, puzzled as to why he didn't feel the wave of relief Electra's engagement promise should have brought him.

The party the following weekend was even better than Electra expected. With the day unseasonably warm and the sky an arched dome of brilliant blue, the decision was made to move the party out to the south lawn, which had been specifically designed for that purpose. White linen cloths, gleaming in the brilliant sunlight, covered tables mounded with food by kitchen servants whose comings and goings were, for the most part, hidden from the guests' view by a square-trimmed box hedge. Rose-covered arched trellises perfumed the air and shaded the marble benches that had been provided especially for tête-à-têtes. At the end of the lawn opposite the servants' gate was a hand-sculpted marble fountain that had been imported from Italy. A similar but smaller fountain on the long serving table spouted streams of Chablis, rosé, and Burgundy into silver ewers. The lawn, rolled as flat as a ballroom floor, had been meticulously manicured. The guests, laughing, talking, and flirting, moved through the outdoor room as if they were royalty and this were their court.

"Electra, you dear thing," said a throaty, feminine voice behind her. "What a madcap idea to have a sit-down dinner outside!"

"I can't take the full credit, Daphne. It was mostly Amelia's idea."

"What a wild, crazy inspiration," Daphne Fitzgerald cooed in her contralto tones. She flicked an ash from her cigarette and drew deeply on the jeweled black lacquer holder. "Amelia has such darling ideas."

"Would you like another cordial?" Electra asked, nodding toward the bar that had been set up on another table for those who preferred beverages other than wine.

"I really shouldn't. I've had two already, and they were awfully strong. I don't know who your supplier is, but you certainly have a good one." Daphne emitted a high-pitched laugh as though some errant thought had amazed her. "Ours was arrested the other day. By Izzy and Moe, no less!"

Electra nodded in commiseration. Local Prohibition agents Izzy Einstein and Moe Smith were as well known as the bootleggers they arrested. "I'm sure Mr. Jones will soon be back at work."

"He always is." Daphne stood with her pelvis thrust forward, her shoulders rolled, and one hand on her hip in the favored debutante slouch, her gaze roaming the crowd. "I didn't expect to see all of Amelia's beaux here at the same party. My goodness, there may be bloodshed."

"It's unlikely. They've all been friends for years. When she finally chooses one, the other two will sulk for a while and then they'll all be friends again."

"Then maybe the rest of us will have a chance." Daphne jested with the confidence of a girl who wasn't at all worried about her popularity. She looked at Electra with a critical air. "I love your dress. Is it Parisian?"

"No," Electra replied with the shadow of a smile. "It's one of my own designs."

"Well, aren't you the clever one? If I tried to do that, I'd never get it to turn out right."

Electra suspected that Daphne's self-assessment was valid, so she didn't comment, not wanting to appear boastful by comparison, though she was proud of her talent. Clothing, fabrics, and designs had always been her passion, even as a child. Her dolls had been dressed in the height of fashion, and though she had long since outgrown the toys, her interest in clothing design had remained. The gown she was wearing was a pale peach georgette crepe, sleeveless and scoop-necked, with a beaded sunburst of peach, pink, and pale rose on the bodice. Her bare arms were covered by a soft silk-fringed jersey shawl in the same shade of peach. Her dark hair was adorned with a clip of sunset-hued feathers; the beaded earrings she'd chosen almost brushed her shoulders. Electra had spent weeks on this outfit, and she knew it was spectacular.

Across the garden she noticed one of her father's younger friends, Robert Hastings, gazing raptly at her, and she nodded to him before turning away. She had known the man all her life, and liked him as she liked most of her father's friends. Amelia had said she felt sorry for Mr. Hastings, because it was common knowledge that his was a loveless marriage, but Amelia tended to dramatize things in order to keep excitement in her life. Electra felt sure Amelia didn't even know the man's wife, for she herself had only seen the woman a time or two. The Hastingses had moved several years ago from Richmond to New York City, and his wife no longer came with him to Willowbrook.

Nearby Electra heard Amelia's bubbling laugh. Naturally, she thought, she would always have room in her home for Amelia. They weren't as close as some sisters she knew, but Willowbrook was large enough to accommodate two households, if Amelia chose to stay after her marriage. They had many great friends in common, and Electra felt certain their husbands would be friends, too. And if Amelia stayed at Willowbrook, they could continue their round of parties, and in time their children would grow up in a happy extended family. The idea left Electra feeling warm and comfortable inside. In her imagination, she could see the next generation of children riding ponies across the lawns and playing endless games.

When the headwaiter discreetly notified Electra that the meal was ready to be served, she called for her guests' attention and asked them to take their assigned places at the table.

Every place setting was marked with a card that had been lettered and hand-painted by Amelia. Each lady's card was decorated with a flower, each man's with a butterfly. Electra had thought her sister's choice of symbolism was a bit risqué, but the cards were pretty, and Amelia had spent hours on them. Amelia was a darling, but she was so romantic and so featherheaded about some things. Fortunately she would soon have a husband to take care of her. She had confided to Electra that her selection was Reggie Smyth-Downs, but she was willing to wait for Electra to announce her engagement first—so long as it was soon. Amelia had giggled over the notion of becoming Amelia Radcliff-Smyth-Downs. Although Electra thought Jonathan Cooper was handsomer and Carleton Edgeworth more intelligent, Reggie was personable and fun, and she was certain he would be a fine match for Amelia.

However, until the announcement could be made, Amelia had no intention of letting her beaux know of her preference. She was sitting amid her suitors midway down the table. The fashionable new shade of emerald green she wore made her hair seem vibrantly red, and she looked for all the world like one of her vivid spring flowers besieged by bees.

Electra self-consciously smoothed her hand over her own black hair. Auburn hair was all the rage, and at times she felt the smallest twinge of jealousy toward her sister. Smiles and gaiety came so easily to Amelia! She never seemed to be at a loss for something to say. She fluttered and blushed and dimpled, and men fell all over themselves in their competition to win her heart. Electra had never found it easy to talk to men, at least not men of her own age. She preferred the more serious conversation of her father's associates.

Not that she would consider marrying an older man. That would never do. An older husband wouldn't fit into her idyllic dream of sharing Willowbrook with Amelia. Older men tended to have had children already and might not be willing to start a new family. And older men weren't as physically attractive to Electra. Their girths were broader or their arms stringier, and she had always had an almost pagan adoration of physical beauty. That's why she would have chosen Jonathan Cooper over Reggie Smyth-Downs, had the choice been hers.

As the waiter sliced a thin sliver of ham and placed it on her plate, Electra recalled her promise to her father. By August she had to choose one of her beaux and give him her hand. But which one? She liked them all in different ways and to an equal degree. Except for Wally Harrison, who truly was tiresome. But given that intelligence was almost as important to Electra as physical beauty, she supposed she would end up choosing Richard Stuart. He was Nordically handsome, with a touch of a British accent that lent an air of sophistication to an already admirable intellect. She glanced back down at Amelia. Besides, if she chose Richard, she and Amelia would still have the same last initial. That would simplify monograms on linens and silver. And she liked Richard as much as any of them.

Electra noticed the musicians had arrived and were setting up their equipment on the adjoining patio. As dusk approached, the lanterns there would be lit, and the dancing would run long into the evening.

Electra looked up again at the mellow rose bricks of Willowbrook. She wanted nothing more than to live here in contentment forever.

CHAPTER 2

AMELIA PRESSED HER LACE HANDKERCHIEF TO her face and tried to stem the tears that still seeped from her swollen eyes. The parlor was somber and dark, and the normal sounds of household activity were hushed as befitted a house of grief. Everything had happened so suddenly, she still felt confused and bereft. One day her father had been as robust and hearty as any man; the next he was dead.

The doctor had determined the cause of her father's death as a massive stroke and had tried to comfort her by saying he was better off to have died than to have lived and been a helpless invalid. Amelia supposed that was true—she couldn't imagine her father not being able to walk briskly and laugh uproariously at all the oddities of life—but his death was still a severe blow.

Dr. McVane had also said it was a blessing that William had died as he had in his sleep. Amelia wasn't so sure of that. She thought he would have preferred to leave this life astride his favorite horse or at one of his parties when he was at his happiest. However, his passing away quietly in his sleep was certainly easiest for the family; she had to admit that. But he had been so young! Not quite fifty! She hadn't known men died of strokes at such an early age. It was all so hard to believe.

Electra was seated in the parlor waiting for her. She, too, was dressed in black crepe, but unlike Amelia, who had found it impossible to adorn herself with any jewelry, Electra was wearing the heart-shaped gold locket her father had given her on her sixteenth birthday, which contained a picture of her father and mother. The locket looked elegant, and because of its sentiment it was appropriate. Electra was always perfectly dressed and able to meet any occasion, a fact that sometimes galled Amelia. But had it not been for Electra's presence of mind to telegraph Robert Hastings in those first hours of bereavement, when Amelia herself had had no earthly notion what to do, they would both have been adrift in a sea of confusion.

It was Electra and Mr. Hastings who had made the funeral arrangements for their father. Amelia had been so stunned by his passing that she wasn't sure she could have dealt with the funeral details alone. Even now, days after he had been laid to rest beside their mother in the family cemetery, Amelia found it difficult to make the simplest decisions. Mr. Hastings had returned to New York the day before, but he had told them to send word if they needed anything at all. Amelia was so grateful, she had cried.

From the hall she could hear the measured tick of the tall grandfather clock. She thought it strange that it still marked time as usual and that April flowers still bloomed in Willowbrook's carefully tended flower beds. Was it only a month ago that they had laughed and danced all night beneath bright lanterns on the patio? It seemed like years.

The mellow notes of the doorbell sounded, and Electra

met Amelia's eyes. "That must be Mr. Dupree," she said. "At least he's punctual."

Amelia dabbed at her eyes again and nodded as they rose to greet him. She hadn't noticed the clock had struck the hour.

Benjamin Dupree, a short man with a pointed gray beard, wore gold-rimmed spectacles which reflected light in a way that was disconcerting to those with whom he was speaking. He had been the Radcliff family's attorney since his father relinquished that position to him some years before, and he had a son and namesake in law school who would, in time, step into his place. People in Catawba Mills weren't fond of change, and among the wealthier families it was assumed that nepotistic succession in a sensitive position was generally the least disruptive.

The sisters greeted the attorney with their voices low, as if their father still lay in a carnation-scented coffin in front of the hearth. Mr. Dupree responded to them in similarly solemn tones, as befitted his mission that day.

When the sisters resumed their seats, Mr. Dupree opened his black leather briefcase and took out a legal document and an overstuffed folder. "I'm sorry to be here on this errand," he said, his eyes no longer meeting theirs.

"I'm sure our father's will holds no surprises for us," Electra said. "Papa never made a secret of the fact that I was to inherit Willowbrook. Naturally Amelia knows this will be her home as well, for as long as she chooses to live here."

Mr. Dupree cleared his throat and shuffled the papers as if he was nervous about what he had to say. "That's close," he managed at last.

"Close?" Electra queried.

"Mr. Radcliff recently added a codicil to his will. It specifies that if you, Miss Electra, are unmarried at the time of his death, his wife having predeceased him, you and Miss Amelia are to inherit everything equally. Including Willowbrook."

The mantel clock ticked loudly in the lingering silence.

"I see," Electra said at last.

"Equally?" Amelia asked.

"Equally," Mr. Dupree confirmed. "I was given to understand that Mr. Radcliff hoped in this way to give an equal dowry to you both."

"I see," Electra repeated.

"Electra, Willowbrook is still yours," Amelia said hastily. "I know how you love it and how you've always known you were to have it. I'm quite content to share whatever else is left."

Mr. Dupree cleared his throat and looked decidedly uncomfortable. Both sisters turned to him, and neither dared speak.

"There's more, I'm afraid. Not in the will. Mr. Radcliff kept that simple and to the point. The problem is with these." He opened the cover of the large folder he had brought with him.

Electra rose and went to him. "What are they?"

"Records, Miss Electra. Bank receipts, bills, and the like."

"Naturally we expect to pay whatever debts Papa owed." Electra's voice was sharp as anxiety constricted her throat.

Amelia couldn't speak at all for fear she would resume crying. Mr. Dupree looked so . . . uneasy!

"I'm afraid it's rather serious," Dupree continued. "The profits from his textile firms sharply declined during this past year, and against my advisement, Mr. Radcliff made some decisions in the last few months that depleted his capital reserve and seriously jeopardized the economic stability of those companies. For months he has been borrowing money to meet the mills' payrolls to avoid firing anyone. Meanwhile, his personal expenditures have been steadily increasing, and much of that on credit as well."

"What are you saying?" Electra demanded. "How much money will be left after the debts are paid?"

"None, I'm afraid." Mr. Dupree kept his eyes fixed on the papers before him. After swallowing hard, he said, "In fact, you'll have to sell all you have in order to break even."

Amelia felt the room spin about her, and she was sure she was about to faint. What would happen to Electra and her?

"I don't believe it!" Electra snatched the papers from Dupree's hand. "Papa would never do this to us!"

"I'm certain he had no idea that this would happen. Mr. Radcliff often gambled with risky investments that paid off handsomely in time, but not in this instance. He was relatively young and in good health, as far as anyone knew, and I'm sure he had every reason to believe he would pull out of this slump just as he had before."

Electra was thumbing through the papers, and by her chalky face Amelia knew Mr. Dupree wasn't exaggerating. The situation was as bad as he had said it was.

"I had hoped Mr. Hastings would be able to stay for the reading of the will, but of course I couldn't ask him to do so without betraying a confidence. Shall I telegraph him to return to Willowbrook?"

Electra turned her back on Dupree as if his words were an annoyance, and she continued to read the papers.

At last Amelia recovered her voice enough to say, "Must we sell everything, Mr. Dupree? Even Willowbrook?"

Electra froze as if she had been turned to stone.

Dupree shifted on the chair. "It may not come to that. As executor I will first sell the factories and mills, but a lot depends on how much I can get for them and how quickly they sell."

"Sell Willowbrook?" Electra's voice was frigid. "Never!"

"Naturally that will be a last resort. No one wants to see you lose your home, me least of all. Why, your father and I were friends. I've visited here often. This hurts me to the quick to have to give you news like this, but you had to know."

Electra lowered herself into her chair, looking terribly weary and about to cry. Amelia was almost as frightened by Electra's display of vulnerability as she was by Mr. Dupree's news. "What can we do?" she asked plaintively.

He closed his briefcase and stood to go. "For the present you're not to do anything. As executor of the estate, I'll put the mills and factories on the market immediately. Then, well, let's wait and see."

Amelia forced herself to stand, and her knees trembled as she walked him to the door. "Thank you for being honest with us, Mr. Dupree. As you say, we had to know, and I have every confidence that you will do your best for us."

He nodded briskly as if his emotions were about to overwhelm him, then left.

Amelia gently closed the heavy door, and for a moment she caressed its satiny finish. In the deep quiet that surrounded her, she could hear the otherwise inaudible movements of the servants as they went about their daily chores, oblivious of this new tragedy. And for the first time in years, as she breathed in, she was keenly aware of the scents of lavender and roses that were uniquely Willowbrook. Sell Willowbrook? Unthinkable! Surely in her grief she had misunderstood. She had never had a clear head for business.

When she returned to the parlor, she saw the silver trace of tears on Electra's pale cheeks and she knew this was no misunderstanding.

CHAPTER 3

"I HATE TO SEE HIM GO," AMELIA SAID FOR THE third time as she ran her hand down the horse's muscled neck. "Cloud is such a lovely animal."

"I know." Electra fed the horse the last of the sugar cubes she had brought from the house. Behind her the large barn seemed strangely quiet now that all but one of the horses had been sold. "But he's not going far. Only to Reggie's."

Though her eyes were misty with tears, Amelia smiled and the dimple appeared in her left cheek. "That's all that makes it bearable. Once Reggie and I are married, I'll have Cloud back again."

"Of course you will."

"I still don't see why we have to sell my horse while you get to keep the Duesenberg." The pout that of late had become a predominant expression for Amelia was back.

"We've been over that. We have to have a car in order to get from one place to another. We could hardly ride double over to Daphne's to play mah-jongg or into Charlottesville to shop. Mrs. Adams couldn't ride Cloud into

Catawba Mills to buy groceries."

The idea of their housekeeper on a horse brought a smile to Amelia's eyes. "I can't see her driving the Duesenberg, either."

"Then we'll keep the Ford as well." Electra hated to see her sister so unhappy, but these matters had to be dealt with. "Shouldn't Reggie have been here by now?"

"I suppose. He said he'd have their groom drop him off here so he could ride Cloud back to his house." Amelia stroked her horse's white velvet nose. "The barn will seem haunted without the horses. Papa would hate to see it."

"So do I. But you know we have to sell all we can in order to keep Willowbrook. The horses were all of fine bloodlines and have brought in good money. Besides, their upkeep was too expensive."

"How much can one horse eat?" her sister argued.

"It's not just the feed, it's the stable boy and the groom, repairs to the barn and fences, and veterinary and blacksmith bills. I tried to explain all that to you. Weren't you listening?"

"Of course I was. I'm not as simple as you seem to think."

"I know you aren't. That's why I've been so put out with you lately. Amelia, it's just the two of us now. There's no one to take care of us except ourselves."

"Well, I don't know about you, but I plan to tell Reggie today that I accept his proposal. If I were you, I'd drive over to Richard's house and tell him the same thing."

"I can't do it like that. I have to wait for the right time."

"He *has* proposed to you, hasn't he?"

"Of course he has. At least he has more or less proposed." Electra frowned at her sister's impatience.

"Then you had better maneuver him into finishing the

job so you can accept." Through the open barn door Amelia saw a car draw to a stop out front. A young man got out and waved the driver away. "Here's Reggie now. You go on back to the house so I can talk to him alone."

Amelia smoothed her small hands over her skirt and the hem of her overblouse. Behind her she heard Electra exit through the gate at the back of the barn.

Reggie strode into the barn with a smile for Amelia. "Mrs. Adams said I'd find you here. I see you have Cloud all brushed and ready for me."

She nodded. "His saddle and things are there in the tack room. His name is printed on the board above the rack."

In a moment, Reggie returned carrying a saddle, blanket, and bridle. Cloud's ears pricked forward.

"Look at him," Amelia said. "He thinks it's just another ride."

"You can come over and ride him, you know. It's not like he's gone forever."

"Thank you, Reggie. I couldn't bear to sell him to anyone but you." She stepped aside while he fit the bit into the horse's mouth. "Would you like to come back for dinner tonight?"

"Aren't you going to Sarah McIntyre's?"

"Why would I be going to Sarah's?"

"She's giving a dance tonight. I assumed you'd been invited."

A sense of foreboding settled in Amelia's middle. Sarah McIntyre was the bellwether of Catawba Mills debutante society. Not to be invited to one of her parties was tantamount to social ostracism. "I suppose the invitation hasn't come yet. You know how madcap Sarah is."

"The invitations were sent out two weeks ago. It's to be a formal party."

Amelia's smile felt stiff. "Since Papa's death last month the house has been in such a turmoil. I'll ask Mrs. Adams about it. She probably mislaid it." She paused to give Reggie a chance to offer her a ride to the party. He turned and began saddling the horse.

Amelia moved nearer and let her hand brush his as if by accident. She smiled up at him as if he were the most handsome and desirable man she had ever seen. "I've been thinking about what you said."

"Oh?" His voice was suddenly distant as if the action of tightening the girth required all of his attention. "About the party, you mean?"

"No, what we talked about at the last party we had here. You know, the one where we ate in the garden and danced on the patio."

He glanced in her direction, but quickly looked away. "We talked about quite a number of things."

Uneasiness crept over Amelia, but she didn't let it show. She dimpled her cheek and lowered her long eyelashes in a way her beaux found irresistible. "You know what I'm talking about. We walked under the magnolia tree. The band was playing 'I'll See You In My Dreams.'"

Reggie patted the horse's rump as he lowered the stirrup and unclasped the buckle so he could adjust its length to his longer legs. "It's a pretty song. It's one of my favorites."

Amelia's smile wavered. What was wrong with him? She was positive he remembered proposing to her under that magnolia tree. How could he have forgotten a thing like that? When she became aware that he wasn't meeting her eyes, her concern deepened.

"I'll take good care of Cloud," Reggie said, too cheerfully. "You know how I love animals."

Under the magnolia he had said he loved her. "Reggie, look at me." When he complied, she said, "You asked me a very important question and I said I would think it over. Well, I have and—"

"Amelia," he interrupted. "I . . . I really have to be going. It's quite a ride back to my house, and my parents will be waiting lunch for me." His eyes were filled with misery, and Amelia's stomach twisted. "We'll talk another time."

"Tonight?" she asked with barely concealed anxiety. "I'm sure Sarah must have meant for me to come—we've always been friends. Perhaps"—she remembered to lower her eyelids flirtatiously—"we could ride to her house together."

Reggie looked away, as if collecting his thoughts, then turned back to Amelia, but failed to meet her eyes. "I've . . . that is, Ida Templeton is going to the dance with me." He shifted from one foot to the other.

"Ida! You have a date with Ida?"

"As a matter of fact, yes. It is a date." He forced a weak smile. "Yes, I guess you'd call it a date."

Amelia stepped back as Reggie mounted the horse. Reggie and Ida? Why, Ida wasn't even pretty!

"I'm sure I'll see you again soon." Reggie gazed down at her as if he felt more comfortable astride the horse, more assured of a quick exit.

"Yes," she replied automatically.

"And as I said, you may come over to ride Cloud whenever you please. Just let me know ahead of time, so I'll be there."

Amelia drew herself up and proudly tilted her head. "You haven't heard my answer to your marriage proposal," she said coolly, pleased to see his increased discomfort. "The answer is no. I can't marry you because I just realized I don't love you."

A muscle tightened in his jaw, and his eyebrows met over the bridge of his nose, but he made no reply.

With a regal toss of her head, Amelia turned her back on him and strode briskly toward the rear door. On one hand she prayed he would call out and stop her, say he loved her and that this date with Ida wasn't what it seemed. On the other, she hoped she never saw him again.

The pounding of hooves on hard-packed dirt told her Reggie was riding away, and pain knotted inside her. This wasn't fair! He had been the most persistent of her beaux. She had decided to marry him!

Amelia ran toward the house, tears welling in her eyes. She would show him! She would accept Jonathan Cooper's proposal. The Coopers were a much nicer family than the Smyth-Downses, and they had more money as well. By the time she reached the house she was crying in earnest.

Daphne Fitzpatrick waved her arm in a dramatic flourish, jingling her thin gold bracelets and spraying a fine powder of cigarette ash onto the Radcliffs' imported rug. "The party was a smashing success," she informed Electra. "You'd have died if you'd seen the dress Ida Templeton wore. Cut clear down to here!" She indicated a spot just above her navel and rolled her eyes. "It was just as low down the back. Honestly, none of us could figure out how she kept it on. And it was the oddest color *green*."

"People with Ida's coloring should never wear green,"

Electra said automatically. "I understand she went with Reggie?"

"Yes." Daphne leaned forward conspiratorially, her long rope of beads looping over her exposed knee. "I thought he was seeing only Amelia."

Electra shrugged as if it made no difference at all. "Our invitations were misplaced in the confusion after Papa's funeral, and Amelia and I thought it might be awkward to come without a card to show at the door."

"Nonsense. You should have simply barged right in. No one would have dared to stop you." She pushed her curly blond hair back under her beaded headband. "You'll never guess who's getting married!"

"How is it you always know the latest gossip before anyone else? Tell me who."

"Richard Stuart!"

Electra carefully replaced her teacup in its saucer. "Richard?"

"We don't have any idea where he found her, but she's from some northern state. Michigan, I think. Her name is Billie something or other. Don't you think that's an odd name for a girl? It sounds as if she's a boy."

Electra noticed her hands were as cold as if winter had returned. In fact, she felt chilled all over. She had planned to marry Richard herself.

"And Wally Harrison is walking out with Betty Sue. I don't know what on earth they find to talk about."

"Knowing Wally, he'll do all the talking. Betty Sue has only to listen." Richard was getting married! She thought of all the time she had wasted in her foolish whim of not rushing into marriage, and now the young man of her choice had turned to someone else. She heard Daphne recounting all the gossip that had been passed about at the last get-together, but Electra's mind was on more somber thoughts.

For the past few weeks neither Electra nor Amelia had been invited anywhere. And recently no one but Daphne had dropped by.

"I suppose you're going to Myrtle Beach again this summer?" Daphne was saying. "My parents are already planning the summer outing."

"No. No, we aren't going this year."

"Why ever not? We always go to Myrtle Beach at the same time."

"I know, but without Papa to act as a chaperon, Amelia and I thought it wouldn't be proper." In truth the house at Myrtle Beach had been the first of the Radcliffs' property to be sold, but Electra didn't want anyone to know that yet.

"Well, I can see how that would be awkward, but what will you find to do around here? Catawba Mills is simply dead in the summertime."

"Who knows?" Electra said with a carefully placed smile. "Maybe I'll fill the time sewing for our trousseaux."

"Are you serious?" Daphne leaned forward so quickly her beads clattered. "A trousseau? Who's getting married? You?"

Electra shrugged but didn't deny it.

"You said 'trousseaux.' Amelia, too?" Daphne removed her cigarette from its lacquered holder and snuffed it out.

Electra looked down at her clasped hands in her lap. She was playing a dangerous game, because Daphne was sure to tell everyone. But curiosity might put their names back on the social lists. Once she and Amelia were invited to parties again, Electra was positive they could become engaged in truth.

Daphne jumped to her feet. "I have to be running. Sarah McIntyre and I are driving over to Charlottesville this afternoon, and I mustn't be late."

"Give Sarah my best, won't you?"

"Of course." Daphne waved as she crossed the room. She had become so excited that she'd dropped the throaty sophistication from her voice and had not realized she'd done so.

Daphne couldn't wait to tell Sarah that there was to be at least one marriage in the Radcliff family. Electra knew they would spend the entire afternoon speculating on who the groom or grooms might be. She hoped she had done right in dropping such a hint. But of course it was only a matter of time before it would be true. Neither she nor Amelia planned to be an old maid.

As soon as she heard Daphne's Bugatti pull away, Electra went upstairs to find Amelia. She was sitting on her bed, working a crossword puzzle while "Cecilia" played on the phonograph.

Electra turned down the volume and said, "I have to talk to you."

"What's a three-letter word that means 'sun'?"

"Please put that down and listen to me."

Amelia wrote "sol" in the spaces and looked up at her sister.

"Daphne just left."

"Oh? I didn't even know she was here."

"That's because you stay in your room all the time these days."

Amelia looked away and crossed her arms over her chest.

"There's nothing wrong in seeking out a little solitude."

"Yes, there is. At least there is for us right now. Amelia, we have to get back into circulation. Do you know what Daphne told me? Richard Stuart is marrying some girl from Michigan!"

"He is? But Richard is one of your beaux."

"Not anymore, evidently. Daphne says her name is Billie something-or-other."

"A lot of girls have boys' names these days. I think it's chic."

"That's not the point. Richard was my favorite beau. And Wally Harrison is seeing Betty Sue."

"Poor Betty Sue. I should send her a card of condolence."

"Can't you be serious? Don't you understand what I'm saying to you?"

"Yes, I do. You're saying we need to find ourselves husbands before all the good ones are gone. Papa would roll over in his grave if he could hear you." She returned to the crossword puzzle. "We both tried to tell you to stop being so picky."

Electra pulled the puzzle away and slapped it down onto the vanity table. "It's not just me who has to worry. Ida Templeton has set her sights for Reggie, and it sounds to me as if she's about to land him."

"Ida isn't even pretty."

"From the way Daphne described her new party dress, Ida won't have to be. You know she has a fortune of her own, and Reggie knows it, too."

"I've decided I don't want him. He's too shallow. Maybe I'll accept Jonathan Cooper instead."

"The same Jonathan Cooper who just left for Europe?"

"What?" Amelia gasped, staring at her sister as though

she couldn't believe what she'd heard.

"I didn't think you knew about that. He's gone to England to study at Oxford."

"He never told me he was still considering that! I thought he had decided to stay here in the States."

"Daphne said he left a week ago."

Amelia's brow puckered as it always did when she was confronted with a dilemma. A moment later she lifted her head and said, "I guess I ought to invite Carleton Edgeworth over for tea. I've always enjoyed his company. He's so witty."

"I've always liked Carleton better than Reggie anyway," Electra agreed. "Reggie can't talk about anything but horses and parties. I'll tell Mrs. Adams to expect him for tea on, say, Tuesday?"

Amelia nodded. "I'll send him a note right away." With a smile she added, "There, now. You were upset for no reason at all. You should write Freddy Knapp and have him to tea as well. His nose is rather large, but he has lovely eyes."

Electra made no comment.

With a giggle Amelia added, "Wouldn't it be terrible if we had to settle for Frank and James Beaufort? I'd just die!"

"Don't even joke about such a thing." The Beaufort brothers were tolerated only because of their influential family and a loose connection through marriage to Daphne Fitzpatrick. "They're both absolute cretins."

Amelia lay back on her mounded pillows and curled her legs beneath her. "Isn't it odd how few invitations we've had lately?"

"Yes, I was wondering about that myself."

"You don't suppose it's because we have had to sell so

many things, do you? I mean, these are our friends. Besides, most of the sales are confidential, according to Mr. Dupree."

"I know, but you know how news of that sort of thing leaks out."

"Someday we'll look back on this and laugh. I'm sure we will."

Electra didn't answer, instead she gazed out the bedroom window in an unconscious imitation of their father. "It's quite serious, you know. I talked to Mr. Dupree yesterday, and he said the negotiations for the mills aren't going well. We may not get as much for them as we had hoped."

"Then we'll sell the factories for more. You're so gloomy these days. No wonder we've been struck off the social lists."

"Don't say that!" Electra snapped. Then more kindly she added, "This is just a temporary problem. Some communication difficulty, perhaps. We haven't been taken off the lists."

"Certainly not. We've all put up with the Beaufort brothers for years and nobody even likes them. I was only joking."

"Most likely everyone is giving us privacy because of Papa's recent death. I'll send out an invitation to Freddy and you send one to Carleton. That will let people know we're ready to pick up our lives again."

"Why stop there? Let's have a party as well." Amelia sat up, her eyes shining. "Let's have a dance."

"You know we can't afford that. The flowers, the band . . ."

"It can be informal—like the one Sarah had last fall. A come-as-you-are party!"

"I hate those."

"All right, a come-as-you-were party."

"I never heard of one of those."

"I know. I just invented it. We'll tell all our friends to wear their favorite clothes, and that way it won't seem strange for us not to have new gowns. It's an inspiration! And we'll ask them to bring their favorite records, and we'll use them for the music. We have plenty of candles to put on the patio, and if the night is rainy, I'll have Mrs. Adams roll up the rugs in the west room. There's plenty of room to dance in there."

"How do you think of these things?" Electra asked with admiration.

Amelia shrugged, though somewhat smugly. "I guess this is my talent, like yours is sewing and designing dresses."

At the reminder, Electra's face became solemn. "I even considered becoming a dressmaker right after we learned of our financial problems."

"You? A dressmaker? Now I *know* Papa is rolling in his grave!"

"If we have to sell everything to clear the debts, we'll have nothing left that will provide an income for us. Haven't you ever considered that?"

"Nonsense. We'll live on our husbands' incomes, as all women do."

Electra nodded in compliance, though she was losing confidence that Amelia's idyllic solution to their predicament would come to pass. There would be time enough to worry if their other marriage prospects fell through, and trying to get Amelia to share her concern would serve only to alarm her. Amelia needed to be protected. "We won't sell Willowbrook," she said aloud. "It will never come to that."

"Of course not. Besides, we made a promise to Papa that it will always stay in our family. Even if, heaven forbid, only one of us marries, there is plenty of room for us both to live here."

"I'm not worried about my ability to find a husband," Electra retorted.

"I never said you were."

"You just write that note to Carleton and send out invitations to the party. I'll worry about the finances." Electra turned and left the room before guilt could force her to apologize. Maybe Amelia wasn't worried, but *she* was. Their best prospects were either choosing other girls or leaving the country.

Needing to be alone to think things through, Electra headed downstairs, her hand trailing lightly on the curved walnut stair rail. As she drew in a calming breath, she felt the pulse and serenity of Willowbrook. Gleaming oak wainscoting and furnishings of cherry and walnut, adorned with silver candlesticks and trays, met her eyes. The wall coverings were of imported damask; the Aubusson rugs had been purchased expressly to cheer and warm Willowbrook's floors and had been a part of her mother's dowry. The crystal chandeliers, now converted to electricity, were still hanging where they had been placed when brand-new. Ten years before the Civil War, a man had come from Raleigh to carve the large newel post at the foot of the stairs. Willowbrook was more than a home to her; it was a heritage, almost a living entity. "I'll never sell you," Electra whispered to the house. "Never! Not even if I have to marry Frank Beaufort."

Surprisingly, both Carleton Edgeworth and Freddy Knapp were unavailable to come for tea. Amelia fretted and pouted over the coincidence, but then buried herself in preparations for the proposed party. Electra was more deeply concerned, but refused to let Amelia know.

The evening of the party arrived, and Electra dressed with care in the peach gown she had worn to the last party before her life had shifted and crumbled. It was her prettiest design, and she knew the cut and color suited her to perfection. Electra hoped her worry was only pre-party nerves and not a premonition.

The hour came and went without a single person coming to the door.

"Where do you suppose they all are?" Amelia asked, her eyes wide with concern.

"I have no idea. Did you put the correct time and date on the invitations?"

"Certainly I did. None of our friends sent word to me that they weren't coming."

"None of them said they were, either."

A knock at the door captured the full attention of both sisters, and in unison they looked up in keen expectation. Amelia went to open it. "Come in," she said with forced gaiety. "Electra, it's the Beaufort brothers."

"Are we the first?" Frank asked in the awkward way that was his style. "I didn't see any other cars out front."

Amelia emitted her tinkling laugh. "You know how everyone loves to make an entrance. I should have known one of these days they would all be fashionably late."

The brothers followed Electra through to the west room and stationed themselves at the tray of canapés. Electra and Amelia exchanged a worried glance as Amelia put "Sweet Georgia Brown" on the turntable of the phonograph.

A second knock at the door sent Amelia rushing to

answer it. In the next half hour, several of the others who had been invited arrived. However, many were noticeably absent, Carleton Edgeworth among them. Electra could see that Amelia's smile was but a mask. She was trying too hard to appear gay and carefree, and she was laughing too much at jokes that were scarcely funny. Her gestures were almost fevered.

Freddy Knapp was hardly through the door before Electra drew him to one side. "Have you seen Carleton? We were expecting him, and I'm afraid he's had car trouble."

Freddy shifted his weight. "He's not coming. Ida is also having a get-together tonight, and he went over there."

"He did!"

"As a matter of fact," Freddy said, consulting his watch, "I said I would drop by there later in the evening."

"You did!" Electra forced herself to smile. "If I had known Ida had planned a party for tonight, we would have made ours for another night."

"It was one of those spur-of-the-minute things," Freddy said.

"I see." Alarms were going off in Electra's head. Their erstwhile friends had chosen Ida's last-minute party over theirs! She felt her anger building, but dared not let it show. Tonight was more important than she had realized. "Would you care to dance?"

Freddy glanced around the sparsely occupied room as if in search of a possible partner. "Not right now."

"Have you seen my gardenias?" she asked in sudden inspiration. "Let me show them to you."

Before he could decline, she took his arm and maneuvered him out into the moonlight. "I love springtime," she said in confidential tones as she pulled her beaded stole about her shoulder against the cool evening air, its silken fringe trailing through her fingers. "Everything seems so full of promise."

Freddy looked around as if he had never noticed that spring was different from any other season. "Most people do, I guess. It leads to summer, though, and you know how hot it gets here."

Electra gazed up at him, copying the mannerisms she had seen Amelia use on her beaux. "You're right, Freddy." She let his name roll off her tongue as if she enjoyed the taste of it. "It does get hot here."

"Winter is worse, though. I've never liked wintertime."

What was wrong with him? A glance revealed only that he looked ill at ease. "Here are my gardenias," she said as she drew a fragrant blossom to her nose. "I think they're especially beautiful in the moonlight. Don't you?" She looked up at him with the most demure expression she could manage. Even a dolt could see the parallel compliment her remark was intended to evoke.

He leaned over and sniffed at the nearest blossom. "Nice."

"You know," she said as if she were thinking aloud, refusing to give up, "the moon seems bigger than usual tonight. Do you know what it reminds me of?"

"What?" he asked as he stared up at the silver orb.

"It reminds me of the night we went rowing on Elkin's Lake. You and I were in one canoe, and Amelia and Reggie were in another. Remember? We paddled about for hours, and you sang me a love song."

"I do remember something about that." He fitfully poked at the flowering shrub, causing the blossoms to tremble.

"You also said you cared for me." Electra hated being so

manipulative, but she had to get him to propose. "I just wanted you to know I care for you, too."

"Electra, I care about both you and Amelia. We've been friends for years. That's why I came here tonight."

"Yes, Freddy?" She kept her voice soft and gentle.

"I wanted you to be the first to know. I'm going to be married."

"What?"

"To my cousin."

"What cousin?"

"Well, she's only a fourth cousin, really. Emma Wayford. You must remember her. She's spent every summer with our family for the past five years."

"That Emma?"

"She's wonderful, isn't she? It's funny that I never saw her in that way before, until last Christmas when I visited with her and her family, and, well, magic happened."

"The Emma Wayford who wears her hair pulled back in a bun? That Emma?"

"That's the one. She's so . . . refined, not at all like those flappers who cut their hair indecently short and go around smoking. Don't you think she will make me a perfect wife?"

"Perfect," Electra said, not daring to say any more.

"I wanted you to know first, because we've always been such good friends. To tell you the truth, I expect Emma may even ask you to be one of her bridesmaids. You and Amelia. I guess you'll find this hard to believe, but she doesn't have many friends. She's shy. All she wants out of life is to make me happy." Freddy was as guileless as any man Electra had ever met, and maybe as spineless, too.

"We had better go inside. Amelia will be wondering where we are."

"Listen, I hate to do this, but could you tell Amelia? I really need to get over to Ida's and tell everyone the news."

"Sure. Go ahead."

"Thanks." He patted her shoulder in brotherly affection. "I knew you'd be happy for me."

Electra stood alone in the black shadows of her patio long after he had left. What was going on here? All of a sudden everyone was pairing off. Had it been happening all along, and she simply hadn't noticed?

She looked up at the looming bulk of Willowbrook, so sturdy and secure against the night sky. Moonlight reflected off the windowpanes as if the house were gazing back at her in supplication. With reluctant steps Electra returned to the west room.

Across the room, Amelia was talking with the two couples who had come in after the Beaufort boys. Frank and James were still at the buffet board, methodically eating their way through the hors d'oeuvres.

Electra wound up the phonograph and put "Ain't We Got Fun" under the needle's arm. As the music began, she drew a deep breath and pursed her lips in a smile. Crossing the deserted dance space, she approached Frank Beaufort and said, "Care to dance?"

"No, thanks."

Gradually she expelled the pent-up air from her lungs and with a sardonic expression said, "Eat up, boys. There's more where that came from."

Frank briefly glanced at her, but James never took his eyes off the silver tray of food. Even her sarcasm had been wasted on them.

The evening was going to be interminable, Electra thought as she tried to join in Amelia's conversation. She might have reached a dead end romantically, but she refused to accept defeat. Something would happen. Somehow she would save Willowbrook. She wouldn't allow there to be any other outcome.

CHAPTER 4

ROBERT HASTINGS LOOKED AROUND THE PAR-
lor he had visited so often, again having to remind himself
that his friend William Radcliff was gone from this place
forever. William's daughters had kept the room exactly as
their father had wanted it, even down to the pipe rack on
the mantel and, next to the fireplace, the easy chair that
still bore William's imprint. The house was so markedly
undisturbed, even though these several months had passed,
that Robert had the uneasy feeling that if he went upstairs
he would find William's outmoded Victorian bedroom still
ready for his reoccupancy. None of this made the task at
hand any easier.

Seated before him on the edge of the sofa were William's
two daughters, looking as dissimilar as was possible for sisters. Amelia was dressed in ruffles and lace, and her hair
was done up in a soft style reminiscent of the Gibson Girl
look. Her wide silver eyes were sweet and expectant, as if
she still held on to wisps of her childhood and might always
do so. Electra, on the other hand, could best have been
described as elegant, her face and eyes as serene as a queen's.

He had watched with interest over the years as these girls grew into young ladies, and had paid particular attention to Electra, for of the two, Robert found her by far the more attractive. Since William's death, Electra had erected an icy barrier that intrigued Robert beyond reason.

"Mr. Dupree asked me to extend his apologies for not meeting with you himself," he began, "but complications from his recent bout with pneumonia have left him quite weak. As I have been working quite closely with him since your father's demise, at your request, he asked me to be here in his stead." He drew a deep breath before continuing. "I'm afraid I have bad news. The last of your father's property, with the exception of Willowbrook and its adjoining acres, has been sold."

"But that's good news, isn't it?" Amelia asked.

"I'm afraid the properties didn't bring in as much as we had hoped."

"How much more do we need?" Electra asked with quiet reservation. "Perhaps we could borrow the money, using Willowbrook as collateral."

"Mr. Dupree told me he has already checked into that with the bank here in Catawba Mills and several in Charlottesville, but none are willing to make a loan, since you already owe more than Willowbrook is worth."

"Banks lend money to men all the time, even without collateral." Electra's steady gray eyes challenged his.

"Men who have jobs and a means to repay the loan, yes."

"I see."

"What can we do?" Amelia asked in a shaky voice. "We can't sell Willowbrook; we promised Papa. Besides, we have nowhere else to go."

Robert thoughtfully fingered his lower lip as he often did when faced with a vexing problem. "Aren't there aunts or perhaps cousins who would take you in? You both had suitors. Perhaps you could marry."

The sisters exchanged a look Robert didn't understand.

"I know it's rather soon after your father's passing, but the rules of mourning aren't as strictly observed these days. No one would think less of you."

"We have our reasons, Mr. Hastings," Electra said. "Personal ones. As for family, we have no one. Papa mentioned a branch of the family in Atlanta, but we don't know them nor they us. We couldn't possibly impose upon virtual strangers."

"Yes," he agreed. "That would be awkward."

Electra rose and walked to the window, her movements fluid and graceful. As she brushed aside the lace panel, sunlight lit her face with pearlescent hues. Robert had always been struck by Electra's beauty, but since William's death his awareness was heightened.

"Could *you* perhaps lend us the money," Electra was saying.

Robert paused. He could afford it, and both sisters knew it. He had considered doing exactly that.

"Don't be silly, Electra," Amelia said. "If we couldn't repay a bank, we couldn't repay Mr. Hastings either."

Electra looked back at him and their eyes met. Robert again recalled the wild, almost foolhardy thought that had come to him over and over in the past few days. "There might be a way around that."

Amelia leaned forward in anticipation, but Electra turned away. Robert paused. He couldn't suggest what he had in mind in front of Amelia.

Without turning Electra said, "Amelia, will you go get the coffee tray? Mr. Hastings always enjoys a cup of coffee, and Mrs. Adams needs help these days." As Amelia left the room, Electra added, "We've kept only Mrs. Adams and one gardener. The work is proving too much for her, so Amelia and I help out whenever we can."

Robert closed the door behind Amelia so no one could overhear their conversation. He hoped Amelia would have to take the time to percolate the coffee, because he wasn't sure quite how to approach Electra or what her reaction would be. "As you know, your father and I were friends for several years. Close friends, even though I was the younger by quite a few years. When your mother died, rest her soul, he asked me to promise him that if he died before you girls were settled into marriages, I would look after you." He tried looking directly at her, but had to avert his eyes. "You're rather mature to need 'looking after,' but I still intend to honor my promise."

"We appreciate all you've done. The assistance you've given Mr. Dupree in settling Papa's affairs has saved Mr. Dupree a lot of time and us a lot of expense. I don't know how we'll be able to pay his attorney's fees as it is."

Robert cleared his throat as he approached her, stopping only a few feet away. "I'm quite concerned about the fix you girls are in."

"So are we. I really don't know what will become of us."

"Your suitors . . . surely . . . ."

Electra tried to smile, but it never reached her eyes. "I didn't want to embarrass Amelia by discussing the subject, but we did consider that. However, it seems our beaux were more interested in the fortune they thought we had than in us. All our friends have more or less deserted us. We haven't been invited anywhere in weeks." She closed her fingers over her father's pocket watch, which she now wore on a velvet ribbon around her neck.

"I see. Perhaps—"

"I've even thought about becoming a dressmaker," Electra anxiously continued, "but that would hardly bring in enough income to maintain Willowbrook, let alone pay the remaining debts."

"You realize that the law requires—"

"If you mean to say we'll have to sell Willowbrook, you'd better forget it! I don't know what we'll do, but we won't sell. There has to be some other way!" She batted back the tears that were pooling in her eyes.

"I thought you would feel that way. That's why I have one final alternative for you to consider."

Electra's eyes, filled with hope and expectation, bored into him as she waited for him to go on.

Robert found it surprisingly difficult to continue. This young woman was the daughter of the best friend he'd ever had, and for years he'd viewed her almost as he might have his own flesh and blood. "As you know, I have always held you in the highest esteem. I'm sure you must be aware that my wife and I are estranged and that our differences are irreconcilable."

Confusion replaced the expectancy in her eyes, but she nodded.

"I get lonely, Electra." He paused to see if she understood the implication of his words, but she remained silent. She wasn't making this easy. "What I'm saying is that I miss female companionship."

"Are you asking that I be your companion?"

With a curt nod, he answered, his palms as sweaty as

those of a boy at puberty and his breathing shallow. He knew he had far overstepped the bounds of propriety, and, for a moment, he was concerned that she might turn him out of the house and refuse to ever see him again, despite her desperate situation.

"I'm a bit confused. As you've said, you're married. Unless I'm mistaken, you're also Catholic and are unable to divorce."

"That is true. I wasn't offering you marriage."

Electra's expression didn't change. He continued, "In return for your companionship, I would agree to pay the remaining debts owed by your father's estate."

Electra broke her silence at last. "That will allow us to keep the house but not to maintain it."

Although her monotone divulged nothing of her feelings, her words indicated she was fully comprehending his proposition. The girl had a good head on her shoulders! "In addition, I would be willing to pay a household allowance for the upkeep of Willowbrook for as long as our liaison should last."

"And Amelia?"

"She would remain here until she chooses to marry. After that her husband would be expected to support her."

"And me?"

"You would come with me to New York." He saw a flicker of interest in her eyes. "I would expect you, in addition to providing me with companionship, to act as hostess at occasional parties and to assume other duties my wife will no longer perform."

Electra looked him straight in the eye. "You're asking me to become your mistress."

Robert nodded. "In exchange you get to keep Willow-brook."

Electra didn't know what to say. Although she was cool and calm on the exterior, her insides were in turmoil. Even the word "mistress" had a forbidden quality. These were women she and her friends speculated about late at night during sleep-overs. Mistresses were kept women; she was pretty sure about that. But the meaning of that term was unclear at best, except that men did the keeping and the mistresses were always talked about in whispers and never among mixed company. She was being offered salvation for Willowbrook in exchange for becoming a mistress, and she didn't have the nerve to admit that she wasn't exactly sure what a mistress was expected to do.

Fortunately Amelia and the tray of coffee arrived before she had to answer. Electra gratefully moved away from the window.

Robert seemed unusually ill at ease, and as soon as he finished the cup of coffee, he excused himself. "Think about what I said," he instructed her as she let him out the door.

For days Electra could think of nothing else. She wasn't eager to leave Willowbrook, but this would be a way—the only way, it seemed—of saving it. As she watched Amelia working about the house, she tried to picture her sister living in a tiny bungalow and holding down a job. The idea was ludicrous. She and her sister had been trained for only one role in life: that of wives capable of overseeing the operation of households of the magnitude of Willowbrook. No one had ever considered they would need to earn so much as pin money.

"I'm going to drive over to Daphne's," Electra said with great casualness. "The Fitzpatricks will be leaving for Myrtle

Beach at the end of the week, and I want to see her before they go. Can I drop you anywhere?"

"No, thanks. I've started a jigsaw puzzle, and I want to work on it."

Electra nodded. Amelia's puzzles, whether jigsaw or crossword or riddles, were a great source of entertainment for her, often occupying her for hours at a time. "I'll be back for supper."

All the way to Daphne's house, Electra tried to decide the best way to bring up the delicate subject of mistresses without having to explain why, but to no avail. Her only hope seemed to be a chance mention of Daphne's brother, Tom, for Daphne had confidentially mentioned one time that he had kept a mistress, and Electra hoped he might have confided something of the arrangement to his sister.

The Fitzpatricks' butler showed Electra into the sun room where Daphne was reading a copy of the satirical magazine, *Life*. When she saw Electra, she tossed the magazine aside and stood to greet her.

Electra sat in the white wicker chair Daphne indicated, and as she looked about, she felt the clock roll back. Being here brought back a flood of memories of the not too distant past when her greatest problem was deciding which gown to wear to the next party. Of all her friends, only Daphne had remained her confidante, and this had come as a surprise because she had never considered Daphne to be particularly loyal to anyone. She was, however, grateful for her allegiance.

Daphne was wearing an awning-striped full cotton skirt and white buck shoes, looking as if she had just come from the tennis court. Her bobbed yellow curls belied the contralto voice she affected. "I haven't seen you in ages," she said.

"I know. I've been so busy these days." Electra had developed the habit of claiming extreme busyness as an excuse for missing the parties. She wondered if anyone believed her.

"Tell Amelia I saw Cloud yesterday and he's in beautiful condition. Reggie is so good with animals, especially horses. I can't imagine why Amelia has let Ida take him over. They seemed so well suited."

Electra smiled disarmingly. "Have you ever tried to talk to the man? He has no mind for anything but horses and parties."

"Strange. I'd have said the same about Amelia."

"She's deeper than she lets on," Electra lied. "You just don't know her as well as I do."

"That's probably true. Cigarette?"

Electra hesitated, then accepted one from Daphne's jeweled case.

"I prefer these because they say smoking Lucky Strikes helps keep your weight down. Not that you have to worry about that, but I do." Daphne lit her cigarette and handed the lighter to Electra as she blew a stream of smoke up toward the ceiling. "I see you're smoking outside the house now that you can make your own decisions."

"Yes, well, I know Papa wouldn't approve, but it's fashionable. In some ways he was dreadfully old-fashioned."

"Aren't all parents?" Daphne rolled her blue eyes. "I have to argue with both my parents about things such as this all the time. My brother Tom is the lucky one."

"I haven't seen Tom lately. Is he still at Princeton?" Electra was amazed at how easily the conversation had turned to him, as she had hoped.

"Yes, and he may be there forever. Father says he's becoming a perpetual student. Truth is he's three hundred miles away from their watchful eyes and having a fine time, if you know what I mean."

Electra leaned forward. "You mean his . . . mistress?"

Daphne glanced toward the door before putting her head near Electra's. "Yes! Isn't it scandalous? It's been over two years."

"Does he plan to marry her?"

"No man would be so gauche as to marry his mistress! Not even Tom!"

"But why? It seems to me after two years he would know her rather well. And he is continuing to see her."

"It doesn't work that way. What man would want to marry a woman who would let him . . . you know?"

Electra nodded, but she still was in the dark. "Have you ever met Tom's mistress?" she asked, not wanting the subject to be dropped before she found out something more definite.

"Goodness, no! I don't even know her last name, just Mae. He met her at a party in New York."

"Do they live together in the same house?"

"No, he has her in a small cottage in Trenton, I think, and he visits her whenever he pleases. That's usually the way it is."

Electra had to risk Daphne's suspicion about her curiosity. Plunging right in, she asked, "Why do you suppose a man would want to keep a mistress? I mean, if Tom wanted this woman's companionship, wouldn't it be better for him to marry her and be with her all the time?"

"Mother would simply die if he married before he finishes

his studies. Besides, if he marries, he has all the responsibilities on his back. A mistress can be discarded at any time."

"True." Electra recalled that Robert had said the bills would be paid only as long as their arrangement continued. She hadn't thought about that. "I suppose if Mae were depending on him and the relationship were to end, she would have to find someone else."

"A mistress can't just advertise, you know."

"Then what future does she have? What securities?"

"None, I suppose. From the way Tom talks about her, I gather Mae doesn't think that far ahead. She sounds foolish, if you ask me. I mean, how can she ever hope to make a decent marriage after she's let another man . . . you know."

Electra drew a deep breath. "No, what?"

Daphne's voice dropped even further. "Let him *sleep* with her." She glanced around again to be sure they were completely alone. "Sarah McIntyre says she believes a married man keeps a mistress so he can have her do things no decent wife would."

Electra's eyes widened. Her mother had died before telling either of the sisters what went on in a marriage bed, and their father had either assumed they knew or been unable to discuss the subject. "What sort of things?"

"Odious things. Things I'm sure you and I can't even comprehend! Why, I don't know all the details yet on what happens in a marriage, let alone with a mistress!"

"You don't?"

Daphne shook her head. "Mother says she will tell me on the eve of my wedding, but from the look on her face, I assume it must be pretty awful. Who knows what *mistresses* have to go through? Of course that's not the case with Tom, since he doesn't have a wife to start with," she added loyally. "I'm sure Tom wouldn't do anything, you know, perverted."

Electra nodded, more confused than ever. "I don't know what happens, either. Since my mother died when I was barely into society, she never told me, and now that she's gone, I may never find out."

"Your husband will know. Evidently all boys know about it, according to Tom. If you don't find out before your wedding night, your husband will explain it to you."

"I suppose. How do you think Mae found out?"

"I guess from Tom. Or maybe someone who would be the sort to become a mistress figures it out on her own. That's something you and I will never be concerned with."

"Certainly not." Electra wondered how she could explain her absence from Willowbrook to Daphne and all their friends if she took Robert up on his offer. "Well, I hate to run, but I must. Tell everyone in Myrtle Beach hello for us, won't you?"

"Of course I will. We'll all miss you and Amelia."

Daphne's last words sounded sincere, but Electra suddenly realized that Daphne no longer initiated any of their visits. It was evident that Daphne was pretending to be a closer friend than she really was. But Electra had a great deal more on her mind. She had a lot to think about before she saw Robert again.

Electra didn't really believe that what happened between a man and his mistress could be as bad as Daphne had suggested, for she couldn't imagine any woman submitting herself to such degradation. But security was another matter, and what Daphne had said about a mistress's uncertain future made sense. At the moment she was young and virginal and thus marriageable, even though her prospects had dwindled along with her fortune. What if she agreed to be kept by Robert and he tired of her? What if the physical duties he expected of her were so unpleasant she couldn't force herself to continue them? Willowbrook would still be forfeit, but by then she would no longer be marriageable.

What she needed was something she could fall back on if the relationship with Robert didn't work out. Not another man to depend on, but a career for herself.

For the next two weeks Electra's sleep was fitful and her appetite waned as she fretted with indecision, hoping some other solution would surface. Amelia blithely went about the daily affairs of Willowbrook, lending a helping hand to Mrs. Adams from time to time and whiling away her leisure reading novels Electra knew she'd read before. Neither of them talked about the inevitable, even when Electra received a telegram from Mr. Dupree telling them the court would order their house put up for sale in thirty days if they didn't do so themselves.

Unable to vacillate any longer, Electra wrote to Robert Hastings at his New York office address requesting that he come to Willowbrook as soon as possible to discuss a business matter. Electra knew she had no choice but to become Robert's mistress, and she had been through periods of intense anger. She had been furious with her father for dying and for having gone so deeply in debt. She had been angry with their so-called friends and, in particular, with their beaux, whose interest in her and Amelia had been so insincere. And she had resented being the one who was responsible for finding a solution. But all that was past now;

she would do what had to be done, but not without trying for one more concession.

Robert returned to Willowbrook even sooner than Electra expected, and as dinner was being cleared away on the evening of his arrival, she told Amelia that she had to speak with him in private about business. Amelia always found business discussions boring, so she was more than glad to go to her room and read.

Electra closeted herself and Robert in the front parlor and sat in the chair her father had always used, with him opposite her. She had worried that her plan to ask him for more than he'd offered might offend him and cause him to withdraw his proposition altogether, but seeing the way his eyes had followed her every move from the moment he'd arrived had assured her the risk of being rejected was minimal. "I've considered accepting your offer," she said in her direct way, "but one other condition will have to be met before I will agree."

"Another? Must I remind you that I'm willing to pay a large sum to remove you from debt and that I have agreed to pay for the upkeep of your sister and Willowbrook?"

"I might point out that I will be forfeiting a great deal as well, but this other consideration will cost you nothing." She noticed he had the decency to blush.

"What else do you want?"

"Security. Our agreement will be in effect for only as long as our relationship lasts."

"True, but—"

"My father told me once that you had friends in the fashion business. I want you to introduce me to the people I will need to know to become a fashion designer."

"Come again?"

"My father must have told you that fashion design is one of my greatest interests. I designed this dress I'm wearing as well as most of my other clothes."

"It's very pretty," he said dutifully. "But fashion design is a difficult profession to break into. We're talking about New York City, not Catawba Mills, Virginia. New York is the fashion capital of the nation. Almost of the world!"

"I know. That's what makes the city so convenient for me. I want to meet the right people and learn from them. Maybe even work for them part-time."

"Work!"

"I promise I'll always put you first, but surely you'll be at your office most of the time."

"That's true, but—"

"A lot of women worked during the war. There's no social stigma attached to it anymore. Besides," she added, giving him a heart-stopping smile, "I would enjoy it, and it would keep me busy."

"You have a point there," he said as he stroked his chin. "I've been concerned that you might get bored while I'm away."

"Then it will work out perfectly."

"If I agree to this additional condition, you will accept my offer?" He leaned forward in anticipation, his eyes intently fixed on her.

"Yes."

"Then it's done. It's a deal." He rose from his chair, looking as if he had accomplished the impossible.

She started to explain that she had little idea what was expected of her, but thought better of it. Soon enough she would know, and she didn't want him to think he'd made a bad decision.

"How soon do you want me to move to New York?"

"I'd like you to return with me now. However, I have to arrange for a place for you to live first. That shouldn't take more than a week—two at the most."

"So soon? Well, I suppose that will give me time to pack and do whatever else I need to do here."

Robert looked as happy as if she had handed him diamonds. "You won't regret your decision, Electra. I'll see to that. I'll put you in a nice apartment and see to it that you never lack for a thing." He took both her hands in his and brought her to her feet. "I'll be kind to you. I know how young and inexperienced you are."

She smiled in relief. "Thank you, Mr. Hastings. I was worried about that."

He laughed as heartily as a man half his age. "Don't you think, under the circumstances, you should call me Robert?"

"I suppose I should . . . Robert."

"Oh, I like that. I like that a lot."

Before she knew what he was doing, Robert pulled her into his arms and kissed her. At first Electra was shocked by the physical contact with him. He was in his mid-thirties but he already had a slight paunch and his hair was prematurely graying. Up close she could see fine wrinkles beneath the deeper and more obvious ones. His hands were broad and his fingers blunt, as if he had done hard physical labor in his formative years. His mouth on hers had left the faint taste of cigar tobacco. The sensation wasn't unpleasant, but neither did it move her romantically.

Evidently he was more pleased with the kiss than she had been, because he stepped back and beamed at her. For the first time, Electra noticed they were almost the same height, and this left her feeling awkward.

"I'll treat you right, Electra. I swear it!"

Before she could respond, he turned and hurried out as if he had a lot to accomplish in a short while. She raised her fingertips to her lips. While his kiss hadn't excited her, it had also not repelled her. And he had promised to be good to her. Surely this would all work out for the best.

Electra went directly up to Amelia's room and rapped on her door before opening it. "He's gone."

"Did you work out all the business details? Honestly, I'm glad you can understand all that. It makes no sense to me at all."

"Mr. Hastings brought me some good news. It seems a fashion designer friend of his in New York is in need of an assistant, and he has offered the job to me."

"A fashion designer? A job?" Amelia's eyes and mouth opened wide in surprise. "Why you?"

"Mr. Hastings told him about my designs, and he's interested in me. I'm to leave for New York in a week or so."

"New York! We aren't moving to New York, are we?" Amelia looked as confused as if Electra had suggested relocating on the moon. "Leave Willowbrook?"

"No, of course not. I'd never expect you to leave our home."

"I don't mind. I'd love to see New York!"

Electra hadn't expected this. "We can't both leave. Who would take care of Willowbrook?"

"Mrs. Adams?"

"She's only the housekeeper and can't be expected to take on more responsibility. Besides, she's getting old. No, I need you to stay here and take care of things."

"While you go to New York?"

"I can't make enough to pay for our expenses by sewing clothes here. I have to go to New York in order to be a success."

Amelia didn't look convinced. "You don't know the first thing about New York."

"That's where Mr. Hastings comes in. He's going to find an apartment for me. To take care of me, as it were."

"Because he and Papa were best friends? That's so sweet of him."

"Yes. It is. Once I'm established there and able to earn a living, we can borrow the money from him to pay off the rest of our debts."

"Wonderful! How long will it take?"

"I don't know yet. In the meantime, you will be in charge of Willowbrook. Do you think you can handle it? I know you're awfully young."

"I'm not much younger than you are. If you can brave New York City, I can certainly manage things here."

"Good. I had hoped you'd say that." She was thankful that Amelia was so naive she never questioned the obvious holes in Electra's story.

As Electra turned to go, Amelia added, "Someday you'll come back and take over, won't you? I've never mentioned it, but I want to travel."

"To travel?"

"That's always been my secret dream, to see the world. After I marry, I plan to have my husband take me simply everywhere."

Electra nodded. "Someday. Now I have to decide what I should take with me."

Once she was in the hall, Electra let out a deep breath. Now if only she could become a great success in fashion design, she and Amelia would be safe.

CHAPTER 5

"YOU'RE TAKING ALL THAT?" AMELIA ASKED AS she watched Electra fill another trunk. "You won't have anything left here."

"I'm moving. You have to take everything when you move. I'll need all I own in New York."

"I don't know how you got to be such an expert on everything. You've never moved before in your entire life," she complained, finally giving verbal expression to the pensive mood she'd been in for days. "Are you taking the furniture as well?"

"No, Rob . . . Mr. Hastings sent word that he has found a furnished apartment for me." Actually he had said he was having one decorated for her, but that sounded too personal for Amelia's ears. In the same letter he had included receipts for the payment of the last of her father's debts and a check to cover Willowbrook's household expenses for a month. It was almost as if he had been afraid she might back out if he didn't quickly get her in his debt. The notion was disquieting.

"I don't know what to tell our friends when they ask

where you've gone," Amelia was saying.

Electra's hands faltered. Did Amelia suspect? "What do you mean?"

"What do you think I mean? No Radcliff woman has ever worked. Even Papa didn't actually have a job, just income."

"Tell them I'm going to be a New York fashion designer and that I'm realizing my fondest dream. As for my having a job, that doesn't mean anything these days. A lot of women are working, and no one thinks a thing of it."

"Not Radcliff women."

"If I had been old enough when the war was still going on, I'd have gone to work to help out, like so many other women did."

Amelia sat on the bed and leaned her cheek against the footboard's tall, spiraling post. "Why didn't you get married when Papa wanted you to? At the time we could have had anyone."

Electra faltered in her movements. "It was because of Mama."

"Mama? What did she have to do with it?"

"You were just a child when she died, but I was old enough to sit with her and take care of her. She used to talk to me."

"About what?"

"About marriage and how much she regretted being married. Not just to Papa but to anyone. She never told me why, exactly, but there was something about it that she found distasteful."

"You never told me that! How could she find Papa distasteful?"

Electra went back to her packing. "I'm sure I don't know."

"Well, *I* don't think marriage would be unpleasant. I'd make a good wife."

"You don't know what you're talking about."

"I do, too. Jenny Allen told me."

"She did!" Electra stared at her younger sister. "How would Jenny know?"

"Her sister Kate is married. Kate told her absolutely everything and Jenny told me."

"I don't believe you."

"The same thing happens between a husband and a wife as happened in Papa's kennels, only it's done from the front and not the back." She smiled triumphantly at Electra.

"That's exactly what I thought!" Electra closed her trunk lid and sat down on it. "That's all that really makes any sense when you stop to think about it." She looked sideways at her sister. "Did Kate say whether or not it hurts?"

"Only the first time," Amelia said authoritatively. "After that it's just like anything else. Kate told Jenny she uses that time to plan the meals for the next day."

Electra pondered what she'd just heard as she snapped the lid clasps shut. "That doesn't sound so bad."

"That's what I said. Maybe Mama just found it boring. Seems like she was always bored about something or other."

Electra didn't answer. Her mother had left the impression of disgust, not boredom. With determination she stood up and started loading the last trunk. "It really doesn't matter, because neither of us is getting married anytime soon."

Amelia lazily reclined on the feather mattress and stared up at the faint pattern on the ceiling paper. "Speak for yourself. I plan to marry, and to do so while I'm young enough to have lots of children."

"You're only eighteen. There's plenty of time."

"Some day my prince will come riding up the lawn and sweep me away to a castle in the clouds."

"You read too many romantic novels. Life isn't like that."

"You have your dreams, and I have mine," Amelia retorted. "How come you think yours are the only ones that can come true?"

How indeed, Electra wondered as she folded her crepe de chine combination undergarments in with her silk hose and Cluny lace brassieres.

When Electra stepped off the train at Grand Central, the first person she saw was Robert. He immediately took charge of both her and her mountain of luggage and had everything loaded into an open-topped automobile he called a jitney. She wanted to ask why it was called a jitney, but didn't want to appear unworldly. It was days later before she learned that the unusual name was the slang expression for a nickel, which was the fare for riding the jitney bus.

Electra had never seen a city larger than Charlottesville and was amazed by the towering buildings. As they made their way up tree-lined Park Avenue, she gazed up with intense curiosity, holding her cloche hat on her head with one hand and bracing herself against jolts with the other. The only building she could identify was a church called Saint Bartholomew's. She wondered if they were anywhere near the Princeton Club, one of the few places she had heard of by name. Her thoughts went immediately to Daphne Fitzpatrick's brother Tom and his mistress. Daphne said they had met at a party there. She glanced at Robert, then turned her attention back to the unfamiliar sights and sounds about her. People were everywhere, as well as more cars than she had ever seen.

"What's in those buildings over there?" she asked Robert, who was watching her with as much interest as she was the city.

He glanced in the direction she had indicated. "Offices, mainly," he said, as if he had personal knowledge of them all. "Accountants, lawyers, engineers, businessmen. Shops are below, of course. Clothing, that sort of thing. I'm sure you'll become well acquainted with those." He smiled indulgently.

"Yes. Yes, I must, if I'm to be a designer. I can hardly wait to meet the designers who work here. Are there any in the buildings on this street?"

"Not the ones I know. They're back behind us in an area we call the Garment District." Then with a rather stern look Robert said, "Remember, Electra, that's not the primary reason you're here."

She glanced at the driver to see if he was eavesdropping, but she couldn't tell. "No, I haven't forgotten. Thank you for sending the check so promptly and for taking care of Papa's . . . final business." She was embarrassed to be talking of their arrangement with a stranger's ears only inches away.

"I'll be prompt in all the payments."

Electra noticed the driver surreptitiously eying her over his shoulder, and she tried not to blush.

Several minutes later the jitney turned right and stopped in front of a building which, to Electra, looked no different from the others, but the name on the red scalloped awning over the door told her that this was their destination—the

Claridge Arms. As they approached the entrance, a portly man in a scarlet coat opened the glass and ironwork door for them.

Once inside Electra stood in awe, for the stone facade of the building had given her no hint of the opulence of the interior. Red plush fabrics, snowy marble, and gleaming brass were everywhere. In the center of the lobby was an enormous chandelier with row upon row of crystal prisms circling a perfect glass globe. Beneath it was a padded circular seat with a raised back, which comically reminded her of a huge velvet juice squeezer. Behind the ornately carved and polished mahogany registration desk was a man she assumed to be the manager, but she could only see him from his top coat button up, because the marble-topped desk was so tall. On the wall at his back were slots for room keys and mail, each behind a glass and brass door with a tiny clasp. Potted palms and ferns and bouquets of freshly cut flowers, strategically placed throughout the lobby, added a sense of homey elegance.

"This is where I will live?" she whispered to Robert.

"Yes. This is your home now."

Almost in shock, Electra followed Robert to the desk, where he introduced her to the manager and showed her how to ask for her mail and for her key, if she chose not to carry it on the streets. At first Electra avoided the man's eyes, as she was sure he was appraising her with the label "mistress," but when she dared look up, he seemed totally uninterested. If he knew of their arrangement, he clearly could not have cared less.

Robert took her to the waiting elevator and told the operator to take them to the penthouse.

Moments later, when the elevator door opened, Electra

was surprised to see a vestibule with only one door rather than a hallway. With a wide grin Robert unlocked the door and opened it with a flourish.

As accustomed as she was to Willowbrook's beautiful Victorian furnishings and dark opulence, her first view of her new home took her breath away. Everything was modern. The couch was a pinkish beige rounded velvet art form, as were the matching chairs. A large crystal ashtray sat atop a black-lacquered coffee table, and smaller replicas adorned each of the matching end tables. The lamps flanking the sofa were made of stacks of crystal pyramids. Sleek, modern statues of various sizes and shapes, along with giant potted plants, seemed perfectly placed.

Robert swept back the wall of sheer curtains, revealing a panorama of the city. Electra blinked and tried to swallow, but her breath seemed stuck in her throat. "I . . . I've never seen anything like this!" she finally managed to say as she crossed the room and pushed open the swinging door that led to the next room.

"Come look at the rest of it," Robert said. As she gazed about the kitchen, with its gleaming white counters, walls, and floor, he said offhandedly, "I've hired a maid for you. If she doesn't suit you, let me know, and I'll get someone else."

She crossed to the bedroom and found it was magnificent as well. The walls, carpeting, and bedspread were all done in the delicate hues of sunrise. The bed had a tufted white velvet headboard and no footboard. A white fur throw was draped over the end of the bed. The dresser and matching bureau were black lacquer with a Chinese design inlay. Here, as in the living room, the lamp bases were all clear crystal.

Electra moved through the room like a sleepwalker. Behind one set of double doors she found a closet the size of a small bedroom. Another door opened into a bath with pink and white tiles, gleaming brass faucets, and a wall of drawers and cabinets. Except for the colors, she felt as if she had stepped into a movie.

"Mr. Hastings, it's—"

"Robert," he interrupted.

"It's too much! What on earth will I do with myself?"

"You don't like it?" He looked crestfallen.

"I love it! But it must have cost a fortune. And it's decorated so beautifully!" She turned to him, her eyes wide.

"It was expensive," he admitted, "but it was worth it. Remember, I said you would also serve as my hostess. In my business I need to entertain, and this is the perfect place for that."

With her head humbly bowed, she admitted, "I don't even know what you do for a living."

"I'm an investor in stocks and bonds, primarily. Also, I own a company that manufactures home furnishings—these are some of my own—and I have a small shipping company as well."

"I see." She looked around the bedroom. To be in here with a man, even one she had known all her life, felt awkward. She had never been in a bedroom with any man. Robert, however, seemed quite at ease.

He opened a pair of cabinet doors in one wall, and Electra was surprised to see a glass shelf slide out on a rack, above which were rows of glasses hanging in front of a gold-veined mirror. "A bar in the bedroom?"

He poured them each a drink as he said, "This place has everything. If there's anything else you need, you have

only to call down to the manager, and he'll send it up."
He handed her a glass of amber liquid.

Electra had never tasted bourbon neat, and the sip she
took made her eyes sting. "This is potent!"

"Only the best." Robert tossed down a swallow as if it
were merely strong tea. "It's from Canada, the best hooch
that can be had."

She took another taste and discovered this one hardly
burned at all. After the third swallow, she found the bourbon went down easily, and soon her entire body felt warm.

"You're a beautiful woman," Robert surprised her by
saying.

She looked up to find him standing right beside her.
"Thank you."

"That's what I like about you. On one hand you look
and act like a cool sophisticate, and on the other there's
the air of a child pretending to be grown-up."

"I'm twenty years old," she said as if in defense. It was
almost true. She would be twenty in August. "I am grown-
up."

"Of course you are."

Robert took the glass from her hand and put it on the
table beside the bed. She was suddenly overcome with shy-
ness. Bravely she lifted her chin so he wouldn't know. He
reached up and removed her hat, then pulled the pins from
her hair and let it tumble down her back. "I don't know
many women who keep their hair long," he said. "If you
want to cut it, I don't object."

With unhurried deliberateness, he unbuttoned her black
linen coat. Her dress was a patterned blue and white crepe
that matched the coat lining. After tossing the coat onto
a padded boudoir chair, he began opening the pearl buttons

down the front of her dress. Electra didn't know what to do. She had never expected him to do this in broad daylight. Was she supposed to help him with the buttons? She couldn't possibly unfasten his shirt in return. The room felt cool as her pale skin was exposed. Frantically she tried to recall what underwear she had put on that morning. All her combinations had been packed, and she had worn only a brassiere and silk panties that hung like a tiny skirt about her hips. Suddenly that seemed shockingly indecent.

Robert slipped her dress off her shoulders and down her arms and let it drop to her feet. "Nice," he said in a throaty voice as he scanned her body. "So nice."

Timidly Electra tried to hide her breasts behind her arms, but he reached behind her and unfastened her brassiere. She was so frightened she could scarcely breathe. "Mr. Hastings, I'm—"

"Call me Robert," he reminded her. "You've done it before. Let me hear you say it."

"Robert," she whispered dutifully.

"There now. That's better." He pulled her arms away from her chest and finished removing the wisp of silk jersey.

Electra couldn't look at him. She was struggling not to cry or to run and lock herself in the bathroom. She had known he would expect intimacy from her, but she had expected it in a dark room at some undefined future date.

"Lovely. I'm glad they're small." He covered both her breasts with the palms of his hands, and Electra sharply sucked in her breath. "A perfect fit."

As he rubbed his hands over her breasts, she felt her nipples harden in automatic response. This seemed to please him. "I'm glad you wear separate garments and not those awful one-piece combinations," he said. "They're too hard to get into."

She wondered if he was referring to other mistresses or to his wife. Somehow she had assumed he had never kept another woman. Now she realized this had been a naive assumption. He was too sure of himself for this to be his first liaison.

He slipped his hands down and under the hem of her panties and kneaded her buttocks. Electra still didn't know what she was expected to do, so she just stood there, hoping the quivering she felt inside wouldn't show. As he started to remove her panties, she had the presence of mind to step out of her heels.

Robert stepped back and looked at her with hungry eyes. "You remove your stockings," he said. "Here. Put your foot up on the bed. Like that."

Electra bent forward and began to roll her stocking down. She could hear Robert's breath rasping in his throat. She had never felt so naked in her life.

"Now the other leg."

She hesitated a moment, then put her other foot on the bed and repeated the motion. After the stockings were off, she looked at him uncertainly.

"God," he gasped, "you're beautiful!"

She bent her head forward, and her hair fell in a thick black mass across her breasts. Robert pushed her hair aside. "I want you to cut it tomorrow," he said. "I don't want anything hiding your body from me."

Silently she nodded.

"Turn down the bed. Slow. As if you were here all alone."

Electra pulled back the pink bedspread and folded it at

the foot of the bed. Behind her she could hear the rustle of clothing and knew he was undressing. Fear gripped her, leaving a coppery taste in her mouth. She slowly drew back the blanket and sheet and lined up the two pillows as if she had all the time in the world. He had paid handsomely for her, and she was determined to give him what he wanted.

"Now lie down."

She did as he said, and saw that he had indeed undressed. His naked body startled her, and she felt a chill tremble through her. He looked so big!

Robert sat beside her on the pale pink sheets, and she lay perfectly still as he ran his hand and his lust-filled gaze over her breasts, her flat stomach, and the nest of dark curls below her navel. "You're so young," he murmured hoarsely. "So pretty."

Electra couldn't say the same for him. His stomach looked larger without any clothes covering it, and his chest and shoulders had whorls of wiry hair on them. His legs were too thin, as were his arms, and the skin looked too pale. She tried not to see his rigid and threatening penis. She closed her eyes and wondered how long this would take.

To her surprise Robert bent over her and began to suck at her nipples. Electra's eyes flew open. Foreplay had never been explained to her, nor had she expected that such a thing would feel so good.

He guided her arms onto his shoulders, and she automatically embraced him. "Does this feel good?" he asked.

Suddenly she understood that he really cared whether she was enjoying it. "Yes," she admitted.

As he flicked his tongue over her taut nipples, an excitement began building within her despite her efforts to remain calm. When an almost inaudible sigh escaped her lips, he seemed pleased. While he kissed her breast with his lips and tongue, he slid his hand lower to touch the triangle of curls.

As he nudged her legs apart Electra held on to him tightly, wondering what would happen next. When his fingers began to explore parts of her body she had never seen, let alone allowed anyone to touch, another jet of fear raced through her.

"It's all right," he soothed gently. "Just relax. Let it feel good."

She tried, but every muscle in her body was tense and trembling. Robert was surprisingly gentle and patient, however, and after a while Electra discovered that his caressing and probing was rather pleasing.

He pressed his finger well into her and smiled. "You're a virgin. I thought you would be."

Electra didn't know how to answer him.

"I'll be easy with you."

He moved his finger in and out until she felt a wet slickness fill her, along with a building urgency, and her body instinctively moved against his in a way that increased her pleasure.

Robert laughed softly. "I thought there was a tiger under that cool shell. I've always thought there would be. Even when you were a child, I suspected it."

She tried not to hear his words or to think what they were doing. She wanted only to concentrate on the delightful new feelings he was awakening in her.

Just when she was sure she was about to explode from excitement, he pushed her legs farther apart and knelt between them. "This won't hurt much. You're good and wet."

Before she had time to object, he had entered her. All the pleasure fled as he pushed deep inside her untried body. Electra cried out as her maidenhead gave way and a sharp burning replaced the sensual enjoyment. Now she held him in panic rather than passion, but he seemed not to notice the difference.

As he pushed in and out of her, Electra clenched her teeth and conjured up the vision of Willowbrook. She could bear this, but only for the sake of her home. For Willowbrook she could stand anything. All at once Robert's whole body stiffened in her arms, and he groaned, then slumped against her.

At first she thought he had died, and terror filled her. His great bulk on top of her was making it difficult for her to breathe, and her heart was pounding against his inanimate flesh. Then, to her great relief, she felt the quick rise and fall of his breathing. He wasn't dead; he was merely finished.

Robert rolled away and after a moment pulled her head onto his shoulder. "Damn! You're the best I ever had." He hugged her as he struggled to get his breath. "I knew we'd be good together. I just knew it!"

She listened to his breathing, without saying a word. In moments he was asleep, but she was wide awake, and the burning inside her was still uncomfortable. Her breasts were tender and her nipples still pouting. For a while there it had felt so good! She had never experienced anything so pleasurable. What would have happened if he had continued to stroke her and suckle her breasts? Electra didn't know.

Gently she touched her breasts and felt a surge of the

desire Robert had awakened. But it was followed at once by an increased burning between her thighs. She let her hands drop back onto the bed. Her new life had begun, and she knew she could never go back from here. In a few short minutes he had altered her life forever.

She eased away from him and went into the bathroom. There was some blood, but not nearly as much as she had feared there might be. She looked at her reflection in the mirror. Except for the expression in her eyes, she looked the same as before. A pink flush colored her chest and breasts, and her nipples were puckered and rosy from Robert's mouth and fingers. Still, he hadn't hurt her any more than was necessary; she felt sure of that.

She drew a long strand of black hair over her shoulder and studied it. Tomorrow she would cut it. Not because Robert had told her to do it, but because she had wanted to bob it for a long time. And she would need more underwear. He had said he didn't like combinations.

Stepping back from the mirror, she wondered what to do now. She couldn't unpack as long he was asleep in the bedroom, so she went into the living room and opened the trunk that held her dressing gown. After slipping it on, she padded across the plush carpet to the expanse of windows and looked out at the city. She felt tiny and invisible in her penthouse perch. Below her feet, the people of New York City went about their daily grind. None of them knew or cared that Electra Radcliff had just been turned from child to woman.

CHAPTER 6

AT WILLOWBROOK, WARM DAYS WERE SPENT IN languid pursuits, but the people in New York City kept up a frantic pace, despite the oppressive heat and humidity, as if they feared winter would return too soon this year and the snows would prevent them from getting their work done. Electra even thought possibly she was adjusting to this faster pace of living, for the days seemed to be growing shorter too quickly for her as well.

Autumn had arrived with little fanfare, other than cooler weather, and had it not been for her occasional walks through nearby Central Park, Electra would have missed seeing the fall colors altogether. Autumn in Central Park was beautiful—no one could dispute that—but it was nothing compared with her memories of the showy Appalachian Mountains surrounding Willowbrook where the vistas were awash in a sea of fall colors. Electra seldom allowed herself to make such comparisons, though, for it left her feeling homesick, and that served no useful purpose.

Robert proved to be a considerate lover, though not one of great expertise. Electra often found herself on the brink of a tremendous sexual discovery during their lovemaking, but as soon as Robert sensed her mounting passion, he came into her and was finished before she could reach her peak. She sensed there was more to lovemaking than she had experienced, but she lacked the worldliness to realize what it might be. Robert was reticent about discussing sex, and Electra soon quit trying to solve the puzzle of her body. Perhaps, she thought, that was really all there was to it. She became aroused, it lasted awhile, then it went away. Robert had said once that it took women longer to "wind down" than it did men.

He was also true to his word. Only two weeks after she arrived in New York, he gave a party at her apartment and included among his guests Anthony Battaglia, one of the foremost designers in the New York fashion world.

That evening, as she often did, Electra wore one of her own creations, a royal blue crepe with a draped bodice sparkling with jet beads and baguettes. A long belt, the ends of which were also beaded with jet, was knotted about her slender hips. Around her neck was a long rope of silvery blue pearls that matched her eyes. The pearls had been a surprise gift from Robert just as their guests were arriving. Electra had protested his extravagance, but he had looped them about her neck anyway.

For some reason, receiving those pearls bothered her more than living in his apartment. The rooms were necessary—she had to live somewhere—but the necklace was not. Somehow she felt bought and paid for by the pearls, perhaps because he had chosen pearls that were not pure white, not symbols of purity. However, it made Robert happy for her to wear them, so she kept them around her neck.

Most of Robert's guests had come as couples, and although many of the men were married, none had brought his wife. With the exception of several women her own age, the guests were all Robert's contemporaries. Although Electra tried her best to talk to his friends, she had nothing in common with them, except for the younger women, who she assumed were mistresses, like her. However, as their arrangements were not a suitable topic of conversation and their only other interests seemed to be the newest picture shows and gossip about people she didn't know, Electra found conversation difficult with them as well. Despite all this, she smiled and pretended to be engaged by the stories she was being told while keeping an eye on the door in anticipation of one particular guest.

Electra knew Battaglia had arrived as soon as he swept into the room with an effeminate young man at either elbow. He loved to make an entrance, and he chose his companions for their cosmetic appeal rather than their mental acumen. Battaglia wasn't a handsome man by any definition. His small black eyes looked like beetles beneath his bushy black eyebrows. His skin, seamed from early years of working in his father's vineyard in the Po Valley of northern Italy, was puffy from dissipated living. His face and square body were those of a peasant; his long, slender hands were aristocratic. Battaglia had little use for women except as mannequins for his clothes, but he had an instinctive ability to dress them to perfection.

Electra was suddenly too shy to approach him, let alone to speak. This was a man whose style she had studied and tried to emulate for years, a man she almost deified. She wished she had not asked Robert to introduce her to him. She was positive she would make some serious social blunder and forever ruin her chances of becoming a fashion designer.

She tried to edge her way toward the bathroom, but Robert caught her eye and motioned for her to come to him. As she threaded her way through the crowd, she nervously fingered her pearls and thought how each sphere was a smooth link in a chain of her own forging. But she had come too far to weaken now, for since she no longer had her virtue, she had to have security of another sort. With an air of determination, she lifted her chin and took her place next to Robert.

"Anthony, this is the young woman I told you about. I'd like you to meet Electra Radcliff. Electra, may I present Anthony Battaglia?"

In silence his black eyes skimmed Electra's face, then perused her gown.

"I'm pleased to meet you," she said with more confidence than she felt. "I've heard so much about you."

"Yes," he said in a manner that clearly showed his disdain for social amenities. "Your gown. Who designed it?"

"Why, I did." With a nervous gesture she touched the draped fabric.

"You?" He looked as if he didn't believe her.

"That's right," Robert said with obvious pride. "Electra designs all her clothes."

Battaglia grunted rudely and started to turn away.

Electra wasn't ready to be dismissed, so she blurted out, "I hope someday to be a fashion designer." When he looked back, she added, "Perhaps I could even work for you . . . someday."

"Battaglia, and Battaglia alone, designs my clothing." He drew himself up to the full height his short stature would allow. "A designer indeed!"

"What she means is," Robert said in Electra's defense, "she wants to work for you. You can see what a seamstress she is. Maybe she could work on cutting out the material or beadwork."

Battaglia narrowed his eyes. "I could use another girl in the workroom. Robert, are you sure you don't object?"

Electra was offended that they were discussing her future as if she had no say in it herself; but when Robert stated he had no objection and the Italian abruptly nodded that the deal was done, her contempt vanished.

"Be at my workshop on Monday morning. Eight sharp. I don't tolerate tardiness, even from friends of my friends." Again his eyes studied the dress she wore. "And let there be no more foolish talk of designing. You'll do no more and no less than the other girls. Understand?"

"Yes, Mr. Battaglia," Electra said, in a tone that was more submissive than she had intended. Amazement that he had so readily accepted her had taken her breath away.

"Not 'Mr.,' just Battaglia. That is how I am called."

"I understand, Mr. . . . I mean, yes." She watched the pompous little man strut away, his young men still in close attendance. She turned her round eyes to Robert. "You did this for me! I'll never be able to thank you enough."

Robert, to her surprise, looked as if he regretted his largess. "Just remember," he said in a low voice, "what you're really here for. Our arrangement must always take precedence over your hobby."

"Naturally." She felt hurt that he saw her aspirations as a mere hobby, but that was all right for now. The important thing was that she was to be admitted into Battaglia's sanctum sanctorum. She planned to learn all she could in as short a time as possible. Despite Battaglia's words to the contrary, she had no intention of remaining in the work-room forever.

The months followed one another like the string of pearls Robert had given her, one sliding by on the heels of the one before, while yet another eased up to take that one's place. Three years passed, and Electra's new life settled in some respects and expanded in others. Her work in the cutting and stitchery room was so exemplary that Battaglia promoted her to layouts of patterns. She was even allowed, on occasion, to assist him as he held up swaths of material on the ever-patient models—he never used plaster man-nequins because of their stiff and lifeless state—and she learned how and why he made the cuts and gathers and seams as he did. All of this information she filed away in the back of her mind, along with everything else she had learned about the business.

Her life with Robert was less satisfying. Although he still treated her with deference and never missed a payment to Amelia and Willowbrook, their relationship had settled into an affair not unlike a marriage.

Electra, over the years, had come to despise herself for having sold her virtue, and she despised herself even more because she knew she would do it again under the same circumstances. Sex had never blossomed into love between Robert and her, though he seemed to have no complaints. She never once refused him, but at the same time, their union had always left her wanting something more. He often spent the night with her, sometimes three or four times a week, and occasionally an entire weekend, but he always returned to his unloving wife. It was in the quiet time after he'd gone that Electra learned to see to her own sexual satisfaction, but she still felt cheated, for she didn't think it was too much to expect that he bring her to her fulfillment at least once. If he had, she might well have fallen in love with him. Or at least fallen into what passed as love in their circle.

Electra had met quite a few women, at Robert's frequent parties, but friendships with the women were discouraged not only by Robert but by his male friends as well. Few of the mistresses were around long enough to become more than brief acquaintances anyway. As for the men she met through Robert, only Battaglia's protégés were her age, and even if they had not changed faces as frequently as did the mistresses, they were interested only in their master and one another. She had, however, made friends among the women who worked for Battaglia. Two women in particular—one a cutter, the other a seamstress—had befriended Electra from the start. If they knew of her relationship with Robert, they never mentioned it. Except for these two women, no one had accepted Electra on her own merit since she left Willowbrook, and she responded to their friendship with deep loyalty.

As she stirred a pitcher of martinis she had made for Robert, she thought about her two friends. Both were being wasted where they were. Lois Dunlap had far greater expertise with a needle than Battaglia would ever let her use. All the designs, including the embroidery and beading, had to be exclusively his and no one else's. Mary Brenner, who cut the patterns and fabrics, worked under the same restrictions. True, the genius was Battaglia's, but he wouldn't tolerate so much as a hint of creativity from anyone else, especially a woman.

Electra glanced at the clock on the piano Robert had

recently added to her furnishings. He was late again. He had been late for the last three evenings.

To pass the time, she sat down at the keyboard and played a simple tune. Like Amelia, she had been taught to play at an early age, although she had never had as much talent for it as her sister. Electra had preferred sketching and solitude, even as a girl.

On evenings such as this when Robert was late and the pulsing city hung between the time when the office workers had left for the evening and the party-goers had not yet arrived, she missed Willowbrook and Amelia. She had gone back to visit with Amelia several times in the intervening years, but always felt awkward, and she was running thin on reasons why Amelia could never visit her in New York. At times Electra was tempted to blurt out the real reason and shock Amelia into a decline, but for the most part, she was glad that her sister's naïveté had kept her from figuring it out—unlike Daphne Fitzpatrick, who had done so in relatively short order. Electra was still upset that Daphne had written to say she knew what Electra had done and couldn't believe she would stoop so low. As wild as Daphne had always been with the boys, she had no right to pass judgment on others.

Pensively she stared out her living room windows. Spring had come again, but unlike the wintertime, which was visible with mounds of dirty snow, and the summer, with heat waves sizzling on the pavement, there was little evidence amid the steel and concrete canyons beyond her window that nature's gentler time had returned.

Electra smoothed her hand over her abdomen, hardly noticing the silkiness of her blue hostess pajamas, for her thoughts were on weightier subjects. At least there had been no child. She had been so naive in the beginning, it hadn't occurred to her that she should worry about pregnancy. That time of innocence seemed so long ago. By the time she had learned how great the risk was, it was far too late to start worrying. At first she was angry with Robert, but soon concluded that since he and his wife were also childless, he must be sterile, and for that she was thankful. If she ever had a child, she wanted it to be born at Willowbrook, fathered by a man who was her husband. Not like that silly Reba person who had embarrassed one of Robert's friends the previous fall.

That thought reminded her of another disconcerting fact. They were still "Robert's friends," not "our friends." At times Electra felt no more important than the clock on the piano—handy but not indispensable.

She paced restlessly into the bedroom to see if the clock in there agreed with the one in the living room. Robert had never been this late before.

At the click of the lock, she hurried back to the living room. Robert was fastening the door behind him. Without a word of greeting, he automatically hung his hat on the brass tree and was opening the evening paper as he said, "What's for dinner?"

Electra's eyebrows drew together. "'What's for dinner?'" she repeated. "You come wandering in two hours late and ask what's for dinner? Where have you been?"

He looked at her over the top of his paper. "Need I remind you that you aren't my wife?"

"No!"

He went back to the column he was reading. "You sound like a wife."

"Robert," she said, forcing her voice to become calmer,

"I was worried about you. Where were you?"

"That's another wife question."

Concern began to build in Electra. She knew him quite well after all this time. "What are you hiding from me?"

"Nothing." He frowned at her. "I owe explanations to my wife, not to you. That's why I so often come here instead of going home."

Electra paced the room, her arms crossed beneath her small breasts. "Is something wrong with Mrs. Hastings?" Even after all this time, Electra couldn't bring herself to call the woman by her given name, Ima.

"I have no idea. We share the same house, but we rarely talk."

Electra moved closer. Why wasn't he meeting her eyes? The pajamas she was wearing were new, the kind that he liked her to wear, soft and thin enough to cling to her body, and slick to the touch. Yet he had barely glanced at her.

She sat next to him on the arm of the couch and ran her hand along its back. Just as she was about to kiss him beneath his ear, she inhaled the scent of perfume. Electra's eyes widened. Again she sniffed. It was on his coat and there was a pale pink smudge on his white shirt collar.

"I don't wear lipstick that color!" she exclaimed as she jumped to her feet. "And that's not my perfume, either!"

Robert paled as he shoved the paper aside. "Now see here, Electra! What are you accusing me of?"

She could only stare at him. Not once had she thought he might be seeing another woman.

"You aren't my wife! You have no right to treat me like this."

"*I* have no right? Who is she!" Electra paced like a caged animal.

"That's none of your business. If you don't like it, you can be replaced."

"I think it is my business!" As she was speaking, his last words—"You can be replaced"—sank into her consciousness. She looked around at the apartment with growing realization. "Is that why you were able to set this place up so quickly? I've always wondered about that. Damn! What a fool I was. You threw out some poor girl to bring me in here, didn't you!"

Robert glared at her.

"You actually did!" Electra felt as stunned as if she were his wife and had just discovered her home was his former love nest.

"Now, Electra, calm down. It wasn't like that. Not really."

"It was, wasn't it!" She sank down on the puffy ottoman. "How many other girls have you kept here?"

"What difference does that make?" he asked, his anger barely controlled. "You have no right to grill me."

"Yes, I do! I have rights."

"Only whatever rights I give you. You're my mistress, not my wife."

"I gave you my virginity," she said as her trembling finger pointed toward the bedroom, "on the same bed where you had other women before me."

"You made a fair deal. I've never paid so much to anyone. Those monthly checks to keep your sister in such grand style aren't cheap, you know. On top of that, I pay an exorbitant rent for this place."

Electra felt sick. For an awful moment she was afraid she would throw up. How gullible she had been! No, this was more than that. "How stupid I've been," she murmured. "How stupid!"

"I don't see what you have to complain about. I'm the one who's spending a damned fortune!"

Her eyes blazed up at him. "I'll pay you back. I'll pay back every cent, if it kills me! All I ever wanted was to save Willowbrook." She bit her lip, knowing she had gone too far.

"I was under the impression you cared for me." Robert's frosty tone spoke more than his words.

"I did . . . do. Robert, I'm angry and hurt. I've said things I never should have said." Desperation was roiling inside her. If he threw her out, she had nowhere to go. "You aren't going to make me leave, are you?"

Pausing to consider all this, Robert went to the chair opposite her and sat down. He could tell she was scared half out of her wits, and hoped he could use this to his advantage. He had no intention of installing his newest lover as his mistress. In the first place, the girl he was seeing was much too young, and in the second, she was probably sleeping with half the boys in the Bronx. Notwithstanding these reasons, she lacked the class Electra exuded so naturally.

"Give me time, Robert," Electra was saying. "Just give me time to think of a place to go."

"There's always Willowbrook," he said cruelly. "I'm sure it's still habitable. I pay the bills." Let her fret some, he thought. She deserved it for treating him as if he were her husband. Electra had been forgetting her place often of late. Letting her get a job had been a mistake.

"If I can stay here a few more weeks," she said, "I can

save enough money to get back home and to pay the upkeep for next month."

He pretended to be considering her suggestion, though he had no intention whatsoever of letting her go. Electra was as polished and as beautiful as a princess, and she was insatiable in bed. She was always still at her peak when he was satisfied, and Robert liked that. "I see no reason to change your living arrangements," he said at last. "At least not as long as you stop acting the part of a jealous wife."

She watched him, her eyes large and wary.

"I'll come and go as I please, see whom I please. You'll live here as my lover and my hostess, and I'll continue to support your sister. That seems fair to me."

Electra nodded slowly. He wasn't going to throw her out. But she had learned an important lesson about her new life. She had no rights where he was concerned and no security past the present moment. She didn't like that.

Robert stood, the bulge in his pants unmistakable. "Come to bed," he instructed. "I have some new ideas I've been wanting to try out."

After an almost indiscernible hesitation, Electra got to her feet. Lately Robert had been going past innovative and into some strange bed play indeed. She wasn't eager to discover what new kinks he had dreamed up now, but she wasn't about to appear reluctant, either. She still needed him, or rather his financial support. She'd do as she was told.

As she went into the bedroom her eyes fell on the black lacquered jewelry box he had bought to hold his gifts to her. In spite of his protests about spending money on Willowbrook, he had no reservations about surprising her with trinkets, some of which were clearly quite expensive. Until now Electra had been reluctant to accept them, because it made her feel like a prostitute. Now she realized they were as good as a bank account.

CHAPTER 7

ELECTRA FINISHED BASTING THE SEAM AND handed the half-finished garment back to Battaglia. He snatched it from her and pulled it on over the bored model's head. "Too loose! Did I not say to stitch it here?" He yanked it off and shoved it back at her.

Electra suppressed a frown. Battaglia had been impossible all morning. He had already reduced Lois Dunlap to tears, and Mary Brenner had whispered that he had threatened to sack Lois and her. Electra ripped open the seam and sewed it a quarter of an inch tighter.

He dressed the model again and pulled the cloth this way and that. "Can't you stand still?" he demanded.

"I was just breathing," the woman protested.

"I'm not paying you to breathe." He stabbed pins in the material to indicate where Electra was to put the next seam. Wielding his shears, he slashed at the hemline. "I want a scarf hem. As tiny as possible."

Electra took the dress and gladly retreated to the opposite side of the room. "He gets so touchy before a show," she complained to Lois as they basted in the seam and worked on the hem.

"Yeah, I know. You'd think it was his time of the month. But this is the worst ever. I've been here five years, and I've never seen him in such a snit," the young woman whispered back.

"Miss Radcliff. Come here!" Battaglia shouted.

The two women exchanged a look as Electra stuck her needle into the fabric and went to see what he wanted. "Yes, sir?"

He was glaring up at the ceiling, his hands clasped behind his back and his feet spread apart. "Do you see anything . . . odd about this gown, Miss Radcliff?" His voice dripped sarcasm.

Electra looked at the chartreuse garment the model was now wearing. It was the one she had finished the day before. As always, she had faithfully sewn over the basted seams, but now the dress sagged on one side and was gathered too tight across the bust. "I don't understand. It fit yesterday. Perhaps this model is a different size?"

"All my models," Battaglia said with barely restrained anger, "are *exactly* the same size. Exactly! Who would hire a model shaped like this dress?"

Electra had to admit one would be hard to find. As thin and as flat-chested as this one was, she could hardly breathe.

"It's ruined! Do you know what this material cost?" he roared.

"Perhaps I could restitch—"

"So now you know how to cut cloth larger? What a miracle you are, Miss Radcliff!"

Electra drew back. "I'm not to blame for this. I sewed it exactly the way I was told to."

"Then how can you explain this?"

"I can't."

"I'm afraid I have nothing more to say to you. You're fired."

"I'm what?" she gasped.

"Are you deaf as well as incompetent?"

"Incompetent!" Her anger flared, and she glared back at him. "Someone deliberately ruined this dress to throw blame on me!"

"Who would do that? Miss Dunlap?"

"Certainly not!"

"Miss Brenner, then? The girl who presses the clothes? One of the models?"

"Don't be ridiculous!"

"Ridiculous! You dare to insult me?"

Electra snapped her mouth shut. There was only one person left who could have ruined this dress, and that was Battaglia himself. Suddenly she remembered the argument she had had with Robert two nights before. He had been angry at her having to work late in preparation for the show and had been furious when Electra refused to quit her job. Robert and Battaglia were friends. "Have you seen Mr. Hastings lately?" she demanded.

"I haven't time to discuss your lover. Now get out!" He shoved his finger imperatively at the door.

First all the blood rushed from Electra's face; then it returned as a painful blush. Until now Lois and Mary had had no idea she had a lover.

Electra snatched up her purse from beneath the counter and stalked out of the workroom, slamming the door behind her. At the elevator, she shoved the tears away with the palm of her hand. She had never been so mortified! How could she go to Robert with this? He was probably behind it! Since the evening she had become jealous that he was seeing another woman, they had been arguing more and more. He wasn't going to get his way over this!

Electra left the building and waved down a jitney bus. Methodically she visited every designer she knew. Although several of them seemed sorely tempted to hire a woman who knew exactly what styles their competition would be showing this season, none was willing to hire her.

Tired and defeated, Electra returned to her apartment. She wasn't sure whether it had been Robert or Battaglia, but one of them had effectively blackballed her from the clique of the fashion world. Robert had won.

After three years with Robert, Electra would have said she knew all there was to know about being a mistress. She had suffered the thinly veiled demeaning comments from his friends and had learned to elude the pats and pinches they attempted when Robert wasn't watching. She had learned to ignore the doorman's penetrating stares after he had correctly concluded she was being kept. She had grown accustomed to the idea of never meeting the wives or daughters of any of Robert's male acquaintances and never going anywhere with Robert where they might run into his wife.

What she had not seen, however, was how completely he controlled her. Because she had displeased him two days before by not being at the apartment awaiting his arrival— the only time it had happened in three years—he had arranged for her to be fired. And Electra had no doubt at all that Robert was behind her dismissal. No one but Battaglia could have had access to that dress at a time when Electra wasn't around. She had been set up.

She considered packing and leaving without telling Robert. He was out of town on business and would be gone for two weeks. This would give her ample time to move out. But how could she support herself? Even if her virtue had been intact, she would still have been out of the marriage market. According to Amelia's letters, all the young men who had courted them were husbands now, and most had at least one child. Electra wasn't about to have made this great a sacrifice for nothing. There was no question of whether she and Amelia could settle now for a life in a cottage as dressmakers.

As she sat on her bed, staring at the door to her closet, she considered trying to trade Robert's patronage for someone else's. She had occasionally talked to mistresses who had done that, but it was invariably the beginning of their downfall. Soon they were considered no better than whores. Electra, however, at this point had known only one man and thus still had some degree of respectability, especially in view of the longevity of their relationship.

But how much longer could it last? By his own admission, Robert was seeing other women, and she didn't know why. Whether it was his attempt to delay the inevitable advancement of years by trying to be as sexually active as possible or whether he was simply tiring of her, she saw she was living in a house of cards that the smallest breeze could topple. The security she had once felt here, in Robert's care, was gone.

Once again a man she had trusted to provide for her needs had let her down, this time through premeditated betrayal, not an untimely death. Knowing that Robert's treachery was intentional was almost too much to bear. Not only had he arranged for her to be fired, but he had chosen a time when he was out of town. She had to take control of her life and trust her future to no one but herself. She would need money to gain her freedom, and for a moment she was at a loss. Then the solution came to her, and she was quickly on her feet. With a sense of keen excitement, she withdrew her jewelry box from her closet and set it atop her dresser. Ceremoniously, she lifted the lid and one by one removed and examined the gifts Robert had given her over the years: ropes of pearls, bracelets, necklaces, brooches, and rings. There was a small fortune here. With the cash from these jewels, she would be able to maintain Willowbrook for two years, perhaps a bit longer, and have enough left for a rather sizable investment.

Determination tightened her jaw, and a glance at the clock told her she still had several hours before stores would close. After working closely with Battaglia for so long, she knew all the right people, all the inside gossip and secrets. Electra put the jewelry box into a shopping bag so it would be less conspicuous and hurried back to the elevator.

"I heard what happened while I was out of town," Robert said with an effort not to appear smug. "I'm sorry for you."

Electra looked up from her glass of Chablis. "Oh, you mean with Battaglia?"

Doubt flickered in Robert's eyes. "I expected to find you devastated. From what I heard, he was rather rough on you."

"Yes, he was. I assumed he would have told you about it." She leaned back on the silver cushions and crossed her long legs at the knee as complacently as if nothing out of the ordinary had happened. "More wine?"

Robert poured himself another glass from the carafe on the coffee table. "I must say you're taking it rather well. I always knew you were a sensible girl."

"Woman," she corrected. "I haven't been a girl for quite a while now."

He pretended she hadn't spoken. "You'll see this is all for the best. It's only proper for you to be here whenever I arrive, and now you have no reason not to be."

"Oh, I wouldn't say that."

His eyes narrowed. "What do you mean?"

"I made a purchase while you were gone. An investment, you might say."

"Oh? An investment?"

"I bought the warehouse over on West Twenty-seventh. You know the one. You've had it for sale for several months."

Robert stared as though her words bewildered him. "*You* bought that? No one told me . . . What on earth do you want with a warehouse?"

The warm smile on her face hid the vengeance in her heart. "It's not going to be a warehouse much longer. It's the new home of Electra, Inc. I've gone into business for myself. Fashion design, of course," she added.

The effect her announcement had on Robert was even more devastating than she had expected. His eyes bugged open wide and his jaw dropped. Meaningless sounds sputtered from his lips as his tongue tried to catch up with his brain.

"Business!" he exploded. "You plan to start your own business? Impossible! I'll never allow it!"

"Too late," she purred. "I've already done it. I've even hired my first two employees, Lois Dunlap and Mary Brenner. Battaglia never realized their true worth."

"Don't tell me you expect me to pay for this?" Robert

yelled as wine sloshed from his glass. "I won't do it!"

"I never asked you to."

"Where do you plan to get the money for this hare-brained scheme? I'll see to it that no banker will lend you a cent—as if they would anyway!"

"No need to. I already have the money." She found she was actually enjoying this. "I sold my jewels."

Robert's face went from scarlet to pasty gray. Slamming the glass down, he ran to the bedroom. Unruffled by his tirade, Electra continued to sip her Chablis. In moments he was back, brandishing an empty jewelry box. "You sold my jewels!"

"I was under the impression that they were mine to do with as I pleased." He had said "my jewels." Had he not intended them as gifts? Suddenly it occurred to her that the jewels, like the apartment, might have been hand-me-downs from his former mistress. Perhaps the jewelry was even part of the Hastings estate, some his wife no longer wore. Whatever the case, what was done was done. There was no turning back. Maintaining her composure, she said, "You have good taste, Robert. They brought in enough for me to buy the warehouse and the materials I needed, with plenty left over to pay my employees' salaries for the first two months."

He looked as if he might suffer apoplexy and drop dead on the spot. Electra rose gracefully. "Calm yourself. I made a good investment. I already know how to design clothing, and with all I've learned about the business as Battaglia's assistant, I can't fail."

"Oh, no? I'll see to it that you're ruined in a month's time," he said. "I'll crush you and leave you in the gutter!"

"Now, that's not good business," she scolded with a

smile. "How can I ever repay you if you do that?"

"Repay me?"

"Certainly. I intend to reimburse you for the jewels and the rest of this month's rent on this apartment and for the amount you will spend on Willowbrook in the future."

"I'm not paying one more cent on that pile of bricks!"

"Then I'll consider the jewels my own, and I won't owe you a penny."

He paced to the window and back. "I can't believe you've done this to me! What would William say if he knew you'd done this?"

Electra laughed. "I imagine Papa would be far more upset with you and what you've done than he would be with me for going into business. After all, you're the one who seduced your best friend's orphaned daughter."

Robert glared at her.

"Now, here's what I propose," she said calmly. "I'll continue living here awhile longer. Just long enough for me to make an apartment for myself in my new building."

"You're going to live in a warehouse?"

"Only temporarily. I'll soon be able to afford a much nicer place. Why, who knows? We might be neighbors in a year or so."

Robert's face went ashen again.

"As soon as I'm financially able to support Willowbrook and myself, I'll begin repaying you. I don't figure I owe you anything for the past three years," she added, "since that was part of our original agreement." She leaned forward and took a cigarette from the gold case on the coffee table and paused while she struck a flame from the gold lighter. "Now we have a new agreement. One that's purely financial."

"You mean . . ."

"That's right, Robert. I'm no longer your mistress." Her eyes took a firm set behind the silvery cloud of smoke. "I'll never belong to any man again. Not ever."

Unmistakable determination in her voice deepened Robert's frown. "I won't agree to any of this."

"No? You have much more to lose than I do if our disagreement should become public. All I have to lose is my reputation, and thanks to you, there's not much of one at stake."

Robert looked as if he wanted to choke her. Instead he went to the door. His hand was visibly shaking as he turned back and pointed accusingly at her. "You'll pay back every cent! Do you hear me?"

Electra clearly had the upper hand and had allowed her features to soften again. "Every cent," she promised. "From this moment on. And, Robert, leave your key, won't you? I'll return it to the manager with mine when I move."

He jerked the key from his key ring and threw it on the floor.

As the door slammed behind him, Electra slowly exhaled, and the smoke floated in a lazy circle toward the ceiling. She had tasted power, and she loved it. From now on she planned to be in control of herself and her destiny. She had no doubt at all that she would succeed.

CHAPTER 8

AMELIA RADCLIFF GAZED OUT AT THE LEAVES of the tree beyond her bedroom window. Three years had passed since her father died and Electra left for New York. Another spring was almost finished. The tender green of the leaves was already toughening into the deeper hues that would see them through the heat of summer. She had described the springtime leaves in the poem she had just completed. "Verdant children cloaked in darker green" was the way she had put it.

She replaced the cap on her fountain pen and pressed the pale pink blotter over the last words she had written. In some ways her poetry seemed to Amelia to be the greatest waste of all. Who would ever see it? Her friend Jenny Allen had once suggested that Amelia sell her poems, but Amelia had never really considered doing it.

Jenny. She was now married to Carleton Edgeworth, Amelia's former beau. Already, after only two years of marriage, Carleton's waist was expanding. Amelia thought it served him right for not being more faithful in his affection for her, but she also felt sorry for Jenny. In time she would be married to a fat old man. But Jenny didn't seem to mind.

Amelia moved from her writing desk to the window seat and read Electra's most recent letter once again. Like all her sister's letters, this one was written on thick, creamy paper and the page was filled with Electra's crisp penmanship. Just looking at the slant and boldness of her sister's script brought Amelia a sense of her sister's determination. Electra had always been the more stubborn of the two. Otherwise she would have married, as their father told her to do, and the two of them wouldn't be old maids now. Amelia hated that term, so she put it from her mind.

Electra had quit her job, the letter said, and was opening a design studio of her own. Soon, she said, her address would be changing. There was no mention of any beau or of when she intended to return to live at Willowbrook.

Amelia sighed and put this letter with all the others in the chintz-covered bandbox in the top of her closet. She dutifully wrote Electra once a week, whether there was anything to report or not. Electra answered when she remembered to do so. Correspondence wasn't one of her strong suits.

She left her room and wandered restlessly down the hall, the Tabriz carpeting silencing her footsteps. Everything about Willowbrook was silent these days. On the money Electra sent, Amelia couldn't afford all the teas and parties that had enlivened the house when her father was alive. Not that Amelia resented it, or so she told herself. No doubt it cost more to live in New York than in the country. But now Electra had started her own business and would soon move to another, presumably nicer, apartment. Amelia couldn't help feeling a bit deprived.

As she went downstairs, she automatically glanced at

the chandelier to see if it had been dusted recently. It had, and that was no surprise. Mrs. Adams had always done a thorough job of cleaning, and the lack of social life at Willowbrook these days had made her job easier. Most of the rooms were closed off now, their furniture hidden beneath old sheets. There was no need to clean rooms that were never used.

Life here had become dreamlike. Time passed, but nothing at Willowbrook changed. Her friends married and traveled and had babies, but her own life was as quiescent as the water in a stagnant pond. She was like a wife to Willowbrook—looking after it, keeping it running smoothly, guarding it against disrepair. Like a wife with no husband.

Having gathered up her straw hat while passing through the foyer, she donned it before stepping from the shade of the deep porch into the sunlight. Although she had no young men coming to call, she was still careful to protect her skin and hair from the sun's harmful rays. She had squeezed too much lemon juice on her skin and smoothed too many jars of cream on her face and hands to let herself burn and freckle now. Her mother had always said the sun would bleach her hair into stripes like corn syrup if she let it. Amelia was proud of her auburn hair, and wasn't going to jeopardize it by being foolhardy. Besides, this was only a hiatus in her life. Eventually, perhaps by autumn this year, Electra would have her business sufficiently under way for her to return to Willowbrook and manage the business from there. Electra hadn't said in her letters this was her intention, but Amelia knew their father had managed his affairs in this manner, and she was sure Electra could do the same. Electra had been gone three years now, and every letter contained a mention of her yearning to move back.

Once she did, Amelia would be free to leave.

As she meandered about the grounds, Amelia planned where she would go after Electra's return. Maybe to the cities her father had promised to take her to someday such as London and Paris. Or maybe to places with wild foreign names like Zanzibar and Siam. And she would marry. She never doubted that. Maybe all the young men around Catawba Mills were taken, but she could have her pick of men in London and Paris. Who would know she was twenty-one if she didn't tell them? Amelia knew she could easily have passed for a girl of eighteen.

Her daydream brought a smile to her face, and for a moment it swept away her melancholy. A loose rock in her path caused her to lose her balance, but her fall was broken by the old ivy-shrouded wall next to her. As she straightened up, mildly chastising herself for not having watched where she was going, she looked at the familiar barrier with interest. She knew what was behind the wall, of course. It was the enclosed garden her great-grandmother had planted when Willowbrook was new. But in all her life Amelia had never been inside. After her great-grandmother's death, the garden had been locked, and English ivy had been allowed to climb the walls unchecked, even to the point of covering the wooden door. When she was a child, Amelia's curiosity about what was within had been thwarted by parental edict and as the years had passed she had come to accept the enclosed garden as merely another feature of the yard, but now she was determined to have her curiosity satisfied.

In short order she fetched the gardener, and together they found the door and stripped the ivy back from it. He struck at the rusted lock with a pickax until it gave way and then shouldered it open. Together they stared at the jungle of plants inside.

"I ain't got time to take this on, Miss Amelia," he complained. "I've got all I can do to keep up the lawns."

She stepped inside. The air here was heavy with the musty scent of decaying leaves, but was laced with the faint aroma of roses.

"Best let me lock it up again," the gardener was saying. "It's a mess in here."

For a long moment she looked about, preoccupied by the intriguing sight. Then she murmured, "A place that time forgot."

"Now, Miss Amelia . . ." the man pleaded.

She turned back to him. "I'm not asking you to work here, Parker." She knew he was not skilled enough for this. Willowbrook hadn't seen a truly talented gardener since their head gardener Randolph Jenkins had quit some years before due to illness. Parker had been Jenkins's assistant, and although he lacked imagination and creativity, her father had promoted him out of a sense of loyalty, and Amelia hadn't had the heart to let him go or the money to get a truly good replacement. "I want to do this myself," she added.

"You, miss?" He stared at her as if she had lost her mind.

"I know there's a lot to do, but I have nothing else to fill my time. If you'll bring me some tools from the shed, I'll get started. I'll need a shovel and clippers. Maybe a rake and hoe."

He looked first at the tangle of growth, then back at her as if he were sizing up her ability to the task at hand. Cocking his head to one side, he said, "Be best if you just set fire to it and start from scratch."

"Would you prefer for me to get the tools myself? Where are they?" Amelia knew he would give in if she put it this way. Servants always had liked her and wanted to please her, because she never ordered them about or otherwise infringed upon their dignity.

Grumbling under his breath, Parker left to get the tools.

Being careful not to become entangled in the thorny undergrowth, Amelia stepped farther into the garden. The area wasn't large in comparison to Willowbrook's expansive grounds, but there was room enough for a huge old willow tree in one corner and for sunlight to brighten the rest. Under the willow was a marble bench encrusted with green and red and gold lichen. A sundial, perched atop a carved pedestal, occupied the garden's center, and in the far corner was an enclosed shed that had probably held tools and potting supplies.

Old-fashioned climbing roses—the kind with blooms as flat as poppies—tangled over one another in a competitive struggle to reach the sun. Honeysuckle, entwined in the ivy, gave the appearance that the ivy was blooming. Bridal wreath and forsythia mounded in huge clumps along what must have been the path. Flame azaleas blazed yellow to orange to pink. A mimosa, spread like an umbrella over the corner opposite the shed, its pink flowers looking like tufts of flamingo feathers. One entire wall was draped in purple wisteria, the trunk of which was thicker than Amelia's waist.

"It's like magic!" she whispered. She discounted the garden's ruin, seeing only its beauty.

Parker returned with the tools in a wheelbarrow. "You'll need this to carry out the weeds, Miss Amelia. If you'll dump them off to the side there, I'll burn them later."

"Did you know all these old flowers were in here?" With gentle reverence she touched a rose's flat face.

"No, ma'am. It's been closed as long as I've been here. I heard Jenkins say once that it had been locked away for as long as he could remember."

"Why would anybody lock up such a lovely place? These must be the very flowers my great-grandmother planted!"

"Most likely. No gardener has been in here for a spell. That's real clear." He looked about in disgust. "There's a passel of work to be done here."

With the shovel, Amelia started scraping the ground so the gate could be swung open and closed more easily. "I won't be needing you, Parker. I'll take care of this."

He scratched his graying head. "This is way too much work for you, Miss Amelia. Maybe you ought to let me do it. I don't really mind."

"No, no. You were right. You have far too much to do already. I'll take my time in here, and I won't push myself too hard. Honestly, Parker. I want to do it."

After a gloomy shake of his head, the gardener left.

Amelia smiled as she tossed a small shovelful of dirt aside. He didn't understand. To him it just looked like work. She saw it as a useful way to spend her empty days. She and this garden had a lot in common, she reflected. It had been shut away and more or less forgotten. Everyone knew it was there, but no one bothered to visit it. All one could see on the outside was a cloak of ivy, but inside, life was flowering and stretching and tumbling over itself. Like the garden, Amelia was in the late springtime of her life. If someone didn't rescue her soon, she would pass into an overblown summer and finally wither away, all out of sight of the world, her passing unmarked and unmourned.

She shoved the blade deeper into the earth. That wasn't going to happen to her! Like this garden she was going to prosper! With increased determination she went back to work.

SUMMER, 1941

'Tis the last rose of summer,
  Left blooming alone;
All her lovely companions
  Are faded and gone.

Thomas Moore

CHAPTER 9

HEAT SHIMMERED UP FROM THE PAVEMENT AS
Electra stepped from the cab and bent to pay the driver.
She noticed that her escort, a handsome young actor who
had been cast as an understudy for an Off-Broadway play,
a play neither Electra nor anyone else cared to see, wasn't
embarrassed in the least that she was paying the fare.

She nodded to the doorman as he swung open the heavy
glass door emblazoned with a golden letter R, centered amid
a laurel wreath—the classic trademark of the Randolph.
She had moved here several years earlier, during the time
between the stock market crash of 1929 and Adolf Hitler's
blitzkrieg across Europe. Electra had viewed that brief era
as a time of innocence—for the world, not for herself.
Electra's innocence was long gone, and she didn't miss it
at all.

The young man with her, who had come to New York
as Bill Wilson of Stratford, Connecticut, but was now
known as William Stratford, paused to buy a paper from a
newsboy standing near the door. Electra removed her beige
cotton gloves and dropped them into her crocodile purse.

When William rejoined her, she led the way across the lobby, her clicking heels muffled as she stepped from the polished oak floor onto the thick carpet beneath the conversational grouping of furniture, then again marking her energetic steps as she and William crossed more bare floor to the elevator. As with the doorman, Electra gave the elevator operator a nod and waited. He was paid to know which was her floor.

"It says here that Germany is laying siege to Leningrad," William said.

"Must we talk about the war in Europe?" Electra asked with an effort to conceal her impatience. "That's all I hear these days."

William obligingly looked farther down the paper. "Tommy Dorsey's orchestra is in town. That young singer, Frank Sinatra, is still singing with him. I don't know what all the girls see in him, personally, but we can go if you'd like."

A faint smile tilted the corners of Electra's lips. She was always amazed at how easily William spent her money. "Not tonight. We can hear them anytime."

William frowned down at the paper. "Why do you suppose he never wears clothes that fit?"

"Do I detect a touch of jealousy?" The elevator man opened the doors and she led William into a short hall.

"Why would I be jealous of a shrimp like Sinatra?" William waited patiently for her to unlock the door, then followed her into her apartment.

The decor of her apartment was unique, like Electra herself. The living room carpeting was white, as were the walls and ceiling. A crystal chandelier was suspended above a large glass-topped coffee table, which reflected its brilliance. The room was saved from austerity by a huge curving sofa upholstered in Schiaparelli pink, more commonly called "shocking pink" nowadays. Masses of verdant palms and ferns, grouped here and there around the room and on the tiny balcony that overlooked the city, provided the only other color.

William went to the glass and chrome wet bar and poured each of them a drink. Electra watched him as she removed her hat and stroked her hand over the cascade of rooster tail feathers on the brim. "How long have we known each other?" she asked.

William paused to think. "We met at Zoe Wharton's Christmas party." He smiled across at her. "You wore that black dress with all the beads on it."

"Yes. I remember the dress. Six months is a long time."

William brought her the drink and gazed down at her. "Not when you are in love."

"I told you not to say that." Electra hated it when one of her lovers pretended to love her when she knew it was a lie. "I told you from the very beginning we would never speak of love."

"I know, but at the time I didn't know you. I didn't know how I would feel about you."

She sighed. "For heaven's sake, Bill, those are the lines from *Heart on Her Sleeve*. Give me credit for some intelligence."

"So what? I mean those words. And I've asked you not to call me Bill. You know I hate that."

"Sorry." She turned away from him and went to look out at the skyscrapers beyond the sheer white curtains at the window. She knew he disliked any reference to his past and that he preferred the formal version of his name. At first she had been fond of all his little pretensions. Now they just seemed silly. "Six months is a long time," she repeated.

"Would you like to see a movie?" he asked.

"Not tonight."

"How about a play? I hear the one at the Morosco Theatre on West Forty-fifth Street is—"

"I would rather be alone tonight," she interrupted.

"You would? Alone?"

"Yes, alone. Sometimes it's pleasant just to be by yourself." Electra had not intended her tone to be so sharp. "I'm sorry," she said. After a moment, she added, "It seems as if we say that a lot here lately."

William's eyes met hers and she could see his disappointment, though she knew he was trying to hide it. "I guess . . . in that case I ought to go. That is, since you want to be alone."

Electra summoned up a smile. "Thank you, William. Perhaps we can get together next week."

"I have rehearsals starting Monday."

"I know." She wondered how she could get him to understand what she was really saying. It was so awkward when she had to come right out and tell a man she didn't want to see him anymore. She had done so more than once, but she always felt uneasy for days afterward. She supposed that guilt, if it could be called that, was the last remaining trace of her genteel upbringing coming to the fore. She managed a convincing smile. "I'll call you."

"You know," William said, "when you talk I can hear the South in your voice. Camellias and honeysuckle and jasmine."

"You must have a remarkable ear," she observed dryly.

She knew only a hint of her Virginia accent remained. And his compliment was borrowed from the lines of his current play. She knew, because she had read his script while he slept last night.

Without comment, William went into the bedroom, and from the sounds she could hear, she concluded he was gathering up the clothes he had worn the day before. Electra had a strict rule that none of her lovers brought more than a single change of clothing. No one was ever allowed to actually move into her apartment any more than he was allowed to question her about the times when she was away from him. Electra kept her independence wrapped about her like a cloak.

When William came back into the room, she didn't turn to look at him. She detested farewells, even when the man didn't recognize it as one.

"I guess I'm going now. Are you sure you don't want me to stay?"

"I'll call you next week." She would, but only to tell him she would be unable to see him for several days. After a few such evasions, William would get the point. He wasn't a fool, nor would his ego permit him to crawl back into her graces. In a couple of weeks he would have convinced himself that the split had been his own idea. Electra liked actors—they were so pliant and so easily led.

She heard the door shut, knowing he would not be back. She never gave anyone her key. That was another of her rules. Without a key, no one could come in unless she permitted it. After those years as Robert's mistress, she insisted on remaining in control.

Robert. She hadn't thought of him in years. She had long since repaid her debt to him, and the few times they had met in public, they had been civil. The crash had almost ruined him, and Electra had magnanimously lent him money, which he was still paying back.

In the mirror that covered one wall of her dining room, she gazed at her reflection. As always she was a perfect size ten. That was more flesh than she allowed her models to carry, of course, but she looked older when she weighed less than this.

Leaning closer, she studied her face and hair. At thirty-six, she was past the bloom of youth, but because of cosmetics and facials, she wasn't wrinkling perceptibly. There were a few lines around her eyes and small ones at her lips, thanks to smoking. At one time she had wondered if the wrinkles would fade if she gave up pursing her lips around cigarettes, but she decided it wasn't worth the effort. Smoking was chic and sophisticated and besides, she enjoyed it.

She pulled a lock of her short hair forward. Fortunately it was still dark, but lately she had begun to find gray hairs at her temples. That could look spectacular if all the rest stayed black. Her sharp eyes, however, found three new ones—right above her forehead. She made a mental note to start having it dyed at her next regular appointment. Now was the best time, before anyone else noticed.

Closing her mind to such thoughts, as one would close a book at the end of a chapter fully intending to resume the reading at some later time, Electra went to her bedroom. The brilliant pink that predominated her living room was repeated here in her vanity stool and robe and bedspread, and the furniture was lacquered a deep garnet to match the drapes. The resulting effect was not unlike that of being inside a huge Valentine. Her bedroom was the only sentimentality Electra allowed herself. She wasn't romantic by nature, though she was sensual, and she liked the color red, possibly because Amelia would have considered it gaudy.

As she removed the navy crepe dress trimmed in beige, she thought about her sister. Amelia had long since stopped asking when she could come to New York for a visit, and Electra was relieved. It would have been awkward trying to explain William and the string of young men before him. Amelia would not have understood, much less condoned such a life-style.

Electra removed her stockings and wriggled out of her girdle.

Why was she so protective of Amelia and her outmoded ways? Electra was known among her crowd as outrageous and unpredictable. Was she somehow secretly ashamed of the way she lived? Electra rejected the idea at once. This was 1941 and New York City. The country was recovering from the privations of the early thirties and beginning to feel the expanded economy from the war in faraway Europe, a war that would increase the demand for American products but would remain far enough removed not to endanger American lives. The new and frenetic pace of life reminded Electra of the halcyon days of her youth when "madcap" and "joy" and "skiddoo" had been familiar terms.

Of course she wasn't ashamed of who or what she was. Electra tossed her dress into the hamper of clothes to be sent to the cleaners and her girdle and hose into the hamper for hand-washables. She was proud of what she had made of herself.

Electra, Inc., was one of the most prestigious fashion design studios in the country. Lois Dunlap and Mary Brenner had been with her over thirteen years now, loyal to her since her first day in business. Lois had shown a flare for hat design and had created the feather-trimmed hat Electra had been wearing. Mary, after years of cutting cloth, was such an expert on fabric that Electra took her on buying trips and occasionally sent her alone to purchase fabric. Electra retained sole right to design the dresses, but she didn't rule dictatorially as had her despotic mentor, Anthony Battaglia.

Battaglia was still around and still had his pretty young men in attendance. Only his highly regarded sense of style kept him from becoming a target of ridicule. At times he seemed to be a parody of himself—wearing outlandish shirts and scarves and making exaggeratedly feminine gestures. But his designs were always at the forefront of fashion. These days Electra considered him her biggest rival.

Electra slipped into one of her own fashions, a one-piece plum jersey with short sleeves and wide culotte-style legs that draped to her ankles. She tied a plum and white sash about her waist and stepped into sandals of braided straw. The day was scorching hot, and even the constant breeze through the balcony door and windows wasn't enough to cool the apartment.

Seeking relief from the heat, Electra went back through the living room and out onto her small balcony. She sat on one of the two chaise longues next to the table and pulled her culottes up, exposing her legs to the air. She hated New York in the summer.

Willowbrook would be cool, she reminisced with longing. With its spreading oaks and lawns and fountains, it would be so cool. The rose gardens would be in full bloom by now, with nodding red, pink, yellow, and white blossoms, and bees humming lazily in the scented air.

The house would be cool, too. The walls had been built thick to keep the house cool in summer and warm in winter. With her eyes closed and her face turned to the breeze, Electra imagined that the air was being stirred by one of the fans suspended from Willowbrook's high ceilings. Baskets of cut flowers would be scenting the room as well. Willowbrook always smelled of lavender and roses and lemon oil. She could almost hear the tick of the grandfather clock and the distant song of a mockingbird.

But then her rebellious senses told her there were no sounds other than the snarl of traffic far below. She opened her eyes and looked down at the tops of cars and buses streaming by. Even though evening was hours away, many of the neon advertising signs were already lit. Not an oak, a mockingbird, or a rose was in sight.

She closed her eyes again. She often wondered if Amelia had any idea how much she had sacrificed for Willowbrook and her. Amelia was thirty-four years old and had never had to earn a penny in her entire life. Thanks to Electra she was living in the luxury of Willowbrook. Electra's generous checks had rehired a small staff of servants to do all the work, and Amelia needed to do nothing but live the easy life and keep Willowbrook running smoothly. At times Electra felt so much resentment over her conscripted exile that she almost hated Amelia. Surely at some point during the past decade and a half, Amelia must have realized what a burden this was on her sister.

Or maybe she hadn't. Amelia still seemed to have one foot in the past and had no conception of what it was like to claw out a successful business in New York. Why, every season could be the last for Electra's designs. There were no guarantees, none at all. And everything Electra knew about running a business she had learned the hard way. No one had ever handed her anything on a silver platter, as she had done for Amelia.

She tried to close out the cacophony of horns from below as traffic snarled at one of the intersections. She had to escape this, even if only for a brief while, and to see Willowbrook and breathe in its elegance. Thinking through her busy schedule, she chose a time when she could manage to be away. Although it was weeks from now, having a specific date in mind would help her bear the grind until then.

This time she wouldn't go alone. She wouldn't take William—that was over for her. She would meet someone new. Someone exciting. She would take him with her to Willowbrook and Amelia be damned! Electra was a grown woman, and she wasn't harnessed to antiquated mores, as Amelia was.

Having formulated this plan to shock her sister made Electra feel better. She had no intention of hurting Amelia, but shaking her up a bit might make her better appreciate what was being done for her. Already Electra's muscles were relaxing, and she was beginning to enjoy the cooling breeze. As she listened to the pulse of the city, she fantasized what Amelia would say and what she might do.

CHAPTER 10

AMELIA PUSHED HER HAIR BACK FROM HER sweat-dampened brow. Although it was only July, the weather was sizzling. Heat hung in the high-ceilinged rooms of Willowbrook like an oppressive lid. Her white eyelet blouse and cotton dirndl skirt clung to her hot body and her shoulder-length hair felt sticky and unpleasant.

Summoning her energy, Amelia decided she would have to go upstairs to pin her hair up off her neck. For several months she had thought about cutting it short—maybe even in a shingle bob—the style her friend Jenny Edgeworth had worn since the mid-1920s. True, such short hair wasn't still fashionable, but Jenny enjoyed its coolness, and on hot days like this Amelia considered forsaking fashion. Electra would have frowned on her rebellion, but then, Electra was one of those who set the ridiculous trends that enslaved women to styles of clothing that were often as inconvenient and encumbering as were hair fashions.

The higher she climbed the stairs, the hotter was the air. Helga Jansen, Amelia's new maid, always cleaned the upper floor early in the morning, and neither of them went up during the heat of the day if they could avoid it. Helga was a newcomer to the area, her family having fled Germany at the first sign of war, and she had not yet grown accustomed to the heat of a Virginia summer. Amelia wondered if anyone ever did, really. The summer before, she had installed an attic fan in the hallway, much against Electra's wishes. Electra was far north in New York City, a place presumably much cooler than the South, and she wanted to keep Willowbrook like a shrine. Amelia was hard-pressed not to resent that. After all, she had to live here and Electra didn't.

She went into her bathroom and stepped out of her espadrilles and onto the black and white tile floor in order to cool her feet. She brushed her hair up from her neck and twisted it into a chignon. Opening her bobby pins with her teeth, she made it secure. Damp tendrils curled at the nape of her neck, but she felt a bit cooler. As yet her hair had no gray, although the coppery highlights of her youth had darkened to a reddish brown. She had put on a few pounds in the last five years—a fact Electra never failed to mention—but the extra weight only served to round out her figure and wasn't unattractive. Still, she mused as she glanced down at the reflection of her waist, it wouldn't hurt to lose a bit. But as Helga had cooked a strudel for dessert that night, the diet would have to wait for the next day, or maybe the following week. Diets were more easily started on a Monday.

Amelia stepped back into her shoes and went back downstairs and into the enclosed porch. Although the glass-louvered windows were cranked open on the shady side of the room and the shades were drawn on the opposite side to block out the sun, the room was still warm. Amelia considered calling Jenny just to pass the time of day, but a glance at her wristwatch told her Jenny would be driving her daughters to their tennis lessons now.

Jenny was Amelia's friend of long standing. An amazing thing, she reflected, considering Jenny had married Amelia's beau, Carleton. Theirs was a steady marriage, and if it had no high peaks, it also had no deep valleys. Jenny seemed contented.

Amelia wondered if she herself had ever been content. She couldn't think of a time. As a child she had always been eager to explore, to experiment, to *do* something. Now she felt almost like a prisoner in a velvet cage. Willowbrook was gracious and comfortable, but Amelia lived a reclusive life. After having been ostracized because of the loss of her family wealth, she had never really rejoined society, not even after Electra had gone to work in New York and the checks had begun arriving and growing larger every year. She and Jenny still visited, but all the other friends of her youth were only coolly polite to her when they passed on Catawba Mills's streets. Amelia no longer blamed them. After all these years she had grown apart from them, and they were less than strangers to her, for strangers at least elicited some degree of curiosity.

Amelia heard the squeak of Helga's crepe-soled shoes on the oak floor in the hall, and she looked around expectantly.

Helga was in her late twenties and was dating a son of Irish immigrants, a combination Amelia found surprising, especially since Helga's English was still sketchy at best. She wore her silvery blond hair in a braid wrapped neatly around her head, and her blue eyes were always open wide as if she still found everything in America amazing. "We are having supper at seven. *Ja?*"

As usual, Amelia wasn't sure if Helga meant this as a question or a statement to be verified. "Yes, at seven."

"I am cooking the roast?"

"Yes, roast sounds good." Amelia would have preferred something lighter in this oppressive heat, but Helga's cooking skills were rather limited. "Perhaps we could have a fruit salad?"

"*Ja*. Fruit salad is good." She smiled at Amelia, showing her even white teeth. She looked as healthy and as wholesome as an advertisement for milk.

"I'm going out to the garden, if anyone should call," Amelia said, speaking slowly so Helga could follow her meaning.

"*Ja*, the garden."

Amelia automatically reached for her straw hat and tied the scarf ends behind her neck as she let the door close behind her. The grass was hot and limp under her shoes. In the distance she could hear the whooshing of a lawn sprinkler at work. She glanced up at the brassy sky and wondered when it would rain again.

The wooden gate in the garden wall swung open easily at her touch. Like the rest of the grounds, Amelia's garden was uncomfortably hot, and some of the plants had begun to wilt. From the potting shed Amelia got a hose and set a sprinkler beneath the mimosa where the spray would also reach the lythrum and delphinium.

Her steps along the brick paths that radiated from the central sundial crushed the petals of creeping thyme that grew in the cracks between the bricks, releasing its pungent aroma.

Sweeping aside the umbrella boughs of the willow, she sat on the marble bench at the base of the large tree. At last she had found relief from the heat. Flanking the bench were banks of impatiens looking impossibly vivid beside snowy sweet alyssum. Amelia leaned back and opened the top button of her blouse to let the air cool more of her skin.

"Hello," an unexpected voice called out.

Amelia sat upright with a jerk. A tall stranger stood in the doorway, his broad shoulders almost touching the ivy-covered walls on either side of him.

"May I come in? I didn't mean to startle you."

His voice was deep and silky with the accent of the deep South. Something about him seemed familiar, but Amelia had no idea who he could be. She tried to remember where her two gardeners would be at this time of day, in case she needed help. The stranger was blocking the only exit from the garden.

"Excuse me?" He sounded doubtful and Amelia realized she hadn't answered him.

"Who are you?" she asked as she stood. She wanted to rebutton the top of her blouse but was afraid to call his attention to the wedge of exposed skin.

"I'm Christopher Jenkins."

"Jenkins?" She stepped forward as she tried to remember. "A Jenkins used to work here. Years ago."

"That was my father." He came closer and sunlight touched his golden hair.

"Christopher?" she asked as if he had not already told her his name. "You're the same Christopher who had a puppy named Max?"

"You remember Max?" He grinned at her, and she felt a warm flush go through her.

She nodded. "I haven't seen you in years."

"After my father had that stroke, we had to move away. We went to live with my aunt in Georgia."

"I remember now." Amelia had liked Jenkins and had cried for days after he left. "How are your parents?"

"Dad is dead now. He never really recovered." He paused and a muscle tightened in his jaw as if the memory was painful. "Mama is still with Aunt Hallie."

Amelia finally recalled her manners. "Come in out of the sun. This bench is the only cool spot I've found."

Christopher crossed the garden and ducked under the weeping branches of the willow to join her. As he turned to look at the ancient tree trunk, Amelia refastened the button on her blouse.

"So this is what was behind all that ivy. I always wondered."

"It was in a terrible mess," she said as she sat on the bench so he could sit down as well. "I've planted a lot of the flowers you see, but I tried to restore the garden as it might have looked when it was first planted. Are you a gardener like your father was? If you're looking for work—"

"I'm a doctor."

"Oh." She felt a twinge of embarrassment. In his casual slacks and open-necked shirt she had assumed him more likely a tradesman than a professional.

"I just moved to Catawba Mills. I heard old Dr. Sportsman had died, and I decided to start my practice here."

"That's wonderful. We need a new doctor here. Dr. McVane is the only one left in town, and he practically has one foot in the grave."

"I didn't mean to intrude on your privacy. I've thought of Willowbrook so often, and I wanted to see if any of the family was still around. I saw you through the open gate."

"You aren't intruding at all." Amelia wished she had put her hair up more carefully and that her blouse were still crisp. She kept stealing glances at him and had to clasp her hands in her lap to remind her not to stare.

"I'm not sure what to call you. I haven't heard your married name."

Amelia tried to keep a blush from rising. "I'm not married. Call me Amelia, just as you used to do."

"Amelia," he said softly as if he were tasting it. "It's a sweet, old-fashioned name. It sounds like lace and flowers."

His blue eyes were searching her face as if he might be wondering why she hadn't married. It wasn't a look unknown to Amelia. She glanced out at the sundial surrounded by bursts of petunias. "We had some reverses a few years back."

"I wasn't trying to pry."

"Anyone will tell you. It's no secret, goodness knows. My father died owing a great deal of money."

"I wondered if he was still around."

"He died in his sleep. It seems like a hundred years ago." Her voice drifted away; then she pulled herself back. "Fortunately Electra had a marketable talent, and she went to New York and became a fashion designer. She lives there still."

Christopher grinned. "It's hard to imagine her in a city. She always seemed rather shy."

"You might say she has changed a bit," Amelia added with deliberate understatement. "She never was really shy, just introverted. I was always the one raising Cain."

"Remember how we used to slip out and play together?"

She laughed at the memories. "You were always the

cowboy and I was the Indian princess, and we went up and down the creek looking for pirates. Why do you suppose we thought cowboys and Indians fought pirates?"

"Who knows. Blame it on *Treasure Island*, I guess."

"Max always gave us away. We would try to hide from whoever had been sent to find us, and he would run out and wag his tail at them." Her smile grew wistful. "I never understood why we weren't supposed to play together."

"Didn't you?"

Amelia lifted her chin as if daring him to say it. "No. I didn't."

"You were a little girl as rich as a princess. I was only a gardener's son."

"That was a long time ago. I'm not rich now, and you're a doctor."

"So are you up to a fast game of sink-the-pirates?"

"Now you're teasing me." He was so close she could see the silver and turquoise flecks in his eyes. His eyes were truly remarkable. A woman could get lost in them and might never want to find her way back out. She stood abruptly and walked into the sunlight.

Christopher followed her. "I wasn't trying to upset you."

"I know." Amelia went to the sundial and touched the warm copper face. "I guess it's the heat. I've felt out of sorts all day." She traced her finger across the marks of the hours. "All those years before I opened the garden, this sundial was in here accurately telling the time, but no one ever noticed. Sometimes I feel like that."

"You're lonely? I never would have guessed that. I assumed you had a fiancé or at least a favorite beau."

She knew he was just behind her, and all her senses thrilled at his nearness. Knowing he was so close made her heart race. "Electra and I stepped out of society when Papa died." She hoped that sounded as if it had been her own choice and not that she had been cast out.

"You're so young to have done that."

"Young?" She laughed mirthlessly. "I'm thirty-four."

"I know. So am I. We're still in our prime."

She studied his face to see if he was teasing her again. His blue eyes were guileless. "Would you like to stay for supper?"

"I can't."

She looked away in embarrassment. So he had been baiting her after all.

"But I can come out later. I have an appointment to discuss a partnership with Dr. McVane. We won't share an office, but he might take calls for me and vice versa. We arranged to meet before I moved here."

Amelia relaxed a bit. "Later would be just fine."

"I'm not sure how long the meeting will take, but I'll make it a point to be here by eight, if that's okay with you."

"Eight is perfect."

Christopher smiled down at her, and Amelia felt her pulse quicken. Then he turned away and left, and she felt a mad urge to run after him. However, she stood perfectly still, her fingers still on the sundial, and watched until he was out of sight.

She had a date! For the first time in years, she would be entertaining a handsome gentleman caller. Best of all, it was someone she already knew she would like. As a child he had been one of her best friends.

She went to the gate in time to see Christopher drive away in a Packard. It wasn't one of the newer models—

she assumed he must still be paying for his medical equipment and perhaps his school expenses—but its shiny black paint had been recently washed. He was a good driver, not taking off in a spray of gravel or creeping from first to second gear. His car rolled smoothly down Willowbrook's catawba tree–lined drive to the highway, then disappeared from sight.

Amelia drew her shoulders back. She wasn't going to make a fool of herself over the prospect of seeing Christopher Jenkins. He probably intended this visit as a means to help him establish his practice. After all, he couldn't take out an advertisement in the paper to say he was in town. Perhaps new doctors always made contact with anyone they had known previously in order to get the word out.

She looked back at the gate and remembered how his shoulders had seemed to fill the opening and how his hair had looked like gold in the sunlight. His eyes had been so blue! She hoped he hadn't noticed her staring into them. She liked what she had seen there.

Amelia had always been convinced that the eyes were mirrors of the soul. She had read that somewhere and believed it implicitly. Amelia had always been a romantic.

She moved the sprinkler to a new position and walked among her roses. She had added only old species to the ones already there. Rosa Mundi with its red petals streaked with white and pink, May Queens that scaled the ivy-covered wall and bloomed with the honeysuckle, pink Four Seasons that went all the way back to the ancient Romans. Their scents blended in the hot air and suggested more romantic times.

This was the prime of her life, he had said. Amelia

touched her cheek, still soft and rounded, her hair still dark even if it wasn't as bright an auburn as it once had been. She wasn't old. Not yet.

Optimism raced through her like the tinkle of a thousand tiny silver bells. She wasn't ready to be put on the shelf yet. She still had years and years to travel and see places she had only read about. Why, she might still marry, and it wasn't too late yet to have children.

Oblivious to the heat, Amelia ran to the house to begin making plans for Christopher's visit that evening.

Amelia sat on the sofa and tried to keep her mind on the radio. In the hall the clock chimed the half hour and began ticking its way toward nine. Helga had long since gone to her rooms above the garage, and the house felt empty and lonely. He wasn't coming after all.

Amelia turned the dial, looking for "Amos and Andy" as she tried to pretend she wasn't disappointed. So what if she had washed and set her hair in the middle of the day and had gone up after supper to put on her prettiest dress?

She picked up a *Life* magazine and thumbed through the usual ads for Vanity Fair slips, whiskey, Bromo-Seltzer, and De Sotos. A Broadway play was synopsized, as was a movie, along with photographs of the various key scenes. The synopses were so detailed Amelia wondered how anyone could enjoy the movie or play after having read them. She usually skipped over the movie details after reading the title, and dwelt on the description of the play, which she had no likelihood of seeing. Interspersed with the magazine's usual fare were articles about the waves of immigrants flooding into America to escape the war. Not all of them were as lucky as Helga had been, and many landed in city slums where they clustered with their own kind, keeping their language and customs intact.

She glanced at her watch and saw nine o'clock was approaching fast. He wasn't coming.

With an impatient gesture she tossed the magazine aside and turned off the radio. There was no sense in waiting for him any longer. She was crossing the entrance hall when a knock sounded on the door.

Amelia paused, her hand on the carved newel post at the foot of the stairs. He was an hour late. She ought not to admit him.

But when the knock sounded again, she hurried to the door. As she had hoped, it was Christopher, the porch light making a halo of his golden hair. He handed her a box of Whitman chocolates.

"I'm sorry I'm late. I had forgotten how long-winded and persistent Dr. McVane can be. I tried to cut short our visit, but couldn't get away any sooner without insulting him. Had you given up on me?"

"I'd hoped you'd come," she found herself saying. All her intentions of coolly sending him away had vanished. "Won't you come in? Helga left strudel on the sideboard. Can I cut you a slice? It's one of the few dishes she cooks really well."

He followed her into the dining room, and Amelia had to struggle to keep her hands from shaking as she cut two thick slices of strudel. Not only had he not stood her up, but he had brought her a box of chocolates! Surely this meant he wasn't here merely to interest her in his medical services.

They went into the living room to eat the dessert. Amelia glanced around the room as if seeing it through his eyes.

The tone was dark, but not oppressive. The chairs and sofa were slightly worn, but looked homey and safe. That was the way the room looked—safe.

As if he had read her mind, Christopher said, "This room looks as if war could never touch it. It reminds me of a more peaceful time."

"We left it as it was when Papa died. He always bought quality furnishings that would last a long time. With war seeming so likely, I'm glad we won't have to replace anything."

" 'We'?"

"Electra and I."

"I thought Electra had moved to New York."

"She has, but Willowbrook will always be her real home. "Do you think we will get into the war? America, I mean?"

"I don't know. I'd hate to be in Roosevelt's shoes right now."

"But Hitler can't be allowed to bully his way across Europe. I was just reading about all the immigrants who have had to leave their homelands. Imagine being driven out of your home!"

Christopher smiled at her. "You've never lived anywhere else, have you?"

"No, I haven't. I plan to travel, though. At least I will after all this war business settles down. Have you traveled?"

"Not really. Not in Europe. I doubt I'll see it. Once I get my practice established, I'll be too busy to be gone several weeks at a time."

"It is a long way over there," she agreed. "I'd like to see things here as well—the Rockies and the Grand Canyon, all sorts of places."

When they had finished the strudel, Amelia said,

"Would you like to go for a walk? It's cool at night."

"Sure. I'd like that."

Christopher opened the front door and held it for her, then closed it behind them. Once they were away from the bright porch lamp and their eyes had adjusted to the silvery light from a full moon, they were able to see quite well, but the enveloping darkness gave an added intimacy to their thoughts.

"I love to come out here at night," Amelia said with a dreamy sigh. "Everything is silver and black and mysterious. When the moon's not so bright, the stars seem almost close enough to touch."

"When I walk outside like this, I always look at the stars and wonder if there's anybody out there like us. All those stars are suns and many may have planets. It seems unlikely that we're the only living things in so big a universe."

"I never knew men thought about things like that."

"You believed only women are dreamers? A lot of men just don't admit it. Dad always said I wouldn't amount to anything, going around with my head in the clouds."

"Yet here you are a doctor."

Christopher took her hand and Amelia closed her cool fingers about his warm ones. She had seldom found anyone who so nearly echoed her own thoughts. As a teenager, she had been the center of attention, but she had been such a proficient flirt that she had seldom talked with her boyfriends about things as personal as dreams. With Christopher such a topic seemed natural. As natural as holding hands with him in the moonlight.

"Come to the garden with me," she said. "There's something I want to show you."

She led him across the lawn to where the ivy-covered

walls loomed black in the darkness.

"Aren't you afraid to walk out here all alone?" he asked.

"There's nothing out here to harm me. We aren't really as alone as it seems. Helga lives over the garage, and the head gardener and his wife live where you once did. Out here in the country we seldom have prowlers. There were a few instances just after the stock market failed when everyone seemed to be living on the road, but the dogs chased them away. Why, I seldom bother to lock my doors at night."

"That doesn't seem safe."

"Electra says the same thing. I guess it wouldn't be safe in a city, but no one in Catawba Mills locks up every night. Our upstairs windows don't even have locks, and neither does the kitchen door."

"It doesn't?"

"The kitchen door is new, and the handyman hasn't gotten around to putting a lock on it."

"You shouldn't tell people things like that. You could be robbed. Or worse."

She laughed. "Doctors don't go around robbing people, and I don't tell everyone I see. I trust you." It was true. All the years they had been apart seemed unimportant. She opened the gate and preceded him into the garden.

The moonlight cast the white alyssum and petunias in sharp contrast with the black shadows. Along one wall hung big white flowers that seemed to glow.

"They're moonflowers," she said. "They only open at night or on cloudy days. Don't they smell sweet?" She bent to brush her fingers over the plants growing beside the walkway. "Lavender, rosemary, and scented geraniums. I love this garden and all its smells. At times I feel more at home here than in the house."

"I never thought you would grow up to be a gardener," he teased. "We seem to have switched roles somewhere along the way."

"I hadn't thought of that!" She smiled up at him. "Wouldn't your father have been surprised?"

"At least as much as yours would have been."

"Shocked is more like it. I never had a hobby I enjoyed as much as I do this garden. Sometimes I feel as if I'm part of it. I guess you think that's silly."

"Not at all. I plan to have a garden of my own someday."

Their eyes met in the moonlight, and Amelia's breath quickened. There was something about Christopher that made her feel as if her soul were part of his. It was an odd sensation that left her warm and exhilarated and shy all at the same time. No other man had ever affected her that way, and she wondered if she could be falling in love with him. To keep him from discerning her thoughts, she said, "What is your house like? Do I know which one it is?"

"It's the small one at the corner of Cypress and Long Leaf. The Mulligans used to live there."

"Why, of course I know the house. The cute one with blue shutters and a porch swing."

"That's the one. It suits me fine for now. Eventually I'll need more space—there's only one bedroom."

"After you marry, you mean." Amelia pretended to study the shape of a moonflower. "Do you have anyone in mind?"

He reached up and brushed her hair back from her face. "Perhaps."

Amelia's heart began to race at the touch of his fingers. "Someone from Georgia? A friend from your school?"

"No. She doesn't know it yet. Until tonight I wasn't entirely aware of it myself."

Amelia's pulse was pounding so rapidly she felt short of breath. Could he possibly mean her? She turned to face him, her head tilted up to meet his eyes.

"Will you have dinner with me tomorrow, Amelia?" he asked.

His voice touched a chord deep inside her. Slowly she nodded.

Christopher leaned forward. Her lips parted as his covered hers. His kiss was gentle but masterful. Her arms circled his neck and she returned his kiss as passion sparked to life between them.

During those first two weeks Amelia learned that Christopher was an ardent suitor. None of her earlier boyfriends had had the nerve to ask her out every night of the week. She was skilled enough in the ways of courtship to know Christopher had picked her out for more than a mere girlfriend. So far he had not mentioned the future except for that night in the garden, but Amelia knew what he had in mind. She had been proposed to by far more casual admirers.

Helga began to expect Christopher for supper more often than not. The dogs became so accustomed to him and his car that they seldom bothered to bark. Amelia let herself trust his affection as one of a lasting nature.

One afternoon, she knew by Christopher's grin that he had something to show her. To her questions he would only reply, "You'll see."

Catawba Mills had a lake by the same name that stretched between rolling hills and forests. On the shore nearest town were boat houses and a restaurant that specialized in fish caught fresh from the lake.

Christopher drove down the row of boat houses and parked beside number fifteen. He came around and opened Amelia's door and led her to it.

"Why are we here?" she asked as he fitted his key in the lock. "Whose is this?"

He pulled open the door and gestured to a freshly painted rowboat that floated gently on the water. In bright white letters on the boat's stern was painted "Amelia." He followed her into the dimly lit interior. "Do you like boating? I bought it last week to surprise you. The paint didn't dry until yesterday."

Amelia put her fingers to her lips as she felt tears sting her eyes. "No one ever named a boat after me. I love it."

Christopher closed the door and put his arms around her. "I love you."

She looked up quickly. "You do?"

"You must know how I feel. I haven't been subtle."

She nodded as the tears gathered rapidly. "I hoped you did."

He bent and kissed her. "Does that mean you may feel the same way about me?"

Amelia realized she hadn't spoken aloud and she threw her arms around him in an exuberant hug. "Of course I do! How could you doubt that I love you?"

Christopher held her so tight she realized he hadn't been at all sure of how she felt. At last he said, "I would have named a boat after you before now if I had known that's all it would take to win you over."

Laughing, they gazed into each other's eyes. "I loved

you even before you bought the boat," she said. "I thought you knew that."

"I was afraid to hope."

She pulled away from him and led them to the side of the boat. "Let's go for a ride."

Christopher took the oars down from the hooks on the wall and shipped them. Then he drew the ropes taut so Amelia could step into the boat. As she eased herself onto the plank seat, the boat swayed and she laughed. Christopher got in opposite her and untied the boat from its moorings. Using one of the oars, he pushed out of the shed. The damp, slightly fishy smell of the dock was quickly left behind as the boat floated out onto the lake.

Amelia didn't care that he hadn't warned her to bring a wide-brimmed hat. The day was somewhat overcast, and she was willing to chance a few freckles for the opportunity to spend time with Christopher. She treasured every moment they were together. Her heart sang with the knowledge that her love for him was returned.

As he rowed with sure strokes, propelling the boat smoothly over the lake's silvery surface, Amelia watched him from the corner of her eye while pretending she was studying the reflection of the puffy clouds in the still water. Christopher had the natural grace of an athlete and made the strenuous task look easy, but their love was so new that she still felt somewhat shy and wanted to watch his every move.

Leaning back, she looked up at the clouds overhead. "What a perfectly marvelous day! I feel as if we own the world. I want to shout to everyone that we're in love."

Christopher paused in his rowing, cupped his hands, and

shouted out over the water, "We're in love! Amelia loves me and I love her!"

Amelia giggled as freely as if she were still a young girl. "What if someone hears you?"

"What if he does?" he countered. "Besides, we seem to have the lake pretty much to ourselves."

"It's a big lake. We have lots of privacy out here. We don't have to worry about Helga or the gardeners hearing us."

Christopher had been heading for a secluded cove where an arm of the lake stretched between tall trees and banks of wild rhododendron. As they floated out of sight of civilization, he rested the oars in the locks and said, "Will you marry me, Amelia? Do you love me that much?"

She reached out and took his hands, nodding happily. "I love you that much and more." She felt as if she might burst from so much happiness. Christopher loved her! He wanted to marry her!

"You're sure? You're really sure? I'm only the gardener's son. Your friends might not accept me."

"Of course they will, and if they don't, then we don't need them." In a more serious voice she said, "I love you, Christopher. I think I have loved you since I first saw you in my garden."

"Only then? I've loved you since we played cowboys and Indians. I never forgot you, Amelia. I've kept your memory near me all these years."

"How could you have loved me then? We were only children."

"I didn't know it was love. But I jumped at the chance to move back to Catawba Mills, and as soon as I was settled in, I came to find you. I was afraid you would already be married."

"I guess I was waiting for you." She breathed in the fresh scents of the shady cove. "Willowbrook will come alive again. Someday our children will be running over the lawns and making playhouses in the azaleas."

Christopher hesitated. "We can't live at Willowbrook. I couldn't afford a home like that. Not yet, at any rate."

"Electra pays for its upkeep. She always has."

"I'm certainly not going to let your sister support us. Besides, everyone would think I was a fortune hunter if I did that."

Amelia's smile wavered. "Leave Willowbrook?" She shook off her flash of foreboding. "Then we'll live in your house. What is it like inside? I've never seen it, you know."

"It's small, but it's pretty. And comfortable. It has a little fireplace in the living room, and I'm told it draws well. The yard had been neglected but we'll soon have flowers growing all over the place. We can pick out new wallpaper and paint the woodwork. You can decorate it any way you choose."

"It sounds perfect! We shouldn't rush into anything as serious as a marriage, though. At least that's what Electra will say. I can hardly wait for her to meet you." She paused. "Would you mind terribly if I tell Electra and have her get to know you before we tell anyone else?"

"Will she object? I never knew her, you know. The two of you always seemed so different, and she never played with us as children."

"She never liked being outside like I did. She wasn't avoiding you. No, I'm positive she will like you."

Christopher looked unconvinced.

"How could anyone know you and not love you?" Amelia asked with a lover's logic.

Christopher smiled and began to row.

CHAPTER 11

AMELIA LOOKED FORWARD TO EACH DAY WITH Christopher, and he spent every hour away from his practice by her side.

"I'd like to have children," she said as they sat beneath the leafy canopy of the willow in her garden. "At least two, preferably a boy and a girl."

He smiled, but she could see the concern in his face. "Perhaps we should adopt," he suggested.

"I'm not too old to have a baby. I'm never sick."

"It's just that if anything happened to you, I don't think I could bear it." He put her hand in his and held it as if she were extremely fragile.

"Nothing will happen to me. I have the best doctor in the world." She leaned over and kissed his cheek. "I hope they both look just like you."

"What did Electra say when you told her of our wedding plans?"

"I haven't actually done that yet."

"Why not?"

"I want to tell her in person. I so often get a bad connection when I call her on long distance. With all the static and crackling noises, I'm sure neither of us hears half of what's said."

"You could write her a letter."

"But then I wouldn't see her expression when she gets the news. She'll be so excited!"

"It's been nearly a month now since you said you'd marry me. Are you sure you aren't having second thoughts?"

"Christopher! The very idea." Amelia nestled her head on his shoulder, and he put his arm around her and pulled her close. "I love you far too much to change my mind. Besides, Electra had planned to come home this week, but she was unable to make it. Something came up at work."

An unsettling thought occurred to her, and she lifted her head and began pleating the loose folds in her full pink skirt. "You know, at times I think Electra is having so much fun in New York that she forgets about me. Surely by now she must have her business well enough organized to run it from here."

"I'm not sure it works that way."

"Well, she has people hired to do the cutting and sewing, and surely there's someone who can do the fittings. All Electra really does is draw the patterns. She could do that here and mail them in. She could use Papa's study for her office if she needed one."

"That's one reason I love you," Christopher said. "The world seems so simple when you're around. Difficult things become easy. You have a way of ignoring all the road-blocks."

"I've always been a dreamer," she said with a smile. "Electra is the down-to-earth one. Too much so, in my opinion."

Christopher stood and drew her to her feet. "I know what we can do. Let's go see my house. You still haven't been there, and I'd like to hear your ideas on redecorating. Why should we care what people may say? We're engaged to be married."

"Yes! Let's do that." She knew it was rather risqué to go there without a third party to chaperon, but after all, they were engaged. She looked down at her left hand and tried to imagine a wedding ring there.

As usual, Christopher followed her thoughts. "Are you positive you want a plain gold band? I could buy you a diamond set and pay it off. I'm not *that* broke."

"No, I want a gold one. Somehow a plain band looks so . . . *married*. You can buy me a diamond dinner ring later. A huge one so sparkling it will blind people across a room."

He laughed. "What was it I was saying about your simple tastes?"

She hugged herself and lifted her face to the breeze. "I want to experience everything! To be simple and gaudy and to travel but to have a home of my own. I feel as if I'm two or three different people all at once. You make me feel young."

"We are young. All our best years are ahead of us. Come on, now. Let's go see your new home."

They drove to town with all the windows rolled down to beat the oppressive August heat, and to keep her hair in order Amelia wore the scarf she kept in his glove compartment. That Christopher had granted her the franchise of storing one of her personal possessions in his car gave her pleasure, as though it were a preview of the satisfaction she anticipated when she would move into his house.

Although Christopher's house was small, it sat on a

lovely, shady lot. Amelia had driven by it often since she and Christopher had begun dating, deriving great joy from the thought that this was the place where he lived and slept and ate his meals. There were flower boxes beneath several of the windows, painted blue to match the shutters, but as yet they were barren, likely because of the heat. "We could put chrysanthemums in the boxes," she suggested. "White ones—no, red. All red. That way we'll have red flowers, blue shutters, and a white house. We'll be displaying our patriotism."

"Do chrysanthemums come in red?"

"I don't know. If not, we could plant begonias. I know they can be red." She could already see herself in a pink and white checked gingham dress behind a snowy ruffled apron, watering the flowers from a spouted can. "I already feel like a homebody," she confessed. "I'll have hot meals for you three times a day, and our house will be spotless."

"You make me so happy when you say things like that. I worry sometimes whether you'll miss having a cook and gardeners."

Amelia smiled to convey a lack of concern, though she was somewhat doubtful. Was cooking difficult to learn? She had never had reason to find out.

Christopher took her by the elbow and led her up the short walk onto the porch which, though deep enough for the swing, was quite narrow. She brushed aside her twinge of disappointment by reminding herself that a small porch would be easier to sweep than one even half the size of Willowbrook's.

She held open the screen door, teasing him with a smile as he labored to unlock the front door. "I'm not as confident about not being burglarized as you are," he said as he finally opened the door and stepped aside for her to enter.

The living room was smaller than she had expected, and while his furniture was new, it wasn't of the quality she had always known. As he had said, there was a small fireplace on one wall, flanked by bookshelves. Through the open door opposite her, she could see into the kitchen. "Where's the dining room?" she asked.

"There isn't one. But come and see." He hurried her across the room into the kitchen. "See? My dining table is in here."

She nodded, remembering to smile. A small round oak table and four chairs filled one end of the room. The sink and counters—the surface of the latter a worn, dull red— were at the other end. A big white stove occupied the wall opposite the door, and across from it was the refrigerator. Although the room had a window above the sink and another by the table, it still seemed dark.

"Light-colored paper in here," she said. "*Very* light. And could we do something about the countertops?"

"Like what?" he asked, looking at them as if he had never noticed them before.

"I don't know. Put in a new surface or something. These are so . . . red." She didn't point out the worn spots where the dark backing showed through. "Pale blue would be nice. Or white. That would look cheery." She looked down at the linoleum floor. It was also red, a paint-spattered design. She made no comment.

"Look out here." Christopher opened a door between the refrigerator and the cabinet, and she saw a screened-in porch. "I sit out here a lot. There always seems to be a breeze."

She followed him out and smiled to see a washing machine. "Isn't that a Bendix? I've seen them advertised."

"You bet. Nothing but the best. You just put in soap and clothes and turn it on. No wringer. And it shuts itself off when it's through. The clothes spin nearly dry, and all you have to do is hang them out on the line."

"Imagine that. At Willowbrook we still use an old Maytag wringer-washer."

He led her back through the kitchen into the living room and pointed at a door across a short hall. "That's the bathroom. The bedroom is down here." He pushed open the door he had indicated and stepped back for her to enter.

Amelia had never seen such a tiny bedroom. Even the servants' quarters at Willowbrook were larger than this. The double bed took up most of the room, and a chest of drawers and a dressing table were crowded into the rest. As she stood beside the bed, she felt the table's stool nudge the backs of her knees. "Everything is very . . . handy," she observed.

"I know it's small, but it's not inconvenient. And look out here." He reached past her and opened the shades. "When you plant those flowers, you'll be able to see them from in here."

"Who is that glaring across the lawn at us?" she asked as she leaned forward so she could see more clearly.

"That's Mrs. Harris. She's a widow woman who has nothing better to do than to spy on me." He grinned. "Until now she hasn't had reason to censure me." He leaned closer and kissed her on the forehead as he pulled the blinds shut. "Now, however, I have a woman in my house, and Lord knows what we may be doing."

Amelia was growing tired of having to force a smile. "I had hoped our neighbor would be the friendly sort so we could visit over the fence and trade recipes."

"Maybe our back fence neighbors will be like that. I haven't met them yet."

"If you've lived here all summer and haven't met them, they couldn't be too friendly."

"Well, we won't live here forever. In a year or two I should be able to afford a nicer place."

"Christopher, we can have a nicer place now. We can live at Willowbrook."

"You don't like my house. I was afraid of that."

"No, no. Don't be silly." She went into the living room and looked around for something to admire. "Look at that fireplace. I can just see us all cozy in front of it next winter. And those bookshelves only need a coat of paint. I can paint them myself while you're at work. Pale yellow, maybe. Do you like yellow? Or white. That goes with everything. They only seem depressing because salmon is such an odd color for bookshelves."

"The bathroom is salmon, too," he admitted glumly. "Salmon tiles with pink swans on the curtains."

"Swans are nice," she managed to say. "Surely the tiles don't go all the way to the ceiling. We can put a cheery wallpaper at eye level." She brightened. "Maybe we could bring some of the furniture from Willowbrook. Half of it is mine, you know."

"Where would we put it? This room is already full, and you saw the bedroom."

"We could put it here instead of this furniture," she said carefully.

"You mean get rid of this? I'm still paying for it."

"It's very nice." She sighed.

"No, it isn't." In exasperation, Christopher ran his hand

through his hair. "Maybe this is all a mistake. You and I are like oil and water. There's no way for us to fit our lives together."

"Don't you say that." She put her fingers to his lips to silence him. "We love each other. We can reach a compromise, surely." She had confidence in her words. No house or furniture was more important than her love for Christopher. If need be, she would give up her life for him. Certainly she could give up a house. But, she thought, there might be a way to compromise.

She sat on the couch and drew him down beside her. "Why are you so dead set against living at Willowbrook? If it's simply a matter of money, you can pay your half and Electra can send smaller checks."

"Amelia, by the time I pay what I owe each month for my office equipment and college loan, I can't afford a place nicer than this. I can't pay half of Willowbrook's upkeep because I don't have enough money. Naturally it won't be this way forever. In time we will be quite well off, maybe even rich. But that's years down the road."

"I won't mind living here. I'll like it."

He continued as if she hadn't spoken. "My father worked at that house as a gardener. Sometimes my mother helped out in the kitchen. They were servants, Amelia. Can't you see why I don't want to live there? I would feel like an impostor or worse yet, a fortune hunter."

"You're no such thing."

"People would think I married you for your money." He cupped her face in his hands. "Can't you see that? I don't have a lot of money, but I do have my pride."

Amelia's heart went out to him. "I know that, Christopher. I can't tell you how much I admire you. This will all work out. Let's spend the next few weeks papering and painting and see how it looks then. Why, I'll bet it turns into a dollhouse. It's already as cute as a bug's ear." She smiled as she kissed the end of his nose. "It just needs a woman's touch."

"I'm sure you're right. As much as we love each other, why are we worrying about something as trivial as where we live?" He stood up. "I'll make some coffee, and we can start planning what we want to change."

Amelia lingered in the room. She felt petty that she cared so much about where they would live, but to her it wasn't a trivial matter. Not at all. Christopher would be at his office or the hospital for long hours, but she would spend all her time at home. What if she wasn't able to improve this tiny house?

She went to the bathroom and peered in. As he had said, it was salmon with pink swans on the plastic curtains. It was smaller than she had dreamed possible, and the iron faucets had dripped a brown stain in the sink and tub. It looked like the sort of stain that would resist all efforts to eradicate it.

Amelia closed the door, put on a smile, and went to join Christopher in the kitchen.

For the next few weeks Amelia spent hours each day painting bookshelves, cabinets, and woodwork, then hurried to air out the house before Christopher was due to return. Paint ruined two sets of her clothes, so she began alternating them from day to day to save her others. Her skin was dry from having used turpentine to clean up the spattered paint, but soap and water wouldn't faze it. However, the house was brighter as a result of her hard work, and Amelia began wondering next how she would learn to hang wallpaper. For a woman who had done so little real work, she was a fast learner and was proud of her accomplishment, and she was sure she could master wallpapering, as well.

"I think I'll learn to sew and make curtains," she said as they left the movies one night.

"You can't sew?"

"Mother taught Electra, but I was always more interested in horses. Surely it couldn't be too hard. I have Electra's sewing machine at home."

"I can't tell you how wonderful you're being about all this."

Amelia smiled and tucked her hand into his arm. Lately a new plan had occurred to her. Christopher admitted the tiny house would be too small once they started their family. Now that she had agreed to move in with him as a newlywed, surely he would humor her by moving into Willowbrook as soon as they needed the extra room. All she had to do was marry him and get pregnant.

Christopher paused as they passed a newsboy and bought a paper. "Roosevelt and Churchill have drawn up a declaration called the Atlantic Charter."

"What is that?"

"They met on a British battleship in the Atlantic and worked out the agreement. I guess that's why it's called that." He glanced down the column. "It says no boundaries of a country may be changed without the citizens agreeing and that there is to be free access to trade and raw materials."

"I don't understand all that. The world is so big; why can't people just be content to live in their own countries and leave everyone else alone?"

Christopher continued to read silently. After a moment he said, "U-boats have sunk an American ship."

Amelia sighed. Talk of war in Europe seemed to be everywhere.

"At this rate we'll soon be in the war."

"Can't we talk about something more pleasant?"

Christopher folded the paper and smiled at her. "Let's go to Willowbrook and walk in the garden. With this haze in the air, the sunset this evening will be beautiful."

Their timing was perfect. Just as they reached the garden gate, the sun was sinking behind the distant hills, and as Christopher had predicted, the sunset was spectacular. Cicadas sang in the nearby trees, and from far away in the woods a bird called out plaintive notes, as if it were sad that the beautiful day was ending and unaware that the next dawn might bring on an even better day. The cooling air was filled with the fragrance of flowers that had waited for a moderation of the temperature before releasing their scent, as if they knew their gifts would be better appreciated when people could turn their attention from their search for relief from the searing sun to the gentler, more aesthetic side of life. Amelia especially enjoyed this time of day, and before Christopher came into her life, she had spent many hours alone in her garden listening to night fall and dreaming of just such a time as this when she would no longer be alone.

Amelia led Christopher to the marble bench, and after she had taken her seat, he joined her. In the gathering dusk, two lightning bugs hovered and blinked across the garden in a carefree manner, as they had done on many summer evenings such as this, but Amelia's heart was not as light as it might have been. Of late much of her day-dreaming time had been supplemented by capricious thoughts of reality.

"On a perfect evening like this, how can there be a war?" Amelia asked as she slipped her hand into his. "If there is a war, you must promise me you won't go."

"I'll promise not to go unless I must. I may not have a choice."

"Let's talk about our wedding. It occurred to me today that this would be the perfect place to have it."

"Here in the garden?"

"The preacher could stand in front of this bench, and we could stand there." She pointed to a spot nearby. "I'm not interested in a big formal wedding. Are you? I'm afraid at my age it would look silly."

"You will be more beautiful than any bride of nineteen, but I want it to be exactly the way you want it. All that matters to me is that you'll be my wife."

"I love you so much." She nestled closer and put her face up to kiss him. "Will your mother be able to come to the wedding? And your aunt?"

Christopher looked away. "Mom's health hasn't been good, and my aunt can't leave work."

"How does she know that when we haven't even set the date?"

He drew in a deep breath. "The truth is, Mom and Aunt Hallie are against the marriage."

"But why? They don't even know me!"

"Mom says I'll be like a goose in a pheasant yard and that she and Aunt Hallie wouldn't fit in any better."

"That's a terrible thing to say!"

Christopher's eyes were filled with sadness. His mother

had a quick tongue as well as a quick temper, and she had said quite a bit more than he was willing to reveal. At one point she had even asked if she and Hallie would be expected to do the dishes after the reception and whether they could be seated down front with the family. Christopher was too proud to burden Amelia with all this. "She didn't mean to hurt you. She's only afraid we won't be happy."

"Well, she's wrong. You and I are more alike than any couple I know. I may have been born in a larger house and given more advantages, but we are a perfect match in all the ways that matter. If our situations were reversed, no one would think a thing about it. Besides, once your practice is established, you'll be rich in your own right. You said so yourself."

"I like the idea of a small wedding. Whether you wear a traditional dress or not is up to you, but I want you to have flowers. I always think of flowers when I think of you."

"Can't we set a date? When I tell Electra, it would be nice to also tell her when the wedding will be. Maybe she will want to design a dress for me! Wouldn't that be nice?"

"How about a Christmas wedding? Christmas Eve."

Amelia beamed. "How lovely! I can carry a bouquet of white poinsettias and holly." But then she frowned. "It may be too cold to have it out here in December."

"As hot as this summer has been, I can't imagine it ever being cold again. How about Thanksgiving instead?"

"Or Halloween?" she teased. "Or Labor Day? If it's Arbor Day I could carry tree seedlings for my flowers."

"Thanksgiving," he repeated. "That gives you plenty of time to have a dress made."

"We should pick out a china and crystal pattern. And

our silver." She added, "Unless, of course, you will agree to use some from Willowbrook."

"I want us to have our own."

"Why are you so closed-minded about that? You'd think my house contained the plague."

"Honey, it's not that." He faced her and took both her hands in his as he said earnestly, "I want to make it on my own. It's important to me. Maybe you can't understand that, having been brought up the way you were, but it's something I have to do." His eyes pleaded with her to understand.

"All right, Christopher. I can't see why that's so important, but if you say it is, I believe you."

He studied her face in the waning light. She had always been so sheltered. She was like one of her flowers—lovely but too delicate for a harsh wind. "I want to take care of you," he said. "I'll never leave you."

"That's all I ask. Just don't ever leave me. I couldn't exist without you."

They sat in the garden until it was too dark to see. "There's no moon tonight," he said. "Look at all those stars."

"'Star light, star bright, first star I see tonight. I wish I may, I wish I might, have the wish I wish tonight,'" she said, repeating the child's verse with her eyes on the heavens.

"What did you wish?" he asked.

"That we would always be like this. Together, in love, happy."

"That's three wishes."

"No, it isn't, because I couldn't have one without the other two."

"I love you," he said. "My only regret is all the years we wasted apart when we could have been together."

"I feel the same way. But maybe it happened like this for a reason. I was quite a flirt in my younger days. You might not have liked me at all."

"Impossible. But I might have been eaten up with jealousy." He stood and put his arm around her shoulders as they wandered back to the house.

The wide porch welcomed them, and he compared it mentally to his postage stamp–sized one. He was still amazed Amelia had accepted his house so readily. That, more than anything else, proved her love for him. He wondered, not for the first time, if he was being too stubborn about not living here. Someday, he vowed, he would give her a house as grand as Willowbrook. Not this far out in the country, of course, for in times of emergency he had to be close to the hospital. He loved her even more for being so reasonable.

They went into the music room, an area almost as large as his entire house. Amelia sat at the piano and uncovered the keys. Playing by ear, she picked out "Chattanooga Choo Choo," a song that always made him smile. By the time she began "High On a Windy Hill," he was singing along with her.

Christopher had a good voice, and with Amelia's encouragement, he sang one of the new Sinatra hits, "Fools Rush In." When he finished, he said, "A lot of people would say that song should be our song. As far as calendar time goes, we haven't known each other very long, only a couple of months, and yet here we are planning to be married."

"It's not as if we're silly teenagers," she protested. "At

our age, we're old enough to know our own minds."

"I'm glad you have no doubts. Pretty soon one of us will have to become level-headed enough to be the head of the family."

"That's your job, thank goodness. Mine is to make you happy and to have beautiful children."

Christopher became suddenly serious. "I still think we should give some thought to adopting. I'm sure there will be mothers who are unable or unwilling to keep their babies for one reason or another. As a doctor, I'll have some idea of the mother's health and mental stability. The adoption could be completely private."

"It wouldn't be the same. Maybe after we have two of our own, we could consider adoption. I want a house full of children. Happy, beautiful children."

Christopher didn't argue with her, though he remained concerned. Amelia was carrying a few extra pounds, but they didn't conceal the fact that her hips were quite narrow. Then there was the danger of a first pregnancy at her age. Christopher knew there was valid reason for concern. She was reasonable, however. Her acceptance of his small house proved that. She would be reasonable about this as well, once they were married. He matched his voice to hers as they sang "Night and Day."

CHAPTER 12

GIVING IN TO CHRISTOPHER'S INSISTENCE THAT she call Electra to give her the news of their wedding plans, Amelia tried once, but when she got no answer, she took that as a sign that she should write instead. Using her prettiest pink stationery and her best fountain pen, Amelia poured out all her love for Christopher, and their dreams. She described his little house in more glowing terms than it deserved and added that within three months she would be a wife and a year after that hoped to be a mother. She finished by asking Electra to be her maid of honor and to make herself a golden yellow dress to match the chrysanthemums that would then be in bloom. She did not ask Electra to design her wedding dress, feeling it would be better to wait for her sister to make the offer.

After driving into town and mailing the letter to Electra, Amelia went to the dry goods store to shop for material for the bathroom and kitchen curtains. She found cloth she liked right away and spent most of the afternoon trying to figure how much to buy. She couldn't recall a time when she had been happier.

Once the material was cut and paid for, Amelia walked across the street to the town's best jewelry store, which had been well established many years before when her grandparents had picked out their china there. It was with no small degree of pride that Amelia would carry on the tradition.

"Christopher will come in to help make the final decision," she said as the saleslady took her to the china. "He's the new doctor, you know, and his time is so rushed. I thought I would choose four or five patterns to speed up the final selection."

"I'm so happy for you, Miss Radcliff. Have you chosen your wedding rings?"

"Not yet. I only wrote Electra this morning—it's all still so new. We'll look at rings when Christopher comes in to see the china." She loved to say his name aloud. The woman seemed quite impressed that she would be marrying the new doctor and had clearly not connected him with old Jenkins, the gardener.

Amelia made her choices, and the clerk dutifully noted the pattern names on a pad in case Christopher should have to come in without Amelia. Then they did the same with crystal and silver plate.

"No sterling?" the clerk asked.

"Mother added that to my hope chest over the years. I already have a complete set."

"Of course you do. How silly of me. I recall your mother and how she did that for both you girls."

Amelia smiled but cast a longing glance at the rows of sterling on display in the case. She had never admitted it to anyone, but she wasn't fond of her silver pattern. It was heavy and had impressive scrolls and curls, but it was too ornate for Amelia's taste. She chose two silver-plate patterns that were fluid and simple. The sterling would be used only for Thanksgiving, Christmas, and formal dinners anyway. She pictured a formal dinner at Christopher's kitchen table and almost laughed aloud.

Her final destination was the church, and as she drove there she saw bags of mail being loaded into an unmarked postal truck. One of those letters was the one she had written to Electra, and it was already on its way. Amelia felt happy inside.

She intercepted the preacher on his way out the door. He recognized Amelia and smiled. He had known her since her baptism as an infant.

"I wanted you to be one of the first to hear the good news," she said as she neared him.

"Good news? I can use some for a change. I've been listening to the radio," Reverend Sullivan said. "All people can talk about these days is war."

"I'm getting married." Amelia felt herself all but glowing.

"You are? Well, that's great news." Reverend Sullivan grinned from ear to ear. "Great news indeed. Who's the young man?"

"Christopher Jenkins. He's the new doctor."

"Dr. Jenkins! My, my. He certainly didn't waste any time, did he?"

"We knew each other years ago, and as soon as he had finished his schooling and such and was ready to set up a practice, he moved here and looked me up."

"I just love it when things work out like that." Reverend Sullivan put his key back in the church door. "Come to my office and let's get you on the calendar. I assume you've set the date?"

"Thanksgiving. Or rather the Saturday after it."

He chuckled and nodded his gray head. "I guess I know what you'll always have for your anniversary dinner—turkey sandwiches."

Amelia wrinkled her nose. "I never thought of that. I guess we'll always have to go out to eat that night."

"Good planning."

They went into the small office, and the minister tipped his head back to read the calendar through his bifocals. "Good, good. The church isn't booked for that day."

"Actually we want to be married at Willowbrook. In the garden."

"A garden wedding? In the autumn?" He looked at her over the top of his glasses. "It rains a lot then. Could be cold."

"If the weather doesn't cooperate, we can have the ceremony inside. We don't plan to have a large wedding, only a few close friends and family."

"No problem, no problem." Reverend Sullivan made a note on his calendar. "Time?"

"Sunset. We want to be married as the sky changes color." She and Christopher hadn't thought to set a time, but she was sure he would agree.

"How about the counseling sessions? I always counsel a couple prior to the ceremony."

"I hadn't thought of that." She paused. "Thursdays? Christopher is off a half day then."

"Thursdays are fine. Three or four sessions are customary, and you have plenty of time for that between now and Thanksgiving." He wrote her name and Christopher's in for the next Thursday. "Two o'clock?"

"That's fine. If Christopher has a conflict, I'll call you."

"Perfect." He held out his hand. "I know you aren't supposed to congratulate the bride, so just let me say I'm happy for you. You've chosen a fine young man, from all I've heard about him."

"I think he's wonderful." She smiled. "I may be a little prejudiced."

The minister laughed. "If you say he's wonderful, I'll believe it. Give him my regards, and I'll see you next Thursday at two."

Amelia all but skipped from the building now that the date was official. She was going to be married.

Amelia's face was wet with tears as she watched Christopher reread Electra's letter. He looked angry enough to bite nails in half. "She has no right to say whether or not we can be married. Who the hell does she think she is!" He glared at the sheet of paper. "What does she mean 'upstart gardener's son'! And telling you to stay at Willowbrook 'where you belong'! she has one hell of a nerve."

"I'm so glad you came out right away. I don't think I could have driven into town without going into a ditch."

"What's her number? I'm going to give her a call and tell her what I think of her."

"No, no! You can't do that. Surely she didn't mean for the letter to sound as dictatorial as it does."

"Hitler would have been more congenial!"

"It says she will be here next weekend. Let's not jump off the deep end. Once I've talked to her and she has had a chance to get to know you, I'm sure she'll change her mind."

"Amelia, that's not the point. She has no right to tell you that we can't get married. She's only your sister, and you're thirty-four years old!"

"I know. But she's also my only living relative. She loves this house as much as I do, and when she went to New York I promised to stay here and take care of it while she earned the money to support it."

"You were what, eighteen years old? She can't hold you to that. Based on this letter, one would think you were married to this house and that she had sacrificed everything for its upkeep. That's sick, Amelia! This is just a damn house!"

"Not to us." She tried to get her voice under control and to keep her temper in check. "Willowbrook is also our heritage. It's been in our family for generations. We expected our children to grow up here and their children after them."

"Does it really mean that much to you?"

She ignored his question. "Our father stipulated in his will that the house be cared for and that it remain in our family."

"He can't do that. Any lawyer can tell you that a stipulation like that is unenforceable!"

"I know. But it was his intent. I promised Electra I would hold up my end of the bargain."

"That's crazy!"

"I think, too, she's jealous. Electra is two years older than I am, and she has no prospects of marriage. Also, I told her in the wrong way. I should have written about you from the beginning, so our engagement wouldn't have been such a surprise."

"Why didn't you?"

"I thought you were too good to be true, that it wouldn't last, that you would grow tired of me. I didn't want her to know that I had had a suitor and lost him."

"I could never tire of you. Surely you know that."

"I do now, but at the time everything was happening so fast."

Christopher sighed and stood up as he tossed the letter aside. He went to the window and looked out. "Now what?"

"Now we wait for the weekend, and you be as charming as you can be, and she will see that we belong together."

"I don't feel charming. And that doesn't have anything to do with you having to stay in this house."

Amelia went to him. "Would it be so terrible for us to live here? I'm sure my leaving Willowbrook is Electra's greatest objection. If we stayed here—"

"Willowbrook is so far from town. If a woman comes into the hospital in the last stages of labor or if someone is dying, I may not have time to get there from way out here. In emergencies even seconds count."

"Then you never want to live here? Not even after we have children?"

"All that is down the road. We can't afford a baby now or for the next few years. The main question is whether you'll marry me without your sister's blessing."

"Of course I will. You're more important to me than Electra. It's just that I want her approval. That's why I thought that if we could live here, so that nothing in her life is changed, she would be more willing to see it our way."

"Why is that necessary?" he asked again.

"Electra pays the bills. I'm sure she intends to move back

here as soon as possible, but the house can't sit vacant or it will fall to ruin."

"Helga can look after it."

Amelia shook her head. "Helga tries hard and I like her, but she's just not capable of running an estate. She knows nothing about keeping the grounds or about repairing the roof. By the time Electra came down to inspect the house, there could be a leak ruining the floors and furnishings."

"It's just a house," he argued. "Sell it. Your father will never know."

"I can't believe you would suggest such a thing. Willowbrook might mean nothing to you, but it does to me and it will to our children."

Christopher sighed. "Let's not fight. We may as well wait until this weekend and see how it goes."

Amelia looked up at him, her eyes round. "We *were* almost fighting, weren't we? How dreadful! Our first argument." Fresh tears rose in her eyes.

"If we never get any angrier than this, we have nothing to worry about." He smiled down at her. "You should have heard my parents go after each other. And my aunt and uncle. It was so bad, they finally got divorced."

"Not me. We'll never divorce. I'll see to that."

"Then you will still marry me?"

"Of course I will, you goose. Electra is sure to come around once she gets to know you."

Electra and her luggage arrived with her usual flurry, but this time she had a man with her. At first Amelia thought Electra had a fiancé of her own; then the man turned his head and Amelia saw he was quite young. Had Electra brought the son of a friend? For what reason?

Helga opened the door, and Amelia entered the hall in time to see Electra's critical perusal of the girl. Hastily she said, "Electra, this is Helga Jansen. Remember I wrote to tell you I hired her when Mrs. Adams left?"

"I remember." Electra turned to her escort. "This is a friend of mine, Carter Symmons. Carter, my sister Amelia."

Amelia automatically held out her hand. "A friend? Are you in the fashion business, too?"

"I'm an actor," he said brusquely, giving her hand a brief squeeze. He looked around the entry as if he were assessing the value of its contents.

"Friends are always welcome at Willowbrook," Amelia said, recovering smoothly. "Helga, put Mr. Symmons's things in the green room."

"Carter will be sleeping in my room," Electra said to the housekeeper.

Amelia tried not to stare. "In your room? I didn't know you had a . . . fiancé?" She looked from one to the other, dreading the answer.

Electra smiled at her the way a cat might smile at a canary. "I don't. As I said, Carter is just a friend." Suddenly her smile was gone. "Now what's all this crap about you marrying old Jenkins's boy?"

Amelia drew herself up. "Christopher isn't a boy. He's a doctor, and he's well respected around here." She tried to ignore Electra's language and her friend.

"In Catawba Mills that's not saying much." Electra walked away from the pile of luggage, Carter close behind her. Helga began wrestling the large bags upstairs. "Careful with that," Electra snapped at the maid. "That's expensive luggage." Helga made an effort not to bump it against the stair risers. "Where do you find these people you hire?" she asked her sister even before Helga was out of earshot.

"Helga is an immigrant. She was barely able to escape from Europe before the war started."

"Ah, yes. The war. Business should soon be booming." Electra opened her purse and took out a gold cigarette case. After taking a cigarette for herself, she offered one to Carter, then put the case back into her purse. She lit both cigarettes with her monogrammed lighter. "Where have you put the ashtrays?" she asked Amelia.

Amelia silently went to the sideboard in the adjoining room and returned with a heavy crystal ashtray. "I wish you wouldn't smoke in here. The smell bothers me."

"Nonsense. Papa always smoked." Electra sat on the sofa and patted the cushion beside her. Like a well-trained lap dog, Carter sat where she had indicated.

Once again Amelia tried to draw Carter into an explanation of why he was there and what relationship he had with Electra. She couldn't believe it could possibly be the obvious one. "Are you in a play near here, Mr. Symmons?"

"Call me Carter. I'm between engagements right now."

"Carter has recently closed on Broadway," Electra said with a smug smile. "Until he gets another booking he's my . . . companion."

"You live together?" Amelia gasped.

"No, he has his own place. I brought him along this weekend so he wouldn't be lonely." She gave Carter a proprietary smile. He returned it with a glowering expression that seemed to be his stock in trade. Amelia thought he looked like a spoiled child.

"I wish you had told me you were bringing a guest," Amelia said, adopting Electra's habit of talking about Carter as if he weren't there. "I'll have to tell Helga to prepare an extra plate."

"Surely the girl can count." Electra flicked her ashes into the ashtray.

Amelia tried not to notice that Carter's ashes were becoming precariously long and that he didn't seem to care. "Christopher will be here for supper. I can't wait for you to meet him."

"I already have. He lived in our backyard for years."

"That was when he was a boy. He's entirely different now."

"Surely he doesn't look like his father. Old Jenkins had a face that would stop a clock."

"Christopher is quite handsome," Amelia said in a testy voice. She could have added he was better-looking than the surly boy who had tagged along with Electra, but her manners forbade it. She wondered how she could get it across to Electra that what she did with this Carter fellow in New York and what she did at Willowbrook were two different matters. Surely Electra was only goading her and had no intention of actually letting him share her bed.

"We've picked out our patterns," Amelia said to break the tense silence. "You'll love our china. It's so pretty. Of course since we aren't having a large wedding, I don't expect to get a full set, but we can add to it over the years."

"I thought I made it plain that you're not to marry that man. You seem to forget all the sacrifices I've made to keep you in the lap of luxury. Now you expect me to welcome this gardener's boy with open arms. He must think he's found a bird nest on the ground."

"We have no intention of living here," Amelia said with bruised dignity. "We'll live in Christopher's house."

"That cracker box? I saw it from the cab as we came from the airport. It's a hovel."

"It's no such thing!" Amelia glared at her sister. "We have it fixed up as cute as a dollhouse inside!"

"Why, Amelia! Have you two been playing house? I'm sure that's why Mother wouldn't let you play in the woods with him when you were a child. I thought you must have outgrown that by now."

Amelia jerked to her feet, anger flashing in her eyes. "I'll thank you to keep a civil tongue in your head, Electra. Christopher respects me and has never made any advances that would spoil my reputation." When Electra mockingly raised her eyebrows, Amelia added, "I think you're just jealous." With that she stormed from the room.

"What a nice welcome home," Electra said ruefully. "I guess it's no more than I expected." She glanced at Carter as she put out her cigarette. "Amelia and I haven't been close for years. Watch your ashes."

He tapped them over the ashtray. "She's not bad-looking for her age. I sure wouldn't have picked her out as your sister, though. You look nothing alike."

Electra had caught his barb about age. Now that she was tinting her hair, she had thought she could pass for close to Carter's age. Maybe, she told herself, he assumed Amelia to be the older sister. "I can just imagine what Christopher Jenkins must look like."

"Yeah," Carter seconded. "A sow's ear carrying a silk purse."

She made no effort to correct his jumbled metaphor. She hadn't picked Carter for his intellect. He bore an amazing resemblance to a new Broadway actor who was all the rage, and he was good in bed. It was not a requirement that he have a brain as well.

Electra realized now she had made a mistake in bringing Carter along with her. What had seemed like sultry passion in New York merely appeared to be bad manners here. She wished she could avoid sleeping with him under this roof, but there was no way out of it without admitting to Amelia she had made a gauche mistake. Electra knew it weakened her case against Christopher for her to have brought Carter, but at the time she had been so angry over Amelia's letter that she hadn't been thinking straight.

"Why don't you go for a walk, Carter? Get some fresh air. I'll call you in time to change for dinner."

"You change clothes for that?"

Electra sighed. "Just don't go into the walled garden. That's Amelia's retreat, and there's no sense in antagonizing her any further."

Carter tossed his cigarette butt into the ashtray and sauntered from the room. Electra reached over and snuffed it against the glass bottom, then went upstairs to freshen up.

She was home at last and she wanted to be alone to breathe in the scents of rose and lavender and to feel Willowbrook's protecting walls about her. Home at last.

Carter had returned from his walk and was upstairs taking a nap when Christopher arrived, and because Amelia was busy in the kitchen, Electra met Christopher alone. As she motioned for him to enter, her gaze swept over him. "So you're Christopher Jenkins. You're not at all what I expected."

"It's good to see you again. It's been a long time."

Electra made no comment. She was still wondering how

old man Jenkins and his scrawny wife had managed to produce a son who looked like an Adonis. She smiled at him, and when he returned the expression, her heart skipped a beat. "Come in and have a seat. Dinner is running a bit late. Amelia hired an immigrant girl who barely speaks English. Goodness knows what she may be cooking or when it will be ready."

As Electra seated herself in a chair opposite Christopher on the couch, her thoughts raced trying to catch up with the changes in her feelings toward this man. Her preconceived notions about him had not taken into account that he would be so handsome. Realizing neither of them was speaking, she said, "I gather you come here often." If she had been right in her assumption that his primary interest in Amelia was her apparent money, then he might be tempted to switch his attention to the wealthier of the two. Electra found herself wishing once again that she had not brought Carter with her.

"I come here as often as I can. My practice keeps me busy."

"I see." Carter didn't have to pose a problem, Electra thought. All she had to do was put him on a train or a bus back to New York. She was keeping him, not vice versa. He would have no choice but to leave. That would give her time alone with this fascinating man.

"Tell me," she asked in a seductive voice, "why did you want to come back to such a tiny town?"

"I like small towns. Especially this one."

His eyes had a directness that stirred Electra, making her blood run hot. Amelia hadn't mentioned Christopher's magnetic sex appeal. "Have you ever been to New York? Once I saw it, I was hooked. All the lights and excitement and places to go—I love it there."

"Then you don't plan to move back to Willowbrook?" His eyes showed a flicker of surprise.

"Of course I will, someday. Just not yet." She smiled at him. "How would you like to see New York? Maybe you'd find it . . . irresistible, too."

"I doubt it." He met her gaze evenly. "My place is here."

"In Catawba Mills? What a waste." She stood for a moment, then sat back down on the couch beside him. "I think you'd be wasted in Catawba Mills." She eased closer and breathed in the spicy scent of his shaving lotion. "Certainly you'd be wasted on Amelia."

Although he stared at her as if he was surprised to hear her make such a statement, she saw no sign that he disagreed with her. Electra smiled and leaned toward him so that her breast rubbed across his arm. She could put Carter on the early bus and have days in which to persuade Christopher his future would be better spent with her than with Amelia. Now that she saw what Amelia's excitement was about, she understood completely. Men like Christopher came along only once in a lifetime. She was amazed to find she was falling in love with him. Love at first sight! Until now, Electra had never believed in it.

"Take a few days off," she purred. "Come to New York with me and let me show you what you're missing." She reached out and caressed his clean-shaven cheek with her fingertips, her eyelids lowered seductively and her lips parted in invitation.

Christopher's reaction was immediate and unmistakable. He caught her wrist and pulled her hand away from her face. His eyes were cold, and the set of his mouth revealed disgust. "I don't know what the hell you're trying to pull, but I'm engaged to marry your sister."

"Engagements can be broken," she quickly retorted.

"I love Amelia, and I have no intention of breaking our engagement, and I sure as hell have no intention of going to New York or any other place with you." He shoved her hand back at her.

Shock and rage began building in Electra as she rubbed her wrist. He was not just refusing her but looking at her as if he found her uninteresting and revolting. She was too astonished to speak.

"I'm not going to say anything about this to Amelia, because it would break her heart. If you're smart, you won't say anything, either. Maybe you're just testing me to see if I can be tempted, I don't know, but whatever your game is, I'm not interested."

Electra had never wanted any man as much as she wanted Christopher Jenkins at that moment. She glared at him as she said, "You've just made a mistake—a big mistake. I'll never condone Amelia's marrying you, and she won't dare do it without my permission."

"Won't she? We'll see about that."

A muscle ridged in Christopher's jaw, and his eyes seemed to penetrate her soul. Electra wanted to cry out for his forgiveness and throw herself into his arms and kiss him until he returned her love, but that, of course, was impossible. With her frustration adding a sting to her words, she said, "You're a fool to think Amelia will ever be happy in that shoe box you call a house. Her home is here, at Willowbrook, and if you had half a brain, you'd know that." Her lip lifted in a sneer. "She'll never marry you. Never!"

Christopher looked as if he wanted to tear her limb from limb, but they were interrupted by the sound of Amelia's footsteps in the hall, and he made a visible effort to conceal his anger. Electra decided she wouldn't give up so easily. Christopher was a man of deep passions, and this, in her opinion, made him suitable for her, but not for the flighty Amelia. Why, Amelia had always changed beaux as easily as she changed her jewelry. Eventually Christopher would see that she was right. All Electra had to do was see to it that no hasty wedding took place. A secretive smile tilted Electra's lips as Amelia came into the room. Electra knew she was the prettier and slimmer of the two, and Christopher wasn't blind. It was just a matter of time.

Christopher tried not to glare across the dinner table at Electra and the man she had brought with her, whom Amelia had introduced as Electra's friend but who Christopher thought looked more like a bouncer at a nightclub. It wasn't that he was bad looking, but he slouched in his chair and had eaten the salad and main course as if he thought he might not see food again for a week. Now he was devouring the last of his sherry tart while the others had barely tasted their own.

Electra was paying little attention to the man, her gaze, instead, still fixed on Christopher as she watched his every move. Christopher was thankful that Amelia had not left them alone again. He was still angry that Electra had tried to seduce him. Amelia's own sister! It was hard to believe, but he knew he had not misinterpreted Electra's suggestion. He was now more determined than ever not to allow himself to become obliged to Amelia's sister for anything, but he couldn't get her words out of his mind. She had said Amelia belonged here at Willowbrook and not in his "shoe box" house, and although Christopher hated to admit it, he knew Electra was right and he wasn't sure what he could do about that.

Helga cleared away the last of the dessert plates, but before anyone had a chance to leave the table, Electra caught Christopher's eye. "I won't beat about the bush," she said. "I've told Amelia, and now I'm telling you both—I won't allow her to marry you."

The hair bristled on the back of Christopher's neck. "You seem to be under the impression that you have some say in the matter. You don't."

"What Christopher means," Amelia broke in, "is that we see no reason why our marriage should affect you."

"Not affect me? Of course it will. You agreed years ago to look after Willowbrook if I would support you."

"That was a long time ago," Christopher said. "Now I'm going to support her."

"Yes." Electra's tone dripped sarcasm. "I've seen your house and have some idea of the style to which she will have to become accustomed."

Christopher leaned forward in a threatening posture, but Amelia's hand clamped down on his thigh beneath the table and he forced himself to sit back.

"Electra, there is no reason for you to be so unpleasant," Amelia responded, then looked away from her sister's glare to Carter. "I don't like having to solve family problems in front of you, Mr. Symmons, but since my sister saw fit to bring you, you'll have to bear with us." To Electra she added, "You have a life of your own, obviously, and you can't expect me not to do the same. You aren't being at all reasonable."

"Who do you propose should manage Willowbrook? Helga? She's only a maid."

"Lower your voice. Her English is better than you appear to think. No, I don't assume any such thing. How about you taking on the job?"

"Me? From New York?"

"No, from right here."

"That's too ridiculous to deserve an answer. I'll move back as soon as I can. You know that. But not now."

"So what's stopping you? Papa managed his affairs from here."

Electra glared at her. "Yes, he did, and he died penniless." Her eyes darted to Christopher. "Did you know that? Amelia dresses in nice clothes and lives in a fine house, but she has no money. You aren't engaged to an heiress."

"I would want Amelia if she were barefoot and living in a tar-paper shack," he growled and was gratified to see the naked envy in Electra's eyes. "I love her, and eventually I'll be able to give her all this and more—without any strings tied to it. She may live comfortably, thanks to you, but she's paying for it in other ways. Why, she's no more than a paid employee. You treat her like a slave!"

"That's not true!" Electra snapped.

"What else would you call a person who isn't free to marry or to move away as she chooses?"

"I expected this sort of scene from a person like you," Electra retorted. "You and Amelia have nothing in common. Nothing at all! Anyone could come in here and romance her off her feet. Ten years from now she'll thank me."

Amelia knotted her napkin into a ball. "Ten years from now I'll have a lovely family and a happy marriage and all you'll have is . . ." She stopped herself before she pointed at Carter, but Electra knew what she meant. Amelia drew in a shaken breath. "I'm sorry. That was cruel."

Christopher covered her hand with his, his eyes on Electra. "I'll do everything in my power to make Amelia happy. As I see it, this house is the only obstacle in our way. I suggest you sell it."

If he had proposed they set fire to it, he wouldn't have drawn a harsher reaction. Electra's disdain was clearly evident in the tilt of her head and the flare of her nostrils. "I'd see you dead before I would consent to sell Willowbrook."

For a moment no one moved or spoke. Christopher fought to stay calm and not to tell this woman exactly what he thought of her and all her family with the exception of Amelia. Then he heard Amelia's uneven breathing and realized she was crying. He turned to her, at once all solicitous. "Sweetheart, I didn't mean to make you cry."

"You didn't." Amelia groped for his hand. "This is all so different from the way I thought it would be. I thought Electra would be happy for us and that you two would like each other. This is a nightmare."

Electra spoke up. "Perhaps you had better go, Mr. Jenkins. My sister is upset. She should go up and rest or she will have one of her sick headaches."

Christopher started to point out to Electra that her medical advice was uncalled for, but Amelia was already on her feet, nodding in agreement.

"You'd better go," she said. "This is all so terrible. I can't stand any more. I feel as if I'm falling apart. Please go."

His jaw was set firmly as he said, "All right, but call me

if you feel sick. I'll see you tomorrow at any rate."

Amelia nodded and he bent and kissed her before he left.

Electra sat watching it all. Amelia was more upset than she had ever seen her, even more distraught than she had been when their father died. She hated hearing Christopher call Amelia sweetheart and watching him hold her hand. And her insides had wrenched when he kissed her.

Christopher let himself out as Electra heard Amelia hurry upstairs, no doubt to cry in her room. He really loved her. He actually cared for Amelia! At least he seemed to think so. She told herself Amelia would never be strong enough to be a doctor's wife, let alone a mother. Since childhood Amelia had had recurring nervous headaches. If it hadn't been for Electra's support, she would never have managed at all. She didn't realize how much effort Electra had expended reminding her to have the gutters cleaned and the furnace inspected. Amelia needed her guidance in everything.

But when Christopher had looked at Amelia, his eyes had been soft with love, and he had known she was crying without having to look at her. Electra could recall no one who had ever cared that much for her. No man called her sweetheart unless it was in response to her having picked up the check or paid a bill he owed. No one kissed her with such gentleness. No one vowed to marry her and love her come hell or high water.

"He's pretty good-looking," Carter said.

"Is he?" she snapped. "I didn't notice." She was still amazed that old Jenkins had produced such a handsome son, but she certainly wasn't going to admit it.

Carter leaned closer to her, making his biceps bunch

under the short sleeves of his shirt. "Ever make love on a dining room table?" he suggested with a grin.

Electra stood up so fast her chair rocked. "Don't be disgusting!" she retorted. "I'm going upstairs."

Carter looked around, as if wondering what he had said wrong. As she started up the stairs she heard him following her. Electra considered sending him out for a walk, but decided against it. Maybe what she needed was to feel a man's strong arms around her and to lose her senses in Carter's athletic lovemaking. She let him follow her to the bedroom.

CHAPTER 13

CARTER MADE LOVE TO ELECTRA AS THOR-oughly as ever, but she wasn't emotionally satisfied. As he stroked in and out of her, she couldn't stop fantasizing that he had blond hair and a captivating southern drawl. When he was spent, she pretended it had been good for her, too.

She couldn't sleep, and after listening to Carter's rhythmical breathing for what seemed like an hour or more, Electra slipped out of bed and put on her robe and slippers.

Careful not to awaken anyone, she went downstairs. The dark house held no fears for her. She couldn't recall a single time when she had been afraid of its shadows and closets, not even the deep one under the stairs where Amelia had once been positive a troll lived.

Restlessly she roamed from room to room, the sound of Christopher's voice haunting her. His tones had been deep and smooth and his accent more Georgian than Virginian. Having heard only northern speech for so long, Electra could easily discern the difference.

Christopher wasn't right for Amelia. She was convinced of that. They had nothing at all in common. She wondered if he had assumed Amelia was wealthy. If that was it, he wouldn't be back, not after Electra had made it so plain that Amelia had no money at all.

Sell Willowbrook! She was still appalled that he would suggest such a thing. She stroked the satin finish on a door frame as if to comfort the house. She would never agree to sell Willowbrook. Thank heaven Amelia had been equally upset by the suggestion. Electra didn't want to have to worry that her sister would do something foolish behind her back.

Although it was dark in the dining room, she could see by the moonlight through the window where each of them had sat. She stared at Christopher's chair. What was it about him that made his memory so persistent? Electra had known many men in many ways, but none of them had been unforgettable. She supposed it was because Christopher had that indefinable quality called charisma. It was as though a person couldn't be in the same room with him without looking at him. Certainly a woman as shallow as Amelia would believe she was in love with him.

Electra crossed through the living room and went out onto the porch. As usual, the porch light was on, but its brilliance was distracting to Electra, so she went down the steps and into the darkness.

A breeze billowed her white robe, and the thought that a casual observer might take her to be a ghost brought a smile to her lips. In a way she felt like a ghost, because she had been absent from Willowbrook for so long. There had been no significant changes in the house—Willowbrook was always pretty much the same—but there were tiny changes that Electra noticed, such as a new set of towels in the bathroom, *Life* magazine where once there had been *Time*, a kitchen door of a slightly different design than the one it had replaced.

Electra's wandering took her alongside the walled garden and when she reached the gate, she went inside. She had been here several times with Amelia but never alone. What her sister found so fascinating about a square of land enclosed by high brick walls was a mystery to Electra. The garden was pretty, of course, but so were the rolling hills behind the house and the avenue of catawba trees leading up to it. When the catawbas were in bloom, the drive was spectacular. The garden reminded her of Amelia—pretty, old-fashioned, and closed away in its own world.

It was Amelia's self-imposed isolation that Electra found particularly annoying. Why didn't Amelia ever want to get out and do anything? True, being at Willowbrook was Electra's idea of heaven, but Amelia could join a club or take a class at Catawba Mills's new college. She could mix with their old friends instead of meeting new and inappropriate ones like this Christopher person.

There he was, back in her thoughts again. How had Amelia managed to meet him in the first place? None of her all-too-frequent letters had mentioned her having been ill, and if she had needed the care of a doctor, she would have gone to Dr. McVane, not some newcomer. Surely Christopher hadn't searched her out.

Electra left the garden, closing the gate behind her as Amelia had insisted be done so some stray dog wouldn't wander in and dig up the flowers. Strolling back to the house, Electra relished the security she felt here at Willowbrook. She would never have dreamed of walking alone at night in New York, especially wearing nothing but her robe. Amelia had no idea how good she had it, thanks to Electra. She was certainly intelligent enough to manage the staff at Willowbrook, but she lacked common sense. When it came to her emotions, Amelia was much too naive. She needed Electra's guidance, and whether she liked it or not, she was going to get it.

For a moment she imagined how wonderful it would be to kiss Christopher and make love with him. Perhaps Amelia already knew and that was why she was so convinced she loved him. But no, Amelia was probably still saving herself for marriage. Electra grimaced. Once a woman was rid of her virginity, it didn't seem to be such an important state. At least Electra had found that to be so. She almost laughed aloud at the thought of Amelia preserving her purity all these years. Yes, Electra thought, making love with Christopher might be an earthshaking experience, and one that she was certain she would enjoy. Once again she regretted having brought Carter. She considered slipping into town, away from Amelia's watchful eye, and seducing Christopher. Surely if he was away from Amelia, she would be successful in winning him. He couldn't possibly prefer Amelia's plump body and laugh-wrinkled face to Electra's perfection. Then she recalled how Christopher had kissed Amelia, and Electra had to admit that she was afraid to take the chance. Later. Later she would go to him, when she could be certain of her triumph.

Miles away, Christopher was also awake, puzzling over how a woman as sweet as Amelia could have such a bitch for a sister. Electra typified all he disliked about the wealthy class and stereotypical city women. She was brassy in a refined way, she was much too aggressive, and she smelled of cigarettes. Of course most people did smoke, but Christopher didn't and he preferred the soft scent of Amelia's perfume.

He wondered if Amelia was safe with her sister in the house. Not that he thought Electra might physically harm her, but there was no telling what ideas she might be putting into Amelia's head. Christopher had felt protective of Amelia since they were children, and by now it was almost instinctive with him. It was as if he had been conceived and designed to love and care for her.

He more than anyone, including Amelia, knew what was right and good for her. Again he thought of Electra's statement about Amelia belonging to Willowbrook. He loved Amelia, and her background and heritage had partly shaped her personality. He was beginning to see he was wrong to take her away from it. If they watched their money and didn't splurge too often, he could pay close to half the cost of running Willowbrook. It wouldn't be as if he were living on Electra's charity if he paid their share. And he might be wrong about not having children as well. Amelia wasn't a prime candidate for motherhood, but neither were many women with families. He smiled at the idea of a little girl with Amelia's laughing eyes and red hair.

Soon Electra and her surly companion would leave, and Christopher anticipated the day. He pictured how happy Amelia would be to hear he was agreeing to live at Willowbrook and to have children. They would be happy together. He was sure of that.

. . .

Electra slid through the crowd in Zoe Wharton's lavish Park Avenue apartment, feeling perfectly within her natural element. Her crimson dress, emblazoned with sequins, molded her slender body like a second skin. Cut daringly low both in front and back, the dress demanded a woman with a perfect body to do it justice, and Electra was showing it and herself off with consummate skill. She knew she was the center of attention and that many of the women there, even some whose bodies were less than admirable, would be clamoring to buy a copy of the dress. However, only a select few of this design would be available the following week, for Electra was an expert at supply-and-demand economics.

Once Electra had completed her rounds through the crowd, she was pleased to note that William Stratford was not there. It was Zoe who had introduced William to her, and it wouldn't have been unusual for Zoe to have invited him to the party. Had William been there, things would have been somewhat uncomfortable, as her escort for the evening was Carter Symmons, and there was no love lost between the two. Carter had recently landed a role that William had also auditioned for, and it was widely known that Carter was now Electra's lover. Electra enjoyed knowing two handsome young men would have loved to fight over her, but she was far too civilized to actually allow it.

As at all of Zoe's parties the liquor flowed freely and there were far too many people. Electra didn't mind that there was no place to sit. Her dress wasn't designed for sitting, and she was here as much to generate a market for the design as to see people. She did, however, dislike having to shout in order to be heard over the crowd and the stage band, and she particularly disliked being jostled.

Zoe was standing on the other side of the room talking to a group of young men. Electra decided to join them. Zoe's career as an actress had lasted only a year, because her face and voice inflections were too similar to Laurette Taylor's and the theater didn't want or need a duplicate. Fortunately, soon after that, Zoe had married a millionaire, and according to her she was twice blessed to have outlived him. Zoe had dyed her hair brilliant red—actually more orange than red and not a shade of orange that could be found anywhere in nature—and was now grasping at departing youth by surrounding herself with young people, preferably men. Through her extravagant parties, Zoe's reputation as a hostess had become as well known as her preference for young lovers. Although Electra liked her personally, she couldn't help but feel sorry for Zoe's failure to do something useful with her life.

As usual, Zoe was talking show business, and her young men, most of them would-be actors, were willing to oblige. "I don't understand it," Zoe was saying. "I simply can't see what bobby-soxers find so fascinating about the Sinatra boy. Even Harry James says he looks like a wet rag, and Harry *discovered* him."

"Yes, but he left James to sign on with Tommy Dorsey," one of the young men reminded her. "Maybe James regrets losing him. Sinatra brings in the crowds."

Zoe shook her head and her huge earrings jangled like silver bells. "If you ask me, he's just a flash in the pan. Five years from now no one will remember his name."

Electra leaned forward with an unlit cigarette and three of the men scrambled through their pockets for their lighters. "Have any of you seen *Bulldog Pike?*" The popular play she referred to was one of the favored conversation openers of the season.

"No," one man said with a grin, "but if he comes in, I'll tell him you asked."

Electra responded to the man's humorous play on words with one of her rare smiles.

"*Bulldog* is another case of much ado about nothing," Zoe said. "It doesn't even have a decent story line, and the performers in that show can't act their way out of a wet paper bag."

"Jealous that you didn't back it?" Electra good-naturedly chided. A large man lurched against her, and when she caught his eye, she cast him a reproachful glance, then turned back to Zoe.

"Electra, you stick to your clothing design and leave the theater to me. Mark my words, not an actor in that play will ever be heard of again," Zoe prophesied. "The writer should be shot."

"True. But the publicity agent deserves an award. Everybody's heard of it, and the tickets are sold out weeks in advance."

As the men surrounding them nodded their agreement, the large man again bumped into Electra, this time sloshing his drink over his hand and sleeve.

Electra glared at him. "Go stand somewhere else," she suggested coolly as she snuffed out her cigarette in a nearby ashtray, "and stop bumping into me."

The man obviously had had too much to drink and his mouth dropped open as he stared down into Electra's cleavage. He swayed unsteadily as if he was about to do a pratfall.

"Come with me," another stranger said, adroitly looping the drunk's arms across his shoulders and pulling him away.

Electra watched the second man haul the drunk to the door, take his glass, and propel him out into the hall. Although Electra didn't know her rescuer at the moment, she intended to correct that oversight, for he was intriguingly handsome. But before she could get over to him, the crowd shifted and she lost sight of him. For another moment or two she looked about, but the man had disappeared.

To ease her disappointment, Electra tried to become interested in Zoe's conversation, but the press of the crowd was making her uneasy. Being familiar with Zoe's apartment, she worked her way through the crowd and down the hall to the bedrooms. The first one she looked into was occupied by a couple who glared at her for interrupting their petting. Electra hastily retreated.

Fortunately, the bedroom at the end of the hall was empty and Electra quickly eased inside and shut the door. In the relative quiet and seclusion of the dimly lit room, she lit a cigarette and after inhaling deeply, she began to relax. As she sat at the dresser studying herself in the mirror, she took a comb from her small evening bag and toyed with her hair, even though it wasn't mussed. Her hairdresser had been right that the new cut she'd done would hold up well at parties, but Electra continued fiddling with her hair because she didn't want anyone to see her idly staring at herself in the mirror.

In the reflection in the mirror, she saw the door open behind her, and the stranger who had come to her aid stepped in. When he saw her, he turned to go, but she stopped him. "Please don't go. I want to thank you for getting rid of that drunk for me. I was afraid he might ruin my dress."

"That would have been a shame. It's a very pretty dress."

Electra turned to face him. "We haven't met. I'm Electra." Of late she had begun using only her first name; she thought it made her more unforgettable.

"I'm Saul Feldman."

"An actor without a proper stage name?" she chided playfully. "I would have expected a Samuel Fields or at least a Saul Mann."

"How do you know I'm an actor?" he countered.

"Easy. You're too handsome to be anything else. Unless you're a male model. Tell me you aren't a male model."

He laughed and stroked his black mustache. "I'm not a model. Now would you like me to call you a taxi? You're a taxi."

Electra smiled at his joke.

"That's better. You're even prettier when you smile."

Electra was intrigued. Most men said she was beautiful, not pretty, and none cared if she smiled or not.

"As to your question, I am an actor but it's only temporary."

"Now you've really surprised me. Usually men say they are only a waiter or a parking lot attendant temporarily but that they are really actors."

"I want to direct."

"Oh? Whatever for?"

He grinned again. "I like playing God. How about you? Are you 'in the business'?"

She shook her head. "I'm a fashion designer."

"You wouldn't be the Electra of Electra, Inc., would you?"

"In person."

"Now I'm the one who's surprised. You aren't at all what I expected."

"Is that a compliment?"

"Yes." He didn't elaborate.

Electra wondered what was being said behind her back that was so unflattering. "Are you here alone?"

"No, I'm with my wife. I thought she might be in here. She's sort of short and has brown hair cut fluffy around her ears. I think she's wearing a green dress. Or maybe it's blue."

Electra laughed. "You'll never find her with a description like that. It fits half the women here."

"I'll run across her eventually."

She found she was enjoying their conversation and was reluctant for him to leave. To detain him she asked the question that was sure to lead to further conversation. "Any news on the war?"

"A U-boat attacked the *Greer* off Greenland. I guess you heard about that."

"Yes, I did. Isn't it terrible?" She wondered if his eyes were as dark as they seemed from across the room or if it was a trick of the dim light.

"It certainly is. Rachel still has family in Europe. We're trying to get them out before travel becomes too dangerous."

"Rachel?"

"My wife."

"Oh." She hadn't met many men who mentioned their wives. Not at Zoe's parties.

"I had a feeling when rubber golf balls went off the market that something like this might happen. Ambassador Grew said more or less the same thing. There are always warnings if you pay attention."

"If there's a war, will you enlist?"

"Of course. Hitler's a crazy man. He has to be stopped."

"But you must be in your late thirties. Surely they will want younger men."

"Rachel's said that, too. The young ones may be preferable, but I'm going as well. You don't have a name like Saul Feldman and not have a reason to hate what that Nazi bastard is doing. I have friends as well as family in Germany, and I don't know how long they'll be safe."

"I don't think there will be a war. Not a big one like the Great War. Someone will stop Hitler. He can't possibly take over the world." She laughed as if such an idea were ludicrous.

"You're forgetting Japan."

"That tiny island? Why, they are farther away than Germany."

"Mark my words, though, they would make a powerful enemy."

"Of course they would if they were as close to us as Canada or Mexico, but their planes can't reach us."

"They could if they were launched off a carrier. The world isn't as large as you seem to think it is."

Distressed, Electra stood and walked across the room. What he said made sense. "Then you think we really will join the war?"

"President Roosevelt can't ignore attacks on our ships. Isolationism is an outmoded policy."

Electra frowned. "Surely Germany and Japan won't be

so foolish as to bring America into the war."

"Nobody ever said war was logical. It makes a lot more sense to mind your own business and to get along."

"Yet you'd fight."

"I'd fight. Some things are too precious to risk and certainly too important to hand over to the Nazis."

The door opened and a short woman with fluffy brown hair and wearing a pink dress poked her head in. "Saul, I've been looking for you."

"There you are! Rachel, this is Electra of Electra, Inc. Electra, my wife Rachel."

"Nice to know you," Rachel said. "I didn't catch your last name."

"I don't use it." She glanced at Saul and added, "It's Radcliff. Electra Radcliff."

Rachel forced a polite smile, as if she had never heard of Electra or her company. "We have to be going, Saul. It's getting late."

Saul nodded to Electra. "It was nice talking to you. Maybe we'll run into each other again sometime."

"Perhaps." Electra saw them out, then shut the door behind them. Frowning, she sat back down at the mirror and stared at her reflection. At one time a wife would have been beside herself with jealousy at finding her husband alone with Electra in a bedroom. But Rachel hadn't even seemed to notice.

Electra leaned closer and studied the faint lines at her eyes and lips. Was she beginning to look old? Rachel was young, but she wasn't pretty, and Saul was definitely handsome enough to cause any prudent wife to be concerned about his interest in and private conversations with another woman.

As she thought how naive it was for Rachel not to have been jealous, a rather startling and confusing revelation came to her: she had been more interested in Saul's conversation than in his body. She couldn't recall ever having wanted a man as a friend and nothing else. What was going on with her?

Again the door opened and Carter stuck his head in. "I've been looking for you."

"I came in here to comb my hair."

Carter walked up behind her and put his hands on her shoulders. "You look great." With an easy motion he pushed the shoulders of her dress down and exposed her breasts. Watching her reflection in the mirror, Carter stroked her nipples until they were erect.

Electra's breath caught in her throat. Carter liked to take chances as much as she did. They both knew that door could open again at any minute and anyone might come in.

Electra saw passion darken his eyes, and she made no move to stop him. By comparison to her ivory skin, his muscular hands looked even more tanned than they actually were. Her nipples peeked like pink buds from behind his fingers. She wanted him and she wanted him that minute, not later.

With the long sleeves of her gown still covering her arms and with her breasts bare, Electra stood and went to the bed. She hiked her skirt above her hips, removed her panties, and lay back amid the pillows and satin bed coverlet.

Carter needed no more invitation. With a practiced

move he unzipped his pants and was entering her before Electra was fully reclined.

She still wore her hose and garter belt, and he hadn't so much as loosened his tie. Excitement roared through Electra, and she matched him thrust for thrust. As his body demanded its surcease, she felt her own climax rush to explosive heights. She fought not to cry out and immediately felt him push one final time into her.

He relaxed, panting, remembering to support his weight on his elbows to keep from crushing her. Electra found she was panting as well.

Carter stood up and drew her to her feet. Her gown dropped back in place over her hips, and she shrugged her breasts and shoulders back into the dress.

Just at that minute Zoe opened the door and stuck her head in. "Come out here and meet someone. It's the writer of *Bulldog Pike*." She rolled her eyes to show her opinion of him.

Electra kicked her panties under the bed and followed Zoe out as if nothing had happened.

"I don't like your sister," Christopher said as they sat on the garden bench beneath the willow. "Maybe I shouldn't say that to you, but it's true."

"Electra has changed so much in the last few years. I hardly know her myself."

"And who was that man with her? I never did figure out who he was."

"He's her boyfriend, I suppose. She said they aren't engaged." Amelia hoped Christopher wouldn't ask the obvious question about the sleeping arrangements. She hadn't been able to sleep a wink with Carter in the house and her wondering what might be going on behind their bedroom door. She was still embarrassed at having been confronted with such a man.

"He seems a bit young for her. He couldn't be out of his twenties."

"I thought exactly the same thing," she confided. "Do you think it's possible that he simply looks younger than he is?"

"He acted like a spoiled child. A starving one at that."

Amelia smiled. "I noticed that, too. I do hope he got enough to eat. I wasn't expecting him, and Helga had already started cooking our dinner."

"He will survive."

Amelia put her hand on Christopher's leg. "I want to ask a favor of you."

"Anything at all, you know that."

"Don't answer before you hear what it is." Amelia avoided his eyes. "I think we should postpone our wedding."

"What? What on earth for?"

"I think Electra is set against it because we sprang it on her so suddenly. If we wait until, say, Christmas, she may come around."

"You also thought she would like me when she met me, but she didn't," he pointed out, not meeting her eyes, because he knew that was far from true. Electra had liked him too well. "If anything, I think we should move it up."

"We originally considered being married on Christmas Eve. Remember?"

"Yes, and we decided against it. The weather may be freezing by then, and it will be too cold for a garden wedding. I know having the wedding in the garden is important to you."

"Let's chance it, Christopher. Please? I want to do all I can to win her over. She's all the family I have."

He sighed. "All right. But I'm warning you that I'm against it. We could wait until hell freezes over, and I don't think Electra will come around on this. But if it will make you feel better, I'll go along with you."

"Thank you. I love you so much for humoring me on this."

His lips curved up in a crooked smile. "If you never ask me for more than this, I'll be a happy man, I guess."

Amelia felt a touch of guilt. She had been overjoyed at Christopher's decision to live at Willowbrook, but she was afraid he might someday regret it. She knew how strongly he had felt about it.

"Where would you like to go on our honeymoon?" he asked.

"I hadn't thought of that. We will get to take a trip, won't we!"

"It will have to be a short one, I'm afraid. Dr. McVane has agreed to take my patients for a week or so, but we won't have much money. I don't like to think of you having to cut corners on things like our honeymoon," he added.

"I don't feel as if I'm cutting corners," she protested. "I've rarely been anywhere, so anything at all will be new to me. Besides, we can pretend to be anywhere. I used to do that all the time. We can go to the mountains and pretend they're the Alps or to the beach and say it's the Riviera."

"Someday I'm going to take you to all those places."

"Yes! And to exotic spots that I've never heard of anyone going to like Zanzibar and Bangkok and the Fiji Islands."

"We'll see them all one of these days," he promised. "When I retire we'll do nothing but travel."

"And we'll show up at our children's houses with armloads of strange gifts for our grandchildren. Naturally we'll spoil them rotten and turn them into little globe-trotters as well." She felt a warm glow at the idea of them having a real family of their own. Christopher had given in on that, too.

"There's so much I want to do!" Christopher exclaimed. "So much I want us to discover together."

"We'll do it all," Amelia promised. "We have years and years ahead of us."

"I love you," he said with a smile. "You're good for me."

"I love you, too." She laid her cheek on his shoulder. "I'm so glad I fell in love with you and not somebody like Carter Symmons." After a moment of thought, she added, "I'm even glad Papa lost all his money, because if he hadn't, I would have married somebody like Carleton Edgeworth or Reggie Smyth-Downs. Then I wouldn't have been available to marry you."

"It really is incredible, isn't it?" he agreed. "Out of all the things we might have done or could have become, we turned out just right to be together."

"Love is full of miracles," Amelia said. "It's every bit as much a miracle as birth."

"That reminds me of something I meant to tell you. I delivered my first new Catawba Mills citizen last night. A little girl. I've delivered others, of course, during my training and internship, but it never ceases to amaze me that so tiny a human can have all its parts in miniature and that everything functions so perfectly."

"I want you to deliver our babies," she said, nuzzling her cheek against him.

"I will. Amelia, if you could just see a baby when it's first born. Watch it turn from pasty white to pink as oxygen gets in its blood. See it wrinkle its face up and let out a yell and wave its little arms and legs for the first time. It's really something."

"I want to raise a miniature of you. As he grows older I want to be able to say, 'That's Christopher's chin, and those are Christopher's eyes.' I want all our children to look just like you."

He kissed her and Amelia floated in the safety of his arms.

CHAPTER 14

THE SUMMER OF 1941 FADED INTO AUTUMN, and with the increased aggression by the Axis powers in Europe, the American people moved inexorably toward an acceptance of the inevitable involvement of the United States in the war—unless a miracle occurred. Congress repealed the restrictive sections of the Neutrality Act of 1939, allowing President Roosevelt the power to equip fighting ships and send them into combat when the need arose.

Thanksgiving came and went. Electra had flown down for the holiday meal, but had gone home the next day. Amelia had been sorry to see her come and relieved to see her go. Since the weekend when Electra had brought Carter down to visit and had been so rude to Christopher, Amelia had treated her with icy politeness. During her brief visit, Electra had been equally cool and had not once mentioned the postponed wedding or Christopher. After dinner that evening, Amelia once caught Electra staring at Christopher's picture in a way that left Amelia feeling uneasy, but as soon as Electra realized Amelia was watching, her fascination turned into a glare and she left the room.

Christopher and Amelia passed Thanksgiving apart because Christopher had no more desire to be in the same room with Electra than she evidently did with him. Amelia tried to point out that he would eventually have to see Electra again, but he still refused to eat the meal with her.

On the following Saturday, as Amelia and Christopher walked in the garden, they concluded that postponing their wedding had been a mistake. Electra was apparently still opposed to the union and had given Amelia the impression she never would welcome Christopher into the family.

With the approach of Christmas season, toys and bright tinsel appeared in the stores and a tree in Catawba Park was festively decorated. The air was filled with a frantic gaiety, as if everyone were trying hard to remember Christmas and forget the war.

On a Sunday morning in early December, Japanese planes launched from an aircraft carrier bombed Pearl Harbor in Hawaii. In less than two hours most of the American Pacific fleet was destroyed.

Amelia and Christopher heard the news over lunch. Like most of the other people in the restaurant, they had just come from church. The owner brought out a radio from a back room, and everyone crowded around it to listen.

"I don't believe it," a woman scoffed. "It's another one of Orson Welles's spoofs." No one answered her.

Amelia's wide eyes met Christopher's as the list of casualties to men and machinery began to come in. Eight battleships and three light cruisers had been sunk or destroyed. One hundred eighty-eight planes had been destroyed. The number of dead and wounded was still mounting, but even the earliest estimates were staggering.

Most of the men had been asleep, many of them on board their ships. The base had been on the lowest level of defense alert. The planes were grouped in bunches when the attack was launched. Antiaircraft guns were still in parks, the ammunition was still in the magazines, most of the ships in the fleet were moored side by side in the harbor. The number of deaths and injuries grew by the minute.

Christopher took Amelia's hand. "I think we had better go."

She nodded, unable to speak. On rubbery legs she followed him to the cash register and stared sightlessly at the gum, candy, and cigars in the glass case. Her mind seemed to be flying in all directions at once, and yet she couldn't have told anyone what she was thinking. It was as if her brain was trying to protect her as long as possible from a thought too dreadful to accept.

When they were in the car, Christopher turned on the radio and tuned in the same announcer. His voice cracked with emotion as he read the names of the destroyed ships: the battleships *Arizona* and *Oklahoma*, the target ship *Utah*, destroyers *Cassin*, *Downes*, and *Shaw*. Many others were heavily damaged. Amelia found herself scarcely daring to breathe as the report continued.

By the time they reached Willowbrook, Helga had heard the news. She was sitting in the front parlor, a damp dishcloth clutched in her hands. The familiar radio announcer droned on and on, now beginning to repeat the story for those who had tuned in late.

After several minutes Helga seemed to remember this wasn't her own parlor and she stood to return to the kitchen. Amelia caught her wrist and motioned for her to sit back down. For the moment class distinctions were meaningless.

"We are here, too, in war. *Ja?*" Helga said. "Just as in my country, we are in war?"

Amelia nodded, without speaking.

"I have friends in the navy," Christopher said. "I've been trying to remember if any were stationed at Pearl."

Amelia still couldn't talk. She felt as if a vise had tightened around her throat. Her mouth was dry and tasted coppery with fear. Gradually her scattered thoughts coalesced into only one—dread. "You'll have to go, won't you." She said it as a statement, not a question.

He didn't answer. He didn't need to. She could see it in his eyes; he would have to go. She laced her fingers together in her lap, and her knuckles turned white from the pressure.

After a while Helga stood again and walked silently from the room, her cheeks stained with tears. Amelia found her own cheeks were wet, but she couldn't remember starting to cry. "When?" she asked.

He shook his head. "I'll call the draft board tomorrow."

"Maybe you're too old."

"They will need doctors. I'm not too old."

"Maybe you won't pass the physical. I've heard you say your knees were ruined by football and . . ."

He put his hand over both of hers. Amelia fell silent. "I have to do it," he said.

She nodded as her tears splashed onto their hands. "I know."

Fiercely he pulled her into his embrace. "I don't want to leave you!" he ground out through clenched teeth.

Amelia summoned up courage she never knew she possessed. "I know you don't. I've known all along, though, that if it came to this, you'd join up." She wanted to cry out to him to wait, to bide his time and let them draft him, not to enlist. True, his country needed him, but she needed him so much more. But instead of voicing these thoughts and revealing how truly selfish she felt, she forced her courage to prevail.

With trembling fingers Amelia turned off the radio. She couldn't bear to hear any more.

"I think we should call Reverend Sullivan and get married right away."

Startled by his words, she stared up at him. "Surely you won't be gone before Christmas!"

"I don't know, but I don't want us to waste any more time. I can't leave you otherwise."

"Maybe he could marry us today."

"We have to get a license," he reminded her.

She wrapped her arms tighter around him. "Promise me you won't leave me until you have to. Married or not, I want you beside me."

He kissed her forehead as he stroked her shining hair. "I won't leave you until it's necessary."

Everyone in town must have had the same idea, because it took Christopher quite a while to get through to Reverend Sullivan. The minister agreed to marry them as soon as they had the license. Amelia stood watching Christopher as he talked to the preacher, her hands clasped in front of her to hide her nervousness.

After Christopher hung up, he silently took her hand and led her outside. Amelia knew where they were going; the garden was so much a part of them that it was only natural for them to go there.

Christopher pulled the gate shut behind them and wedged a twig in the latch so it couldn't be opened. They walked on the brick path around the sundial and toward the potting shed. With the flowers gone now, the only color in the garden came from the bronze leaves of the creeping thyme and the deep red of the sedum ground cover.

Christopher opened the shed and took out the quilt they used for picnics or as a cushion on the marble bench. Amelia asked no questions. He spread the quilt beneath the willow tree, covering the alyssum and thyme, then turned to her.

Slowly Amelia began unbuttoning her dress. They had planned to wait until they were married, but in a world turned topsy-turvy the old standards didn't seem to apply.

The air was cold on her skin, but Amelia didn't mind. Now that the first shock of the news was over, she felt hot from head to toe. As she slipped the dress from her shoulders, she stepped out of her heels and onto the quilt. Christopher had removed his coat and tie and was opening the cuff links on his white dress shirt.

Amelia helped him with his cuff links and began unbuttoning his shirt. Christopher's hands caressed the silk and lace of her slip, an urgency in his touch. "You're sure?" he asked as she opened his shirt and kissed the smooth skin of his chest.

She raised her eyes to his and nodded. "I want you. We never should have waited this long."

Christopher bent his head and kissed her with all the love in his soul. Amelia pressed her body tight to his, and her breasts mounded on his warm flesh. Christopher's urgency was quickly communicating itself to her. When his tongue touched her lips, she opened her mouth and eagerly sought his tongue with her own.

She let Christopher remove the rest of their clothing until they stood naked in the weak warmth of the sun. The stripped boughs of the willow draped around them to the ground, creating a semblance of a lacy chamber. Almost reverently Christopher reached out and touched her throat, trailing his fingers over her chest to the swell of her breast and brushing her nipple. He didn't speak, but she saw his love shining in his eyes. It was as if their hearts and souls were one and there was no need for vocal communication.

Slowly he drew her into his arms and kissed her again. Amelia felt his body hot against hers, his manhood hard and seeking.

They lay on the quilt, and Amelia laced her fingers in his golden hair. "When I first saw you here in the garden, I thought you looked like an angel," she said.

"I thought almost the same thing about you. I hadn't expected you to have grown so beautiful."

"I love you, Christopher." She gazed up into his eyes as she stroked his shoulders and chest. "You feel so good."

Christopher kissed her again, and Amelia felt passion surge through her. When he lowered his head to her breasts and took one of her nipples into his mouth, she felt as if she would explode with her desire for him.

He was a skillful lover, and he taught her the pleasures of loving as if they had all the time in the world. The quilt kept them insulated from the cold earth, and the sun high above warmed their bare skin. Amelia had never known such ecstasy, as Christopher showed her how to be a complete woman.

When he entered her, the pain was much less than she had anticipated. Her love for him was so strong that she forgot the discomfort almost at once. Together they moved in the ancient rhythm of love, their bodies matched and as one.

Unexpectedly, she felt the spiraling release of her passions, and she held tightly to him as her body was rocked with greater pleasure than she had ever known. Her climax triggered Christopher's and he pressed tight against her as her body accepted the libation from his.

As the world re-formed around them, Christopher pulled the side of the quilt over their bodies and held her close to him. "I love you, Amelia," he said. "I love you more at this moment than I thought it was possible to love. I hope you never regret that we didn't wait until our wedding night."

"In our hearts we are already married," she said as her fingers traced the line of his chin and jaw. "I think we have been from the very beginning. No, I'll never regret this. What could have been more perfect than to have consummated our love here in our garden?"

He smiled, but his eyes were sad and she knew he was remembering the war. "You're getting cold," he said. "We had better get dressed."

She admitted she felt chilled now that her passion was spent, and they dressed hurriedly. Amelia ran her fingers through her hair to straighten it as Christopher folded the quilt. When they left the garden, she felt as if she must look different somehow, and it made her feel warm to think that the evidence of Christopher's love was still within her.

Hand in hand they walked back to the house.

The war officially began with the words "Yesterday, December 7, 1941, a date which will live in infamy . . ." Christopher was one of the first to enlist, and he was told to report to his induction center early on December 15. On the twelfth he and Amelia were married in the garden by

Reverend Sullivan in a ceremony that lasted only six minutes. Helga and Dr. McVane were the only witnesses. After the ceremony Helga went back to the kitchen and the doctor and Reverend Sullivan returned to their offices. Amelia and Christopher stayed in the garden, their new rings feeling strange on their fingers.

Amelia looked down at her shiny gold band, a smaller replica of Christopher's. "We did it. We're really married." She still couldn't quite believe it.

"It's a shame your sister couldn't come."

"All the planes are full of soldiers," she said. They both knew Electra had made no effort to get there.

"Do you regret not having a white dress and all the trimmings?"

"No, this is better." She smoothed the skirt of her pink dress. "I would rather remember I wore a cheerful color. If I had really wanted a white dress, I wouldn't have put off having it made until the last minute."

"It may be a while before you have any new clothes. There's already talk of rationing cotton to make uniforms."

"And gas. But that won't be so bad. It will keep me from gadding about all over the place." Amelia was struggling to keep their conversation light so she wouldn't cry. She couldn't cry and spoil things, and more important, she had to appear brave for her Christopher, her husband, who showed no fear as he faced the grave danger ahead.

Christopher brushed the hair back from her face. "What will you do to keep busy while I'm gone?"

Amelia put on her brightest smile and looked up at him, but couldn't make direct eye contact for fear that she would be unable to continue holding back her tears. "Jenny Edgeworth says there will be scrap drives to collect metal and paper and grease. I'll help her. I can't for the life of me see why the army needs bacon drippings, though."

"Grease is used in making explosives."

Amelia turned her face away and rose. Silently Christopher followed her lead, and together they walked along the familiar path that led around the sundial and to the gate.

"Maybe I'll join the Red Cross," she said in an effort to direct their conversation back to matters she could deal with. "I'll sew one of those flags with a star on it to hang in my window. Next spring I'll plant one of those victory gardens like the ones we read about in the paper. Or maybe by then it will all be over and things will be back to normal." She looked up at him hopefully, but he didn't meet her eyes. "I'm good at gardening. Maybe I'll grow extra food and give it to people like Jenny, who can't seem to grow anything."

At the gate they paused, and Christopher looked back at the garden. "I always think of you, of us, here. I first saw it in summer, and now I've seen it in all the seasons but spring."

"You'll like it then," Amelia said. Her resolve not to cry weakened, and her eyes filled with tears. "The mimosa and azaleas bloom then. That's its prettiest season."

"You're more beautiful than all of them," he said, pulling her into the security of his embrace. "I like to think of you like this garden—changing, yet never changing. Everlasting. I wish this could be our whole world."

"I'll bring all of your letters here to read them," she promised, as her unchecked tears stained her cheeks and dampened the lapel of his wedding suit. "It will be as if you're here beside me. And whenever I write you I'll send you a leaf or a pressed flower so you'll always have the garden with you, too."

"Do that, Amelia," he said softly. "You do that."

She found there was too much she wanted to say, so she said nothing at all.

Christopher left for basic training at Fort Benning on the fifteenth, as planned, and afterward he was able to return home for two brief days before leaving to join his unit. Amelia took a snapshot of him standing tall and straight in his uniform and another, more casual one, of him leaning forward and grinning at her with one foot propped up on the garden bench. His starched khakis made him seem taller and broader of shoulder than ever, and the sight of him in uniform instilled a fierce pride in Amelia.

All too soon Amelia had to drive him to the train station to see him off. After a long, passion-filled good-bye kiss, he started to board, then ran back for another quick embrace. As the train began pulling away, he hurried on board and waved to her until he was out of sight. Amelia somehow managed not to cry until she was back in the car.

Before she left town, Amelia drove by Christopher's little house at the corner of Cypress and Long Leaf. Another couple had already moved into it, and the young woman was painting the shutters a bright green. Amelia drove away without a backward glance.

Immediately and with a vengeance, she plunged into her work at Willowbrook, but at first it seemed that nothing would ease the pain of their separation. A week after Christopher left, she had evidence that their long nights of loving had not left her pregnant, and her regret was deep. She missed him even more than she had thought she could.

With each letter she sent him, she included a leaf from their garden. At first there were only the thyme and gardenia and sedum leaves, but soon she could include leaves from the willow and bridal wreath as well. As each flower made its appearance she pressed a perfect specimen and sent it to Christopher. As her victory garden grew, she also included leaves from it. At times she felt as if she were mailing Willowbrook to him leaf by leaf.

Christopher's letters were always cheerful, though he couldn't always say where he was or where he was going. She saved each one in a curly-maple box she had emptied just for that purpose.

As the war dragged on toward the end of summer, Amelia offered the use of Willowbrook to the military as a convalescent home for wounded soldiers, and they were quick to accept. One of the large upstairs rooms she converted into a workroom. Two days a week women volunteers from all around the county joined her there to organize scrap drives, plan blood donor drives, and to mend clothes for civilians who were commuting to nearby cities to work in factories. On Wednesdays the women rolled bandages and boxed them for the Red Cross.

Amelia offered her roof to the local civil defense unit for use by aircraft spotters as they watched for enemy planes. She was thanked for her patriotism, but was told the spotters preferred the better vantage point of the nearby forest fire watchtower. Determined to do all she could, she loyally extinguished her porch light and blacked out her windows every night, and her victory garden was so productive she was able to supply food for two other households as well as Willowbrook. At times she had to laugh at what Jenkins would have thought about the irony that his son had become a doctor and his daughter-in-law a gardener.

As Christopher had predicted, gasoline rationing became a fact. The East Coast began restricting supplies in May, and by December the entire country was affected. The government said the cutback was necessary not only to preserve gasoline supplies but to save on tire rubber as well, for both commodities were desperately needed abroad to keep the armed forces mobile. Amelia put the "A" designation she received in her car window, and although the restriction to three gallons of gasoline a week would significantly curtail her driving, she was determined to accept the inconvenience without resentment.

Ration books of colored stamps were issued for the purchase of meat, coffee, butter, cheese, and sugar. The point system was as confusing to the grocers as it was to Amelia, and she wondered how anyone had devised it in the first place.

She helped organize the collection of everything from old newspapers to bacon grease to metals of all kinds, even including empty toothpaste tubes. Jenny's husband Carleton had gone overseas during the summer of 1942, and Amelia found her friendship with Jenny strengthening. Together they hosted a scrap party, the admission price being a bundle of rags or a box of scrap metal.

With every bandage she rolled and every piece of salvaged material she hauled, Amelia thought of Christopher and felt encouraged that she was doing so much to speed his victorious return.

Electra Radcliff felt like a salmon swimming upstream. Although the war had created a demand for a line of clothes for the new tide of working women, which Electra was quick to supply, rationing was preventing her from turning them out in the quantity she thought best for her business, and she had little tolerance for things that interfered with her determination to succeed at everything she did.

Sitting on the edge of one of Zoe Wharton's most comfortable chairs, Electra frowned over the rim of her glass of rum and Coca-Cola at her hostess, verbalizing yet another of her complaints. "Do you know how difficult it is to make a dress with no zipper or metal fasteners? Regulation L-eighty-five is a damned nightmare!"

Zoe, who had become accustomed to Electra's tirades, only smiled to acknowledge that she'd heard and continued sponging makeup on her legs.

"I've never been wild about patch pockets, and having only one on a blouse makes it look unbalanced. I suppose I don't mind hems being limited to two inches but having no more than seventy-two inches around a skirt makes it look skimpy."

Zoe padded barefoot across her plush carpet to her cheval mirror and critically surveyed her legs to be sure she hadn't missed a spot. "I'll be glad when this damned war is over," she said, "and I can buy stockings again."

"I did design some things I'm proud of for the fall show. It's a line of double-use clothing. The dresses are simple, with tailored jackets for the office. After five o'clock you leave off the jacket and add flashy glass jewelry, the brighter the better, and you're ready to go out on the town."

"Whatever happened to 'less is more'?"

"Too Oriental. Since no one can buy real jewelry these days without feeling guilty, the style is to wear flashy fakes."

"You can keep up with styles for me. It's all I can do to manage my theaters." Zoe owned two and with her male managers away at war, she was trying to juggle the responsibilities of both by herself as well as to produce plays.

"Any news about that friend of yours, what's-his-name? You know the one with the mousy wife." Electra pretended to suddenly recall his name. "Feldman. Saul Feldman."

"I believe he's somewhere in the Pacific." Zoe picked up an eyebrow pencil and leaned back and drew a line up the back of each of her legs to represent the missing hosiery's seam. "You'll never believe this, but I've heard that his wife is seeing someone on the sly."

"Rachel? You're kidding! While Saul is in combat? That's terrible." She seemed to be absorbed in her thoughts for a minute, then continued, "Who is it? I can't recall anyone interesting who's still around here."

"He's an old friend of yours, actually. Robert Hastings." Zoe was the only one who knew how Electra had first happened to come to New York.

"*Robert?* Why, that old devil!"

"Since his wife died last spring, he's been seen in public pretty often. There's talk that Rachel may divorce Saul and marry him."

"How awful!"

"Saul won't be the first or the last to get a Dear John letter, more's the pity."

"I never figured a plain girl like Rachel would Jap Saul. Robert's tastes have certainly changed."

"Well, she's young and who knows but that she might be a tiger in bed. Did I draw this seam straight?"

"It looks fine. Does Saul know all this?"

"*I* certainly haven't told him. I hope he doesn't hear. It may all blow over before he comes home."

"I hate this war," Electra said as she sipped her drink.

"It's helped the economy. I only wish I could find more plays to produce with all-female casts. Do you know how hard it is to find leading men these days? When I do come up with one who isn't under eighteen or over eighty, all I hear is how he ought to be fighting instead of entertaining the wives at home."

"I still can't believe William is dead," Electra said. "And I hear Carter has lost a leg from the knee down. He was so handsome."

"At least he's going home to Indiana alive."

Electra thoughtfully stared at the condensation streaming down the side of her glass. The war had gone on for well over a year now, and Amelia had never once written her about whether or not Christopher was well. Amelia seldom wrote her at all anymore. There had been a short letter informing her of their wedding date and another to say the wedding had gone as planned and that Christopher would leave before Christmas. Electra hadn't answered either letter, and Amelia had rarely written since.

Electra had never gone so long before without news from home. Years before when Amelia had written volumes, Electra had wished she would stop. Now that she had, Electra missed the letters. "I think I'll go to Willowbrook for a few days."

"Oh? I thought you and your sister weren't on speaking terms."

"We aren't. Thinking of William and Carter made me realize how precarious life is."

Zoe arched her brows in surprised doubt. "Or maybe you'd like word of your brother-in-law?"

"You know too damned much about me," Electra grumbled.

"What are friends for? Nothing bad has happened to him or Amelia would have written."

"I suppose. All the same, I think I'll go. Lois and Mary can oversee things for a couple of days."

"By the way, did I tell you about the play that's beginning rehearsals? It's called *Oklahoma*! these days. I don't know how good it will be with music, since it wasn't all that hot as *Green Grow the Lilacs*, but it might be fun. Richard Rodgers wrote the songs with Oscar Hammerstein, of all people, but Agnes De Mille is the choreographer so it can't be all bad. And you do remember, don't you, that we have tickets to *False Steps*?"

"Sure. I'll be back in plenty of time. Amelia and I have never been able to bear long visits with each other, especially not these days."

"Does she know you have a thing for her husband?" Zoe gave Electra a piercing look.

"What are you talking about? I can't stand him."

"Don't tell me that. I've already heard the other version over rum punch."

"I detest rum. I'll be glad when the world gets back to normal."

"Maybe this is normal. Remember the Great War?"

"Only too well." Electra drew a line in the frosty side of her glass. "Forget what I said that night. Okay? Christopher is married to Amelia and that's all there is to it."

"You know you can trust me. Besides, you aren't the first woman to want what you can't have."

Electra's smoky eyes met Zoe's. "He doesn't even like me."

"From the way you described the evening you met him, I'd say that's hardly surprising."

"They shouldn't have sprung their courtship on me so suddenly. I had heard nothing of him being back in the area, then all at once he's back and they're getting married!"

"I suppose you prepared Amelia for Carter? Really, Electra, you can't expect a country woman to know how our crowd lives. From what you've told me about Amelia, she sounds like a holdover from the Victorian Age."

"She is. I can't see how she ever got Christopher's attention. I'm telling you, by comparison, he makes Carter look homely!"

"Family gatherings should be quite lively when he comes marching home."

"I'll see that you get a ticket to the event."

"I hate to chase you off, but I have to dash to the theater. Ticket sales start tonight and you'd think nobody down there could itch unless I'm there to scratch for them."

"I should be leaving anyway. I don't like to travel at night these days. Soldiers leaving for Europe or coming home would just as soon drag you into an alley as not."

"Sounds interesting."

Electra put her drink on the tray and went to the mirror to adjust her hat to the proper tilt. She and Amelia had to make up eventually, she reasoned. Besides, it was worth swallowing her pride to get some word on how Christopher was doing.

Electra's trip home wasn't an easy one. Before finally getting a flight to Charlottesville, she was bumped three consecutive times by servicemen with travel priority who were being shuffled from one military base to another. She tried not to be angry for the delay, but she was.

Then the bus from Charlottesville to Catawba Mills was

delayed two hours because of a mechanical breakdown and the difficulty of getting replacement parts. At last she arrived in Catawba Mills, thinking her travel difficulties were over, only to be turned down by four taxi drivers who refused to use their precious gasoline to go all the way out to Willowbrook for a single fare. The fifth she bribed with a generous tip in advance. Once the cabbie deposited her bags on the drive at Willowbrook, for they no longer had the time—or, Electra thought, the courtesy—to carry them inside, Electra paid the fare and the driver hurried away. The war, with all its privations and inconveniences, had become her personal enemy.

Electra stood there in the drive a long moment, staring at her home. For all its years, Willowbrook's grandeur was undiminished. The rosy bricks were warm and inviting, the tall white columns as impressive as ever. The huge oaks and magnolias were magnificent, as always. But everywhere she looked, there were men—men in pajamas and robes playing checkers and cards on the wide porches, men with arms and legs bandaged or missing being pushed about in wheelchairs by men with less debilitating injuries, men on crutches hobbling over the grounds where she had played as a child. They were soldiers, but not like the men bustling about, bumping women from airplane seats. These soldiers had been ripped and torn apart by this mindless war.

Electra picked up her suitcases, finding them heavier than she remembered, and slowly mounted the front steps. The soldiers nearest her nodded a greeting and a few smiled. She nodded back but found a smile was beyond her capability.

Inside, the house was in an orderly but efficient bustle. More men were coming and going on the stairs. Wheelchairs whispered over the oak floors. Voices could be heard everywhere. The library and front parlor were filled with rows of beds, some neatly made, others occupied. Nurses in crisp white uniforms scurried about, responding to doctors' orders.

Resentment rose within her. What had Amelia done? Electra recognized Helga by the coil of blond braids atop her head and stopped her long enough to ask, "Where is Miss Radcliff?"

"Mrs. Jenkins is upstairs. In the sewing room."

"The sewing room?" Electra's cool voice accurately reflected her displeasure.

"The green bedroom, Miss Radcliff."

Still carrying her luggage, Electra went upstairs and down the hall. Putting down her bags, she opened the door to what had been her father's room. A dozen women sat there, some using sewing machines, others doing handwork. When Amelia saw her, she rose with a smile.

"Electra! I didn't expect you until tomorrow. How was your trip down?"

"Damn the trip. Who are all these people?"

Amelia looked a bit uneasy. "Why, surely you recall Jenny Edgeworth, Carleton's wife? And here's Sarah McIntyre and Ida Smyth-Downs." As she introduced the other women, Electra nodded the briefest of greetings to the women who had married her and Amelia's former beaux.

Amelia picked up a rectangle of cloth on which she was sewing. "Let me get you a needle and you can help us. Goodness knows you've always been better at sewing than most of us." Amelia's voice sounded strained as if she was trying to hide her real feelings in front of her friends.

Electra felt no such need. "Why is our home full of men?" she demanded.

"I told you about that on the telephone. They are convalescing soldiers, men who no longer require hospital care but who aren't yet ready to return to their families. Don't you remember?"

"You said a few soldiers. I thought that meant three or four. You've turned Willowbrook into a damned hospital!"

Amelia smiled at the staring women and hustled Electra out into the hall. "What are you trying to do? Cause hard feelings? Surely you don't begrudge doing all we can to win this war. The hospital beds are needed for the more recently wounded, and there aren't many private houses large enough to be used as convalescent hospitals." She bent to pick up Electra's bags. "I've put you in Mother's wardrobe."

"In the wardrobe? You expect me to sleep in a closet?"

"It's a very large closet. Once I cleaned out all the old clothes, it was almost the size of a small room. There's a cot in there already."

"Cleaned out what clothes? You can't mean you threw out Mother and Papa's clothes!"

"No, I gave them to a scrap drive. They were so hopelessly out of date that they were unwearable. They've been put to use to end the war."

"Quit going on about the war! You gave away everything? And why can't I sleep in my own room?"

"Because it's full of wounded soldiers. And this house isn't a shrine. Of course I got rid of their clothes. It should have been done years and years ago."

They entered a small room that connected what had been their parents' separate bedrooms. Amelia put down the luggage with relief. "These new hard-sided bags look nice, but they're heavier than the old soft ones. Were you able to find a cab without much trouble?"

"Don't change the subject. What else have you done to my home?"

Amelia drew herself up and gave Electra an icy blast of retribution. "This is my home, not yours. You live in New York."

Electra's anger swelled until her temples pounded. "Willowbrook is my home! It will always be my home. I work my fingers to the bone to provide for it and to give you a place to live, and look what you've done! You've turned it into a damned hospital."

"There's no need to shout. I'm sure the ladies in the next room can hear you, and once you've come to your senses you'll be embarrassed at having acted this way."

Electra was so furious she stammered. "How—how dare you do this! To—to—"

Amelia cut her off with a glare. "You have no right to criticize me! Do you think I never found out how you earned your living when you first went to New York?" Amelia spoke barely above a whisper, but her words rocked Electra. "Daphne Fitzpatrick learned about it, and she made sure everyone else heard, too. All those ladies in there know you were a kept woman, and it's taken years for me to overcome that."

Electra tried to speak but found she couldn't.

"And then you had the nerve to bring one of your lovers here to Willowbrook! Did you think I was so stupid I wouldn't know what you do in New York?"

"Carter didn't keep me," Electra said with all the dignity she could manage. "I kept him. And you're a fine one to talk about lovers. At least I didn't take up with a servant's son."

Amelia didn't try to hide her disgust with Electra's imperious behavior. In a shaky voice she said, "You can stay here for as long as you wish, but don't cause trouble and don't do anything to embarrass me." With that she left, slamming the door behind her.

Electra eased herself down on the bed, the springs protesting with a squeak. Everyone knew about her being Robert's mistress? How had Daphne found out? Even though all that was years ago in her past, Electra was awash with embarrassment. Everyone knew and apparently had known for years. Every time she had come to Catawba Mills, there must have been whispers and perhaps even laughter behind her back.

Electra lifted her head and straightened. She had nothing to be ashamed of. She had done what she had to do to save Willowbrook and provide for Amelia. If her sister was ungrateful, then so be it. Electra had put Robert far behind her. Now she was the one who kept lovers, not the other way around. If the people of a backwater town like Catawba Mills, Virginia, couldn't see that, why, it was not her problem. In New York she was important; her designs were in great demand. New York was a much bigger pond than Catawba Mills, and she was a leader there.

Electra stood and picked up her suitcases. She wasn't going to stay here and sleep in a closet and be made to feel ashamed. She marched down the hall without a glance at her father's former bedroom or a word of good-bye to Amelia. Ignoring a soldier's offer to help with her bags, Electra went downstairs and phoned for a taxi.

While she waited for a cab to arrive, Electra sat on her

bags on the porch and ignored the wounded men who stared at her with frank curiosity. She had come here for rejuvenation and to hear some word about Christopher. Obviously both were now impossible.

When the cab finally arrived, Electra gave the upper windows a quick glare. Although Electra couldn't see her, she knew Amelia was up there sewing away and chatting, as if keeping up appearances was the most important thing on earth. Electra decided then and there that she owed Amelia no fealty whatsoever. When Christopher came home, she was going to give Amelia a run for her money. Unless she was very much mistaken, she could take him away from her sister. Then let Amelia talk about appearances and put on self-righteous airs.

Electra got into the cab, and as she rode away she made her plans to seduce Christopher.

CHAPTER 15

THE WAR DRAGGED ON, AND AS THE WOUNDED soldiers at Willowbrook learned to use their crutches and artificial limbs and gained the strength to be on their own, they were sent away and more soldiers with the same frustrations and griefs and pains took their place. Amelia learned to help some with their physical therapy, and she read to the blinded soldiers or helped them write letters home. In the four years since the United States entered the war, she had learned to do things she would never have dreamed of doing as a child. She even wrote Christopher and told him of her plans to become a nurse so she could help him in his profession. He replied with glowing appreciation for her decision.

On May 7, 1945, Germany surrendered and would soon be occupied by the armies of the four major powers. Roosevelt had died of a cerebral hemorrhage less than a month before, and Truman had become president. Some were afraid the war would linger on without Roosevelt but others thought Harry Truman would bring it to a swift close.

Amelia was too excited to sit still after she heard the

news that the war in Europe was over. Christopher would be safe now, and as soon as possible he would be home. She began planning where she would meet him, what she would say, and which dress she would wear. He had asked her to wait for him in the garden so he could see her as he had on the first day, but she wasn't sure she could wait that long. She didn't know yet whether he would be coming by plane or train, but she was sure she wanted to be reunited with him at the earliest possible moment.

Amelia and Jenny Edgeworth were alone in Amelia's sewing room and were straightening it for the next day's work. All the other women had gone home to be with their children.

"Jenny, do you think I've aged any?" Amelia asked as she fidgeted with her hair. "It's been four years since I've seen him. I'm thirty-eight years old. Almost forty. It doesn't seem possible." She looked at her reflection in the sewing room mirror and touched her cheek. "Almost forty," she repeated.

"You certainly don't look it."

Amelia lifted a strand of her hair. "Do you see any gray?"

"Not a bit. Do you put something on it?"

"No, I've just been lucky."

"We both have. I got a letter from Carleton this morning. He's to be mustered out next month. It's been so long since we've seen him! Terry is twelve now and Rita is nine. Rita says she can barely remember him."

"I'm glad he's coming home so soon. I haven't heard yet when Christopher will be discharged."

Jenny smiled shyly. "Carleton looks so nice in his uniform. He's lost a lot of weight."

"He always has been fine looking," Amelia said. In a

sadder tone she added, "I feel sorry for Ida and Emma." Both Reggie Smyth-Downs and Freddy Knapp had been killed in the war. "Betty Sue Harrison said Wally has been badly wounded and may never walk again. She said they may have to amputate his leg after all. She was beside herself."

"How terrible it's been," Jenny agreed.

"Terrible," Amelia echoed. "War really is like hell."

The doorbell chimed and Amelia looked up in surprise. Since Willowbrook had become a hospital no one had bothered to ring the doorbell. From the top of the stairs she saw Helga, her arms still loaded with clean towels, open the door. The caller was a teenage boy wearing a loosely fitting Western Union uniform. A cold knot formed in Amelia's stomach.

Jenny had followed her, and as she caught sight of the messenger whose uniform had become synonymous with the worst of bad news, she clutched Amelia's hand. From the icy chill of Jenny's fingers, Amelia knew her friend was filled with as much fear and dread as she was.

Appearing reluctant to do so, Helga took the envelope the boy offered and closed the door.

"My parents know I'm here," Jenny whispered. "You don't think it's Carleton, do you? That my parents told the boy to come here?"

Amelia pulled her hand free. As she walked stiffly down the stairs, never taking her eyes off the telegram, she said, "It could be from Electra. She might have sent it."

When they reached the foyer, Helga handed the envelope to Amelia. With trembling fingers she opened it.

"We regret to inform you . . ." it began.

Amelia couldn't see for the tears, and there was a ringing

in her ears. Numbly she sank down onto the stairs and stared unseeing at the square of paper. Her mind refused to accept the dreaded news.

"Christopher," she heard Jenny saying as if she were far, far away. "Near Remagen in Germany."

"I've never heard of Remagen," Amelia said in a dazed voice. "I don't even know where that is." She knew she was crying because her cheeks were wet and her vision was blurred, but she couldn't connect with the fact. The piece of paper lay in her lap, crumpled between her hands.

Jenny gently pulled the telegram from Amelia's hand so she could read all it said. Helga stood in the doorway to the living room, gripping the towels to her chest.

"There must be some mistake," Amelia said. "If Christopher were . . . I'd know if something had happened to him." She turned her eyes from one woman to the other. "I'd know if it had," she repeated.

One of the convalescing soldiers, a major, came to them. "Is something wrong?"

Jenny silently handed him the telegram.

"It's a mistake," Amelia explained, tears still streaming down her face. "I'm sure it's a mistake, Major. The war in Europe is over. Christopher will be home in a couple of months. Nothing has really happened to him or I would have felt it myself."

The major read the telegram, then said, "If you'd like, Mrs. Jenkins, I can make some phone calls. Try to get some details."

A cold numbness crept over Amelia, and although her tears continued to fall, she felt oddly peaceful. "If you'd like, you may. But I know it's a mistake." To prove how confident she was of it, she managed a smile. "Just a silly mistake. A red tape snafu."

The major's face was solemn as his eyes met Jenny's. "Perhaps you'd better take Mrs. Jenkins up to her room where she can lie down." He offered the telegram to Amelia, but she looked at it as if it had no connection with her.

Jenny took the telegram for her. "Come on, Amelia. I'll sit with you until you feel better."

"I feel fine," Amelia protested as Jenny helped her to her feet. She had the curious and rather unpleasant sensation of being unable to hold on to her thoughts. Her mind was like a movie screen on which images flickered and then disappeared. She wondered if she should mention it to someone, but that seemed to be too much trouble. She let Jenny help her up the stairs.

Amelia noticed she was in her room, though she had no memory of walking down the hall. Her room was dim with the blue-gray light of evening. She sat on her bed and lay back, surprised at how exhausted she felt.

Within what seemed to be the blink of an eye she saw that one of the army doctors had come into her room and Jenny was showing him the telegram. Amelia closed her eyes and decided not to think about it.

"I'm afraid she's in shock," Jenny was saying to the doctor. "She cried some, but then she stopped. She keeps denying that it's true."

"Repression and denial are common in grief," the doctor said.

"I know that. I see it here every day," Jenny replied, "but this is different. I think she really doesn't believe it."

"Tired," Amelia murmured. "So tired."

The doctor frowned down at her. "I came prepared to administer a sedative, but she doesn't seem to need it. I'd say she's taking the news pretty well. Some women just aren't that attached to their husbands."

"That's certainly not the case here," Jenny snapped. "She and Christopher were newlyweds when he left. He's all she ever talks about."

"If he's been gone several years and they weren't married long before that, she may not be facing the feelings of a wife of long standing. A lot of couples rushed into marriage before the man had to ship out. This is the way it seems to me."

"You think it's normal for a woman to want to go to sleep minutes after hearing her husband has been killed?" Jenny demanded.

"Sleep is a way of escaping. Another form of denial. Believe me, Mrs. Edgeworth, the best thing for her is for us to leave her alone and let her rest."

Jenny could not have agreed less, but he was, after all, a doctor. "I'll stay here with her just in case."

"If you really want to help her, you could call the rest of her family and save her the misery."

Jenny picked up the telegram and stared at it. "There can't be a mistake, can there? She seems so positive that it isn't true."

"The War Department doesn't make mistakes like that. Telegrams such as this aren't sent out without careful review. Women make a lot of to-do over knowing if their husbands are safe or not. Believe me, Mrs. Edgeworth, I've seen hundreds of wounded men here and overseas and there is no invisible cord connecting them to their loved ones. I'm only surprised they would only now be informing families about a battle that took place two months ago."

Jenny detested the man's attitude, but he seemed to be positive that he knew best. "I could call her sister. As far as I know, she's all the family Amelia has. I don't know Christopher's family or how to get in touch with them."

"Her sister will know. Families keep up with things like that." The doctor glanced back at Amelia, who appeared to have fallen into a deep sleep. "I have to get back downstairs. There are patients I need to check before I'm through for the night."

Jenny nodded, her eyes remaining on Amelia. Regardless of what the doctor said, she knew Amelia wasn't behaving normally. Perhaps, she thought, men in combat had different symptoms from newly bereaved women.

After the doctor left, Jenny went to the address book lying next to Amelia's bed. Listed under *R* for Radcliff she found Electra's number.

To keep from further disturbing Amelia, Jenny went to use the extension phone in a small alcove down the hall. On the fourth ring a woman answered.

"Electra? This is Jenny Edgeworth." When there was no reply she added, "Jenny Allen—Amelia's friend."

"Of course." Electra sounded cool and distant, as if she might have recognized the name without the explanation but hadn't wanted to admit it. "How are you?"

"Fine, thanks. I'm calling about Christopher."

"Christopher?" Electra broke in before Jenny could explain. "Has something happened to him?"

"I'm afraid so. I hate to be the one to call you, not being family and all, but Amelia is in no shape to do it and—"

"What happened! Is he wounded?"

Jenny paused. Amelia had told her that Electra hated

Christopher and that that had been the cause of their rift. From the sound of Electra's voice, Jenny suspected that the opposite was true. Suddenly this phone call became terribly difficult.

"Hello? Hello! Are you there?" Electra demanded.

"Yes. Yes, I'm sorry. Electra, Christopher is dead."

There was a stunned silence over the phone. Jenny rushed on. "The telegram just arrived. It says he was killed at Remagen. I think that's in Germany, but I'm not sure. We're trying to get more information. Amelia . . . well, she's not taking it very well." She hesitated. "Hello? Electra?"

"Yes. I'm here. What did you say about Amelia?"

Jenny raised her voice over the static on the line. "I said she isn't taking the news well. She's too quiet. I'm afraid for her."

"Yes. Well . . ." Electra's voice trailed off as if she still hadn't comprehended Jenny's concern. At length she said, "I can't believe it. With the war almost over I had hoped . . . You say the telegram came today?"

"That's right. Only a few minutes ago. Major Hodgart has agreed to make some calls and try to find out the details." Jenny hesitated again. "Could you come home? I realize how difficult it is to travel now, but Amelia—"

"She doesn't need me," Electra cut in, her voice bitter. "Now of all times she doesn't need me."

"But you're her sister. You're all the family she has."

"Did Amelia ask for me?"

"No," Jenny reluctantly admitted. "She hasn't said much of anything, really. She's asleep in her room. I'm calling from the hall phone."

There was another long pause. Then, when Electra

spoke, her voice sounded strained, as if she was trying not to cry. "Tell her . . . Tell her I'm sorry about . . . Christopher."

"All right. Should I say you're on your way here?"

"No. No, this would be a particularly bad time for me to come. I need . . . Amelia needs some time to herself. Perhaps later."

"Listen, Electra," Jenny said in some exasperation, "I don't know what's going on between you two, but she needs you!"

Another long silence crackled over the phone wire. Jenny said, "Do you know how to reach Christopher's parents? They aren't in Amelia's address book. Do you think I should call them? Surely it's not my place to—"

"Or mine. The army will have sent them a telegram. I have no idea where they live." Electra's voice was firm again and as cool as ever. "Thank you for calling me. Again, tell Amelia I'm sorry."

The phone went dead. Jenny stared down at the silent receiver in her hand for a moment, trying to figure out what could possibly have happened between the two sisters to keep Electra away at a time like this. Certainly it wasn't because Electra had hated Christopher, or she wouldn't have cried at the news of his death. Electra had cried. Jenny couldn't imagine Electra, whom she had never particularly liked, shedding a tear for anyone. Why, she had been dry-eyed at the funerals of both her parents.

Jenny replaced the receiver in its cradle. Whatever was going on, Amelia needed someone, and Jenny was the only one around except Helga. She went back to Amelia's bedroom and sat in the slipper chair trying to think of some way to comfort her and imagining how grief stricken she would have been had the telegram been about her Carleton.

•   •   •

In August President Truman ordered an atomic bomb dropped on the Japanese city of Hiroshima. The effects were so astounding as to be unbelievable. Three days later another bomb was dropped on Nagasaki. On August 14 the war ended.

As the news spread, people went wild. Electra and her employees ran out into the streets of New York, joining a sea of others doing the same. Horns blew in celebration, ticker tape streamed from skyscraper windows, and everywhere there were smiles and laughter. Total strangers stopped one another and exchanged pleasantries and shook hands. A young man in a corporal's uniform grabbed Electra and, even though she had never seen him before in her life, gave her a kiss right on the lips. When he released her, he did the same to Lois Dunlap and Mary Brenner, who were staring at him in surprise. Electra gasped, but she laughed when she saw he meant no harm.

Electra knew there was no point in trying to carry on business, so she closed for the day. Mary, who had a sweetheart in the navy, had already caught a cab home to sit by the phone. Lois was excitedly speculating on whether the wave of returning soldiers would supply her with a husband. Being neither young nor particularly attractive, Lois had no boyfriend, though she was fond of telling people that she had had one, of course—a fiancé—but that he had been killed in one of the first battles of the war—so sad. Electra hoped Lois would finally meet a man who could see past her physical plainness and glimpse her inner beauty.

Not bothering to hail a cab, Electra set out on foot toward her apartment. As she walked she waved and smiled at other smiling and waving strangers. Her heart felt light and free for the first time since Christopher's death.

At Willowbrook the recuperating soldiers were as jubilant as everyone else. Those who were able hurried from room to room, shaking hands and shouting that the war was over. Only one room was off limits.

Amelia sat in that room gazing sightlessly out the window at the drive, much as she had every day since the telegram had come. It was as if something in her had died with Christopher and the rest of her still didn't believe he was gone.

A few of the soldiers looked in, but they all knew of Mrs. Jenkins's bereavement and had too much respect to intrude on her obvious grief. Only Jenny came all the way into the room and went to sit on the window seat near Amelia's chair. "Did you hear the news?" She wasn't sure these days what Amelia's mind would accept and what it wouldn't.

Amelia nodded. "The war is over. The boys will be coming home."

"Carleton was so excited he and the girls drove all the way out from town to tell me in person. He wanted to come speak to you, but I told him you were resting."

Amelia made no comment and continued looking out at the drive.

"He says he's glad now that he was mustered out early so he could get a place in Ben Dupree's law firm before all the other men arrive looking for jobs." Jenny leaned over and touched Amelia's cool hand. "Are you all right?"

"Of course." Her voice at last had a touch of wryness in it rather than the flat tone Jenny had come to dread.

"I know this has been hard on you. I'm going to keep coming out here until all the soldiers have gone on their way."

"Soldiers?" Amelia's deep-set gray eyes looked confused.

"The patients." Jenny studied her with growing concern. This wasn't the first time she had noticed the disorientation in Amelia's thoughts. Jenny was worried, because the confusion seemed to be worsening. It was as if Amelia were willing herself away into some uncharted land of the mind.

"Why don't you come out and talk to the men?" Jenny suggested. "It would do you a world of good."

After a long pause, Amelia said, "Not now. Not yet."

"Amelia, look at me." Jenny grasped Amelia's chin and turned her face away from the window. "Honey, you can't keep on like this. You've got to snap out of it." She drew a deep breath and added, "Christopher wouldn't have wanted you to grieve so deeply. He would have wanted you to get on with your life."

Amelia merely looked at her.

Jenny felt a chill run through her. "Can you hear me?"

"I can hear you."

"So why do you sit here day after day? Amelia, you've sat in this chair and stared out the window for months! If I didn't find you in fresh clothes each morning, I'd swear you'd never moved."

"I'm waiting for him," Amelia said as she turned back to the window. "He said he would come back to me, and I'm waiting for him."

Jenny knelt by her friend's chair. With deep concern she said, "Christopher isn't coming back. Don't you remember? He died at Remagen last spring."

"He promised to come home to me, and he will."

"Remember when the lieutenant brought you his belongings?" Jenny retrieved one of Christopher's medals from Amelia's dresser. "See? His things are here. We had a marker put up in your family cemetery."

"Christopher isn't there."

Jenny bit her lower lip. A mortar shell had blown up the jeep in which Christopher was riding and there had been no body to return. Jenny couldn't bring herself to remind Amelia of that. "Maybe I should call Electra," Jenny suggested. "She says she isn't still upset with you. We've talked several times these past few months."

Amelia made no sign of having heard.

Jenny went down the hall and tried to call Electra, but all the New York lines were busy. When she finally succeeded in ringing Electra's apartment, there was no answer.

"You are calling Miss Electra?" Helga said from behind her.

Jenny jumped. "I didn't hear you walk up. Yes, I was calling Electra, but she isn't home. I suppose she's out celebrating."

"Ja. Is very good, war being over. Maybe I soon hear from my family." Helga added quickly, "My brothers, they were on Russian front." Helga was always careful to make that distinction.

"I hope they came through safely." Jenny cast a worried look back down the hall.

"Miss Amelia, she is no better?"

Jenny shook her head. "If anything, she's worse. How late does she sit there?"

"I put her to bed before I go to my rooms. She is like obedient doll. She will undress when I say and put on gown when I say, but nothing does she do for herself." Helga glanced back at the closed door. "Mornings I find her back at window. I am not knowing how long she sleeps."

"Even the doctor now agrees that something is wrong," Jenny said, "but he can't treat a civilian. Dr. McVane has been out, but he says there's nothing physically wrong with her. I'm worried sick."

"She is needing a different kind of doctor."

"A psychiatrist, you mean? Unfortunately they don't make house calls, and Amelia refuses to leave her room. I'm afraid it would be harmful to force the issue. Besides, there is no psychiatrist in Catawba Mills, and if she went to Charlottesville she would have to be committed. There's not enough gas to drive her back and forth."

"Maybe in time she gets better," Helga said doubtfully.

"In the meantime I'm going to find Electra and insist she come to help Amelia. This ridiculous feud has gone on too long." Jenny gave a decisive nod.

Electra was at home when she received the phone call from Jenny. After a long and sometimes heated conversation, she agreed to come home.

Electra knew there was no point in trying to travel by rail. All the trains were filled with exuberant, singing soldiers. She went to the airport, resigned herself to waiting for the first plane that would take her to Charlottesville, and prayed the bus service to Catawba Mills had improved. A day and a half after leaving her apartment, she arrived at Willowbrook.

There were still soldiers everywhere, and to her eyes they looked no different than they had when she had come here more than two years before. On closer inspection, however, she noticed that the bedding on a number of the cots was neatly rolled up, indicating that the beds were unoccupied. Evidently as many of them as possible had been sent home as a celebration of peace.

She went into the back parlor, leaving her bags at the foot of the stairs. Helga was busy cleaning and enthusiastically singing as many words as she knew of "The Surrey with the Fringe on Top." When she saw Electra she exclaimed and hurried to her. "You are come!" she said.

"Where is my sister?" Electra wasn't sure if Helga had become proficient in English, so she spoke slowly.

"She is being upstairs in her room." Helga preceded Electra to the stairs, pausing only long enough to scoop up the suitcases. "She is always in her room. That's why Miss Jenny and I are having worry."

Electra had no intention of discussing her sister with the German maid. If it had been up to Electra, the girl would long ago have been replaced with an American. She remained as aloof from Helga as was possible.

Helga nodded toward the closed door to Amelia's room. "She is being in there. I will put your things in your room."

Electra noticed Helga was taking her bags into her former bedroom, not the large closet, and she let out a sigh of relief. She wasn't sure she could have managed those closed spaces and a cot after her exhausting trip.

She tapped lightly on Amelia's door and went in. The room was dim except for the sunlight that splashed in the windows. Amelia sat there in her slipper chair, facing out toward the gardens. "Amelia?" she said. "I'm here."

Amelia made no sign of having heard.

Electra put her purse on the bed as she passed and sat on the window seat. Amelia never glanced in her direction.

"What are you watching?" Electra said, following her sister's gaze. "The driveway?"

Cold dread began building in Electra. Until now she had assumed Jenny was exaggerating, perhaps even meddling in their private affairs in order to make peace between them. Now Electra realized Jenny had understated the problem.

Amelia had lost weight. Her cheeks, which had been plump now looked hollowed, her eyes were sunken, and her dress hung loose at her waist. Her hands lay clasped in her lap, the skin on them almost translucent in the sunlight. Electra could see the pale blue tracery of veins on the backs of Amelia's hands where soft flesh had once been.

"I'm here now," Electra said in a dazed voice. "I'm home for as long as you need me."

Amelia's unnatural quiet was unnerving. "I'm sorry I couldn't come to the funeral," Electra said, "but I was afraid, under the circumstances, it would upset you more. Oh, hell, Amelia, I didn't come because I knew it would upset me. That's the truth."

She went to her purse to get a cigarette, remembered Amelia didn't smoke and therefore had no ashtray, and returned the cigarette to the pack. She paced back to the window. "Jenny Edgeworth told me it was a nice ceremony. I wondered why you didn't call." Now she could see why, and she fell silent for a minute.

"Jenny says there's nothing wrong with you physically. You just have to snap out of this."

"He's coming home," Amelia shocked her by saying. "He promised to come back to me."

"Christopher? Amelia, Christopher is dead! He *can't* come home."

Amelia closed her lips as if to end the discussion.

Electra tried to get her to speak again, but Amelia remained silent.

Days passed. Electra, Jenny, and Helga spent hours in Amelia's room, each trying in her own way to break Amelia's shell. Amelia rarely spoke, and then only to reaffirm that Christopher would be coming home.

At last Electra reached the end of her patience. She and Jenny had spent the morning trying to get Amelia to eat the toast Helga had sent up. "She's starving herself to death!" Electra blurted out. "That's what it is. She's doing it on purpose! She just wants to be with Christopher!"

"That's a terrible thing to say!" Jenny retorted. "Can't you see she can't help it?"

"Nonsense!" Electra grabbed Amelia's chair and pulled it around to face her. "This is it, Amelia! You're going to stop this nonsense and you're going to stop it now. I love you, and damn it, I even loved Christopher, but I'm not going to spend the rest of my life trying to get you to eat a piece of toast. You've always had gumption, and it's time you used it. Now, you can come back to the land of the living or I'm sending you to the mental hospital at Charlottesville!"

"Electra!" Jenny gasped. "You don't mean that!"

"I do!" Electra felt tears course hotly down her cheeks. "I love Amelia too much to let her waste away. I'm going to call the doctor now and set up an appointment for her." She strode across the room and out the door, with Jenny protesting at her heels.

The door slammed and Amelia was left alone. She blinked. Go to Charlottesville? Leave Willowbrook and her garden? How could Christopher find her there?

Slowly Amelia forced herself to stand, moving carefully, as if she wasn't sure her muscles would support her. For a minute she paused and looked down at the catawba-lined drive. Leave Willowbrook? She couldn't do that.

As silently as a ghost Amelia went to the door and out into the hall. She could hear Jenny and Electra arguing in the room across from her, but she ignored them. With her hand on the walnut rail for support, she went downstairs. She crossed the entryway and stepped out onto the porch. A hot breeze touched her cheeks, and she blinked again. The last time she was outside, the air had been cool and scented with spring. Jenny and Helga had taken her to the cemetery for a service of some sort.

Amelia went down the front steps and across the lawn. As her eyes caught sight of the familiar ivy-covered walls of her garden, her steps grew stronger.

She went in and looked around. No one had been here in months, and the garden showed its neglect. Weeds grew where she had always planted begonias, and trailing fingers of grass stretched beneath the willow where a few alyssum struggled for survival. Dead petunias clotted the base of the sundial, and untrimmed runners of the rambling roses reached out toward their more sedate cousins.

Slowly Amelia walked down the red brick path. The scent of thyme rose from beneath her feet. She bent and stroked her fingers through a rosemary bush, then inhaled its aroma.

She brushed aside the long trails of willow and sat on the bench. It was cool here. Even in the hottest part of summer it was cool on the marble bench, here in the deep shade.

She drew in a deep breath. With it came a new sense

of calm. Not the deadening numbness she had suffered all summer, but a gentle familiarity. Amelia's eyes widened, and a spark lit within them. She looked about with growing eagerness. She couldn't see Christopher, but she could feel him. She put out her hand as if she might touch him, but even though she didn't, the sense of being with him continued. It was as if Christopher was all around her, not in any one spot but throughout their garden.

Emotion swept over her, and she began to sob as she hadn't since she heard of his death. At the time she got the news and in the months since, she hadn't believed it, but now she knew it was true. Christopher was dead; he would never physically return to her.

Yet he had returned. She could feel him in every breeze and see him nodding in every flower. Amelia cried until she was empty of grief. Then she stood on rubbery legs and went to the nearest flower bed. Kneeling on the ground she began pulling out the weeds.

"Miss Amelia's gone!" Helga cried out as she burst into Electra's room.

"Gone!" Electra pulled herself away from her heated argument with Jenny and glared at Helga.

"What do you mean, gone?" Jenny demanded, her cheeks flushed with anger.

"She is not being there!" Helga waved her hand toward Amelia's room. "No one is being in there."

Electra and Jenny rushed past the maid and all three ran down the hall. As Helga had said, the room was empty.

"Where can she be?" Jenny wailed. "She never leaves her chair."

Helga had lapsed into German and was wringing her hands.

Guilt assailed Electra. She should never have said what she did in front of Amelia. She had known Amelia could hear her, but at the time she had thought she couldn't or wouldn't comprehend the meaning. Now she was gone. "Search the house," she commanded.

Electra hurried to the bathroom and shoved open the door. In Amelia's state of mind she might try suicide as a means of escape. The room was empty, as were all the others upstairs.

Those soldiers who could move about were enlisted in the search, and soon it was obvious Amelia was nowhere in the house.

"We have to search the grounds," Electra said, "especially the stream behind the house."

"You don't think she would try to drown herself!" Jenny exclaimed. "The stream has almost dried up from the heat."

"It only takes three inches," one of the soldiers said grimly. "I've seen it happen."

They hurried outside and across the lawn toward the stream. Electra saw the garden gate was open and she hesitated as the others rushed past. The wind could have blown it open, she thought, but then she caught Jenny's arm and pointed. "Look."

They exchanged a glance and ran toward the gate.

Amelia was there on her knees, calmly weeding the flower beds. When she heard them she looked up. They could tell from her red and swollen eyes that she had been crying, but for the first time in months they also saw alertness. She sat back on her heels and said, "I can't leave here now. Not and leave everyone who loves me."

A faint smile came to her lips as she looked around the garden.

Electra forgot her sophistication as she dropped to her knees next to Amelia and threw her arms about her sister and hugged her tightly. "You scared us half to death! Are you okay?"

Amelia nodded and put her arms around Electra. "I'm all right now."

A warm breeze eddied about them and the flowers nodded in agreement.

AUTUMN, 1959

The long sobs
Of the violins
Of autumn
Pierce my heart
With monotonous languor.

Paul Verlaine

CHAPTER 16

"OH, AMELIA! HAVE YOU HEARD THE NEWS? Lucy and Desi are considering a divorce."

"Lucy who? I don't know a Desi." Amelia's coffee cup clinked against its saucer as she picked it up for another sip. In the foyer her grandfather clock chimed the hour.

"Lucille Ball and Desi Arnaz," Jenny Edgeworth said as if she thought everyone must know that.

"*That* Lucy and Desi." Amelia put her cup and saucer on the side table. "I guess that means the end of 'I Love Lucy' if he doesn't anymore—love her, I mean."

Jenny gazed into her coffee cup as if she were reading tea leaves. "I can't believe it. That show has been on for eight years. Since 1951! They're like family."

"You watch too much TV," Amelia chided with a fond smile. She and Jenny had been through so much together— the war, Christopher's death, and Amelia's subsequent breakdown, and now Carleton's struggle with cancer.

"I'm telling you, Amelia, there's divorce everywhere. Daphne is in her third marriage now, and she hasn't buried a husband yet."

"Divorce is accepted these days."

"All too true. Even my sister Kate. I never thought I would see them break up."

"It happens."

"At least that's something you didn't have to face. Christopher would never have left you," Jenny affirmed with the loyalty of a lifelong friend.

"No. No, he wouldn't have left me. It took a world war to take him from me. We had such a love, we..." Her voice trailed away when she remembered that Jenny and Carleton had had marital problems and had even separated for a while. "How are the girls?" she asked, choosing a safer subject.

"Fine. Just fine. Terry's baby is due next month, and I'm to go stay with them a week before. She and her husband are already nervous wrecks. She's carrying low, so I'm sure it will be a boy, but Terry is hoping for a girl. Rita is finally graduating from college at the end of this fall semester." Jenny shook her head at the perplexities of youth. "She has an art degree! Now I ask you, what can you do with a degree in art?"

"I don't know. Be an artist?"

"Sure. Like artists can make a living." Jenny had adopted some of her daughters' slang. "She'll be living at home forever."

"You know you don't mind."

Jenny smiled. "You're right. At least she won't find as many causes to protest once she gets back to Catawba Mills. I told Carleton she must have majored in art because she painted so many picket signs."

"At least she stands up for what she believes in. Not many of our old gang did that."

"Well, really, Amelia, what did we have to protest? The world was still sane then. We didn't have singers like Elvis Presley shaking his hips at us or rigged game shows like 'The $64,000 Question' or rockets blasting off into space. One of these days one of those things will miss the ocean and land on somebody's head. You mark my words."

"I worry more about Castro and Cuba than I do about being hit by a falling rocket."

"I worry about that, too. So does Carleton. We still keep fresh canned goods in our fallout shelter."

"Jenny, did it ever occur to you that if the bomb hits anywhere near here it will wipe out so much land and make this whole area so radioactive that you won't be able to come out of your shelter again? If you did there wouldn't be anything left to eat."

"We could stay in the shelter until we were rescued," Jenny argued. "I still say you should have built one."

"Pooh! I'm not afraid of dying. I'd be much more afraid of being closed up underground and not being able to get outside."

"I still say you're taking unnecessary risks."

Amelia smiled. She really wasn't afraid of death. "How is Carleton feeling?"

"Better. He says he's better. Of course the girls and I still worry. Cancer is so terrible, and we aren't sure yet that the operation was successful. I'm sure old Dr. McVane could have cured him right away. I don't have much confidence in Dr. Brockfield. He's so young."

"I'm sure he's quite capable."

"But it's in Carleton's lungs. He only has one left now. You can't do without lungs." Her brow wrinkled with worry.

"But you said yourself that he's better. He wouldn't have

been released from the hospital unless it was true."

Jenny nodded but said, "Sometimes I don't think they tell me everything."

"Nonsense. You're imagining things."

"Have you heard from Electra lately?"

"I got a letter yesterday. She's better at correspondence than she used to be."

"My Rita loves her teen fashions. She has several pairs of Electra's jeans. They cost an arm and a leg, I don't mind telling you. Your sister could retire on that jeans line alone."

"I wish she would. At the rate it's going, I'll be too old to travel by the time she gets around to retiring." Amelia laughed as if that thought didn't bother her.

"You still want to see the world? I would have thought you'd given up that idea by now."

"That's because you've been places, seen things. I never go anywhere at all." She rose from her chair and went to a framed photo of Christopher that stood on the mantel. "We planned to travel, Christopher and I. Oh, we knew we wouldn't have been able to do it at first, not with his medical practice and all, but we were going to eventually." She reverently touched the black-and-white photograph of his smiling face. "People shouldn't put off doing the things they really want to do."

"As I recall, you didn't put off much. All of Catawba Mills was talking about the whirlwind courtship you two were having."

Amelia smiled down at the photo before replacing it beside the two of Christopher in his uniform. "He swept me off my feet all right. I would have done anything for him."

"Speaking of husbands, I have to run. I told Carleton

I'd only be gone thirty minutes, and I've been here an hour." She hurriedly pulled on her cardigan sweater. "He says I never learned to tell time. Can you imagine? This from a man who used to be on the golf course in all kinds of weather. Well, that's the difference between husbands and wives. We have to give schedules of departures and returns just as if we were airplanes."

Amelia laughed as she escorted Jenny to the entry. As she opened the door, her mood turned pensive. "Remember how crowded and noisy it was in here during the war? I used to stand here at the door and think Willowbrook had come alive."

"It's peaceful here now. Well, I'm off. See you in a day or two." Jenny hurried on her way.

Amelia shut the door and again looked around the entry, becoming increasingly melancholy. It was too quiet here these days. At times the silence grated on her nerves, and she longed for the bustle of activity of years before that had had her aching tired from head to toe every night when she tumbled into bed. There had been less time to think then. The silence now was broken only by the metronomic ticking of the clock and the distant sounds of Helga working in the kitchen.

Amelia fetched her sweater off the hook on the hall tree and called out toward the back of the house, "I'll be in the garden if there's a phone call." Hearing no answer, she shouted Helga's name. When Helga still didn't reply, Amelia shook her head. Helga's hearing was beginning to go, a fact Helga always disputed most vehemently. If Helga needed her and couldn't find her, she knew to look in the garden.

The day was cool for early October, with a fretful wind

tossing the arms of the trees and rustling over the dulling grass. When Amelia buttoned the sweater, she found it was more snug about her middle than ever. She had gained weight again. She supposed she should go on a diet, but there really was no reason for it—she wasn't trying to stay attractive for a man and her health was excellent. Electra would complain when she came for her next visit, but Electra couldn't understand that every woman didn't have a desire to be as flat and angular as a young boy.

The wind tugged at Amelia's skirt chilling her knees. Cold weather bothered her more of late, causing aches and pains to settle in her knees and hands. Amelia didn't consider this ill health, though. She could still ignore the twinges, and the discomfort didn't affect her way of life. At fifty-two years of age she reasoned she could expect her body to feel different than it had at twenty-two.

Once she was inside the garden's high walls, with the gate closed, she was sheltered from the autumn winds. She smoothed her hair back toward the bun she wore low on her neck and tucked the loose ends into place. The year Christopher died, her hair had turned completely gray, and although Electra had insisted she should dye it, she refused. She thought gray hair looked more natural and dignified on a woman her age than Electra's black, and obviously dyed, hair.

Because of the growing rebellion in her knees, Amelia had replaced the scented geraniums with asters of various colors, which would return year after year. Likewise she had let chrysanthemums and daisies take the place of the begonias. She still loved the garden, but she no longer enjoyed kneeling on the hard ground.

Autumn had begun to strip the mimosa and bridal wreath

of their leaves. The forsythia was already bare, and the willow had turned to brilliant gold, its boughs cascading as gracefully as ever. She brushed aside the trailing leaves and sat beneath the willow on the marble bench.

After a while she said aloud, "It's like sitting in a shower of gold coins here beneath this tree."

She could feel Christopher near her, agreeing with her observation. She always felt him here in what had been their special place.

"Jenny was here," she said to Christopher. "She's so worried about Carleton. I know you could have found a cure for him, but this Dr. Tom Brockfield, I don't know about him." Her eyes lit up as she recalled in detail Christopher's handsome and virile countenance. "Brockfield looks like a mere boy. This is his first practice. Old Dr. McVane is still alive, but I guess you know that. He's in a nursing home, you know."

Amelia surveyed the sanctuary that surrounded her. "I certainly never intend to go into one. If you ask me, it's cruel to put a person in an old folks' home, even if they do call them nursing homes these days. At least I don't have to worry about that. Willowbrook will always be here."

She fell silent as she gave consideration to what Helga and the gardeners would think if they walked by and heard her. She had developed a habit of speaking aloud to Christopher when she was in the garden because he seemed so real to her. It was as if he were there, just out of sight. She felt less lonely speaking to him aloud, and she was always careful not to do it in the house, even though she occasionally sensed his spirit there as well.

"They would think I had gone dotty and lock me up," she said in amusement.

"Jenny said Lucy and Desi are splitting up, but I guess you wouldn't know who they are." She liked to keep Christopher apprised of all the latest news. "There's a new show on television that I think you'd like. It's called 'Bonanza.'" She thought back over her day to see if there might be anything else Christopher would like to hear about.

"I wish Electra would offer to send me on a trip again. She has such awful timing. The only times she has ever suggested I leave were times when I needed to put plants in the ground or when Jenny and Carleton were having all those arguments, and I couldn't desert Jenny at a time like that. Or when Helga's youngest brother came to the States for a visit. Helga would have been so disappointed if I hadn't been here to meet Klaus. He was so nice. He has blond hair a shade or two lighter than yours."

She touched her hair. If Christopher had been there, would she have been so adamant about not dying it? A part of her rebellion had been to upset Electra just a bit. She wondered if her gray hair bothered Christopher. With her fingertips, she studied her face. She had a few more wrinkles than when he had seen her last, but her skin wasn't the type that wrinkled badly. Electra's was, but for some reason her face was still perfectly smooth.

"Do you suppose Electra has had plastic surgery?" she said aloud. "No, surely she would have mentioned that to me. We're closer now, you know. I look back on those years when we didn't speak, and I wonder how I got through them. I was busy, of course, and I had our life together to look forward to. I still don't see why she objected to you so strongly. Electra wasn't brought up to be such a snob." She wasn't entirely sure this was true, so she stood up and shook a few golden leaves off her skirt. "I guess I should go back to the house before Helga notices I'm out here without a scarf. Just because the wind gives her earaches, she assumes it does that to everybody."

Amelia let herself out of the garden and found her head gardener, Bob, and the boy he was training standing near the gate. She nodded pleasantly, and they greeted her in return.

When she was gone, the boy turned to the older man. "Who was she talking to? There's nobody else in there."

"I know it and you know it, but Miss Amelia ain't so sure." He went on clipping the ivy runners that threatened to spread into the grass.

"You mean she's off her rocker?"

The older man straightened and fixed the boy with a reproachful frown. "Jerry, you're a good kid and you have the makings of a fine gardener, but if you ever say a word against Miss Amelia, I'll see to it that you'll be looking for another job."

"But if she's talking to herself—"

"After the war Miss Amelia hired me when nobody else would. I was all shot up in the war, but she said it didn't matter to her if it took me a mite longer than the average person to get my job done. Helga and Martin feel the same way as me. We'd work until we dropped for her. If she wants to talk to somebody you and me can't see, why, that's just fine. You understand me?"

"I guess so."

"Just don't ever let on you hear her. Near as we can tell, she's talking to her dead husband. Helga reckons it's sort of like praying. You just think of it like that. Like she's praying out loud. And if you ever hear her in the garden and see somebody coming, especially if it's Miss Electra, you go to singing. Let her know she's not alone." Old Bob looked toward the house where his employer had gone. "We look after her, and you'll learn to do the same. You hear?"

"Okay," Jerry said, though he was still puzzled. "I want to keep this job, and I like Miss Amelia a lot. She's good to work for."

"You bet she is." Bob went back to work on the ivy. "Here at Willowbrook we take care of our own."

Electra draped the pebbly wool over the dressmaker's dummy. In the same manner as her former boss, Anthony Battaglia, she used live mannequins for the final fittings, but she was too kindhearted to insist a model stand motionless for hours while she worked out the original design, as Battaglia had done. One of the many things she had detested about the man was his lack of compassion, not only for his models and his female employees but for the women who would ultimately wear the clothing he designed, whether it was comfortable or not. She was working on a coat for the 1960 fall fashion line. Electra always tried to stay a full year ahead to avoid last-minute rushes and panics.

"I'll need a good stiff interfacing for this, Mary," she said over her shoulder. "Will you get it for me?" In the past five years Mary had come to play a larger role in Electra, Inc., and was now Electra's assistant.

"Sure thing."

Alone for a moment, Electra paused to reflect on how lucky she had been to arrive in New York when she did. She had been able to make a place for herself in the fashion industry and had become well established before the war turned the world upside down. By following her instincts and remaining flexible, she had weathered depression, war, and changing tastes, and she was now considered one of the foremost New York designers. Her name was world renowned for her adult women's fashions, and recently she had added insurance by opening a new line of clothes expressly designed for youths.

Mary and Lois had both expressed doubt that such a line would be profitable, as teenagers had never been a group with much money. Electra took that into consideration and made the new line, Butterflies, a reasonably inexpensive mass market product. She hired young advisers to keep her in touch with current fads, and she geared her line toward the trends that seemed most likely to last awhile. Teens responded by pouring money out of their parents' pockets and into Electra's.

The coat she was now designing, however, was for the adult market. It was to have a mandarin collar and three-quarter-length sleeves, and it would stand out from the body like a bell. She had chosen banker's blue for the wool, but the lining was to be brilliant red, her signature color.

Mary returned with a bolt of the new pressed fiber interfacing. "Isn't that rather short?" she asked as she studied the hemline.

"I'm predicting shorter skirts for next year. The dress to go with this barely reaches mid-knee."

"Surely no woman will want to show her knees," Mary argued. "Knees, toes, and elbows are ugly."

"Men don't agree, and women dress to please men." Electra had also learned a useful philosophy of dressing while she was Robert's mistress. That philosophy was one reason she had stayed on top in the fashion world. "I may not agree with the idea, but it's true. I'm convinced that's why the cocoon style didn't last. The dresses were comfortable—they didn't touch anywhere but at the shoulders and knees—but the woman's body was hidden, and men didn't like that." She picked up the scissors and began cutting out the armholes on the wool. "Beneath this coat will be a sheath that fits her like a second skin. And, Mary, be sure the color matches the red lining exactly. That last shipment seemed to be off just a bit. Have you taken care of it?"

"I sent it back this morning."

"Good. Will Betty be in today?"

"She's to come over right after school."

"Perfect." Betty was Mary's fourteen-year-old daughter and was one of Electra's most reliable sources for teen tastes. "Let me know when she comes, and I'll show her the sketches I did last night."

Electra gathered up the wool and went into the next room, where Lois and two other women were sewing on other garments for the next year's show. Lois now sewed only the finest details and supervised the other seamstresses, who put in the seams and darts. Electra showed Lois how the coat was to go together as Mary put the interfacing on the worktable.

Electra beamed with satisfaction as she looked about the workroom. Her employees, all women, were happy, and she had never had a problem with loyalty. They were all excellent seamstresses, and she made no secret of the fact that she approved of their work. Hanging near the wall were the racks of clothes being made for the fall show. The spring clothes were already finished and were locked in a closet until time for the show. Electra trusted her workers, but not so much that she left completed garments hanging about to tempt them. The fashion business had its cutthroat side.

After glancing at her father's pocket watch, which she wore on a filigreed gold chain around her neck, Electra rushed to get her own coat and hat. "I'm meeting Bret for lunch, and I'm running late," she told Mary and Lois. "If there are any calls, put the messages on my desk." Neither of the women said anything about her meeting Bret Harley for lunch, but Electra felt their disapproval. Mary and Lois didn't like him, but Electra didn't care, because she was in love.

Like most of her young men, Electra had met him at Zoe Wharton's apartment. Bret was another of the actors who seemed to flock to Zoe in droves. He was unusually handsome and had a delightful personality. Bret could always make her laugh. Because he was in his late twenties, Electra felt young when she was with him. He had once guessed her age to be thirty-nine and she hadn't corrected him. Electra knew she looked younger than her fifty-four years, thanks to her hairdresser and her plastic surgeon, and on the inside she felt as young as Bret.

She put on her pillbox hat and pulled on her short beige gloves as she was leaving the sewing room. Her studio was still in the warehouse she had bought from Robert so many years before, and even though it wasn't far from the restaurant where she was to meet Bret, she was late so she hailed a cab and handsomely tipped the driver for hurrying as she had asked him to do.

Bret, who was already in the restaurant's lobby, looked peeved, but when he saw her he smiled and Electra's heart did a flip-flop. He was so handsome he made her ache inside and although he bore more than a passing resemblance to

Christopher Jenkins, Electra hadn't noticed the similarity until she nearly called him by the wrong name. From that time on Electra had known she loved Bret. It was as if fate had given her another Christopher.

"Sorry I'm late," she said as she stood on tiptoe to kiss his lips. "I was cutting out a coat and lost track of the time."

"I was afraid something had happened to you." Bret's voice was deep and smooth, with every hint of the accent he had developed during his childhood neatly erased in favor of the carefully enunciated speech necessary for his work on the stage.

"I didn't mean to worry you. I should have phoned ahead."

They were taken to the table Electra had reserved near the atrium, and she was pleasantly aware of the attention they stirred among the other diners. Part was for her, of course, because she was well known for her fashions, but the envy on the women's faces was because of Bret. Electra felt a sense of power, knowing he was here with her rather than with a younger woman. Age had always been Electra's enemy, and with Bret she felt she was the winner.

When the waiter had taken their orders, Electra said to Bret, "Have you reconsidered your decision not to move in with me?" For Bret she had been more than willing to relax her rule about living alone.

"No, we've already discussed that. Remember?"

Electra cast him a coy glance from under her eyelashes. "I know, but I don't agree with your decision. It would be so much nicer if we lived together."

"I agree," he said smoothly. "But my apartment is near the theater, and it's much more convenient to my work.

Cab fare would eat me alive."

"You could pay for the cab out of the money you'd save on rent." She knew exactly how much that was because she had had to help him pay his rent a few months before when he was between plays. "I should have insisted that you move to my place before you were cast in *Gazebo Spring*. I could help you learn your lines," she tempted.

"I already know my lines."

Electra reached across the table and covered his hand with hers. Even through the fabric of her glove she could feel the heat of his body. "I love you, Bret. I want to be with you."

"I know, darling, but we have to be reasonable. What if it doesn't last between us? I'd have nowhere to go."

She loved it when he called her darling. "It will last. I know it will. I've never been so happy."

"I'm glad," he said, bestowing on her another of his heart-stopping smiles. "I want you to be happy."

Electra gave his hand another squeeze and straightened in her chair. She knew they shouldn't hold hands like lovesick teenagers. Not in a restaurant.

She removed her gloves and laid them on her clutch purse as the waiter arrived with their Caesar salads. She always ate a salad at lunch in order to keep her weight down, and Bret did the same to show his support. He was so wonderful, she thought. What would he think if she were to propose?

As she ate and half listened to him telling about his morning, she toyed with the idea of marrying him. She was past the age for having children, of course, so that wouldn't be a problem. With her life-style, she had always felt she should never have children, even when she was young enough to do so. But he might find out her real age when they applied for a license. She wondered if it would be possible to apply in private so Bret wouldn't know what she put in that blank. Or maybe he wouldn't care. If he loved her—and she was sure he did—her age wouldn't matter. Perhaps she would even tell him herself. No, she thought, there was no reason to let him know she was older than he thought.

"When will the play open?" she asked as if she had been listening.

"It goes up November eighteenth. You don't have plans for that night, do you? I want you in the front row on opening night."

"If I do, I'll cancel them. Your first Broadway play is more important than anything else."

"I appreciate you asking Zoe to put in a good word for me with the director. I might not have been cast otherwise."

"Nonsense. With your talent? Of course you would have been."

When they finished eating, Electra discreetly paid the waiter, and Bret offered her his arm as they left. Electra felt envious eyes on her back and she smiled. These days she found herself smiling often.

"I know!" Bret said as they left the restaurant. "Let's go for a walk in the park. I'm off for the rest of the day and it's nice out. Call Mary and tell her you won't be back this afternoon."

"I can't do that. We're in the middle of working up that fall show. Besides, I'm wearing new heels, and they aren't comfortable enough for walking."

Bret looked as disappointed as a four-year-old who had just been denied an ice cream cone. Electra patted his cheek. "Don't be blue. We can go to the park on Saturday."

"All right. I know you're right."

"One of us has to be sensible," she said with a smile.

"You? Sensible? That sounds like a pair of old shoes. You're a butterfly—free and unfettered." He grinned down at her.

"I'm a butterfly when I'm with you," she agreed. "You've taught me how to be one. That's what inspired the name for my teen line of clothes."

"I'm glad I've been a good influence."

"Goodness knows I've needed one," she said with a laugh. "For a while there I was burning my candle at both ends. I'm much happier with you than I was when I was playing the field."

"So I'll see you tonight?"

"Of course. Why don't I drop by and pick you up when I leave work?"

"No, don't do that. I'll meet you at your apartment. Wear your red kimono—I'm bringing Chinese."

"Great! And egg rolls. You forgot them last time."

"And egg rolls," he repeated. He whistled for a cab and opened the door for her. "Behave yourself," he said as if she were a young girl, "and I'll see you tonight."

"Yes, Bret," she said obediently. She leaned up and kissed him good-bye, her lips lingering daringly on his. "Until tonight," she whispered.

As he sauntered back onto the sidewalk, she closed her own door and gave the driver her work address.

CHAPTER 17

"I HAVE A SURPRISE FOR YOU," ELECTRA TOLD Bret.

"Oh?" His blue eyes lit up almost as expectantly as those of a child on Christmas morning. "Where is it?" He looked around the bedroom.

"Not a gift. It's much better than that. I'm going to take you to Willowbrook."

"Willowbrook? What is that, a hospital or something?"

"No, silly. Willowbrook is my home. My real home. It's in Virginia near a little town named Catawba Mills. It's where I grew up."

"Oh. Well, you know I have rehearsals every night next week and—"

"Of course I know that. You forget how much money I've invested in *Gazebo Spring*." She cuddled closer and laid her cheek on his chest, the hair there, surprisingly dark considering Bret's blondness, tickling her nose. "That's why I booked a flight for today. We have the whole weekend."

Bret was silent.

Electra lifted her head and looked for a response in his face. "Aren't you pleased?"

He smiled and stroked her dark hair back from her cheek. "Of course I am."

"You'll meet my sister. Amelia lives there and looks after the place, since I have to stay in New York."

"Is this a big place?"

Electra put her head back on his shoulder, and with her voice softening as if she were describing a lover, she said, "It's very big. At one time it was the showplace of the county. It's at the end of a long avenue lined with old catawba trees. In the spring they are covered with white blossoms. The house is surrounded by rolling lawns and gardens. One is a yew garden that Papa kept rolled as flat as a floor for outdoor parties. It has a fountain at one end." Wistfully she added, "We had our last great party there just before he died. It was during Prohibition, and we had a table fountain, a replica of the large one, that showered three kinds of wine."

"Prohibition?" he said with a laugh.

Electra realized her mistake. With a short laugh she said, "Not *that* Prohibition! I meant my father had prohibited us to serve wine. I was very young—too young to drink."

"Well, I wondered. I mean Prohibition was way back in the twenties. We studied it in school."

"Then you should have realized I couldn't have meant that," she said sharply.

She tried to pull away, but he drew her closer and rolled so that his upper body covered her bare breasts. As he kissed her, Electra felt her anger dissolve. She could never stay angry at Bret for long.

•　　　　•　　　　•

The flight to Virginia was turbulent, and Electra believed this to be the cause of Bret's ill temper. Not that he said anything to indicate he was in a foul mood, exactly, but he wasn't as talkative as usual, and when he was unaware that she was looking at him, his expression was sullen and he sat with his shoulders hunched. She was looking forward to introducing him to Amelia and hoped he would cheer up soon.

Instead, when they entered the town of Catawba Mills, Bret stopped talking altogether and his face clouded with disappointment. Trying to see the town from his metropolitan point of view and without the nostalgia she felt for Catawba Mills, she had to admit to herself it wasn't the prettiest town she had ever seen. Most of the downtown buildings had been built before World War II—some of them long before—and to an outsider they probably looked like just a jumble of old buildings. Bret had no memories connecting him to these time-worn structures, as Electra did.

As she looked around, she realized that the current city-improvement campaign to modernize the appearance of Catawba Mills's business district by covering the building fronts with new aluminum facades in neutral shades would someday strip away her memory link to the town where she had grown up. Then only Willowbrook would remain as it always had been. Catawba Mills had grown in population and changed considerably since she moved away, and Electra wasn't happy with the results. Circumstances beyond her control had kept her from being here to participate in the decisions that had brought about these changes, but someday she would return, and perhaps then she could do something to restore Catawba Mills's dignity and charm.

Until then, she had no choice but to accept Catawba Mills as it had become.

A short time later, as they approached the gates of Willowbrook, Electra leaned forward on the cab seat in eager anticipation. As always, the black iron gates between the red brick pillars were open. Electra had never seen them closed, and she wasn't sure such was even possible.

As the cab drove up the curving avenue of trees, she could hardly curb her excitement. She put her hand in Bret's and tried to instill him with her happiness.

But not until Willowbrook came into sight did she feel Bret's awakening interest. The house was as stately and as magnificent as ever, and she was sure Bret shared her opinion. "We're home," she said with a sigh. "This is Willowbrook."

Electra paid the cab driver as Bret carried their luggage up the steps. He was looking around as if he couldn't believe his eyes. In this setting, Electra noticed, he looked more like Christopher than ever.

Instead of walking in unannounced, Electra rang the doorbell so she and Bret could make an entrance. She wanted to savor every moment of her homecoming. When Helga opened the door, Electra beamed at her. "Is Amelia here? I wired her that we were coming."

Helga was staring at Bret. "Ja, she is here. I am going to get her. Please to sit in the parlor." She closed the door behind them and left Electra to find her way into the parlor, while she bustled away to find Amelia.

"I don't know why my sister is so adamant about keeping Helga," Electra confided to Bret. "She seems to be a competent housekeeper, but she acts like a member of the family. At least her English has improved."

Bret sauntered over to a marble-topped end table and casually picked up an exquisitely decorated egg from its golden pedestal. "What is she, Swedish?"

"German."

He looked more closely at the art object in his hands. "Is this a Fabergé? A real one, I mean?"

Electra glanced at it. "Yes, I gave it to Amelia for Christmas a few years back. It reminded me of one Papa gave to Mother."

"Where's the original?"

"We had to sell it after he died. That was before I went to New York."

Electra went to the mantel for a closer look at Christopher's smiling face in the three photos. He had been a handsome man, but the camera hadn't done him justice. So much of his charm had been in the way he moved and spoke. Electra had almost forgotten that her every encounter with Christopher had been one of anger. She glanced over at Bret. Yes, the resemblance was striking.

Amelia came hurrying into the room, her face wreathed in a smile, but when she saw Bret, she jerked to a halt and appeared to be struggling to maintain her pleasant expression.

Electra let her stare for a moment, then said, "Amelia, I'd like you to meet Bret Harley. Bret, my sister, Amelia Radcliff."

"Jenkins," Amelia amended. "I'm Amelia Jenkins."

"Of course. How silly of me," Electra said smoothly. "I assumed you would have taken back your maiden name by now."

A hint of a frown tarnished Amelia's smiling face. "Why on earth would I do that?"

"Well, after all, you were only together a few weeks."

"I was married," Amelia snapped, her smile all but gone.

Electra felt the hair on the back of her neck bristle, but she forced her voice and features to remain calm. "Bret is playing the lead role in the Broadway production of *Gazebo Spring*."

Bret nodded. "I play Tony. Electra is one of the primary backers, so I have to be extra good." Bret flashed Amelia the smile that always won female hearts. "She's our angel."

"Angel, is it?" Amelia didn't look at all captivated.

"He means—" Electra began, but Amelia cut her off.

"I know what he means. We have a little theater group in Catawba Mills."

Bret looked amused, as if amateur theater had no correlation with Broadway.

"We can only stay for the weekend," Electra said. "Bret has to be back for rehearsals on Monday." To Bret she said, "Be a darling, won't you, and take up our bags? It's the room two doors down from the head of the stairs, on the right."

Bret replaced the egg on its stand, leaving it sitting askew, retrieved their bags from the foyer, and headed up the stairs. "Isn't he gorgeous?" she asked Amelia.

"You're staying in the same room?" Amelia queried, trying to sound casual as she repositioned the Fabergé egg.

"Now don't start that again," Electra cautioned as she unsnapped her purse and took out a cigarette and lighter. "Where's an ashtray?"

Amelia got an ashtray from the sideboard in the dining room and thrust it at Electra. "I don't mean to start anything, but isn't he too young for you?"

"No, he isn't," Electra snapped. "Bret is older than he

looks." Her critical eyes took in Amelia's gray hair and aging skin. "Why don't you put a rinse on your hair? You'd look years younger."

"How old is he?"

Electra went to Amelia and put her arm around her sister's shoulders. "Now, let's not fight. Aren't you glad to see me?"

"Yes, I'm glad to see *you*."

Electra let her arm drop. "I wired you that I was bringing someone with me."

"I thought you meant another woman, not a boy. If you had called, I would have talked you out of it."

"That's why I sent a telegram. I didn't want to argue." Electra angrily flicked her cigarette ashes at the ashtray. "It's important that you get to know Bret."

"Why? Are you planning to adopt him?"

Electra glared at her. "No, but I may marry him."

Amelia's mouth dropped open. "Marry him! That boy?"

"He's not a boy!" Electra could no longer keep the anger out of her voice. "I should have known you'd act like this, that you'd be jealous."

"Jealous? Of him?" Amelia looked genuinely perplexed.

"Doesn't he remind you of anyone?"

Amelia looked back toward the stairs as if trying to freshen her memory of him. "No, no one. Should he?"

"Skip it."

"Has he actually asked you to marry him?"

"Not yet. Maybe I'll ask him this weekend. Why, we could spend our honeymoon right here at Willowbrook!"

"That's out of the question!"

"It is not! Willowbrook is my home, you may recall."

"Only half of it. Papa left the other half to me."

Electra's frown deepened. She had forgotten that. Years ago when the lawyer had read their father's will, Amelia had said Electra could have her share of the house, but in the worries and turmoil that had followed, Electra had never had the deed changed. "Then we'll only honeymoon in my half of it!"

"Why would you even consider marrying someone so young? You can't possibly have anything in common."

"As a matter of fact, we share a lot of interests," Electra said in her defense. "You're only trying to cause trouble because I didn't welcome Christopher with open arms."

"Christopher? What's he got to do with this?"

"Just never mind. Skip it. I don't need you to tell me what to do." With an angry jerk of her head, Electra stormed from the room in search of Bret.

Amelia stared after her. Then in an equal burst of anger, she bustled out to her garden. She banged the gate shut behind her and went to the bench, shoving aside the willow boughs. "Electra is acting like a pigheaded fool!" she said to the air in the general direction of the tree trunk. "We had gotten along so well lately, too."

She was so upset she fidgeted on the marble bench. "Do you know what she's done now? She's brought a young man—a *very* young man—down to stay with her, and she says she's going to marry him! You should see him! I'll bet he's not even thirty years old."

Amelia stood and paced restlessly beneath the willow's overhanging branches. "I thought she was finally too old for all that nonsense. Bringing her boyfriends down here for a romp in the hay! Papa and Mother must be rolling in their graves."

She sat back down on the bench, glaring at the tree

trunk. "He looks like one of those pretty boys on television. I'll bet he's no better than a . . . a gigolo! The older Electra gets, the younger her boyfriends are! I've never seen the likes of this."

A new thought struck her, propelling her to her feet. "I hope Jenny doesn't take it into her head to visit us. I told her Electra was coming this weekend. Jenny will tell Carleton, and then it will be all over town that Electra is making a fool of herself."

Over the fence came the robust melody of a song called "Tom Dooley." Amelia scowled in the direction of the disturbance. "I don't know why Martin has to sing so loud," she confided to Christopher's memory. In a louder voice, intended for Martin's ears, she said, "You'd think he was trying out for the opera or something."

When Martin showed no sign of lowering his voice, Amelia sighed and headed for the garden gate. With so much noise going on, she couldn't think straight, much less talk to Christopher. As she opened the gate, she saw Electra standing nearby as if she had been listening. Amelia stepped out and firmly closed the gate behind her.

"Who's in there?" Electra asked. "I heard you talking to someone."

"People who listen at garden gates deserve to hear bad things about themselves."

Electra eyed the gate a moment, then reached for the latch.

Amelia brushed Electra's hand aside. "No, you don't. This garden is on *my* half of the estate."

"I have no interest at all in whom you were talking to in there."

Amelia knew she was lying, but she had no intention

of giving Electra an explanation. At least, she noted, Martin had finished his song and was back to weeding the lawn.

"I came out here to make up with you," Electra said. "But if you'd rather not . . ."

"No, no. I don't want there to be hard feelings between us. We're apart so much of the time as it is. I may not have been fair in my assessment of your . . . young man."

"Bret. His name is Bret Harley."

"Of course. I remember now. I may have been unfair to Bret. But, Electra, don't rush into anything you may regret. Don't marry too quickly."

"You're a fine one to say that," Electra retorted. "Look how you let Christopher sweep you off your feet."

"I know, but I had known him as a child, and things were different then. I was still young enough to have children, and we were on the brink of another world war. You shouldn't feel such an urgency."

"By the way," Electra added with carefully modulated tones, "Bret thinks I'm a little bit younger than I really am. Let's allow him go on thinking that. All right?"

"How much younger?"

"He thinks I'm thirty-nine."

Amelia stared in disbelief. "Thirty-nine!"

"Stop glaring at me like that. You know I've never looked my age."

"Neither does Jack Benny," Amelia retorted. "He's thirty-nine, too."

"I thought we were going to make up."

Amelia sighed. "Okay. I'll go along with your being thirty-nine, but only if you promise me you'll wait a few months before you marry him."

Electra crossed her arms in a decidedly defensive stance, but said nothing.

"If it's really love it will still be there a few months from now. That was the advice you gave Christopher and me. Remember?"

"Okay. I'll wait a while longer. But if he proposes to me before then, I'm going to accept."

Amelia nodded. Surely Bret wouldn't really want to rush Electra into a marriage. At least she hoped not.

For the remainder of the weekend Amelia, Electra, and Bret were civil to one another. Bret even did his best to charm Amelia, but Electra wasn't jealous because his friendly attitude toward Amelia was the same one he would have shown an aunt. He assumed, and Electra let him, that Amelia was her elder sister, and Electra even went so far as to hint that she herself was a late-in-life child.

By the time the weekend was over, Electra was pleased to see that Bret was enjoying himself and was even cheerful about returning to New York and the grind of rehearsals for *Gazebo Spring*. As she packed to leave, not trusting Helga to get their things into the proper bags, she considered how she would redecorate this bedroom to reflect Bret's masculine taste. By the time they slept here again, they might be husband and wife! Electra hugged herself as exuberantly as a child. She and Bret had made love each night and every morning, and although she was exhausted, she felt warm and glowing inside. She loved sleeping beside him all night and waking up to him in the morning. Her only concern was that his youthful stamina exceeded her own. This, she told herself, was proof of his love.

The closer they got to New York, the more cheerful Bret

became, and by the time they landed at La Guardia, his eyes were sparkling with laughter. Electra believed the weekend had done them both a great deal of good. Even though she wrinkled her nose at the acrid smell of exhaust fumes as they walked across the tarmac to the terminal, she clung to the fresh memory of the easy graciousness of Willowbrook.

"Someday," she said as they slid into a cab, "I'm going home to Willowbrook, and I'll never leave it again."

"You'd like to live there? You wouldn't miss the city?"

She shook her head. "Not for a minute. You should have seen the way Willowbrook looked when we were having parties. We rolled up the rugs for dancing and used candles for light instead of electricity, and it looked like wonderland."

"When was that?" he asked a bit too casually.

Electra glanced at him, suspicious that Amelia might have dropped a hint to him about her age. "When I was a teenager. Of course."

"I never had that much fun when I was growing up."

"You never talk about your childhood at all," she observed. "I really know very little about you."

"You've read my publicity kit. I'm from Missouri and grew up on my parents' farm. I graduated from the University of Missouri at Columbia, and here I am."

"But that's what I mean. If you grew up on a farm why didn't you recognize that old cultivator we found in the barn, and why did you have to ask what caused the crib marks on the stalls?"

"We had new equipment and no horses," he replied easily. "How should I know horses will chew on wood?"

"It just seems odd that a farm boy would never have had

even a pony. Amelia rode all the time, and while I never particularly enjoyed riding, I knew how."

"We weren't regular farmers," he evaded. "I guess you'd say Dad was a gentleman farmer."

" 'Was'? Has he passed away?"

Bret shook his head. "Retired."

"But how do you retire from—"

"What are all these questions all of a sudden?" he interrupted, his eyes growing wary. "Are you checking up on me?"

"Of course not." She laid her hand on his thigh to calm him. "I believe you. It's just that I want to know so much about you and you never volunteer anything."

"I'm a man of mystery," he teased, his good humor restored. He leaned forward to tell the driver, "Let me off at the Wharton Theater on Broadway."

"At the theater?" Electra couldn't keep the disappointment from her voice. "Surely you don't have to be there today. I had assumed you'd come home with me."

"I've been with you every minute of the weekend," he said in a reasonable tone. "I need to go over my lines before tomorrow."

"I can help you do that."

He leaned over and lightly kissed her. "You know one thing leads to another with us." He winked at her. "We would never finish those lines."

Electra had to smile because she knew it was true. Bret's sexual appetite was apparently limitless. "Will I see you tomorrow?"

"We'd better make it Tuesday. After being gone all weekend I have some things I need to catch up on."

"Tuesday, then." The cab slowed to a stop in front of

the theater. "And, Bret, give some more thought to moving in with me."

He kissed her fully on the lips before swinging his long legs out of the cab. "Don't press me, darling."

The kiss and endearment kept her so warm she didn't notice the coolness of his tone until after the cab driver had deposited Bret's bags and driven away.

Electra saw the driver glance at her in frank curiosity as she settled back in the warm spot Bret had left on the seat. She suppressed a smile. Because she was so powerful in her own right, she rather enjoyed having Bret say no to her from time to time. When he was being masterful, she could let herself be soft and yielding. This sort of role-playing had added spice to their lovemaking.

Tuesday afternoon Bret called to say he wouldn't be able to see her that night after all. The director had called a longer rehearsal than usual, and he was to go back to the theater after dinner. Electra was disappointed, but she eased her loneliness by going into Tiffany's and looking at wedding rings.

She had never thought she would marry, or even that she would ever want to be a wife. Not after Robert. She had seen at too early an age how monogamous men were— or rather how monogamous they were not. As much as she didn't want to be some man's mistress, she wanted even less to be a cuckolded wife. Now, however, she was in love, and she wanted to be Mrs. Bret Harley almost as much as she wanted to be to the American fashion world what Chanel was to the French.

The saleslady took out several boxes of rings, each more brilliant than the last. Electra tried one on the ring finger of her left hand and studied the effect. All the rings were beautiful. She wished Bret were there so he could give her his opinion. After long consideration she chose an engagement ring with a brilliant ruby. The wedding band fit around it, making a circle of diamonds. "Put this away for me, will you?"

"Certainly, Miss Radcliff." The clerk recognized Electra as she did all of Tiffany's regular customers.

Electra wrote out a check as a deposit on the ring. She was positive Bret would like it. He always said she had impeccable taste.

She left the jewelry store feeling as giddy as a schoolgirl. She knew she should have waited for Bret to shop for the ring with her, but he was so busy. He often rehearsed until after the stores had closed. Electra almost laughed aloud as she realized neither she nor Bret had actually proposed. She had promised Amelia she wouldn't rush into a marriage, but that wasn't the same as an engagement.

As she walked along the crowded sidewalk, her thoughts turned to Amelia. On two separate occasions she had overheard her talking to someone in the walled garden. Was it possible Amelia had a boyfriend? Surely if she did, she would have tinted her hair and lost some weight. Electra had been hard pressed not to suggest a sensible diet for Amelia. But if she had a man friend, who could it be? Of their old beaux none seemed likely. Richard Stuart had retired in Catawba Mills, but Amelia had said he was still married and still stuffy. Carleton Edgeworth practiced law in Catawba Mills, but Electra had seen him recently and knew he was fat and bald as well as in poor health. Besides, Amelia and Carleton's wife, Jenny, were good friends.

Electra stopped in her tracks and was almost run over

by a woman behind her carrying a big shopping bag. Surely Amelia wasn't taking up with another gardener! No, that was silly, she told herself. Martin was married, and Bob wasn't at all attractive. Jerry was only a high school boy. As she resumed her brisk pace down the street, she convinced herself her ears had been playing tricks on her.

As she passed a Chinese restaurant she paused. Although Bret had to work that night, he still had to eat, so she went in and bought a take-out meal for two.

From experience she knew the theater's lobby doors would be locked at this time of evening, so she had the cabbie drop her off near the stage door of the theater. The guard at the door stopped her. She lied saying that Bret Harley was expecting her, and when the guard recognized her, he let her enter.

As soon as she reached the wings, she could hear Bret's voice on stage. The play was about star-crossed lovers, and he was delivering the lines intended to persuade his girlfriend to come back to him. Electra stepped carefully over the coils of rope, guy wires, and discarded props that cluttered the backstage area. When she was in a position where she could see the stage, she stopped to watch.

The red, white, and blue gelled lights overhead gleamed off Bret's pale hair, and their intensity made his skin appear to be paler than it really was, even a bit washed out. But she knew that the greasepaint he would wear during the actual performances would return his natural tan, so she didn't worry. His muscles rippled under his tight T-shirt, and his frown made him look ferociously sexy. Electra shivered to think this handsome young god was her lover.

The female lead was being played by a pretty young girl who looked too innocent to be away from home. Bret had told Electra that the girl's name was Jody Kemp, but he had described her as rather plain. Electra could see for herself that nothing was further from the truth. As Jody agonized over whether to return to Tony or to marry an older, established man, Electra saw a yearning in her eyes that seemed much too real for the performance she was giving. Electra reflexively stepped farther back into the shadows.

In tears, Jody exited the stage on the side opposite Electra, and when Bret finished the scene, he followed her off.

Electra had hoped Bret would come offstage on her side and save her the trouble of having to hunt him down, but he hadn't, so she began carefully winding her way back through the organized clutter of the stage crew.

She caught sight of Bret in a corner filled with costumes from the fitting room, talking to a young man Electra vaguely recognized from an earlier play. As she passed behind a grove of Masonite trees, she heard the other man say, "You're playing with fire, Bret."

"No, man. I know what I'm doing. Hell, I've got the best of both worlds." He had dropped his stage accent, and the distinct Bronx twang that remained jarred Electra's nerves as much as the implication of his words. Her amazement made her pause.

"One thing worries me, though," Bret went on. "The old broad's getting pushy. She keeps trying to talk me into moving in with her."

The other man laughed. "Jody would have your balls! How did you ever explain to her why you were gone all weekend?"

"I told her it was a sabbatical, that I needed to be alone with my thoughts. I wish to hell I had been. Electra's the horniest old woman I've ever seen."

Electra's insides turned to cold, clammy stone.

She wanted to run away, but she was afraid one of the men would see her.

"I brought Jody a gift and that calmed her down. It's a gold egg. Fabergé."

Electra stiffened. Amelia's Fabergé egg? None of this made any sense.

"Pretty spiffy. If you have to be kept, that's the style to choose. My old woman isn't that generous."

"Sweet talk is the key. Just do like I told you. And keep a hard-on."

"That's easy for you to say."

"Shit, man. You're an actor."

Electra closed her eyes and prayed that she wouldn't faint. Her heart was pounding so hard she felt as if it might burst.

The sound of footsteps alerted her that the conversation was over, and she tensed up until she realized the actors were moving away from her. Not wanting to confront them, she remained motionless several minutes longer. Finally she remembered to breathe. There had to be another explanation. Surely she had misunderstood what she had heard. Maybe these were lines from the play. That must be it!

Feeling more confident with each passing moment, Electra made her way through the stored scenery toward the back of the building where the dressing rooms were.

Bret's name was on the door of the first one she came to, and as she hesitated in order to calm down, she congratulated herself for not having accused Bret prematurely of using her and playing her for a fool. Her impulsiveness had sometimes caused her trouble, but perhaps the restraint she'd shown by waiting until she'd had time to think this through meant that she was winning the battle. Or had she been the victim of artful deception, and now of self-deception as well? There was only one way to find out for sure.

With cold fingers Electra turned the knob and pushed the door open. Bret wasn't at the makeup table, but her worst fear was realized by the mirror's reflection of what Bret and Jody were doing on the couch.

Electra froze for a second, then quietly closed the door. The hammering that had begun behind her eyes was increasing in frequency and intensity, and her stomach was churning. Convincing herself that discretion was the better part of valor, she set the bag of Chinese food in the doorway where Bret would have to see it. Then he would know she had been here, for he often teased her about her fondness for Chinese food. She hoped he would deduce that she had discovered his deception, but she no longer took it for granted that he would be so intelligent as to do so.

She straightened and tilted her head at a proud angle. All she wanted now was to get out of there before anyone noticed her.

By the time she reached the street, she thought she might be sick on the sidewalk, but sheer will kept everything down during the cab ride home.

She made it into her building's elevator before the tears started, and she held off the sobs until she reached the sanctuary of her apartment. Lying in the darkening room, she cried away the remainder of the evening. Her face swollen and her body sore from tension, she opened a bottle of bourbon and drank her way through to the dawn. She stayed awake long enough to call Mary and say she wouldn't be in that day, then collapsed on her bed in a drunken stupor.

CHAPTER 18

ELECTRA WAS TOO WISE A BUSINESSWOMAN TO let Bret's infidelity affect her backing of *Gazebo Spring*, but she made it clear to Zoe Wharton and the rest of her friends that she and Bret were no longer an item and that it would definitely be a faux pas to invite them to the same parties. As a result, Bret was dropped from the social lists, and it seemed likely his career would end in the mediocrity his acting ability deserved. Electra knew this wounded Bret more deeply than the scene she could have caused in his dressing room the evening she caught Bret and Jody together, but because of the pain she had suffered, she wasn't the least bit sympathetic.

Electra had honestly loved Bret and believed he loved her, and the hurt ran so deep that in order to protect herself, she had pulled back from her theatrical acquaintances, Zoe being the only exception. Therefore, when Saul Feldman called, she was caught off guard.

"Dinner tonight? At Vargo's?" She tried to think of a believable excuse for declining, but she was so rattled by the sound of his voice, she couldn't think straight.

After a moment with no response, he said, "We could go somewhere else if you'd rather."

His deep, mellow tones, friendly, inviting, reminded Electra of how lonely she was, but her rising expectations were tempered by doubt and suspicion. "Vargo's is fine. Shall I meet you there?"

"Great. Say at eight o'clock?"

Electra suppressed a sigh. So it was his intention for this to be a business dinner, not a social evening. As she hung up, she told herself to be glad. She was vulnerable now and didn't want to fall for anyone on the rebound. As she dressed, she reminded herself she didn't need a man to make her happy and that having a new lover would hamper the work she needed to be doing. But the real truth was that she felt more alone than ever before.

Vargo's was an elegant restaurant set high above the city, its floor-to-ceiling glass walls affording a spectacular view of New York's lights. Electra easily spotted Saul and was taken to his table. As he rose, he smiled in greeting and held her chair for her.

In the years since the war, Saul's hair had gone from black to silver, making his dark eyes a remarkable contrast. He had been a nice-looking man in his youth, but was even more handsome now. Electra had seen him here and there from time to time, but they had seldom talked.

"It's been a long time," Saul said. "How are you?"

"Fine, thanks. And you?" She watched him take his seat opposite her. His suit fit impeccably, and he was clearly at home in this expensive restaurant, unlike the young men she had dated. This was business, and he had invited her, and Electra was elated that she, for once, wouldn't be expected to pick up the check.

"Can't complain. I saw *Gazebo Spring*'s opening performance."

"Oh?" she asked, keeping her voice cool and detached as she inhaled deeply on the cigarette Saul had lit for her.

"I believe you have a hit there."

"I haven't seen it." Her eyes met his, challenging him to ask why.

Saul merely smiled. "As long as everyone else sees it, the result is the same. Zoe tells me you might be interested in backing other shows now that money is more or less secured on that one."

"Perhaps. I gather you have one in mind?"

"Yes, it's a new three-act play by Carter Symmons."

Electra betrayed herself by the flicker of her eyes. "Carter Symmons?" she asked carefully.

"I doubt you know him. He was a rather promising young actor before the war, but he lost a leg and that ended his career. He wrote two plays last year, and both of them were well received. Now he has a new one called *Mary's Promise* that I believe will be a hit."

Electra hesitated. She had known Carter so long ago. It seemed like another lifetime. Did he remember her and expect a favor for the relationship they'd once had? "Did Carter suggest you come to me?"

"You know each other? I had no idea. No, he never mentioned your name."

"We were acquainted once, years back. So he's a playwright now. And this play, *Mary's Promise*—it has a part you're interested in?"

Saul laughed. "I'm not an actor anymore. I want to direct it. I directed *A Season of Fools* and *The Glass Rainbow*."

Electra gave him a speculative glance. "I'm impressed.

Last year everyone was talking about *The Glass Rainbow*. I had no idea you were connected with it."

She paused while the waiter placed their food before them. "I haven't seen you in a long time. Do you and—Rachel, was it?—go to Zoe's these days?"

"It was Rachel and we're divorced now. She's remarried. A man named Robert Hastings."

Electra lowered her gaze and pretended to be interested in her plate of scampi. "Now that you mention it, I believe Zoe did tell me something about that." So Robert had finally married one of his mistresses. She wondered if Rachel had the impression that he could be trusted. To have been reminded of two of her ex-lovers so unexpectedly left Electra uncomfortable.

"It was a fairly amicable divorce, if there is such a thing. It seems she had been seeing him behind my back for years. Once I found out about it, I certainly didn't want to stay married to her. She evidently knew Hastings would marry her, and he did."

"You don't seem to be exactly broken up over it."

"I was mad at the time, but that was a year ago. Now I'm glad she's gone."

Electra lifted her wineglass. "Here's to freedom."

Saul joined her in the toast. "So what do you think about backing *Mary's Promise*? We need an angel, and while there are no guarantees, I expect the play to be a good money-maker."

"I want to read it first. I assume you have a script?"

"Of course." He took a copy of the play from the leather attaché case he had brought with him. "This is an extra, so there's no rush about returning it, but I would like to know what you decide as soon as possible."

Electra put the bound script under her purse. "I'll read it tomorrow. Tell me what you find so fascinating about it."

As Saul went over the story line of the play and told her how he believed it should be presented, Electra ate her meal and reflected on how coincidental it was that Carter Symmons had cropped up again in her life. She would never have guessed he had it in him to write anything more complicated than his name.

"So," she said, "have you remarried?"

"No way. Once was enough for me. How about you?"

"No, not even once." She had a pang of regret about Bret, but put it firmly out of her mind. Dwelling on what was past was unproductive. "I like my freedom too well to share my life with anyone else on a permanent basis."

"I couldn't have expressed it better myself," he agreed. "I hadn't realized how much of what I wanted to do with my life was curtailed because I was living with Rachel. If I feel like eating dinner at midnight or if I want to read in bed all night, there's no one to complain about it."

"Exactly," Electra agreed with an emphatic nod. "If I don't want to put on makeup on the weekend, I don't have to."

"I can walk around my apartment in my socks and squeeze the toothpaste from the middle."

"Or wear jeans."

Saul grinned. "I can't imagine you in jeans."

Electra proudly jerked her chin up. "I didn't say that I *do* wear them, only that I could."

"I'll bet they look good on you."

She knew he was teasing her, and she actually blushed. Electra couldn't remember the last time a man had made her blush. Nor had she ever admitted that she occasionally wore the jeans she designed for her teens line. At first she had worn them in order to verify that the design would produce a comfortable fit, but now she wore them simply because they were comfortable. Still, a woman of her years shouldn't admit to dressing in such youthful clothes.

Saul ordered a dessert for them both—a chocolate-cinnamon torte for which Vargo's was famous—despite Electra's automatic protest. Although Electra couldn't remember the last time she had had a dessert, she found herself eating this one with enjoyment.

Over coffee they gazed out at the spectacle of lights from the New York skyline. "When I first came here," Electra surprised herself by saying, "I couldn't believe there could be so many people all in one place. I couldn't begin to imagine what all of them did for a living." She laughed. "I still can't."

"I guess I take it for granted. I've lived here all my life. In fact my apartment is within a few blocks of my parents' apartment, where I grew up."

"Are they still there?"

"No, they retired years ago and moved to Arizona. One of those new retirement communities."

"I'm going to retire someday," Electra said. "I'll move back home to Virginia. Have you ever seen it?"

"Not from the ground. From an airplane it all looks pretty much alike."

"You should go there sometime."

"It's hard to picture you anywhere but here in New York."

"Is it?" Electra's eyes filled with her amazement. "I've

always considered myself a Virginian."

"We all have our roles, don't we? Even when the roles don't fit. I always thought Rachel was the perfect wife, and then I found out she had been cheating on me during most of our marriage. I cast you as the City Woman, and I have trouble seeing you in any other role."

"That's because you've never seen Willowbrook. That's my family home and my roots are there."

"I'd like to see it someday."

Electra sized him up a moment before responding. "I only take special people there, people with whom I want to share a part of myself."

"I'd like to see it someday," he repeated.

Electra felt an enveloping warmth. He was flirting with her, and she was actually enjoying it. Saul was older than her usual run of lovers, but she was able to be herself around him, and she found that refreshing. She didn't have to remember not to recall events that occurred before he was born, or worry about making a slip that might give away her age. "Would you like to come home with me tonight?" she invited, her tone sultry and confident.

Saul glanced at his watch. "For a nightcap, you mean? I'd better not. I have to be at the theater early tomorrow."

Electra blinked. She couldn't believe he had actually turned down her invitation. Was it possible he had misunderstood her offer? Again she felt a blush rising, and this one wasn't pleasant. Perhaps he had understood, but didn't find her physically attractive.

"How about tomorrow?" he asked. "How long has it been since you visited the Statue of Liberty?"

"I don't think I ever have." She stared at him.

"Then it's high time you did. Why don't I pick you up at, say, three o'clock?"

She thought of all the things she had expected to do that day. It would be Saturday, so none of her employees would be in the office. She had intended to sketch some preliminary drawings for a show she was putting together for a television special. "All right. Three o'clock. Do you know where I live?"

"No, but I will after I see you home." He smiled. "I'm not in that much of a hurry."

Electra was confused all the way back to her apartment. Saul made no move to take her hand or to put his arm around her. Did he intend to come upstairs with her after all? Electra was accustomed to being the assertive partner in all her relationships, and she wasn't too sure she liked being off-balance this way.

At her apartment building, Saul slid out of the cab and held the curbside door for her, but when she got out, he didn't shut the door. She looked back at him questioningly.

"See you tomorrow," he said and climbed back into the cab.

As the taxi drove away Electra realized she was staring after him. She now recalled what it was about Saul Feldman she found so intriguing: his unpredictability. She abruptly turned, and as the doorman opened the door for her, she nodded. When she reached her apartment, she let herself in and went straight to the nearest mirror.

She leaned close and studied her reflection in minute detail. Rigorous dieting kept her figure slim and her cheeks pleasantly hollowed. Both of her cosmetic surgeries had been done by experts; her skin neatly cupped her jawline and her forehead was smooth. Her hair was black by comparison to her pale skin, but her coloring had always been dramatic. She pulled down a short lock of hair for a closer examination and frowned at it. Maybe her hairdresser was using too black a dye. Jet black hair looked false after a woman reached a certain age, regardless of her skin tone. She examined the roots carefully. No gray was showing.

So why hadn't Saul wanted to come up to her apartment?

Maybe, she thought, he was one of those men who weren't attracted to women. He had been married, but that proved nothing, especially since Rachel had left him for another man and had had at least one lover during their marriage. Electra frowned again. She didn't think Saul was that type, but anything was possible. She examined everything she had said to see if she had made a fool of herself. No. Her invitation had been oblique.

She carried her purse and the script into her bedroom, and after undressing, she put on a rose-colored negligee with a matching sheer peignoir. Even when she was sleeping alone, she liked to look pretty. And since she had discovered Bret's unfaithfulness, she had been alone every night.

To keep from dwelling on her loneliness, Electra curled up in bed and began reading Carter's script.

By three o'clock the following afternoon Electra was ready for Saul's arrival. She had found Carter's play an intriguing and poignant love story. Knowing Carter as she did, Electra suspected that some of it must be autobiographical, and she felt a jealous jab at whoever the innocent young Mary might be in real life. She was still amazed that Carter possessed such a sensitive soul, and she was definitely suspicious that his sullen, half-barbaric attitude had been no more than a thorough job of acting.

Had they all lied to her, and had she been so gullible as to be taken in by their deceit? This script was proof that Carter Symmons was more than he had seemed to be. And Bret. She had loved Bret and had never guessed that he saw her only as a meal ticket and that he had a younger lover on the side. She blamed herself for not having learned the lesson from Robert that men were not to be trusted. She had never yet found an honest one.

She belted her garnet silk shirtwaist dress and spread the full gathered skirt so it gracefully covered her petticoat. The lines were flattering, accenting her small waist, slender legs and curving breasts. The vibrant color complemented the dramatic contrast between her ivory skin and ebony hair. She wondered, as she slipped on her garnet heels, why she was going to so much trouble to dress attractively when she had sworn off men and was almost positive Saul wasn't interested in another intimate relationship with a woman.

Her phone rang. She knew it was Saul. Drawing a calming breath, she answered it and told him she would come down and meet him in the lobby. Not wanting to keep him waiting, she quickly shrugged into a boxy black and white plaid coat with three-quarter-length sleeves, tucked her red purse and the script under her arm, and pulled on her black kid gloves as she left the apartment.

Saul was waiting for her across from the elevator. He was wearing navy slacks and a shirt with blue and fawn stripes beneath a stone-color cardigan sweater. Electra couldn't help but think it was a shame that such a handsome man wasn't interested in women. As she stepped off the elevator, Saul came forward to greet her.

"I read the script," she said as she handed it to him. "I liked it."

"Then you'll invest in it? Good. You won't be sorry."

"Yes. But remember, Carter is not to know I'm the angel."

"I won't breathe a word. Now that our business is done, let's be on our way."

The day was as perfect as an autumn day could be. The air was crisp without being cold or soggy, and the sky was deep blue with puffballs of white clouds. The ride to Battery Park was surprisingly quick, since the Saturday traffic was light.

At the ferry landing they mingled with the crowd of tourists waiting to board the boat.

Less than fifteen minutes later, Electra and Saul boarded the ferry and Saul guided her to the stern railing. As the boat pulled away from the Battery, sea gulls, seemingly from out of nowhere, began trailing them in rising and falling swoops. From the attaché case Saul seemed always to have with him, he produced several slices of bread wrapped in waxed paper, half of which he handed to Electra. She stared at the bread a moment, then asked, "What are these for?"

"The birds, of course. You mean you never feed birds either? What do you do for fun?" Saul tore off a corner of a bread slice and tossed it into the air. Several gulls dived for the morsel, and the one whose timing was best caught it and gulped it down, then rejoined the flock.

What *did* she do for fun? Electra wondered that herself. She enjoyed drawing designs for clothes, but that hardly constituted fun. She liked to visit with Zoe and her other friends, but sitting around smoking and drinking wasn't all that stimulating. She was rather taken aback when she realized she did nothing that really fit into the "fun" category. She pulled off a piece of bread and tossed it up in imitation of Saul. Even as the bread was rising, it was plucked out of the air—lunch for another greedy gull.

As they approached the coppery green Statue of Liberty, Electra breathed deeply of the salty air. She had seen the statue from a distance many times, but she had never been to Liberty Island. She wondered why that was; certainly she had spent enough spare hours in this town to have done this before now. She glanced at Saul who had obviously been on this ride before but who seemed to be thoroughly enjoying himself. He didn't seem to care if he looked like a tourist. Saul knew how to make the anonymity of New York work for him. She looked about at her fellow passengers. If they recognized her, they gave no indication of it. Electra felt more freedom here on this ferry with Saul than she ever had away from Willowbrook.

After docking at Liberty Island, they strolled around the base of the huge statue. Everywhere cameras were clicking and children were dashing about. Many of the people were conversing in foreign tongues. Electra felt a rush of patriotism when she gazed up at the statue's placid features. Saul reached into his attaché and brought out two bags of peanuts, one of which he gave to Electra.

"For the pigeons?" she asked.

"No, for you."

Electra laughed as she ate the roasted peanuts, not giving a thought to the calories packed into each nut. Something about being with Saul Feldman liberated her, not just physically but mentally, as well. "You come here often, don't you?"

"Sure. I like being outside. My father used to bring me here regularly. Both my parents immigrated to America, and the Lady had almost a religious meaning to them. I heard the story dozens of times about what they thought the first time they saw her. She was a part of my childhood that was important to me. During the war I often remembered walking here as a child and looking up at her. It helped me keep up my courage." He laughed. "I guess you think that's corny."

Electra shook her head. "I wasn't thinking that at all. As a matter of fact, she makes me feel the same way."

Saul only smiled. He didn't know how much she needed courage. To her surprise, he reached out and took her hand. After an instant's hesitation, Electra closed her fingers around his, but had hardly done so when he released her again. She was puzzled, but dared not look directly at him. Was he wanting more intimacy with her, or wasn't he? And why did she care one way or another?

"Do you want to climb up to the crown?" he asked.

She craned her neck to stare at the crown, high above them. "In these heels? You must be joking."

"Next time wear flats. And maybe jeans." He winked at her.

She couldn't tell if he was teasing or serious, and unexpectedly she felt self-conscious. She was standing here in full sunlight—the same sunlight that was notorious for exposing otherwise invisible wrinkles and age spots—and until now she had been careful to meet men indoors where the lighting was kinder. With Saul, however, she hadn't given it a thought. "You're teasing me," she said defensively.

"Actually, I wasn't. I think you'd look cute in tight jeans."

Electra stopped in her tracks and frankly stared at him.

Saul grinned. "That time I was teasing." When she started walking again he added, "What I meant was I think you'd look damned beautiful, not cute."

She felt her mouth drop open, but he was already on another subject.

"Look at that," he marveled as he stared at the skyline. "Don't you wish you had invented concrete? You'd never have to sew a seam again."

Electra looked across the water at the mountains of concrete and steel and glass. "I could certainly retire to Willowbrook," she agreed. "In fact I would never have had to leave it."

"But then we wouldn't be here together," he pointed out, "and that would be a shame."

"Would it?" she asked. "We hardly know each other."

"It's all relative. Sometimes you meet a stranger and you know him better than you know some of your friends. You know what I mean, don't you?"

"No, I don't."

He looked at her. "No? I could have sworn that had happened to you. When we met for instance."

"That was nearly eighteen years ago!" she protested. "Before the war. Why, I'll bet we haven't seen each other a dozen times all together!"

"I know," he said confidently. "Some people have to work at a relationship, and with others it's just as natural as breathing."

"And with others it doesn't happen at all," she retorted. "You and I fit into the latter category."

"No, we don't. I know you felt exactly what I did the night we met. I remember it in detail. You had on a shiny red dress, and I kept a drunk from spilling a drink on you."

"How do you remember that? That evening you couldn't even remember what color dress your own wife was wearing, as I recall."

"See? I knew you remembered."

Electra abruptly closed her mouth. It would seem she did indeed remember. "That doesn't mean a thing," she said at last.

Saul stepped closer to her. Before she knew what he was about to do, he pulled her into his arms and kissed her. Electra felt her lips part beneath his, meeting his passion in kind, and when he released her she felt as dizzy as a schoolgirl. She was aware that people were staring and grinning at them, but she ignored them. "I thought you were . . ." She caught herself in time.

"Because I didn't go home with you last night?" He not only seemed to intuit what she had been about to say, but didn't seem offended by it. "You're wrong."

He took her hand again and this time he held it firmly and in a way she couldn't mistake. She could feel the heat from his palm tingle all the way up her arm.

"Everybody doesn't go around doing the same things in the same way," he explained. "I want to be your friend, Electra, as well as your lover."

"My friend," she stated, disbelief evident in her voice.

"It is possible, you know. Men and women can be friends, and they can enjoy each other on more than one level." He smiled at her. "I want more from our relationship than an affair, and I want it to grow into something that will last."

"Oh? Then what was all that last night about not wanting to get married again? I don't think you know what you want."

"Everything doesn't have to be black or white," he said. "Right now I have no intention of remarrying."

"But you just said—"

"I also have no intention of being a one-night stand."

Electra's temper flared as she thought of her own numerous one-night stands. "You really have a nerve! Of all the—"

"Calm down, Electra. I'm trying to say I have more respect for you than that."

Unabashedly she stared at him. How long had it been since a man had respected her? She felt a foolish urge to burst into tears. Could it be that Saul honestly didn't know of her numerous lovers, each younger than the one before? Electra felt a deep sense of shame. She hadn't experienced that emotion since she turned the tables on Robert Hastings so many years ago.

"I think I need to go home," she said in a strained voice.

Saul drew her back and quietly said, "We have a lot of friends in common besides Zoe."

He knew. Electra's eyes narrowed defensively.

"I knew the night we met that there would be something between us," he went on. "At the time I didn't see how that could be, but now I'm single and here you are. We can make it be anything we choose for it to be—friendship, an affair, maybe both. What do you say?"

"I say you're as mad as a march hare, and I'm getting out of here!"

But all the way home she thought about what he had said, and when he walked her to her door, she let him kiss her again. This time she didn't ask him to come in. She needed time to think. She had never before met anyone like Saul Feldman.

CHAPTER 19

ELECTRA LEANED OVER HER DRAWING TABLE and penciled in a full skirt. After a brief hesitation she sketched a sleeveless V-neck top. She had a feeling jumpers would become fashionable in the coming year, and her instincts toward fashion were rarely wrong.

Pausing in her work she gazed out the window. The sky was a dull pewter color, and rain had been falling steadily for several hours. Winter was on its way—the season Electra liked the least. Winter not only meant freezing legs between the door and the taxi, but that time had run out for designing and sewing the next season's fashions. Her two major shows, spring and fall, were complete except for a few hems and the addition of some beadwork. Her TV style show was another matter.

Electra didn't know of any other designer who had had the inspiration to book a style show for television. In the first place there was the problem of color. Although many broadcasts were done in color, the colors on individual TV sets would likely all be different, and what model with green skin could wear anything that would look appealing? The announcer would have to describe not only the style but the subtleties of colors in terms most people could understand. Then there was the matter of price. Most of the people who would watch the show couldn't begin to pay her designer prices. For that reason Electra was aiming the show at her teen market. Since the entire show couldn't revolve around jeans and blouses, she had to work up some dresses as well. The dresses would have to be casual enough for school and be made of fabrics that could be laundered. After so many years of designing in luxurious materials for women of high fashion, Electra was hard pressed to switch to casual dresses.

She looked back at her sketch and drew in a turtleneck sweater. What color should the ensemble be? This year the most stylish color had been green. A pity, really, since it was a color that didn't work with most complexions. Electra penciled in "charcoal gray corduroy" beside the jumper and "pale pink" for the sweater. She made a few more cryptic notes in the margin, which Mary and Lois would have no difficulty interpreting after their years of practice, then pulled out a fresh sheet of paper.

She did several quick sketches of sweater sets, some round-necked, some modest V lines, even a couple with boat necks and turtlenecks. The sweaters worn next to the body were all short-sleeved, the cardigans all long-sleeved. She chose the best of the sketches and began drawing in finer detail. She made a note that the collar made of the new mouton would be detachable so it could be worn over the plain neck of a different sweater for added interest.

On another sheet of paper she worked up a finished drawing of the more basic round-necked set, which was a staple of all teen girls' wardrobes. Most owned several sweater sets in a rainbow of colors. The trick was to make this set different from the others, yet alike enough to fit the teenagers' need for conformity.

Electra drew in a butterfly on the top sweater. She was sorely tempted to have Lois sew it in her exquisite beadwork, but this would drive the price well above the range of her customers' pocketbooks. She made a more detailed sketch of a butterfly in one corner of the page and a note to have a number of these appliqués reproduced. After a moment's thought she added instructions to make the butterflies in three sizes. She would put butterflies on all the sweaters as if they had paused there in flight. On the sketch sheet she drew butterflies near the waist ribbing on one sweater, on the shoulder of another. She even drew a large appliquéd one on the skirt of the jumper, reminiscent of the poodle skirts of several years back. She made a note to place several scatter pins of enameled butterflies on the sweater's turtleneck.

Satisfied, Electra sat back in her chair. This gave her several new ideas she could draw up on Monday. A glance at her watch told her half the morning was already gone. On Saturdays she often came in to work practically at dawn. It was her way of combating loneliness. This day was too dreary, however, for her to spend the rest of it alone.

On impulse she dialed Saul Feldman's number. "Saul? How would you like to go to Willowbrook with me? Yes, I mean today. We can catch the noon flight. No, I'm not kidding." She paused while he made up his mind. "Great. Meet me at the airport at eleven-fifteen."

She hung up and drew a deep breath. For several days she had tried to sort out how she felt about Saul but had been unable to reach a conclusion. Maybe taking him to

Willowbrook would help. She then called Amelia to tell her to expect them for supper. After a moment's hesitation she added that Helga should prepare two rooms.

So far she and Saul had not become lovers, and he seemed to be in no hurry to make that commitment. Electra simply couldn't figure him out.

Amelia was perplexed by Electra's phone call. Two rooms? The few visitors she had brought to Willowbrook had been young men, and they had stayed in Electra's room. Amelia never made any attempt to hide her disapproval of such improprieties. Perhaps, she thought, this guest was a woman. Based on Electra's history, that was all that made sense. It seemed doubtful that she was finally beginning to act her age.

With Helga's hands full with cooking supper and cleaning, Amelia took it upon herself to put clean sheets on the beds. Helga was also developing arthritis in her knees, and the stairs were difficult for her, although she rarely complained. Amelia had her own share of aches and twinges, but she paid them little heed.

Since she had forgotten to ask Electra if her guest was a man or a woman, and wasn't certain her guess was correct, Amelia put the rose sheets on Electra's bed and the white ones in the guest room.

Willowbrook had long ago returned to normal, but at times Amelia recalled what it had been like when the rooms were filled with convalescing soldiers. This had been the room for the burn cases. The wheelchair patients had had to use the lower floor. If she closed her eyes and concentrated, she could almost hear the men's voices, especially the one they called Mack. He had been recovering from wounds that would leave him crippled for life, but he always had a joke to tell or something to say that would make the others laugh. She wondered where he was these days and whether he was still alive. A few of the soldiers had sent her Christmas cards at first, but gradually they had become immersed in their civilian lives, and the cards had trickled to a stop.

Amelia spread the sheets tight across the bed, automatically making the hospital corners, as she had been taught. The sheets were old, but still serviceable. Her mother had told her to buy the best in linens because they would last far longer than the cheaper brands. Evidently she had been right, because the sheet was worn so soft it felt like silk, but the fabric was still strong.

Over the sheet she spread two matching green blankets. None of her family had done much quilting. It hadn't been considered dignified. Amelia was the exception. At times Helga stayed to watch television when one of them was feeling lonely, and Helga, who had embraced everything American, had taught Amelia to quilt. Most of their joint efforts had been sent to Helga's nieces and nephews in Germany. When Amelia first realized she enjoyed hand sewing, the idea made her laugh aloud, because as a girl she had been such a tomboy and had vowed that she would always have more interesting things to do than sew. How naive she'd been.

The bedding had the powdery floral scent Amelia favored in her perfume. In her younger years, she had begun making linen sachets from the flowers in her garden. Now it was a custom of long standing.

She spread the white counterpane over the bed and tucked it under the pillows. Who was Electra bringing down? Likely a woman this time. Amelia wished she had thought to ask her. At times she was forgetful of the simplest things.

Between Amelia's and Helga's efforts, the house was shining clean by the time the cab pulled up out front. Amelia opened the door and stepped out to greet them. Beside Electra stood a man Amelia had never seen before. He wasn't much taller than Electra, and to her amazement he appeared to be about her age. Amelia's apprehension about this visit began lifting. The man was handsome, but he wasn't like the pretty young men Electra usually brought with her. Maybe, Amelia dared speculate, Electra had finally met The One.

The cab drove away and Electra preceded the man up the steps. "Amelia, this a friend of mine, Saul Feldman. Saul, this is Amelia."

Amelia held out her hand to shake his. "Welcome to Willowbrook, Mr. Feldman."

"Please, call me Saul. You have a beautiful home." His voice was rich and deep, his smile warm.

"Thank you. Won't you come in?" It was enjoyable to meet someone old enough to have been taught manners like her own. Amelia beamed at Electra to show her approval.

"I thought we would never get here," Electra said. "We hit air pockets all the way. And the rain! It's coming down by the bucketful between here and New York."

Amelia glanced at the sky. "We've had nice weather here. Maybe you want to walk in the gardens and stretch your legs."

"Not yet. First we have to get inside." Electra gave her sister a probing look.

"Well, of course you do. Just put your suitcases there by the stairs, Mr. . . . Saul. Helga will carry them up."

Helga had come into the foyer and Saul, seeing her age, said, "I don't mind taking them up. Where should I put them?"

"My room is the second door on the right," Electra said.

"I've made up the green room for you," Amelia added quickly. "It's across the hall from Electra's."

As Saul took the luggage upstairs, Amelia leaned toward Electra and whispered, "I like the looks of this one."

"Hush!" Electra murmured back. "He'll hear you." As soon as she was sure Saul was out of earshot she said, "We're just friends. As I said, New York is dismal this weekend. I invited him on the spur of the moment."

Amelia nodded and smiled. She didn't believe a word of it. This was the first man of an appropriate age she had seen with Electra in years. "I hope he likes baked ham. That's what Helga is making, baked ham." Suddenly her eyes widened in alarm. "Did you say his name is Feldman? Maybe he can't eat pork! Oh, dear!"

"Relax. He's not religious." Electra was walking in the parlor and looking about with obvious relish. "God, I miss this place. You don't know how lucky you are not to have to leave it."

"I sometimes wish I could," Amelia hinted. "You know, to travel. Jenny says she and Carleton plan to send their oldest daughter on a trip to Europe when she graduates from college. Wouldn't that be nice?"

"All young people seem to go to college these days," Electra mused. "It's not like when we were growing up, when most girls just got married instead. I never missed it, personally."

"I wanted to go," Amelia admitted.

"You did? You never mentioned it."

"I knew we couldn't afford it at the time, and after that there never seemed to be an opportunity." Amelia thought she had long since buried that resentment, but some remnant of it remained. If she had gone to college, she would have had to travel at least a little way, as there wasn't a college then in Catawba Mills and she could have refused to go to the one in Charlottesville. Maybe, she thought, the travel was the main reason why she had wanted to go to college.

"We all have some regrets," Electra pointed out. She went to the end table and gazed down at it.

Amelia remembered the Fabergé egg that used to sit there. She had noticed it was missing after Electra brought down that last young man. Bret, that had been his name. Amelia was positive he had stolen it, but she hadn't mentioned it. Electra would probably have accused her of misplacing it and of falsely blaming Bret. Now she noticed Electra was noting its absence, and she almost hoped Electra would ask where it was. She didn't.

Saul came into the room and smiled at Amelia. "This is the most beautiful house I've ever visited. I hope it was no imposition for me to show up at the last minute."

"No, no. None at all. Why, when we were growing up we had people in and out of here all the time. Papa used to threaten to put in revolving doors," Amelia said with a laugh. "It's much too quiet these days."

Electra gave her a wry look. "You just don't appreciate it. You should try to keep up with the rat race every day. Traffic and people everywhere, and the noise!" To Saul she said, "When I first get here each time my ears ring from all the silence."

He laughed. To Amelia he said, "Electra has told me so much about you, but you aren't at all the way I pictured you."

"Oh?" Amelia wondered what Electra had said and whether this disparity was a compliment.

"You look nothing alike," he said in explanation. "I expected you two to bear more resemblance to each other."

"I suppose you're right," Amelia said with a look at her sister. Electra's black hair, slim body, and elegant clothes were a far cry from Amelia, who wore black slacks with her shirttail out to minimize her weight and whose long gray hair was pinned up in a bun. "We both have the Radcliff eyes. Electra took after Mother, and I look like Papa."

"You must have had handsome parents," Saul gallantly commented.

Amelia gave Electra an I-told-you-so smile because Electra was staring pointedly at Amelia's waistline. It was none of Electra's business if she preferred desserts to dieting, and she hoped Electra wouldn't take it upon herself to lecture her again this time.

Saul breathed in deeply. "Is that a Virginia ham I smell?"

Amelia nodded.

"Great! I haven't had ham all week."

Amelia relaxed. "I'll go give Helga a hand. Why don't you two walk in the rose garden until we get the food on the table."

Electra and Saul went out onto the porch. "Looks as if we should go for a walk whether we feel like it or not," she said.

"It's clouding up. If we don't get out now, we may not have a chance later." As they went down the steps he said, "I don't think I've ever seen two sisters who look less alike."

"It's her hair," Electra told him. "It went gray the year her husband was killed in the war—almost overnight, as a matter of fact. I suppose it was a combination of shock and grief, although they hadn't been married very long."

"Sometimes that's harder."

"I never thought he was right for her. Anyway, I've tried to persuade her to dye it or at least cut it short, but I can't tell her a thing. Now I see she's started wearing slacks!"

"That's okay these days. You should know that better than anyone."

"We're moving toward a youth culture," Electra argued. "In a few years anyone over thirty will be considered ancient. That's why I can't understand her reluctance to fix herself up."

"I like her hair," Saul surprised her by saying.

"You do?"

"Yes, I do. She is obviously over thirty, and I see no reason for her to pretend otherwise. There's nothing wrong with growing old." He caught a lock of his gray hair between his fingers and tugged. "See these? I earned every one of them. I was telling someone that the other day, that every gray hair on my head is inscribed with the date of a performance or the name of a would-be actor. These are my battle ribbons."

"That's fine for a man, especially a director. It's different with women."

"It shouldn't be." Saul shook his head as if this was indeed a perplexing problem. "It just shouldn't be. Take you, for instance. When your hair finally goes white, you're going to be even more beautiful than you are now. You'll be spectacular."

"The George Washington Bridge is spectacular," she retorted. "I'd rather be twenty again and beautiful."

"Well," he said as he looked down at one of the last roses of the season, "we all would rather have that. But we can't, so there's no use whining about it."

Electra stared at him. Saul was unlike anyone she had ever met before.

The next morning when Amelia came downstairs she found Electra in the breakfast room alone. Amelia asked her, "Are you going to marry him?"

"Marry him! Of course not." Electra was so accustomed to working early in the morning that she found it impossible to sleep late. "Where did you get an idea like that?" She took an English muffin off the plate of breakfast breads and began to eat it without butter.

"He's so different from all those others." Amelia reached for another blueberry muffin and began buttering it. "How old is he? About fifty? He reminds me of someone. Doesn't he you?"

"No, and I have no idea how old he is. It's not a thing you ask a person."

"Well, I think you should marry him. It's obvious he likes Willowbrook."

"What if he does? We couldn't live here, even if we did want to get married, which we most certainly don't. Saul is a director. A very successful one. He could no more live here than I can."

"But you will retire someday, won't you? Someday soon? You're already fifty-four, you know. Don't people usually retire at fifty-five?"

"A few do, but most company retirement plans don't begin until age sixty-five, which is what I have set up for my employees. As for myself, I haven't even thought about retirement. After all, I'm only now reaching my peak." She frowned at the butter on Amelia's muffin. "Besides, if I were to retire, who would feed and clothe you?"

"Papa always said it was good business sense to put money in the bank so you could live off the interest. You've been doing that, haven't you?"

"Of course I have a savings account," Electra snapped. "But the interest isn't enough to support a house of this size or to pay the staff required to run it."

Amelia ate the muffin and ignored Electra's grimace as she reached for another one. "I wish I could remember who it is he reminds me of."

"Who?"

"Saul, of course. Don't you just hate it when some memory or another is just barely out of reach? I do."

"My memory is perfect, thank you."

"What sort of plays does Saul direct? Comedies? Mysteries?"

"All kinds. He's extremely talented. At the moment he's rehearsing a drama called *Mary's Promise*." Electra almost laughed as she added, "You'll never guess who wrote it—Carter Symmons."

"I don't know any Symmons."

"Yes, you do. You met him before the war. He came down with me the weekend you told me you wanted to marry Christopher."

"Him? The one who ate with his elbows on the table and didn't seem to own a tie?"

"That's the one."

"Whoever would have thought he could write a play?" Amelia marveled. "I'd have been willing to bet he didn't know the alphabet."

"He wasn't that bad," Electra retorted defensively.

Amelia became silent as she recalled that weekend. It had been one of the worst in her life. As it had turned out, she could have married Christopher as they had first planned and had those extra months with him. Her eyes brightened. That was who Saul reminded her of! Christopher! Not physically, of course, but his personality.

She shot a sideways glance at Electra. Did she see the similarity? Surely not or she would have dropped Saul like a hot rock. She had hated Christopher on sight. Amelia restrained her smile. She certainly wasn't going to point the likeness out to Electra. If she did, Electra might never see him again. She could hardly wait to go out to the garden to tell Christopher about it.

"You look like the cat that swallowed the canary," Electra observed with a wary tilt of her head. "What's on your mind?"

"I was thinking how nice it would be if you married Saul," Amelia said to bait her. "We could have the ceremony here in the parlor."

"For God's sake," Electra grumbled, "don't start on that again."

"You have to admit he's different. He even sleeps in another room."

"How would you know?" Electra retorted. "Maybe he slipped across the hall during the night."

"If he did, he slipped back again, because the door to your room was open when I came downstairs. Your bed was empty."

Electra glowered at her. "Why should it matter to you if I get married or not?"

"Of course it matters! I want you to be happy, to have someone to take care of you as you grow older."

"I'm far from senile, and I don't need anyone to take care of me." Electra spoke as if the notion were absurd. "If anyone needs a keeper, it's you. I saw you going out to that garden of yours last night, and it was misting rain."

Amelia didn't deny it. She had gone out to tell Christopher that Electra was home and had brought an adult male with her this time. "You've never been married. You don't know the pleasures of having a husband."

"Oh, no? I'll bet I do."

Amelia's expression was an odd mixture of scorn and sympathy. "That's entirely different. I think it's sad the way you live."

"You do, do you! And how did you get to be such an expert on married life? You and Christopher were only married a few short weeks before he was shipped overseas."

"True, but they were the happiest weeks of my life! Christopher loved me. Really loved me! If he had come home . . ."

"You have no way of knowing what would have happened if he had." Electra's eyes flashed with anger, reminding Amelia of icy daggers. "He might have left you for . . . for someone else." She pulled back as if she was sorry she had said too much.

"No, he wouldn't," Amelia said, her own voice tight from provocation. "That's the difference in a couple who are really and truly married to each other. A lot of people go through the motions—with or without a proper ceremony," she added pointedly. "But Christopher and I were like parts of the same puzzle. We fit together in our hopes and plans and love, and there wasn't any room left for a third person to come between us."

"Hogwash!"

"Elegantly stated," Amelia said as she rose with dignity from the table, "but wrong as usual." She turned and stalked out of the room.

There was only one place for Amelia to go where Electra wouldn't follow her. Once she was inside her private garden, Amelia paced and stewed over their argument. Because of the rain the night before the bench beneath the willow was too wet to sit on. Besides, she hadn't stopped to get her sweater and moving around helped dispel the cold.

"She has certainly become bad-tempered in her old age," Amelia muttered. "Imagine her even suggesting you might have left me for another woman!" The breeze touched her face gently, and Amelia felt some of her anger dissipate.

"I wish you could meet Saul. I finally figured out who he reminds me of—you! No, I won't breathe a word of it to Electra. As mean as she is these days she might bite my head off. You know she would never see him again. I feel sorry for him in a way. Electra has become so brash after living in New York."

At once Amelia felt a twinge of guilt. She had been brought up to know it was rude to call people brash, even if they were. "I surely thought Electra would turn out different than she has. But then, I never expected half the things that have come about in my life—Papa dying penniless, me finding you only to lose you again."

She lifted her face as the breeze stirred again. "But I haven't really lost you, have I? If I had never felt your presence here in our garden, I think I would have lost my mind."

As her pacing slowed, her thoughts grew calmer.

After a while she heard the gate open, and she turned to find Saul standing there. "Am I intruding?" he asked. "As I opened the gate I thought I heard you talking to someone."

"You aren't disturbing me." Breaking one of her own rules, she invited him in.

"Electra seems upset, and I thought something might be wrong."

"Electra is frequently upset when she comes to Willowbrook. We've never been close, you see. I suppose Electra and I are as different as two people can be who have grown up in the same family."

"She's a complicated person," Saul admitted.

"But you like her?"

"I like her a great deal." He looked around the garden. "What a wonderful place. Did you plant it or was it here before?"

"A little of both. Do you like gardens?"

"I've never had one. I've lived in New York all my life."

"This one is special to me," Amelia said as they walked along the brick path. "I bring all my problems out here. Also all my triumphs and sorrows. Christopher and I met here."

"Christopher?"

"My husband. He was killed in the war."

"I'm sorry."

Amelia gave him a smile but didn't try to explain that he had come back to her, in a manner of speaking.

"Actually we knew each other as children, but we hadn't seen each other in years. It was as if we were meeting for the first time. We were married over there by the willow tree. In a way I feel as if it happened yesterday."

"I know what you mean. I have memories like that, too."

"And in other ways it's as if I've known him forever."

"It's too bad he didn't come home."

"What?" Amelia realized she had been talking too freely. "Yes. A shame." She went back toward the gate. "We should go back to the house and put Electra in a better mood."

Electra was watching from the window when Amelia and Saul came out of the garden. At once she was torn by jealous suspicion. Was Amelia trying to steal Saul away? Electra would have thought it was impossible if it wasn't for the way Saul had admired her the evening before. Although she didn't admit it even to herself, Electra was still smarting with jealousy over hearing Amelia say that Christopher would never have looked at another woman.

When Amelia and Saul entered the house, Electra said, "You two look like long lost friends. Were you actually in the walled garden?"

"Amelia was showing it to me," Saul explained. "In the summer it must be terrific."

"Actually spring is its best season," Amelia said.

"I wouldn't know." Electra reached for the ashtray. "Amelia rarely lets me go into it. As far as I know, she no longer shows it to anybody." There, she thought. Let Saul see that Amelia has set her cap for him and then see how fast he runs.

Saul was looking at Amelia. "I had no idea. I'm flattered."

"I'm not quite as bad as Electra thinks. My friend Jenny has been in the garden as well as an occasional workman. But it's true I only ask special people to see it."

"We should go," Electra said abruptly. "There's a flight out in an hour."

"So soon?" Amelia protested. "Helga has already put a roast on for dinner."

"We need to leave now," Electra firmly reiterated. "I have a dozen things I need to do and some sketches to finish for tomorrow."

Saul looked confused but he nodded. "I'm afraid Electra is right. I hadn't planned to be gone this weekend, and there are things I should be doing, too." He smiled at her. "I've enjoyed my visit. Thank you for having me."

"My pleasure." Amelia returned his smile.

Electra lit a cigarette and shot a stream of smoke toward the ceiling. Amelia and Saul certainly seemed close all of a sudden. What had they been talking about in that damned garden? She hated to feel jealous. For some reason Amelia could trigger it in her when no one else could.

She glanced at Saul. She should never have brought him here. She wasn't even sure why she had. They weren't lovers, and he seemed so determined to be her friend that she wasn't sure they ever would be. Saul was much too confusing. Now that Amelia had brought it up, he did remind her of someone, but she couldn't for the life of her figure out who it was.

She decided it would be in her best interest to forget Saul ever becoming her lover and to find someone less complicated. Someone who wouldn't have such an emotional impact on her life.

CHAPTER 20

TRUST NOT BEING PARAMOUNT IN HER RELA-
tionships with men, Electra decided to attend Saul's auditions for *Mary's Promise* to make sure Bret Harley didn't
get a part. His play was scheduled to run several more weeks,
but Saul's rehearsals weren't scheduled to begin for two
weeks. She had heard of actors double-booking themselves
on the assumption they would be free by the time they were
needed to rehearse the new play. Bret was amateur enough
to try this. She also wanted to be sure Jody Kemp wasn't
cast. She felt small-minded for being so vengeful toward a
woman whom she had never met and who almost certainly
didn't know of her affair with Bret, but Electra couldn't
deny her hurt feelings.

She waved at Saul when she entered the theater, but
chose to sit at a distance from him because he was working
and needed all his concentration. Taking a seat in the back,
she settled down to watch. On the front row she saw a man
who resembled her memories of Carter Symmons. She
hoped he wouldn't look back and see her. It wasn't likely
that he would unless he came up the aisle.

Nearly an hour into the auditions, a young man eased into the seat beside Electra, and she glanced at him and nodded a hello. He was probably in his early twenties and had a Nordic handsomeness of the type that Electra found appealing. His blond hair was cut shorter on the sides than most youths seemed to prefer, but he wore the tight, faded jeans and body-hugging T-shirt that were the trademarks of his peers.

"Mind if I sit here?" he asked.

She inclined her head in silent agreement. She could feel his vitality even though several inches separated them.

"I'm Troy Summers," he murmured in a low voice so he wouldn't disturb the others. "You're Electra, aren't you?"

She nodded, her interest piqued. "How do you know who I am?"

"I heard someone backstage talking about you. I hear you're a backer for this show." His piercing gaze sent a tingle up her spine. "Do you have a last name?"

"Of course, but I never use it."

"So does that mean you aren't married?"

"It wouldn't matter if I were, but no, I'm not." She appraised him more carefully. In a suit, he would be strikingly handsome. "Are you married?"

He grinned, his teeth white and straight. "Not me. I've never met a woman like you before."

Electra allowed just a hint of a smile onto her lips. He was good at this game. "There aren't many women like me."

"How about if we get out of here and go somewhere for a drink?"

"What about your audition?"

He shrugged. "I've done one reading. He can call my

answering service if he wants me." His sultry blue eyes traveled over her body in an undeniably suggestive manner. "Or maybe you could put in a word for me with Feldman."

"No, I won't do that. If you want a part, you should go back with the other actors and read again."

"I'll take my chances," he said with a wink.

As Electra stood and preceded him out of the theater, she considered mentioning his name to Saul, then decided against it. She didn't want it said that she backed shows in order to provide vehicles for her young men. She had heard that said about Zoe Wharton, and it wasn't flattering. Besides, she had no idea whether Troy could act or whether he was right for a part.

There was no doubt, however, about his looks. If he could act at all, Electra thought he would go a long way. He exuded sexual magnetism.

She considered Saul and what he would think if she had an affair with this young actor. At once she frowned. Why should it make a difference to her what Saul would think? He had no hold over her. She wasn't even sure he cared for her at all other than as a friend.

"I have a better idea," she said as they stepped out into the sunlight. "Let's go to my place, and I'll make you one of my specialties."

Troy grinned and whistled for a cab.

By the next morning Electra was congratulating herself on her choice of a lover. Troy had proved to be as good in bed as she had hoped he would be. She stretched her lissome body and molded it against his. Expectantly she raised her head, but found he was still fast asleep.

She slipped out of bed and reached for her robe, feeling

past the age where she could comfortably walk around naked.

She closed the bathroom door behind her and surveyed her reflection in the mirror. The night before she had left on her makeup in order to look her best, but their lovemaking had smudged her mascara into dark circles beneath her eyes. After locking the door behind her to ensure her privacy, Electra removed her makeup with cold cream. Without it she looked older and more vulnerable. Having seen too much already, Electra looked away from the mirror and turned on the shower.

By the time Troy began stirring, Electra had made up her face, combed her hair, and dressed in black slacks and a red and white sweater. She rarely wore slacks, but today she felt too youthful for hose and heels. "Get up, sleepyhead. It's a beautiful day."

Troy squinted up at her and dropped his head back onto the pillow. "Oh, God. I feel as if I've been run over by a truck."

Electra laughed and pulled the covers off him. "Take your shower while I make us some breakfast. There's a razor in the medicine cabinet and shampoo in the shower." She leaned over and playfully patted his bare buttocks. "Nice view." With another laugh she left the room.

As she poached them each an egg and toasted English muffins, she could hear the shower running. She wondered where he lived and whether he would want to stop by there to change into fresh clothes. Not that he had been dressed all that long the day before.

The shower stopped, and she pictured him using one of her thick white towels to dry his body. She was tempted to go in and offer to do it for him, but if she did, they would probably end up in bed again. Electra smiled. They would make love again; she was sure of that. But later. After they had walked together in the park and she had thoroughly enjoyed this exhilaration she was feeling. Every time she took a new young lover it was as though she had found the fountain of youth.

Thoughts of Saul came into her mind, and she wondered if he had seen her leave the theater with Troy. She hoped he had. A little jealousy was good for a man. Besides, she thought defensively, she and Saul weren't lovers, and for all she knew he had a woman on the side. Saul wasn't a man to be ruled by his passions, but she knew him well enough by now to know he was no eunuch.

She heard a muffled voice and realized Troy was using the extension in the bedroom. Who could he be calling this early in the morning? He had no wife. Perhaps, she reasoned, he was calling the theater to see if he was to return for another reading. Each director had his own system for auditions, and she wasn't sure if Saul handled them in this way or not. Certainly it was too soon for him to have posted the names of the cast.

Knowing it was none of her business, but overcome by her curiosity, Electra pushed open the bedroom door to find Troy engaged in an intense conversation. When he realized she was there, he jerked up his head and gave her a wary look.

"Breakfast is ready." Alarm bells were going off in her head. Who had he been calling for him to look so guilty?

Troy said an abrupt good-bye and hung up the phone. He wore only a towel around his hips and his hair was damp from the shower. "My roommate," he said. "I was telling my roommate that I won't be home until later."

"You have to check in with your roommate?"

"Yeah, well, Mike worries. He thought something had happened to me when I didn't come home."

"You could have called him last night." Electra felt a wave of relief to hear his roommate wasn't a woman. "I wouldn't have minded."

Troy grinned at her and winked. "I had more important things on my mind last night."

She smiled. "Get dressed. Your breakfast is getting cold."

To Electra it was a huge breakfast, accustomed as she was to only a cup of coffee. Troy looked around as if he was still hungry even after she toasted him an extra muffin. "We'll have an early lunch," she promised. "The day is too beautiful to waste."

Central Park was full of people who had the same idea as Electra. She had hoped to find some privacy, but there were people everywhere. Troy didn't seem to mind. He strolled beside her with his arm draped around her shoulder, as if he wanted everyone to see they were a couple. Whenever they passed an elm tree he gave her a kiss and told her with mock earnestness that it was good luck to do so. Electra was happier than she had been since Bret left her life. Troy was sexy and exciting, and she thought he might already be halfway in love with her. She didn't even worry about having relaxed her rule about being seen in the sunlight. Age was a phantom that didn't exist when two people were lovers.

When they grew tired of the park, they walked down the street, window-shopping. Troy had a boyish excitement that kept Electra smiling. As thrilled as he was at everything he saw, she thought he must not have been in town long.

"Where are you from?" she asked.

He tightened his arm and hugged her as if she were too precious to be taken for granted. "Saint Louis. I'll bet you grew up here in Manhattan."

"You lose. I'm from Catawba Mills, Virginia."

Troy grinned. "So it's true what they say about southern women being hot to trot."

"I never thought of myself in quite those terms."

He ignored passersby and kissed her on the forehead. "Look over there. Now, that's one good-looking suit!"

She followed his gaze to a navy suit with narrow pin-stripes. "You would look wonderful in that."

He laughed and shook his head. "I can't afford anything that nice. With my income, I have to shop at Sears."

She wrinkled her nose. "You have to buy the best in clothes. First impressions are terribly important for an actor. Come on inside and I'll buy it for you."

"What? Why, I can't let you do that." He put his arm around her and gave her a brief hug. "It sure looks great, though." His voice was filled with longing.

Electra winked and put her arm around his waist. "Nonsense. I insist."

After a weakening argument, Electra overcame his objections and they went into the store. She easily caught a clerk's eye and coolly told him Troy wanted to buy the pinstriped suit. The clerk found the suit in his size and took him away toward the dressing rooms. Electra sat on one of the sofas to wait. Buying something special for him gave her a warm feeling. She was reasonably sure he wasn't from a wealthy family.

In a few minutes he came out to show her how the suit looked. "What do you think?" he asked as he turned around for her inspection.

"It's perfect," she pronounced.

"He has excellent taste," the clerk agreed.

A woman with graying hair on the opposite end of the sofa also looked at Troy with approval, but Electra ignored her.

"What do you think about the color?" Troy asked.

"Couldn't be better," the clerk said. "It brings out the blue in your eyes."

Electra and Troy exchanged an amused look. "Do you like it?" she asked.

"I'll say! I feel like I'm ten feet tall."

She laughed. "It's yours."

As Troy and the clerk went back into the fitting area, the other woman smiled at Electra. "They grow up so fast," she said wistfully.

Electra shot her an icy glare. When the woman lowered her eyes in confused embarrassment, Electra stood and went to a cubicle stacked with men's shirts. Surely that woman hadn't mistaken Troy for Electra's son! Electra pretended to be engrossed in choosing a dress shirt to go with the suit.

By the time she had chosen two ties, Troy and the clerk had returned. Electra had him charge everything to her account, as this was a store she frequented. "We would like to pick up the suit by closing time today," she said as she signed the sales slip.

"Today?" The clerk looked doubtful until he read her signature. "Very well, madam."

"I could have waited until tomorrow for it," Troy said as they left the store. "Did you see how impressed he was at who you are?"

She smiled. Fame had its privileges. "There's no need to wait. I have somewhere I want to take you tonight."

"Tonight?" he asked doubtfully.

"Zoe Wharton is having one of her extravagant parties. If you intend to make a big splash on Broadway, it's imperative for you to get to know Zoe. More careers are made in her living room than on the stage."

"Oh? You'll introduce me to her?"

"Of course." Electra hugged him companionably. "But keep your distance. Zoe can be a shark when it comes to men like you. If you get too close, she'll eat you up."

"Well, now. That's a good idea. Would you like to eat me up, too?"

Electra laughed and matched her steps to his.

Electra knew that, as always, Zoe's party would be crowded. Electra had often teased her about planning her parties as if she lived in a mansion rather than an apartment. But Zoe's guests never seemed to mind the crowding, for the more people there were the greater the chance of rubbing elbows with a director or an agent or some other person of influence. Hopeful actors would do almost anything to get on her guest list.

"How do I look?" Troy asked nervously as he and Electra left the elevator.

"Perfectly marvelous," Electra said in an exact imitation of an actress they both knew.

Troy smiled, but Electra noticed he was still nervous. She would have thought that after making love all afternoon he would have been too tired to be anxious. She ached pleasantly from head to toe. But stamina was a small price to pay for having a lover whose skin was still tight and whose muscles were hard.

Zoe answered Electra's knock and greeted her as if they

hadn't seen each other in years. Then her eyes traveled speculatively over Troy as Electra introduced them. Troy was covering his nervousness with nonchalance, and as he smiled at Zoe, he draped his arm around Electra's shoulders.

Electra was wearing a deep red dress made of layers of chiffon. It had as full a skirt as the waistline could accommodate and transparent sleeves over the barely concealing bodice. The dress was meant to float with her movements, but with Troy's arm wrapped around her the dress didn't float, and the deep V of the neckline gaped. Electra shrugged off his arm as unobtrusively as possible.

As Zoe was asking Troy what plays he had performed in, Electra searched the crowd for familiar faces, nodding a greeting to several. Finally Electra found the one she had hoped to see. Saul Feldman was standing by the punch bowl. Their eyes met and Electra acknowledged him with a nod and a hint of a smile. Saul appeared to be alone, and she knew he hadn't failed to notice her escort. She hoped jealousy would make Saul realize she wasn't a woman to string along forever.

Zoe was leading Troy through the crowd to introduce him to a theatrical agent who had recently arrived. As Troy neared Electra, he reached out and grabbed her hand and pulled her along in his wake. She was amused to think he might be afraid of losing her. Troy had an agent already, but this one was far more prestigious. Electra had spoken to him on several occasions and the man was almost as gifted in discovering talent as he thought he was.

As Zoe introduced Troy, he again wrapped his arm around Electra's shoulders as if they were a high school couple going steady. Becoming uncomfortable with his physical demonstrativeness, although it was ego-inflating to think one of the most handsome men in the room was unmistakably proclaiming himself to be her lover, she eased away from him as she greeted the agent and the producer beside him. She noticed several heads turned in her direction and she believed she saw envy in their eyes. Certainly she and Troy were attracting attention.

"I've heard a lot about you," Troy said to the agent. "They say you're the best."

The man shrugged but grinned. "What can I say?"

"Who do you represent? I'm thinking about changing agents."

"When you make up your mind, then we'll talk," the man said evasively. Then, "Do you really have an agent?"

"Sure. William Stevens."

"Ah," the agent said as if that explained everything.

Troy turned to the producer. "Do you have anything new in the works?"

"Yes, as a matter of fact, I do. A musical."

"Hey, you're in luck! I can sing." Troy grinned as if he and the man had been friends from birth.

The producer didn't crack a smile. "So you're not cast at the moment?"

"Well, Saul Feldman wants me for *Mary's Promise*, but I can get out of it. When are auditions?"

Electra stared up at him in disbelief. He was committing professional suicide.

"Young man, I'm not casting anything—that's the director's job—and even if I were, I wouldn't do it tonight." He made as expansive a gesture as he could in the crowded room. "This is a party. Enjoy!"

"Gotcha." Troy winked as if he thought some sort of deal had been made.

Electra caught his hand and pulled him away with the excuse of wanting punch. "What are you doing?" she demanded when they were a safe distance away. "You can't tell a producer you'd abandon a show if a better offer comes along!"

"Hey, honey. It happens all the time."

"Yes, but nobody comes right out and admits it like that. He'll remember what you said from now on."

"And it may get me a role in a musical. I have a great voice. I dance good, too."

He had again draped his body familiarly about hers. Electra brushed his arm away, this time not as unobtrusively. As she readjusted her dress, Troy said, "Hey, is that Naomi Petra over there?"

Electra followed his gaze to a tall woman with black hair and red lips. "Yes, it is."

"Introduce me. Okay?"

"I don't know her except by sight."

He narrowed his eyes speculatively. "Is it true she arranges it so that her lovers play opposite her?"

"That's the rumor. By the way, you didn't tell me Saul cast you in *Mary's Promise*. That was really fast. Congratulations."

"He hasn't. I lied. The cast won't be posted until tomorrow."

Electra stared up at him. "You lied? I thought you were telling the truth."

He shrugged. "I'm an actor. I lie for a living."

Trepidation began creeping into Electra. "You're awfully good at it."

"Look. You wait here and I'll go get us some punch."

"All right." She noticed he was still staring at Naomi Petra.

As Troy threaded his way through the crowd to the refreshment table, Electra watched him closely. What else had he lied about?

Troy poured two cups of Zoe's punch, which was rumored to be no more than straight liquor with coloring added. He paused at a bowl of bright-colored pills. Electra felt her stomach tightening. This bowl was a new fad that had drifted in from Hollywood. The bowl contained various pills, some harmless, some quite potent indeed. Dipping into it was a form of Russian roulette that Electra found distasteful. She was about to work her way to Troy to warn him when he picked through the bowl's contents and selected two pills. He popped them into his mouth and washed them down with punch.

Electra stared. He had done that as if he knew exactly what he was doing. He refilled his glass and began working his way through the crowd. But he was heading for Naomi Petra, not Electra. When he reached her side he offered her the other punch glass. Naomi gave him an interested smile.

"He seems to have made friends," a voice said beside her.

Electra turned to see Saul watching Troy. "Knowing Naomi's reputation, that's not all he'll make."

Saul laughed. "Jealous?"

"Of course not," she snapped. But she was. "He's just a friend."

"When I saw him hanging over you like a shawl, I thought he might be more than that."

Electra glanced at him and smiled. "Now who's jealous?"

"Of him? Nah." He took her elbow and escorted her through the crowd. "Come on. I'll get you some punch."

At the table Electra frowned down at the bowl of pills. "What are all these? Do you know?"

Saul shook his head as he poured them each a glass. "Who knows? All I know is they're big trouble. Especially mixed with this punch." He took a sip. "Go easy. Zoe's outdone herself tonight."

Electra put the glass to her lips as her gaze sought out Troy. He had tossed down a glass of punch as if it were water and she saw he was well into the refill. And that was on top of at least two pills.

"Stop staring at him like that," Saul advised. "People will think you care."

She immediately dropped her gaze. Turning her back to Troy she said, "Have you cast *Mary's Promise?*"

"Yes. He didn't get a part."

"He didn't? But he looks perfect for the part of Matt."

"Yes, he does. He gave a good reading, too."

"Then why didn't you cast him?"

"Someone else gave an even better reading, and Troy left before auditions were over. I didn't like his attitude. We're down there to work, not to act like prima donnas."

Saul added, "The boy's his own worst enemy. He came in as if he knew the lead was his and as if he thought I was working for him. He told me he was there to read for Matt and that he wouldn't take a smaller role. Matt was the only role he would have been suited for anyway, but he was stupid to tell me that. And all that from a boy straight off the bus."

"I thought he might be new in town."

"I don't know how long he's been here, but I checked

and he wasn't cast for a single one of the parts that he wrote down on his résumé."

"He lied about that?" Electra felt her mouth drop open.

"I guess he never thought I'd check. Maybe he acted in all those plays in high school."

"Or college," Electra added.

Saul laughed. "He never went to college. Where did you get that idea?"

"From him. He told me the name of his fraternity and what drama classes he took and—"

"And you believed him. He couldn't have gone to college. He's not old enough to have had the time."

Electra stared up at him. "How old is he?"

"According to him, nineteen."

"Nineteen!"

"Of course he could be lying about that, too."

Electra snapped her head around and stared in shock at Troy, who was still several yards away and deeply engrossed in conversation with the actress. That explained a lot. His physical demonstrativeness, for instance, and his naïveté. But to Saul she said, "That's nonsense. Utter nonsense. Of course he's older than that. He was just trying to get the role of Matt."

"Nineteen is the age he tried to cross out. Matt is twenty-four, and that's the age he wrote above it." Saul grinned. "That's why I'm not jealous. If you made him your lover, you'd almost be guilty of contributing to the delinquency of a minor."

Electra felt slightly sick. All at once she wanted to leave the party and be alone. She was about to tell Saul as much when there was a commotion in another part of the room. She turned to see that Troy was no longer beside Naomi

Petra and that the actress looked more than slightly offended.

"What happened?" she asked Saul.

"I don't know."

A young man came to her side. "Excuse me, but your
son is sick."

"I beg your pardon?" Electra's voice was laced with ice.

"He's throwing up in the bathroom."

Electra lifted her head with dignity. Troy was disgracing
her as well as himself by being sick in Zoe's bathroom. And
this young man thought Troy was her son! Electra felt a
roomful of eyes staring at her, and embarrassment flooded
over her.

"Let's go see about him," Saul calmly suggested.

Electra walked ahead of him, the crowd parting to allow
them to pass. As soon as they were in the hall she heard
the conversation behind them resume and knew she and
Troy figured largely as subjects. No one who came to Zoe's
parties ever made a spectacle of himself by getting sick. It
was too gauche even to be considered.

They found Troy in the bathroom, half lying, half
crouching on the tile floor, his arms hugging the toilet. He
looked as miserable as anyone she had ever seen. He looked
almost as bad as she felt.

"Thank God you made it in time," she said dryly. "Otherwise I could never have faced those people again."

Troy groaned.

"We have to get him home," Saul said. "Where does
he live?"

"I don't know." She sat on the edge of the tub. "Troy,
what's your address?"

He could only moan and grip the toilet as if it were a lifeline.

"What the hell did he take?" Saul asked, staring down at him.

"Who knows? I saw him swallow something from the bowl. Troy, do you know what pills you took?"

He managed to shake his head. "Green. And red. Three of them."

"Three?" Saul exclaimed. "And then you drank Zoe's punch? Hell! You're lucky you aren't dead."

Electra searched Saul's face. "Do you think he's in danger? Should we take him to a hospital?"

"All they could do is pump his stomach and there's no reason for that now. If he doesn't know what he took, they can't do much else." To Troy he said, "Where do you live? We have to get you home."

Troy shook his head again.

Zoe hurried into the bathroom and stopped just inside the door. "What's wrong with him? What happened?"

"He swallowed three of those fancy pills and two glasses of punch," Electra said.

"He did! Everybody knows not to take *three*. Good God! Which kind were they?"

"I have no idea. Red and green was all he said." At the moment Electra didn't care much for her friend. The young man who was evidently Zoe's newest lover was standing in the doorway looking curiously over her shoulder.

"Well, he can't stay here." Zoe looked nervously down the hall. "He has to leave."

Electra's eyes narrowed. Zoe was uncharacteristically upset. She suddenly realized those pills weren't as harmless as Zoe had assured her they were. Nor as legal. Electra felt as gullible as Troy. She stood and said, "He can't or won't tell us his address, but I have his phone number. I'll call his roommate."

"No!" Troy protested weakly.

In no mood to coax the address out of him, Electra ignored his wishes, went to Zoe's bedside phone, and dialed Troy's number. When a man's voice answered she said, "Is this Mike?"

"Yes," the voice drawled out in a lisp. "Who is this?"

Electra paused. Many of her male models affected a lisp exactly like this, and she knew what it meant.

"Hello?" Mike repeated.

"Troy is sick and I need to get him home. What's the address?"

"Troy's sick? Oh, my God! What's wrong with him?"

Electra closed her eyes and gripped the phone until her hand shook. Mike's evident anxiety told her that he and Troy were more than friends.

Saul had followed her into the bedroom. "Electra? Are you okay?"

She managed to nod. To Mike she said, "He's had too much to drink. Give me your address, and I'll send him home in a cab."

"Yes, yes. Do that. I'll make some black coffee and get the bed turned down," Mike said. "Who is this?"

"It doesn't matter."

Electra wrote down the address on Zoe's notepad and tore off the page. To Saul she said, "Will you help me get him downstairs?"

"Of course."

Saul went back to the bathroom and pulled Troy to his feet. He looped Troy's arm over his shoulder and commanded the boy to walk. Zoe looked on in obvious disgust.

Electra braced herself, lifted her chin, and forced herself to walk back into the crowd. She had made a big mistake with Troy. She realized how foolish she must have looked with Troy pawing at her like an adolescent. Her skin was clammy; her embarrassment almost overwhelming.

As the crowd parted once again to let them through, Electra heard a woman giggle, but she dared not react. Her mind was besieged with the recollection of disparaging remarks others had made about Zoe and her penchant for young lovers. Electra was certain people were thinking the same of her, if not already saying such things about her behind her back.

Once Saul and his besotted charge were out the door, Electra quickly followed, closing the door behind her, wishing she could somehow erase this event from her mind and the minds of all those witnesses. Hurrying past Saul, she pressed the elevator button. "Thank you for helping me," she said through clenched teeth, so mortified she could hardly talk.

"No problem. This isn't the first drunk I've rescued you from at one of Zoe's parties. He's probably not the last, either."

"Yes, he is," she ground out. She refused to meet Saul's eyes, instead keeping her vision glued to the plastic arrow above the elevator door. "I'm not coming to any more parties here."

"He's the one who made a fool of himself. Not you." The elevator doors opened, and Saul maneuvered Troy inside.

Electra stepped in and pushed the lobby button. Thankfully there was no elevator operator, no one she would have to pretend to ignore. "You're wrong," she said as the elevator began descending.

Troy groaned as if he would be sick again and Saul eyed him warily, but apparently the boy's stomach was already empty. Electra pretended she hadn't heard him.

"You know, I never noticed how young he really is," she said. "I never thought how odd we must look together."

Saul didn't comment, but his silence confirmed her fears. Electra fastened her eyes on the lighted numbers and counted down the floors in silence.

The elevator stopped with a stomach-lurching jolt. Troy looked as if he wanted to die. Electra tried to disregard her thoughts about how expensive the suit had been and her concern as to whether Zoe's punch would stain it.

At the curb she hailed a taxi and gave the driver the slip of paper with Troy's address as Saul folded Troy into the back seat. After a brief hesitation, Electra gave the driver a bill large enough to pay for the fare and a tip. She didn't know if Troy or Mike could afford to pay, and the driver looked none too pleased to have a drunk in his backseat.

As the cab pulled away Electra waved down another one.

"You know," Saul said as they waited for the cab to pull to a stop. "It would simplify everything if you and I got married."

Electra stared at him in silent disbelief.

"It may not be in the best taste to say so, but neither of us is getting any younger. We like each other, and we have a mutual respect. Right?"

She nodded.

Saul opened the cab door for her. "So what do you think? Do you want to marry me?"

"I don't want to marry anyone. Especially now."

She was getting in the cab but Saul detained her. "The Troys of the world aren't the way to go."

"I know that," she snapped. "I need to think about it. I need to be alone."

"Give me a call." He let her get into the cab and slammed the door as she gave the driver her address.

Electra stared at him as the cab pulled away, hardly able to believe her ears. She had never received a stranger proposal.

When she finally stepped into her apartment and closed the door against the outside world, she took a deep breath and tried to collect her thoughts. She was exhausted physically, mentally, and emotionally. As she looked around, she felt thankful that her maid service always left her apartment impeccably clean and all of her things in order. It was a pity no such service existed to put one's life in order. But if one did exist, she knew she would never use it. She had to live her life her way.

Gathering strength from her determination, she made a quick inspection of her apartment and was relieved to find that Troy had left nothing behind. She would never have to see him again. The only problem was that the essence of Troy still lingered. Somehow she had to rid herself of that as well.

Moving quickly, Electra went into the bathroom and gathered up the shaving cream, deodorant, and razor she kept for overnight guests and threw them all into the trash. That made her feel better. Enough was enough. She wanted no more handsome young men in her life. The lesson she should have learned with Bret had finally hit home with Troy.

She took off her dress and tossed it on the bed, then went back to the bathroom. Leaning over the basin, she washed off all her makeup and took a long, searching look into the mirror.

Struggling for objectivity, she saw a woman who looked good for fifty-four but who was well past the bloom of youth. Thanks to her surgeon's skill, her wrinkles were minimal and her chin line was firm, but her skin had lost much of its tone. Her hair was the same shade it had been in her youth, but in contrast with her older skin, it appeared too dark and glossy.

Electra picked up her brush and worked the teasing out of her hair. Again she studied her reflection. Parting her hair, she could see a fine line of gray at the roots. It was time for another touch-up. She ran her long fingers through her hair and tried to picture it in its natural color. Amelia's hair had a yellowish tint, but auburn hair often grayed that way. Her hair might be closer to silver. She wondered if it was possible to dye it silver or if she would have to let it grow out.

"I'll find out first thing Monday morning," she promised her reflection.

She was going to have to change her life-style and that was all there was to it. She wasn't so sure she wanted to keep the same circle of friends, either. She and Zoe had known each other for years, but thinking back, Electra realized they rarely shared confidences any more. She was more likely to share her more intimate thoughts with Saul than with Zoe.

She went back into her bedroom and undressed. After

slipping on her nightgown and robe, she put away the clothes she had been wearing and lay down on the bed.

Saul. He had asked her to marry him.

Electra rolled over onto her stomach and leaned her cheek on the palm of her hand, even though she knew that caused wrinkles. What was she going to do about Saul?

She had meant it when she said she didn't want to marry anyone. Often she worked weekends or late at night or sat up all night sketching designs as the ideas came to her, most often around midnight. She didn't want to have to check in with someone or call with an excuse for working late. She had no interest in cooking and even less in housework. Husbands tended to expect their wives to quit work and become homemakers. Electra knew she would not only hate that but would refuse to do it.

Her business was going well. Great, in fact. She was known and respected worldwide. She would hate to let anything interrupt her life.

And Saul couldn't move to Willowbrook. Electra had always promised Amelia, as well as herself, that when she retired, she would come home to stay. Saul couldn't live there and continue directing plays, and he loved his work as much as Electra did her own. In fact he hadn't been all that impressed with the idea of Willowbrook as a home. He was a city boy, born and bred, as he put it, and he saw no advantage in country living.

But he had asked her to marry him. Even after seeing what a fool she had made of herself with Troy, he still liked and respected her. She was sure Saul wouldn't have asked her to marry him if he didn't love her. She knew that just as she knew she loved him. But theirs was a quiet and easy sort of love, like a favorite sweater or comfortable shoes.

Their love was steady and satisfying, but it lacked the heady leaps of passion Electra found so exhilarating.

She pulled a pillow from underneath the cover and hugged it to her. When she noticed it still smelled faintly of Troy, she tossed it onto the floor and pulled out the other one. Troy had given her all the exhilaration she hungered for, and that was one reason she was so miserable now. Two people in one day had mistaken her for his mother! Electra groaned and rolled onto her back.

All too clearly she saw herself advancing into old age with impossibly black hair and foolishly young gigolos. And they *were* gigolos, the young men like Troy and Bret. Troy had been unemployed since his arrival in New York, living off gifts from women like her. Or men. She recalled Mike's lisp and groaned again. The frantic concern in his voice was unmistakably that of a lover. She had never considered that she might be sharing him with a man! That made her feel worse than Bret's nubile young actress had.

She would have to change her phone number, but that would not be a problem; she had changed it often to avoid calls from former lovers. It was, of course, unlisted, and no one had it but her closest acquaintances. Mary and Lois at work, Saul, Zoe, and her current lover. Now she would need to tell only three people of her new number. And Amelia. She had almost forgotten about Amelia.

For a few minutes she considered going to Willowbrook to rest, but she decided against it. She needed to finish the sketches for the television style show within the next week so her seamstresses wouldn't have to work in a raw panic.

Then there was Saul. She couldn't leave without responding to his proposal.

As much as she disliked the idea of marriage, part of her

wanted to say yes. Marriage wouldn't suit her, but it would be so nice to have someone to come home to. Someone to sleep beside when it was cold and rainy outside, someone to hold her hand during her rare illnesses. Someone to talk to face to face. Yes, in a way she would like to marry Saul.

They were compatible. They had rarely disagreed. When they didn't see eye to eye on a subject, they discussed it or argued about it, but never to the extent of losing their tempers. Saul would be easy to live with. She even liked his apartment—a loft near the theater district. He had divided the open spaces with screens, and his taste was so similar to her own.

But marriage?

Electra gazed up at the ceiling. She had to say no, at least for now. Saul would understand. She couldn't change everything from her hair coloring to her life-style and take on the challenge of marriage all at the same time.

She was certain Saul really would understand.

WINTER, 1986

And Winter slumbering in the open air,
Wears on his smiling face a dream of
Spring!

Samuel Taylor Coleridge

CHAPTER 21

"I'VE DECIDED," ELECTRA ANNOUNCED OVER her morning cup of coffee. "I'm going home."

Saul looked up from the paper. "Home? You are at home."

"To Willowbrook. I'm going to retire."

"Retire?"

"Why do you keep repeating everything I say?" Electra asked with some exasperation. "I'm eighty years old. I should have retired years ago."

"That's true, but when you didn't, I assumed you never would." Saul turned back to his newspaper.

"Would you put that paper down and listen to me? What do you think about it?"

"I give it a week, two at most."

"I knew you'd say that," Electra said triumphantly. "So I didn't tell you until I was certain. I wrote Amelia back in September. She's not too pleased, I can tell you."

Saul looked at her carefully. "I can see her side of it. Can't you? After all, she's had Willowbrook to herself for over half a century."

"You needn't put it that way. You make me sound like a museum piece."

"We both are. It's occurred to me that we're both such successes because we've outlived all our competition."

"Speak for yourself. I have a wild pack of young designers yapping at my heels."

"You should have married me," he told her, amusement twinkling in his eyes. "I could have supported you all these years, and you wouldn't have had so many worries about staying ahead of the pack. The apartment manager must wonder about us—me coming here every morning for the past quarter of a century."

"Will you stop that?"

Saul chuckled and Electra smiled. She knew he was teasing her. "Maybe I should have married you. Made an honest man out of you," she said.

"The offer still stands. If you're going to take me up on it, though, you'd better hurry. I'm seventy-three. A man won't wait forever."

Electra threw her napkin at him. As far as she was concerned, they had the perfect relationship. Saul had been her lover, her only lover for twenty-six years. Their earlier passion had mellowed into a love deeper than that shared by most couples who really were married. Saul kept his apartment, just as Electra kept hers. Sometimes they spent weekends together; sometimes they didn't. Always they met for a morning cup of coffee, usually at Electra's apartment, to plan their day or simply to see each other.

"I don't think you believe me," Electra said.

"You're right," Saul answered from behind the paper.

"Well, this time you're wrong." Electra stood and paced to the large window with its view of New York City's mountains and canyons. "This time I mean it. I've even given notice on my apartment."

"You what? Electra, that was a damned fool thing to do. There must be a dozen people waiting for an opening in this building."

"I told you I was serious," she said with what Saul had always called her smile in miniature. "I'm leaving in two weeks."

She finally had his attention. "You're serious!"

"Christmas is over, so is New Year's. There's nothing left here but wintertime, and winter in New York is no picnic." Her voice softened. "You know how beautiful Willowbrook is in the winter. Snow lying in unbroken drifts over the lawns and fields, the ice in the stream behind the house."

"Snow is snow," Saul said bluntly. "Spare me the poetry."

"No, it's not. It's different in the country, in Virginia."

"What about me? What about us?"

Electra went behind Saul's chair and put her arms around him. Bending, she kissed the top of his silvered head. "You can retire, too. Come to Willowbrook with me."

"I can't do that. I have a play in production. You know that—unless you're going senile on me."

"Don't be so grouchy." She gave him a hug. "You can come down when the play doesn't need you anymore."

He snorted his contempt of the notion. "As soon as this one is under way, I've agreed to do Carter Symmons's new one. I can't go gallivanting off to Willowbrook." He stood and caught her hand and drew her to the window. "Look out there, Electra. Take a good look. How can you consider giving up all this? Let Amelia live at Willowbrook in peace. This is your home now."

"How can you say that? You know my heart is at Willowbrook. It always has been."

"Bull! You're just too stubborn to see things the way they are. You always have been. There are no Broadway plays in Catawba Mills and no other night life to speak of. You'll be so bored you'll go crazy inside a month."

"No, I won't."

"And nobody there will go for you having just one name, either."

"I have two names when I'm in Catawba Mills. Electra Radcliff."

"It should have been Feldman long ago. Marry me and forget this nonsense about moving to Virginia."

"I'm going, Saul."

"What about your designs? Are you going to let Electra, Inc. fold after all these years?"

"Not entirely. Betty Marlow—Mary's daughter, remember?—is taking over the business. I've agreed to send her sketches from Willowbrook. From my notes she'll be able to keep the company solvent."

"So you aren't retiring after all. You're just leaving me behind."

"I'm doing no such thing. I had assumed you would come with me. Besides, Betty is too loyal to me to switch to another designer. I'll keep the business as long as she cares to work."

"Too bad about her mother," Saul said.

"Yes, it is. Mary was so talented. I miss her. And Lois, too."

"We're getting old," Saul commented as he gazed down

at the traffic below. "Symmons tells me Zoe Wharton is in the hospital. Intensive care. Her heart, he said. They doubt she'll recover."

"That's sad. And in the end, she's all alone."

"Yeah, she probably turned down one too many proposals," he replied pointedly.

"Maybe I'll marry you if you'll retire to Willowbrook with me," she tempted.

Saul laughed. "Maybe *you* won't go crazy in a month's time, but *I* would. I can't stand all that peace and quiet."

Electra felt a keen disappointment. "Then you really won't come with me?"

He shook his head. "My home is here. Is your mind really made up?"

She nodded, not trusting herself to speak.

He turned back to the window, and she could tell by the tone of his voice he was feeling sad. "You'll come back from time to time, won't you? To see me?"

She put her arms around him. "Of course I will. And you'll come down to visit me."

He hugged her. "It won't be the same, honey. It just won't be the same."

"I got another letter from her," Amelia informed Christopher in the garden. "Two weeks. She says she's coming in two weeks." Amelia paced to the sundial and back to the willow tree. The cold hurt her joints, and she had to take much smaller steps than she had when she was younger. "Why now? Why not thirty years ago when I could still have gotten away from here and traveled?"

Amelia shoved her hands into the pockets of her coat. "If you had come back, it would have been different. For one thing, we might not have lived here. I know, I know," she said as if he had disputed her words. "I know I said I wanted to bring up my children here and all that, but you would have changed my mind."

She smiled, and a dozen years lifted from her face. "You always could talk me into anything. Remember the time when we were kids and we decided to dam up the stream? It was your idea, you know. I would have been happy to make our pirate ship in that oak tree but no, you had to have a raft." Amelia chuckled at the memory. "I told Papa I did it. He was mad at me, but I think he was impressed with what a good dam we'd made. I couldn't tell him you thought it up, or you would have been in trouble."

She ducked under the slender, bare limbs of the willow tree and sat on the bench. She knew it was too cold to be out here, but she didn't want to go back to the house. Not yet. There wasn't much to see in the garden at this time of year. The only plants with leaves still on them were the ivy, the old gardenias, and a few of the herbs. To look at the garden now, a person would never imagine all the flowers that would burst out of the dirt and seemingly dead branches come spring. Winter had always been the garden's worst season as far as beauty was concerned. But the resting period was as necessary as the flowering one. Otherwise the plants might have burned themselves out in one continuous flowering spring. She and Christopher had discussed this often of late.

The garden wasn't as well kept as it once had been, she had to admit that. Her knees could no longer withstand the bending and kneeling it took to keep the beds in order. There weren't many weeds, though. Sometimes she wondered about that. She had finally reached the conclusion that Jerry must come in here after hours and weed for her, even though she'd told him she wanted to do it all herself. The thought of Jerry as a young boy, not knowing one end of a hoe from the other, brought a smile to her lips. But he had persevered and had developed into a fine gardener.

"I went to see Jenny yesterday. She's not doing very well. Since her girls moved her into that nursing home, she hasn't done well at all. I know she's forgetful, but so am I these days. We all are. Everybody but Electra." Amelia grimaced. "I wish she'd forget to move here.

"Anyway, Jenny's daughters said it wasn't safe for her to live alone. Why, Jenny's lived by herself for years. Carleton's been dead forever, seems like. Now all of a sudden they say she can't be alone." Amelia shook her head in dismay. "Maybe it's a good thing we never had those kids I wanted. Maybe if we had, I'd be shut up like Jenny. She sure is looking bad. She's aged a lot these last few years."

Amelia looked up at the bare branches silhouetted against the pale sky. "Jenny's not as lucky as I am. Once Carleton died, he was gone. Not like you. I tried to get her interested in gardening, but she never cared much for it. But then, neither did Carleton, so he might not have been around her even if she had planted something."

For a while Amelia was silent. Then she said, "Even without the war, you might be dead by now. I've tried to imagine what you would look like if you were my age, but I can't. You'd be handsome, though. No doubt about that. You always were."

She took her hands out of her pockets and rubbed her aching knees. She knew she should go back into the house and get warm, but still she lingered. One light snow had already come and gone. Soon there would be others. When snow was on the ground, Amelia stayed inside. She wasn't as agile as she had once been, and she was afraid of falling on the ice. "Before long I won't be able to get out here as often," she reminded Christopher. "Then, too, Electra will be underfoot." She shook her head as she levered herself up from the bench. "I'll never know why she would take it into her head to retire now, of all times."

Still shaking her head, she left the garden and began the walk to the house. The distance that had seemed so short in her youth was much longer now. She had to pause several times along the way to catch her breath. Amelia didn't especially mind growing old, but it had its disadvantages.

Willowbrook still looked the same. She had had the house painted the summer before, and Jerry saw to it that the other gardeners kept the grounds the way they always had been. Some of the catawba trees leading up the drive had died and been replaced so the lined drive no longer looked as uniform as it once had. The stream behind the house had much deeper banks now, but was seldom more than a trickle these days. Eventually she supposed it would play out altogether and be nothing but a ditch. No matter. There were no longer any children on the place to play beside it, nor were there horses to drink from it. Amelia considered going down to the old horse barn just to look around, but she decided against it. Her knees were hurting, and her memory of the barn was better than its reality, for in her mind the stable still held Cloud and all the other fine horses of her youth. These days it was used as a garage and storage for the lawn equipment.

Amelia slowly made her way up the steps, her hand sliding along the rail Jerry had installed for her safety. She told herself she used it only to make him happy. She had teased him about needing it himself. Jerry was well into his forties now and developing aches and pains of his own.

When she was finally on the porch Amelia hesitated and looked around at Willowbrook's lawns. They were all so familiar to her. She felt as if she personally knew each blade of grass and every twig. "I should have traveled," she mumbled, then realized she wasn't in the garden and closed her mouth. Turning back to the house, she went inside.

Helga spotted her right away. "There you are! I am looking everywhere for you." Helga came to Amelia as swiftly as she could these days. "You have been outside in this cold. *Ja?*" She frowned accusingly at Amelia.

"*Ja.*" Amelia smiled as she reached under her chin to untie her head scarf.

"I am having a fire in the parlor. You go in there and get warm." Helga helped Amelia out of her coat and opened the door to the coat closet. "You sit close to the hearth now and get warm. You are hearing me?"

"I hear you." Amelia knew Helga assumed that since she herself was deaf, everyone else was, too.

The fire was burning brightly and popping cheerfully. Amelia had to admit to herself that she really was cold. She pulled a chair closer to the fire and stretched her legs out to soak up the heat.

Helga came in and sat opposite her. "You have had another letter from Electra?"

Over the many years they had spent together, a strong bond of friendship had developed between Amelia and Helga, and only when they were around other members of the household staff did they revert to the formality of their positions as mistress and housekeeper. For several years now

Helga had had a younger woman working for her, doing the more strenuous tasks. These days Helga was more a supervisor and cook than a housekeeper. Amelia often wondered if Helga's cooking had improved or if her own tastes had changed to fit the menu.

"You know I have," Amelia said reluctantly. "She still intends to retire. Says she will move home in two weeks."

"Two weeks! *Ach Himmel.*"

"My sentiments exactly," Amelia said. "Well, I guess we have to make the best of it."

"*Ja.*" Helga stared at the fire.

"Any word from your nephew?"

"He is being happy at Harvard now."

Amelia smiled her approval. The boy was really Helga's great-nephew, and Helga was proud of the fact that he was the first of her nephews and nieces to be born in America. "Write and ask him to visit us during spring break. I miss him."

"*Ja.* I will do that." Helga looked into the fire as she said, "What if Electra is not wanting Karl to come for visit?"

"We'll tell her it was already arranged. This is your home, too. Of course he can come. And maybe Gretchen as well."

"I have not been seeing Gretchen in nearly a year," Helga said. "It would be good to see them both."

"Then it's settled. Write your brother and tell him before they make other plans."

"*Ja.* I will do that," Helga said again.

Amelia looked around the room. The Aubusson rug was spotless and every knickknack had been dusted. Even the crystals on the chandelier were kept sparkling, thanks to Helga's keen eyes and the maid's dexterity. The house was serenely silent except for the crackling of the fire and the ponderous ticking of the grandfather clock in the hall. Electra would be a disruptive influence in the house, and Amelia knew Helga was dreading her arrival, too.

This room, like the library opposite it, was paneled in oak rather than papered. Amelia liked being surrounded by wood, and she enjoyed the lemon smell of the wax Helga used to polish it.

"Once Electra gets here, I suppose this room and all the others will smell like cigarette smoke."

"Is a dirty thing, smoking," Helga firmly agreed. "Is not too much to ask that she smoke only in her room or outside?"

"I agree and I intend to tell her so." Amelia dreaded the confrontation. She disliked conflict, whereas Electra seemed to thrive on it. "As soon as she gets settled in, I'll tell her. As you say, it's not too much to ask." She gazed up at the framed photos of Christopher on the mantel. She wished he were there to bolster her courage. Although she would never admit it, Amelia was somewhat afraid of Electra.

Helga looked across at Amelia, a deep frown burrowing into her brow. "She is not bringing one of her 'friends,' is she? I am not eager to have one of them around."

Amelia's eyes widened. "Surely not! I mean, not to actually *live* here." She shook her head vigorously. "No. No, of course not. Electra is much too old for that sort of thing." She hoped it was true. "Saul is the only one she has brought down for years."

She raised her eyes to an oil painting of the Muses that adorned the wall. "Have you ever noticed how much that one looks like Jenny when she was younger?"

Helga obligingly turned her head. "A little, maybe. Jenny was never so fat."

"True. I've always wondered why all the women in old paintings are so plump." Amelia laughed and patted her rounded stomach. "I guess I was just born too late to be in style."

"You look nice," Helga said protectively. "My own mother, she would have made two of you, and she was known as being a beautiful woman. I am not liking to see a woman too thin. Like boys, they are."

"Well, you may as well get used to it. I'm sure Electra is still thin as a shadow."

"We will fatten her up, you and me." Helga winked conspiratorially.

"Maybe so," Amelia said with a nod. "Maybe so. Mother was always thin, you know. No, you couldn't know that. Mother died long before you came here." She sighed. "Sometimes all my memories run together. Anyway, our mother was thin like Electra. I took after Papa. When I was a girl, I had to watch every mouthful. That's one good thing about growing old. We don't have to try to fit into a mold we weren't designed for."

Helga nodded. "If one of her 'friends' come with her, I will make prune Danish every day until he leaves."

Amelia smiled and nodded. "That should do it."

Electra, in a flurry of excitement, hired a limousine to drive her from the airport to Willowbrook. This was no ordinary visit, and she wanted to arrive in style.

As they headed up Willowbrook's gracious drive, she leaned forward for a view of the bare arms of the catawba trees and wished the young ones would grow quickly to catch up with the old ones. She was afraid the drive would never be as impressive as it once had been.

The driver stopped out front and she paid the fare. As he drove away she paused to savor the moment of home-coming for as long as she could.

A blustery wind was blowing, and she could smell rain on the way, perhaps snow. Inside Willowbrook would be warm and protecting and peaceful. Electra had hungered for this day most of her life. She had come home. Home to stay.

Slowly she climbed the steps. In a week, maybe two, the movers would have all her other things boxed and delivered to Willowbrook. She was really home at last.

As she reached the porch, she tried not to think of her parting from Saul. He had been gruff in a vain attempt to conceal the fact that his eyes were shinier than usual over her going, and Electra had felt teary herself on the flight down. Only now did she fully realize there would be no Saul here with whom to share her morning coffee or with whom to talk late into the night or to ride with on the ferry. Saul liked riding a ferry better than anyone she had ever known. She was rather alarmed to see how much she was already missing him. Electra had always preferred to travel with little emotional baggage.

To mark the beginning of her new life, Electra rang the doorbell. Perhaps it was her long-term association with the theater, but she had a definite flare for the dramatic. She could have walked in unannounced, but until she actually crossed the threshold, she was still Electra of New York.

Amelia opened the door, and she didn't look all that pleased to see Electra. For a moment it appeared that she wasn't even going to invite her in. "For heaven's sake,

Amelia. It's cold out here. Didn't you hear me drive up?"

Amelia stepped aside, and Electra hurried in out of the blustery wind. "Where's Jansen? She's supposed to open the door." She hoped to draw a smile from her sister.

"If you mean Helga," Amelia answered as she closed the door, "she's in the kitchen, I expect. Her hearing isn't what it once was." She looked at Electra, taking in the silver fox coat, which exactly matched the color of Electra's hair, and the stylish navy dress. "I don't know why you've taken to ringing the bell as if you're company, anyway."

"Good heavens, but it's hot in here! Why do you have the thermostat set so high?" Electra had kept her apartment on the cool side since the power shortages of the mid-seventies, and after the biting wind outside, the house felt witheringly hot.

"It feels quite comfortable to me. Take off your coat and you'll be cooler."

Electra slipped out of the coat and draped it over the hall tree. She breathed in Willowbrook's remembered scents and smiled in deep contentment. She was home!

They went into the parlor as the clock chimed the half hour. Amelia said, "I expected you earlier."

Electra made all the proper responses as she and Amelia drifted into small talk. For some reason Amelia seemed determined to be in a gloomy mood. Electra had never had much patience with depression. She was determined not to let Amelia pull her mood down as well. "I've dreamed of this day since I left here that first time. Do you remember, Amelia?"

"I remember."

Electra wondered what was wrong with her sister. Surely there hadn't been problems with the help. Amelia had always been able to keep employees longer than anyone Electra had ever known. Was Amelia sick? She looked a good bit older than Electra remembered from her last visit, and she seemed determined to talk about how dull it would be here and how all their friends were dead or in nursing homes. She had hoped Amelia would be happier to see her. No matter what Amelia might think, however, Electra was home. Home at last.

After supper Electra went up to her room, using the excuse of being tired. She wanted to be alone with her thoughts as she unpacked. Not that Amelia seemed all that talkative. Electra supposed this was a momentous day for them both.

Someone—Helga, Electra assumed—had already lined the drawers in her dresser and put in sachets of rose and lavender. Electra meticulously put away her clothes as if it were a ritual. A century seemed to have passed since she had packed up and gone away. She had been such an innocent then. These days no girl of twenty would be so naive as not to know what went on between a man and his mistress. Thinking back on it, Electra could hardly believe she had ever been so innocent. That had been such a simple time.

A photograph of her, taken before Papa died, sat on her dresser in the same frame it had been in for sixty years. She studied it for a moment, then compared it to her reflection in her dressing table mirror. She had changed, of course, but she could see a hint of the girl she had been in her carriage and in the shape of her face. In a rare moment of introspection, she asked herself if she had any regrets. Her answer was no; she had none. Not really. She couldn't think of anyone she had willfully harmed. Some of her young men had been angry when she dropped them, but they had been using her as much as she had used them. Then there was Saul. She missed him more than she had expected, but it had been her choice to leave him. There was, however, one small disappointment—one she could never voice to anyone. She regretted that she hadn't met Christopher Jenkins as an adult before Amelia had, so that she might have had a chance to make him love her.

In a way, her young men had been the result of her efforts to find another Christopher. Almost all of them had been tall blonds with Germanic good looks. All but Saul. But then, Saul was the exception to every rule. She wondered if she would have given him a different answer to his proposal of so long ago if he had been taller and had blond hair. Electra shook her head. She wasn't that shallow, surely, and Saul was handsome in his own right.

Besides, she was through with all that. From this point on, she planned to simply enjoy living at Willowbrook and forget about men and how they had complicated her life.

She dressed for bed and turned out the light. Instead of lying down, however, she went to the window seat and sat with her legs drawn up under her as she had done when she was a girl. Beyond the windowpane rain was falling— a gentle rain without the passionate outbursts of thunder. The drops running down the glass crazed the lights from the barn and outbuildings. Like a child, Electra traced the path of one of the drops with her fingertip.

From now on everything in her life would be simple and serene. She was home.

•   •   •

Down the hall Amelia lay in her bed, staring up at the same ceiling she had known since she was a child. Her body ached with the familiar twinges that cold and rain always brought with them.

After Electra had gone upstairs, Amelia and Helga had had a long talk in the kitchen. Both had agreed that having Electra in residence would hamper their way of life. For one thing, Electra always treated Helga like a servant. And Helga still remembered when Electra had made Amelia so unhappy about marrying Christopher. Helga's loyalties were long and they ran deep. Amelia knew Helga's loyalty to her was all that kept the housekeeper from quitting on the spot earlier that evening when Electra mentioned the roast was tough and too highly seasoned.

Amelia sighed and rolled over, curling her body around the extra pillow. She had slept like that for years, ever since Christopher left for the army and she had had only his pillow for company in bed. Like Helga, Amelia had a long memory, and she wasn't sure she trusted Electra where Willowbrook was concerned. Amelia knew all there was to know about the place and how to run it. She knew all the small idiosyncrasies of how to treat the people who worked for her and how to keep the place running smoothly. Electra had always been bossy and opinionated, and she was certain to want to make changes. Amelia dreaded the next few days.

Rebelliously she whispered, "Why couldn't she just have stayed where she was?" At once she felt guilty because Willowbrook was as much Electra's home as it was hers. Her resentment toward Electra was also uncharitable, because they only had each other. All their other relatives were dead and buried long ago.

Amelia, however, wasn't thrilled over sharing her daily life with her sister. "There will be trouble," she murmured to her pillow. "Mark my words, there will be trouble."

CHAPTER 22

ELECTRA WAS STILL HAVING DIFFICULTY SLEEP-
ing. It wasn't that Willowbrook was too quiet—her apartment had, if anything, been quieter. The bed was softer
than the one in New York, but it was, after all, her bed.
She had been back home for a week, which was longer by
several days than any visit to Willowbrook since she left as
a young woman, and she couldn't understand why she was
having trouble sleeping.

But the lack of sleep hadn't slowed her down much.
During the short time she had been home, she had made
several improvements in the place. With the help of the
two younger gardeners she had rearranged the furniture in
the back parlor. Amelia had been miffed that Electra had
taken the room for her own use, but it was necessary because
of the available sunlight in the room. And the furniture
had to be rearranged because her drawing table wouldn't
fit into the room without shifting the sofa and chairs. Amelia kept the house as if it were a museum, especially where
the furniture and its arrangement were concerned. Electra
liked change and was accustomed to changing her furniture

arrangement on a regular basis. She had also ordered new wallpaper for her bedroom and new paint for the woodwork. The room had been decorated for a young woman, and Electra's tastes had changed.

She had tried to pension off Helga, but Amelia had become so outraged that Electra had backed down. Helga was nearly as old as her mistress, and her hearing was marginal at best, but Amelia insisted that she be kept on. In an effort to compromise, Electra hired a young woman to cook and elevated Helga to merely overseeing the housekeeping. This satisfied both Amelia and Helga and provided Electra with decent meals. Helga might be of sterling character, but she simply couldn't cook.

After the first couple of days, Electra had settled back into her usual work routine, but quickly discovered that being at Willowbrook wasn't conducive to fashion inspiration. Surrounded by the sights and smells of her youth, Electra found herself wanting to sketch overblouses and low waistlines and accent them with ropes of pearls. She had never realized how much her surroundings affected her designs.

Soon she was hungering for crisp forms in aluminum and glass, for anything that was less than seventy-five years old. All Willowbrook's newer furnishings had been bought by her parents around the turn of the century. Pieces original to the house were even older. Electra had always preferred furniture with clean lines and a spare look. Now, as much as she loved Willowbrook, she found her senses overburdened with heavy oak and walnut furniture, velvets and brocades, and wallpaper on all the walls that weren't paneled. Amelia not only liked it this way but became extremely agitated when Electra suggested that plaster and paint might improve the walls. She wouldn't even agree to putting down wall-to-wall carpeting in place of the floral wool rugs. In fact, the suggestion had made her so angry that her face turned beet red. Electra had given in for fear of sending Amelia into seizures. She was, however, determined to repaper and paint her own bedroom. A person could live only so long with faded roses and violets.

Most of all she missed Saul. Every morning he was her first thought and her immediate disappointment. She considered flying to New York to see him, but she had only been at Willowbrook a little over a week. Saul would tease her unmercifully if she ran back to the city so soon. And she didn't want to go back, she told herself. She was at Willowbrook at last and that was exactly where she wanted to be.

Electra pushed aside her newest drawings. All the sketches looked like flappers and were wrong for the show she was preparing for the coming fall. She rested her chin on her palm and stared down at a blank sheet of paper. After the fringe and basics fad of the 1970's Electra had discontinued her Butterfly line. Fashion had blurred into a more consistent look for teens and adults. Now she almost wished she had kept it going. Maybe she could have started a new flapper craze for teenagers. Some of the sketches she'd done since coming home were quite good for period pieces.

Electra tossed her pencil into the acrylic pencil holder. She was supposed to be retired, and yet here she was, working as relentlessly as she had in New York. She should have been enjoying her new freedom, not sketching dresses that would never be made.

She paced to the window and brushed aside the curtains.

The sky was clear and the day crisp but not frigid. It was one of those days that came so rarely in January, the ones that suggested there might someday be another spring. Electra had always detested winter with its chilling winds and drab colors. She decided to go for a walk and enjoy the brief respite from rain.

After donning a warm coat and a knitted cap, she stepped out onto the porch. It was colder than she had expected. Somehow she always had pictured Willowbrook with moderate temperatures and green grass. Shoving her hands into her coat pockets for warmth, Electra went down the steps to the side yard.

Her first stop was the area of lawn her father had created for outdoor parties, an outdoor room of sorts, with walls of greenery defining its limits. The large fountain near one end was still there, though it obviously had been drained until the threat of freezing temperatures had passed. She and Amelia had had so many parties here. The gardeners still kept the area clipped and mowed, but the ground was no longer as perfectly flat as it had once been. She doubted that it had been rolled smooth since her father died. This had always been her favorite garden. It had clean, precise lines and no clutter of flower beds or walkways. Perhaps in the spring, Electra thought, she would have another party out here and invite all their old friends.

But Amelia had said all their friends were dead now or in nursing homes. Surely Amelia had exaggerated. They couldn't all be gone.

As Electra left the hedged enclosure she lowered her head against the wind. She circled around the rose garden, now looking barren and brambly in the winter cold, her feet crunching on the gravel of the drive.

Ahead was Amelia's walled garden. Jerry, the head gardener, was working near the gate. Amelia, Electra was sure, would allow him to work at Willowbrook for as long as he pleased, if her loyalty to Helga was any indication. Electra wondered what he found to do when no plants were growing. Was she pretending to work in order to justify his salary? She decided to take a closer look.

As soon as he saw her approaching he began to sing. The nearer she came the louder he raised his voice. Only when she was a few feet away did he break off his song to say, " 'Morning, Miss Electra."

"Good morning. What are you doing?"

"I'm loosening the dirt in this bed. It don't do to let it pack down."

"Wouldn't it be better to do that in the spring? Nothing is growing in it now."

He looked uneasy as if she had caught him in a deception. "No point in waiting until the last minute."

Now that he wasn't singing, Electra could hear a voice that sounded like Amelia's in conversation with someone she couldn't hear at all. Electra listened more closely. "Is that my sister in the garden? Who is she talking to?"

The gardener glanced uneasily at the gate. "I wouldn't know, Miss Electra. I'm out here minding my own business."

"Well, she must be talking to someone. I didn't know we had company." Electra's spirits rose at the prospect of a visitor, and she stepped toward the gate.

"I wouldn't go in there if I was you," Jerry said. "I mean, Miss Amelia, she likes her privacy."

Electra put him back in his place with a look cooler than

the day. "See to your gardening." She walked briskly to the gate and swung it open.

Amelia was there but she was alone. When she saw Electra she broke off in mid-sentence and stared at her.

"Who are you talking to?" Electra exclaimed. "There's no one here but you."

"What are you doing in here?" Amelia demanded at the same time. "You know this is my private garden."

Electra glanced over her shoulder at Jerry, who slowly went back to breaking the half-frozen soil. He looked as upset as Amelia. Electra turned back to her sister. "I came over to see what Jerry was doing, and I heard you talking to someone." She looked around the garden again, but still saw no one and there was no place here to hide. "Who were you talking to?"

"Christopher," Amelia said after a long pause. "I was talking to Christopher."

Electra felt the blood drain from her face. Was Amelia losing her mind? "Christopher has been gone for years."

Amelia shook her head. "No, not really. At first I felt that way, too. But then I came out here and, well, here he was."

The hairs on the back of Electra's neck prickled.

"I've been talking to him out here for years and years. Can't you feel him?"

"No." Electra glanced around uneasily. Amelia sounded so certain. "No, of course not. There's no one else here."

"Well, maybe not physically. But he's here just the same. I was just remarking to him how fortunate we are to have such musically inclined gardeners. I don't know what it is about this place, but after men work here for a while they all start to sing. Jerry has a particularly good voice, don't you think?"

"Yes." Electra cast an accusing glare at Jerry. She couldn't tell because his skin was so tanned, but she thought from the humbled tilt of his head that he might be blushing. "Yes, I find it most remarkable."

"Christopher and I agree."

Electra snapped her head back around to Amelia. "Stop talking like that. Surely you can see no one is here but us. For you to talk to Christopher—" She bit back her words. Confronting Amelia with an insinuation that her behavior suggested insanity might not be the wisest course.

A prim smile spread across Amelia's wrinkled face as if she had a secret that eluded Electra.

Carefully Electra said, "Why do you think Christopher is here?"

"Why, because I can *feel* him. Can't you? But then, you never really knew him, did you? Maybe you don't know what to look for."

"And he's been out here for years?"

"Ever since he died," Amelia confirmed with a nod.

Electra didn't know what to say. It was obvious to her why Jerry and the other gardeners sang. They were signaling Amelia that someone was approaching. Did that mean that half of Catawba Mills was aware of Amelia's foolishness or had already concluded she was crazy? Electra knew all too well how hired help liked to gossip.

"Maybe if you come over here, you could feel him better," Amelia suggested. "He always stays close to me."

"And you talk to him. Aloud. Surely he doesn't answer." She hoped to show Amelia the impossibility of what she was saying. "If he doesn't answer, he isn't here."

"Why would you assume that? Two people can be together and one of them not talk. Besides, he *does* answer me."

"He does?"

Amelia nodded. "At first I couldn't hear him, but now I can. I don't know how to explain it, really."

Electra was speechless. It had never occurred to her that Amelia's mind might be slipping. Now she recalled dozens of times when Amelia had mistakenly called her Jenny or some other friend's name, or when Amelia had forgotten or mislaid something. Until now Electra had seen all these incidents of forgetfulness as irritating but normal. Now they added up to something far more alarming.

Electra eased back, her hand fumbling behind her for the gate. She actually heard herself saying, "I didn't mean to intrude."

Amelia smile slowly faded as if her mind was already on other matters.

Once Electra was outside the garden, she stared at the wooden gate, trying to decide what to do. Turning, she glared at Jerry and motioned for him to follow her. When they were out of earshot of the garden, Electra asked, "How long has this been going on?"

Jerry's jaw slackened, and he looked thoroughly miserable. "As long as I've been here, and I started to work here back in 1959. A man by the name of Martin was working here then. He died in '71."

"Yes, yes. I remember him."

"Martin told me to sing whenever anybody was coming so it would hush up Miss Amelia. Used to work, but it don't now."

"Didn't you think it was odd for my sister to be talking

to herself?" Electra demanded in exasperation.

"Yes, ma'am, I did at first. Then I come to see it as being just a regular peculiarity, like Helga throwing salt over her shoulder if she spills any or my brother wearing the same old beat-up cap whenever he goes fishing."

Electra frowned at him.

Uncomfortably shifting his weight from one foot to the other, he added, "We've all got quirks. I reckon this is as harmless as any other one I've ever seen."

"Having a conversation with a man who has been dead for forty years is a bit more than a quirk," she snapped. "Who else knows about this?"

"All the gardeners, of course. And Helga."

Electra groaned. "In other words, it's all over the county!"

Jerry drew himself up and met her frown with one of his own. "No, ma'am, it ain't. Me and the boys, we don't talk bad about Miss Amelia. She's a saint on this earth, if there ever was one. Why, she kept Bob Newsome on when nobody else would hire him and when my youngest girl come down so sick here a while back, Miss Amelia went to the hospital to sit with her and read to her so me and my wife could get some rest. She sat with her many a night before she was well enough to come home. Every one of us that works here has a story like that. If Miss Amelia wants to talk to her flowers or whatever, why, that's up to her."

Electra glared at him in disbelief that hired help could or would be that loyal. She turned on her heel and stalked toward the house. She needed to talk to Saul.

She dialed Saul's number in the privacy of the back parlor, and when he answered, she felt a wave of relief.

"What's wrong?" he asked, obviously picking up on the

anxiety in her voice. "Surely you're not tired of Shangri-la already."

"No, I'm not," she answered testily. "It's Amelia. I'm worried about her."

"Amelia? What's wrong? Is she sick?"

"Yes. I mean no. Saul, I'm not sure." Lightening her tone, she asked, "Would you consider it abnormal for someone to talk to herself?"

"They say it's okay as long as no one answers."

"That's just it. He does. I mean, she thinks he does."

Saul was silent for a minute. "You're kidding. Right?"

"I wish I were. Amelia is convinced Christopher is in the garden. I guess she means his ghost or something. She knows he's dead."

"Christopher was her husband. Right?"

"That's right. He died back in World War Two. Evidently she has been talking to him ever since." She let out a strangled laugh. "I used to think she was meeting a lover out there. God, it must have been Christopher all along!"

"Okay, okay. Calm down. Let me think."

"Maybe it's Alzheimer's or just plain senility."

"Has a doctor seen her?"

"No, I doubt it. Certainly not for this. I just found out about it and came in to call you. I don't know what to do."

Saul was quiet for a minute as if he were trying to digest all this. "I've never known a single time in all these years when you really needed me, when you weren't completely in charge."

"Don't be silly, Saul. I can think of dozens of times."

"Not when you sounded like this."

"Well, of course I'm upset! This is my *sister*." Electra sat on the edge of her correspondence desk and caught her lower lip between her teeth. "It's a good thing I came when I did. Amelia shouldn't be left alone. I've got to do something."

"I thought you said she has been talking to . . . him all this time. Is she distraught or so depressed she might try suicide?"

"Certainly not! You know how Amelia is. She's like an aging Little Mary Sunshine."

"Why not make an appointment with a doctor and take her in for a checkup?"

"How am I supposed to get her there? Tie her up and drag her? She thinks *I'm* crazy because I can't hear him. Besides, I doubt there's a psychiatrist in Catawba Mills, and I wouldn't know who to call in Charlottesville."

"Take her to the family doctor. If he suspects that she has Alzheimer's, he can refer her to a psychiatrist."

"Yes. Why didn't I think of that?" Electra relaxed a bit. "It's so good to hear your voice. I guess I was rather going off the deep end."

"I miss you like hell."

Electra wrapped the phone cord around her fingers. "I miss you, too."

"Why don't I come down for the weekend?"

"Could you? I know you must be in the middle of rehearsals."

"Not over a weekend. Not yet."

"I'd love for you to come down," she said with undisguised relief. "Saul, do you think Amelia will have to go into a nursing home?"

"I hope not. She's as attached to that pile of bricks as you are. Probably more so."

"No one loves Willowbrook more than I do." Electra's

guilt sharpened her voice. In the last few days she had started noticing how drafty the old windows were and how much the drab, dark wood and old wallpaper got on her nerves. "You know I'm not qualified to take care of her if her mind is going. I wouldn't know how to begin. I've never been any good with sick people."

Saul laughed. "There's my Scarlett O'Hara."

His teasing put a smile on Electra's face. That was Saul's pet name for her when she was being stubborn or self-centered. "You just haul your rear end down here to Tara and help me figure out what to do," she retorted.

"I'll catch the late flight on Friday. Is that okay?"

"Yes, that's fine. I'll be waiting up for you."

After they hung up, Electra leaned her head back and massaged the tight muscles in her neck. Worry over Amelia had already given her a headache, but knowing Saul was coming down helped her to relax. Not that she needed him or any other man, she told herself firmly, but Saul was her friend. Together they could decide if Amelia needed to be put into a nursing home for her own good.

In the intervening days until Saul's arrival, Electra could visit nursing homes in the area so she could make an intelligent choice if such a decision became necessary. She tried to imagine Willowbrook without Amelia, but found it was impossible. Amelia was as much a part of the old house as the oak paneling and Aubusson rugs and grandfather clock. Willowbrook had existed without Electra for more than half a century, but she wasn't sure it could do without Amelia. The idea wasn't a comforting one.

For the first time Electra thought of her own and Amelia's mortality in connection with Willowbrook. She was eighty years old and Amelia wasn't much younger. Who would look after the house when they were gone? Electra had never considered this before and the idea was staggering.

There was no one, not a living soul, to whom she could bequeath Willowbrook.

Electra stood and wandered around the room and into the library, looking at the house as if for the first time. Not many people could afford to buy, let alone to keep up, a house and grounds like Willowbrook. She couldn't bear the idea of it being divided into apartments or of letting it lapse into disrepair. Once they were gone, who would wax and polish and dust all this oak and walnut and mahogany?

She lovingly caressed the spines of her father's books. Thanks to Helga, the library had been kept in excellent condition, but dust gathered fast, particularly in houses with drafty windows and loose doors. And who would want these books? Here in Willowbrook's library they looked like old and trusted friends, but taken individually their titles were faded and their spines cracked. They would be tied in bundles and sold by the lot to whoever would haul them away. The thought made her sick.

For the first time in years, Electra felt the full weight of Willowbrook's responsibility. As in her youth, Electra couldn't count on Amelia. Then she had been too featherbrained, and now she seemed to be losing her grip entirely.

Electra sat in the leather chair that had molded itself to her father's bulk. How often she had seen him sit here. He had left this chair that last night and gone upstairs to meet death. But the cushions of the chair still remembered his weight and shape and were ready for him should he return.

He had never considered that neither of his daughters would marry. Of course Amelia had married, but that had been so brief as to scarcely count. Amelia had never left Willowbrook. She had been its caretaker for so many years. Their father had assumed they would marry and have children, preferably sons, and would pass Willowbrook on to them. Electra had expected it herself, as had Amelia. But that had not happened, and now there was no one.

Electra sighed as she stroked the worn leather of the chair's arms. As she had before, she would think of a solution. As always, the burden of logical thinking fell to her. She wondered if Amelia ever had a thought of the responsibilities of Willowbrook's future. Probably not, she decided. Amelia had always been so sheltered. She had probably had few, if any, serious thoughts at all. Electra tried not to feel envious.

CHAPTER 23

AMELIA WAS AWARE OF A CHANGE IN ELECTRA from the moment she admitted she had been talking to Christopher in the garden. She had thought Electra would understand, but evidently she hadn't. Amelia never knew when she might look up from a book and find Electra staring at her or watching her rather than the television. At times she felt certain Electra was standing just outside the room she was in, and when she looked out, she would usually see Electra walking away with studied nonchalance.

A dozen times Amelia started to explain to Electra that she didn't actually hear Christopher audibly but rather intuited his thoughts, but each time she stopped herself, reasoning that Electra might find that admission even stranger.

She also noticed Electra had begun pacing like a caged lion, going from room to room, window to window, as if she were bored to distraction. Amelia tried to get Electra interested in hobbies she herself pursued to while away the day, but Electra had never been one for putting puzzles together or crocheting. As for herself, she thought as she examined her red knuckles, her own crocheting days were numbered.

For years now she had found great pleasure in sending anonymous gifts, usually lap covers or shawls she had crocheted, to patients in the Catawba Mills hospital, but lately there were days, sometimes weeks, when her fingers were too sore and stiff to handle the yarn and needle. Before long she would have to give up her handwork, and she thought that was a shame, since the hospital was her last link with the life she might have led with Christopher.

Amelia sat by the fire in the front parlor and gazed at the old photographs of Christopher on the mantel. She still wished they had had a child. At least then she would have had a living part of him. She paused to count up the years. The child would have been forty-three now. There would have been grandchildren, maybe even great-grandchildren.

She looked around at the room that had been too quiet for too long. As she did almost every day lately, Amelia wondered who would inherit Willowbrook, since Christopher's child had never been born. Christopher was silent on the subject, but she recalled he had never particularly liked the house. After all these years of being personally responsible for the upkeep of Willowbrook, Amelia didn't want strangers in it. Unbeknownst to Electra, she had sent letters to their distant cousins in Georgia all of which had come back marked "Addressee Unknown." If any of that branch of the Radcliff family still existed, she had no way of locating them.

Absently Amelia moved the fire screen toward her to block the heat from her face. She needed to discuss Willowbrook's future with Electra, but she was reluctant to do so. She had talked to Helga about it, and they were both of the opinion that since Electra had always cared so little for Willowbrook, she might take it into her head to sell it. Amelia had lived in the house all her life, and she had no intention of moving away now. Helga felt the same way. As long as Amelia had a breath left in her body, Helga was determined to stay beside her.

The prospect of death was no stranger to Amelia, but she was in no hurry to rush it. Not anymore. She had never bothered to make out a will, since there was no one to be a beneficiary. Helga had said she would move near one of her brothers if Amelia was the first to go. Helga's loyalty pleased Amelia. These days hired help seemed to move from place to place like bees in a flower patch, but the people who worked at Willowbrook were remarkably constant.

Amelia saw Electra pass the parlor door, glancing in yet again as if to be sure Amelia was still in there. She was sure Electra's pacing would wear holes in the rugs, and she dearly wished her sister would light someplace—preferably back in New York. Yes, she wished Electra would just pack up and leave again.

Now Electra had it in her mind to start redecorating Willowbrook! Amelia had, of course, raised Cain over it, but she was almost positive Electra had ordered wallpaper and paint for at least her bedroom. Amelia didn't really object to her sister making her bedroom look nicer. That room faced west, and the wallpaper was sadly faded. But Electra had even talked of new paper in the downstairs rooms or—Amelia shuddered at the idea—of plastering Sheetrock and painting that and the paneling as well in shades of beige and off-white. Amelia had been so upset she had almost had one of her bad spells. Thankfully she had managed to outargue Electra, but she didn't trust her. She was afraid that if she died first, Electra would paint the whole house beige and sell it off, piece by piece, as condominiums or whatever. The mere notion left Amelia lightheaded.

She reached for the small pill bottle in a drawer of the table beside her chair and placed a glycerine tablet under her tongue. Thinking too much about Electra and the future wasn't a good idea. She waited calmly for her spell to pass.

Electra could hardly wait for Saul to arrive. She had kept a close eye on Amelia and had taken note of every lapse of memory and every article she misplaced. One of the young maid's regular tasks appeared to be locating and retrieving Amelia's lost glasses or crochet hook or her book. The girl was evidently accustomed to doing this, because she was amazingly adroit at discovering books under chair cushions and eyeglasses in vases. Electra had been diligent at recording every eccentricity she observed in the notepad she had begun carrying in her pocket. She had never been around anyone whose mind was slipping, and she wasn't sure what questions the doctor would ask her about her sister's behavior.

It was close to midnight on Friday when Saul arrived. Electra immediately escorted him to his usual room, and once the door was closed so they could talk privately, she gave him her notepad.

"What's this?" he asked.

"I've jotted down all the weird things Amelia has been doing." Her eyes searched his face anxiously as he read the first few pages.

"Electra, you can't be serious. These things are no different from what you or I or anyone else might do from time to time."

"I have never put a crochet hook in the butter compartment of a refrigerator, and I daresay neither have you."

"I'll admit it's a bit odd, but it's no reason to have her committed."

Electra bit her lower lip. Until now she had avoided even thinking of the word "commitment." She had considered only the possibility of moving Amelia to a nursing home, not a mental hospital. "Do you think commitment will be necessary? I mean, can't I just have her kept in a nursing home?"

"I'm sure a nursing home won't keep Amelia against her will unless she's certified incompetent."

She sat on the end of the bed and crossed her legs. "I never thought of that."

After scanning a few more pages Saul said, "I think you're brewing up a tempest in a teapot."

"That's because she isn't your sister. I'm worried sick over her. All she did this afternoon was sit in the front parlor and stare at the fire. I have no idea what could have been running through her mind."

"Maybe she was wondering why you've started writing down her every move and is planning to have *you* committed."

"Very funny."

Saul smiled. "Look, honey. There is nothing we can do tonight. Let me talk to her tomorrow and see what I think."

"I suppose you're right."

"Do you want to sleep in here or in your room?"

Electra smiled. "I'd like to sleep with you. God, Saul, you have no idea how much I've missed you."

"I'll bet I do. Go get ready for bed and let's get some sleep."

With a lighter heart, Electra changed into her nightgown and rumpled her bedcover so the maids wouldn't suspect she'd slept elsewhere and be needlessly shocked. She almost laughed at the thought that in her youth she had flouted tradition and now she was trying to keep up the appearance of modest behavior for the sake of maids whom she barely knew. She supposed that her only predictable trait was her unpredictability.

The next morning at breakfast Amelia was pleased to find Saul at the table. "I had no idea you were coming. Electra, you should have told me, and I would have asked Helga to make those blueberry pancakes he likes so much."

"You spoil me," Saul said with a smile.

"It's good for a person to be pampered now and then. I'll ask Helga to make your favorite chocolate cake for supper."

"The one with the whipped cream filling?" His smile broadened into a boyish grin.

"I'll go tell her now." Amelia got up and hurried from the room as fast as her stiff knees could carry her.

"Helga, you'll never guess who's here," Amelia said as she entered the kitchen. "Saul!"

"I know. I just saw him."

"Why, that's right. You would have seen him when you carried in his breakfast. I promised him that cake he likes. You know, the recipe you cut out of that magazine."

"*Ja*. Already I have thought of it. I will send Nadine into town for whipping cream when she is finished making up beds. Is good to see him again, is it not?"

"Yes, it is. Very good."

When Amelia went back into the dining room, Electra was leaning toward Saul, obviously engaged in earnest conversation. But before she could hear what was being said, Electra abruptly straightened as if she had been caught doing something wrong. Amelia glanced from one to the other as she resumed her seat. "Can you stay with us for a while this time?" she asked Saul.

"Only for the weekend, I'm afraid. I have a play in rehearsal."

"You should bring all your actors down to Willowbrook one of these days," Amelia suggested, but with a teasing smile. "Helga could stuff them with blueberry pancakes, and they could put on a play at the high school in Catawba Mills."

Electra looked to Saul as if to be sure he was paying attention, then turned back to Amelia. "You know that's impossible. Surely you know that."

Amelia searched her sister's face. "I wasn't serious, for goodness' sake." There was something strange going on here, and Amelia wasn't sure she liked it. She passed the plate of biscuits to Saul.

"So, Amelia, what have you been up to since I last saw you?" Saul asked, feigning nonchalance.

"Oh, the same old stuff. Nothing much changes around here, you know."

Electra put down her fork. "I'd say there's been one big change. I moved back home. Remember?"

"Well, of course I remember," Amelia testily responded. "You're sitting right there, aren't you? Saul asked what *I* have been doing, and I haven't done anything new to speak of." She could have added "Except for having to put up with you," but good manners forbade it. "Why don't you two get married and go on a world cruise or something?" she grumbled. That would get Electra out of the house for a while.

"Amelia!" her sister gasped.

"I've asked her to marry me," Saul said. "She keeps turning me down."

"You shouldn't take a chance on losing a good man like Saul," Amelia said to needle Electra. "You know what happened to Richard Stuart when you put him off."

"What happened?" Saul asked with amusement.

Amelia was enjoying their banter and Electra's discomfort. "Nothing. Absolutely nothing."

"She's talking about a boy I used to date when Papa was still alive," Electra explained in a tight voice. "I haven't thought of him in years."

"He had a British accent. Married a girl from Michigan or Minnesota or someplace like that. I met her a time or two. She was rather nice. Had fluffy hair, the kind that sticks out from the head."

"How can you remember that when you can't remember where you put your slippers?"

Amelia looked at her in confusion. "My slippers are in my closet. What makes you think I lost them?"

Saul looked as if he was choking down a laugh.

Electra stood and tossed her napkin down on the table. In a frigid voice she said, "I'm going for a walk. If you'll excuse me?" Not waiting for a reply, she stalked away.

"Now, why do you suppose she's acting like a wet hen?" Amelia wondered aloud.

"Don't pay her any attention."

Amelia lowered her voice. "Electra is driving me to

distraction. She wanders from room to room and won't sit still five minutes running. I don't know what can be wrong with her."

"As a matter of fact, she's worried about you."

"Me!"

"She says you talk to Christopher," Saul ventured, "and that he answers you."

"Oh, for Pete's sake! Come with me. No, bring your biscuit with you." Amelia led him through the house and grabbed her coat from the hall tree. "I should have known she would go off the deep end over that. Put on your coat. It's cold out."

Saul held the biscuit between his teeth as he shrugged into his heavy coat, then followed Amelia outside. "Looks like snow is coming," he commented as they crossed the lawn.

"Probably. It would be an odd winter if it didn't come."

At the entrance to her garden, she pressed down the latch and swung open the gate. "Come inside," she urged when Saul hesitated. "Get in before Electra sees us and comes barging in." She closed the gate behind them and preceded Saul down the brick path. When she was beneath the willow tree she sat on the bench and patted the cold marble beside her. "Sit here."

Saul did as she instructed.

Amelia folded her hands in her lap and drew in a deep breath of cold air. "There, now. Can't you feel him?"

"Who?"

"Christopher, of course. Oh, not in the flesh, but his essence." She shook her head. "No, I suppose you can't, since you never met him. But being near Christopher made me feel like this garden does—calm, yet full of life. I come here and I talk to him. If I hold my mind just right I can hear him answer. I know how he feels about a thing."

"You hear him?" Saul gently asked.

"Not with my ears. With my heart. I hear him in my heart."

Saul studied her profile. "You must have loved him with a rare devotion."

She nodded. "I never met any other man like Christopher. When I was with him I was, well, more than I am. Do you know what I mean? I was braver and more patient and happier."

"It's been a long time," Saul reminded her.

"It's been a lifetime and then some. He's been dead longer than he was alive. When I heard he'd been killed, I prayed to die. I really did. If it hadn't been for Helga and my friend Jenny, I think I would have."

"No one dies from a broken heart."

"Whoever said that has never had one. Part of me did die with Christopher. Maybe that's why I can feel him here with me. A part of me is with him."

"Why here? Why not in the house? Didn't you two live there for a while?"

"Christopher never liked Willowbrook. That was one of the few things we disagreed about. We met here in the garden, or we were reunited here, I should say. We knew each other when we were children, you know. We were married here in this garden. The minister stood here and we stood there." She pointed to a spot a few feet away. "He was so handsome with his hair all golden in the sunlight and his eyes so blue and full of love." She let her voice trail away as she remembered that day. "We always came out here to the garden when we wanted to be alone. He proposed here." She laughed. "We even made love out here, if you can believe that, coming from an old woman."

"I believe you."

"I was young then," Amelia said as if he hadn't spoken. "My hair was still auburn and I wasn't wrinkled or sore in the joints. I planned to have children, even though we were getting a late start. Christopher worried about that, but I know I would have been all right." She looked sideways at Saul. "All we ever had was a beginning. No middle and no end, just a beginning. So I come out here and I talk to him, and whether it's strictly true or not, I believe he answers me. What harm is there in that?"

"None. No harm whatsoever." Saul covered her hand with his. "Let's go back to the house. You must be half frozen."

Amelia had to let him help her up. Her knees and hips were rebellious when they were cold. "Snow is coming, as you said. I can feel it. Maybe you'll get snowed in and we can keep you here for a while."

"Maybe so," he said with a smile.

"But if not, I wish you'd take Electra back with you. She's driving me crazy."

Saul laughed.

When they returned to the house, Electra was waiting for them in the front parlor. Having seen as much and more of Electra than she wanted, Amelia made the excuse of needing to tell Helga something and left them alone.

"Well?" Electra demanded when Amelia was gone.

"She's as sane as we are. She just misses her husband."

"After forty-some-odd years? It's morbid to grieve that long for someone she barely knew."

"She loved him." Saul warmed his hands by the fire. "I

wish I thought you would grieve that long for me."

"You ought to be happy that I'm more sensible than she is. What about the way she talks aloud to him? And what about him answering her? You can't convince me that's normal!"

"It's not the way you think. She knows he's dead. She is as normal as you are."

"Thanks for nothing! I don't care what you say, I'm taking her to a doctor as soon as I can get an appointment!"

"You're taking me to a doctor?" Amelia said from the doorway. "What's this? What doctor?"

Electra wheeled around to face her. "I thought you went to the kitchen!"

"I forgot to hang up my coat." She let Saul take it from her and carry it to the hall tree. "What's this about a doctor?"

Electra drew in a deep breath. "I'm worried about you."

"About my mind, you mean," Amelia said, her voice rising. "You think I'm crazy! That's it, isn't it?"

Electra's temper flared. "Talking with a dead man isn't exactly sane, especially when he *answers* you. And you're so forgetful these days, I'm afraid you'll wander off and freeze in the woods or turn on a gas jet and blow us all up!"

Amelia stared at her for a long moment as if considering her response. With her eyes fixed on Electra's, she said, "If anybody is crazy around here, it's you for talking like that!"

Saul hurried back in and stepped between the angry sisters. "Now calm down, both of you."

"Don't tell me to calm down, Saul Feldman!" Electra snapped.

"You're just causing trouble," Amelia said to her sister. "You always have, bringing in those boys the way you did and begrudging me not only Christopher but his memory as well."

This was close enough to home to sting. Electra clenched her hands into fists and planted them on her hips. "At least my lovers were flesh and blood and not some . . . some *ghost*."

"Christopher is not a ghost and don't you say he is!"

"Ladies!" Saul interjected. "Please! Sit down so we can work this out."

Electra paced to the window as Amelia sat on the edge of the love seat.

"Electra, you too. Sit in that chair."

She glared at him for a long time, then did as he said. She and Amelia exchanged a look of pure animosity.

"Now, there's obviously more going on here than whether Amelia talks to herself. What is it?"

"I talk to Christopher. Not to myself."

"See? She admits it!" Electra resisted the urge to leap to her feet.

"So what?" Saul asked. "Why do you care?"

"She's my sister. I've always had to take care of her! When Papa died we would have lost everything if it hadn't been for me." Electra trembled with rage. "I even sold myself so she could live here in comfort. I sold myself!"

"No one asked you to," Amelia snapped. "I never asked you to do that. I would have moved to a smaller house. I would have taken a job."

"Doing what? Neither of us ever had been taught to earn a living."

"Someone would have hired us. You can't blame me because you agreed to be Mr. Hastings's mistress! All these years I've waited for you to come back and take over Willowbrook, as you promised you would, so I would be free to travel, but you stalled until now, when I'm too old to leave. You didn't even want me to marry Christopher for fear you'd lose me as caretaker."

"Caretaker! That's the thanks I get for working myself half to death all those years?" Electra was so angry she could scarcely talk.

"I never asked you to! I told you I wanted to get away from here! I kept Willowbrook going for you."

"And I offered you a chance to travel. I did! Several times! But you always turned it down. You said you had to put up preserves or oversee a repair or whatever. You had your chances to travel!"

"And you were able to design your clothes," Amelia retorted. "That's all you ever wanted to do—design clothes. You were so engrossed in drawing dresses that you put off getting engaged until all our beaux found other girls! Don't try to tell me you sacrificed anything!"

Saul reached out and took each of them by a hand. "Do you two hear what you're saying?"

Both turned at once and glared at him.

"Electra, you got to follow your dream. You became a designer of the first order. You could never have done that without moving to New York, now, could you?"

"That's not the point! I—"

"Yes, it is." Saul kept his voice calm to soothe her. "And you, Amelia, got what you wanted, too. You got security. In the garden when you were telling me how you felt, you were describing security. Would you be happy away from your garden?"

Amelia looked doubtful. "That's not the same. I—"

"If you hadn't been here at Willowbrook you would never

have seen Christopher when he came back."

"That's true," she admitted reluctantly. "And I always planned to return to Willowbrook after my travels. I never wanted to live anywhere else."

Saul turned back to Electra. "Would you have been happy if you'd never left Catawba Mills? Can you honestly say you're glad to have moved back home?"

Electra looked away. "I love Willowbrook."

"I know you do, but do you love it in large doses?"

"She wants to change everything," Amelia put in. "She wants to paint it beige and off-white."

Saul grinned at Electra. "Come on, now. Admit it."

"All right," Electra said angrily. "So I miss New York. I lived there most of my life. Of course a person misses what she's become accustomed to."

"I think it's more than that. Betty tells me you're sending her sketches nearly every day. That you're working on a new show."

"I told you I wouldn't shut down Electra, Inc. until Betty decided to retire. She has to have sketches or there won't be any dresses to sell. And since when have you started talking to Betty about me?"

"I was curious to see if you had really retired. Betty says there's a woman in your office who is quite capable of creating designs."

"She is not! I am Electra! I won't have my name on some garment I didn't create. Surely you can understand that."

"Yes, I can. The only thing I can't figure out is why you wanted to retire in the first place."

"Well, hell, Saul. I'm eighty years old! Did you think I would work forever?"

He laughed. "As a matter of fact, I did. Come back with me. You know you're bored sick out here in the country."

Amelia leaned forward eagerly.

"I'll do no such thing," Electra said. Amelia sat back.

"You admitted you miss New York," Saul prompted.

"I've let my place go. All my furniture is on the way down here."

"Move in with me. Hell, I'll even marry you." Saul grinned at her as if he had never proposed such a thing before.

"I'm tired of work." She couldn't make her words sound convincing even to herself. "The air is clean here. I can breathe."

"Come back with me," he repeated.

Electra wavered. Then she saw Amelia surreptitiously reach into the drawer beside her and take out her heart pills. "No. I've moved home and I'm staying." Amelia had said she took the pills regularly as a precaution, but Electra suspected the problem was more serious than Amelia would admit. She couldn't leave until she'd had a chance to talk to Amelia's doctor. "I have no intention of leaving," she repeated.

Saul, who hadn't seen Amelia take the medicine, shook his head, perplexed. "It's just a house, Electra. Just bricks and wood and furniture. Not a shrine."

"What will happen to it when we're gone?" Amelia suddenly blurted out. "What will happen to Willowbrook?"

Stunned, Electra looked at her. This was exactly what she had been asking herself lately. "How should I know? There's no one to inherit it. I suppose whoever settles our estate will dispose of it."

"Sell it, you mean." Amelia's jaw set into stubborn lines.

"Well, we can't pack it up and take it with us," Electra burst out. "After we're gone, it shouldn't matter. We won't be here."

"Nobody around here could afford Willowbrook. It will be chopped up and sold in acre lots the way the Knapp estate was. The house fell to ruin and was finally sold for scrap lumber."

Electra looked around the room. "No one would do that to Willowbrook."

"The Knapp place was almost as nice as this. If it didn't sell, this one won't either."

Electra frowned. "There must be some provision we could make. Someone to look after it."

"It's only a *house*," Saul put in.

"No, it's not," Electra replied. "It's more than that to us." She looked at Amelia and tentatively smiled. "Amelia and I have based our entire lives on the welfare of this house. Right or wrong, it's important to us."

Amelia nodded. "It's our heritage. And more."

Saul sighed. "Okay, then, do you know anyone who could afford its upkeep? Maybe the children or grandchildren of friends?"

"I'm so out of touch," Electra said. "I have no idea who has children or what they may be like."

"Jenny has two daughters, but I wouldn't leave anything to them, not after they put Jenny in that nursing home."

Saul's face lit up in inspiration. "What about something like a historical society? Surely Catawba Mills has something like that."

Amelia nodded with interest. "There is a preservation society! I remember a campaign last summer to save the old depot from being demolished."

"Will they take this house, do you think?" Electra asked with growing excitement.

"I can call and ask," Amelia said. "I'll call right now."

Electra leaned forward and clasped both of Saul's hands as Amelia started from the room. "That was an inspiration! It's the perfect solution."

Saul shrugged, but he looked proud of himself. "I had to think of something. I couldn't have my two favorite ladies so unhappy."

Amelia stopped at the door and looked back at Saul. "That's it! That's what I wanted to tell you, but I forgot until you said that. You remind me of Christopher. You always have."

Electra stared at Saul. "What are you talking about? They look nothing at all alike."

"No, but he reminds me of Christopher, nevertheless." She continued on toward the hall and the phone.

Electra was still surprised, and yet on one level she knew it was true. She had just never been able to admit it before. Saul was like Christopher. Only Saul was like the part of him that Electra had loved, not the part he had given to Amelia. "You know," she said softly, "I think she's right."

CHAPTER 24

MRS. OLIVIA SIMPSON, PRESIDENT OF THE CAtawba Mills Historical Preservation Society, sat on the velvet love seat in Willowbrook's front parlor and she was wearing an expression that indicated she felt she had died and gone to heaven. "Beautiful!" she exclaimed again. "Simply beautiful. I can't tell you ladies how honored our society is to be named your beneficiary."

"Electra and I have already spoken to Ben Dupree—he's our lawyer, you know—and all the papers are in order. Electra has arranged for an endowment to keep up the house." Amelia clasped her hands in her lap and smiled at Mrs. Simpson. She vaguely remembered the woman's mother from her high school days. Olivia seemed to have more sense than her mother had had, and this pleased Amelia. She wouldn't have been comfortable leaving Willowbrook to a group run by someone without common sense.

"Do you have any questions?" Electra asked. "All the furniture is to remain in the house. Naturally Willowbrook won't be handed over to you as long as either of us chooses to live here."

"Perhaps it's indelicate to ask this," Mrs. Simpson said, "but what about your personal belongings? Clothes, linens, and so forth?"

Electra spoke up quickly. "Well, of course, there are a few things of sentimental value which we have specifically included in our wills, such as Papa's pocket watch, which I have treasured all these years. I want my friend Saul Feldman to have that. And there are a few things of Amelia's that would mean a lot to her housekeeper, Helga, who has been with her since before the Second World War. Your society may keep whatever you choose of those unlisted items to display in the house."

"There are some lovely old gowns in the attic room," Amelia reminded her. "They date back to early in the century and if you look in the old trunks under the south eave you'll find our great-grandfather's Confederate uniform and some other clothes that go all the way back to when the house was built."

"Whatever you don't want is to be given to charity," Electra added.

Amelia hesitated, then said, "I do have one further stipulation. All our help here are very loyal to us and to Willowbrook. I must insist they be kept on here for as long as they wish. Helga has her rooms over the garage, and one gardener and his family live in the cottage. I don't want them to be sent away."

"No, no. Of course not," Mrs. Simpson said. "Actually, having them here will be a distinct advantage to us in that we won't have to train new people to keep up the place.

Besides, I'm sure it will be years and years before any of this is necessary."

"I wouldn't be so sure of that," Amelia said. "Neither of us is a spring chicken. Electra is eighty."

Electra frowned her disapproval, but Amelia ignored her. At their ages, Amelia thought it was silly to pretend they still had an indefinite life expectancy.

"Well, I must be running along," Mrs. Simpson said. "Again I want to thank you for your extremely generous gift and for showing me around the house."

"Your acceptance of our home has relieved us of a great deal of worry," Electra assured her.

Amelia watched as Electra walked Mrs. Simpson to the door. It was done. They had signed their wills that morning in this very room. Ben Dupree had brought everything to the house, saying it was for their convenience, but Amelia thought it more likely he had been afraid that with snow in the forecast, she and Electra might have an accident on the way to town and die intestate, putting him in the onerous position of having to wade through a mountain of legal work to settle their affairs.

She had never felt quite as comfortable with Benjamin Dupree IV as she had been with his grandfather, perhaps because he was younger than she and Electra and had not been through such difficult times with them as had the elder Dupree. And he seemed to be so much busier than his grandfather or even his father ever had been, never having time to sit and visit. But then, everyone seemed to be pursuing life at such a rapid pace these days that Amelia wasn't surprised the divorce rate was so high and so many of them seemed discontented. Somehow Electra seemed to have been caught up in that same hectic life-style. She wasn't sure whether it had been Electra's fault for always trying to be younger than she was or whether it had happened because she had lived all her adult life in a big city. Whatever the reason, Amelia felt sorry for her and thought what a shame it was that they had never been close.

With considerable effort, she got to her feet and tottered to the window, a painful process on such a cold day. Brushing aside the lace curtain, she looked out across the lawn. Snow was beginning to fall, and as the ground was already frozen, the big flakes were rapidly blanketing everything. Amelia had always liked snow, and even though the accompanying cold weather had begun to affect her adversely, she still thought it was pretty. But then, Amelia liked all the seasons for one reason or another.

She let the curtain fall back into place over the frosty glass. In the hall behind her she could hear Olivia Simpson thanking Electra again, and knew Electra was trying to get the woman out of the door before more cold air rushed in. Amelia had to smile. Electra always took everything so seriously. The furnace would soon warm the hall.

After the front door closed, Electra called from the doorway, "I'm going upstairs to write Saul. I promised to let him know when everything was done."

"I'll go up with you."

Amelia crossed the room, letting her hand caress the carved back of the settee as she passed it. She was relieved to know the house would continue. "Isn't it odd to think of tourists coming through this house? I suppose the society will put up velvet stanchions in the doorways and cover the carpet in the hallways with one of those horrible vinyl runners."

"Maybe not. Everything is in such excellent condition

they may use it as a hands-on exhibit. Hire it out for weddings and teas and so forth."

"There will probably be a plaque on the door to your room saying 'Electra slept here' or some such nonsense."

"Do you think I should leave my drawing table here? It looks out of place with all the antiques."

"Of course you should. The tour guides will probably make up all sorts of stories about how you learned to design at that very desk and how that set you on the path to international fame."

"But it's not true."

"So what? If you weren't so famous the society might not have wanted this house. I'm sure they feel your name will attract more tourists than . . . than mine."

As they climbed the stairs, Electra slowed her steps to match Amelia's. "Whoever would have thought things would turn out the way they have? When we were growing up, I never had an ambition to be a famous designer."

"I wanted to be a writer," Amelia confessed.

"You did? You never told me that!"

"There was nothing to write about, I guess. I thought I would travel and be inspired by all those exotic places. I never told Jenny either. Maybe I was afraid to try and fail. Christopher knew. I told him."

Electra was silent until they reached the top of the stairs. Hesitantly she said, "Amelia, there's something I need to get off my chest. I didn't hate Christopher. I guess, well, I guess I was jealous. You see, when I met him as an adult, I felt . . . that is, I found myself falling—"

"Don't say any more," Amelia broke in. "Some things aren't meant to be said aloud. I know what you're going to say. For a long time I didn't, but then I finally figured it out. That's one reason I pointed out to you that Saul reminds me of Christopher." Her eyes met Electra's and she repeated, "Some things just aren't meant to be said."

Electra nodded and went into her room. Amelia stared at her closed door for a moment, then continued down the hall. She hoped Electra wasn't going to start unburdening her conscience right and left. Amelia had no intention of reciprocating. For the first time in years she felt as if she loved Electra, and she didn't want blatant honesty to sneak in and destroy that love again.

She closed the door to her room and got her jewelry box from the closet and took it to the window seat where the light was better. She didn't own much jewelry because she had never been particularly fond of wearing it. Her wedding band, now worn paper-thin, was the only ring she always wore. Inside the box was the short string of pearls that had been practically mandatory with silk shirtwaist dresses and the little black dresses of several decades earlier, and the pearl stud earrings that matched the necklace. Beside these was the gold locket that had belonged to her mother, the one that contained tiny photos of both her parents. In the tray beneath were a sapphire and diamond ring her father had given her for her coming-out party, a diamond dinner ring, and one with an opal surrounded by diamonds. She took out the opal ring and her pearls and closed the lid. Eventually the other jewelry would go to Electra, but she wanted to give these to Helga.

She slipped them into the pocket of her dress and began the trip back downstairs. She recalled a time when the trip up and down had been nothing, when she had made the journey as if walking on flat ground. Now she planned her trips to her room to avoid needlessly climbing the stairs.

Helga was in the kitchen rolling dough for apple strudel, singing a German song slightly off-key as she worked. As it was the cook's day off, Helga had the room to herself. Amelia had entirely crossed the room and touched her arm before Helga knew she wasn't alone. Her last note ended on a squeak.

"You are scaring me half out of my wits," she said as she saw it was Amelia.

"I'm sorry. I wanted to give you these." Amelia put the pearls and ring on Helga's floury palm and closed her fingers around them.

"What are these?" Helga stared down at the jewelry.

"I want you to have them. I put it in my will that they are to go to you, but I decided to give them to you ahead of time."

"But these are yours! I cannot be taking them." Helga tried to give them back.

Amelia shook her head and put her hands behind her back. "If Electra should go before I do, there might be some mix-up and you might not get them. Lately I'm so absent-minded I might put them someplace where no one would ever find them. This way I know where they are."

"But is too much!" Helga stared down at the handful of jewels. Then she said suspiciously, "You are feeling bad? Ja?"

"No, I feel just the same as I always do. I guess it was signing my will this morning and showing Bertha Cates's daughter around the house—whatever her name was. Simpson, I think. Anyway, it struck me that this is a day for tying up loose ends. Haven't you ever felt that way?"

"Ja, I am knowing the feeling. But Miss Electra might think I took these."

Amelia shook her head. "I'll tell her when she finishes writing Saul. Remind me."

"I will put them away in a safe place," Helga said. "Thank you."

Amelia smiled and nodded. "Good, good."

She left the kitchen and went back toward the front of the house. Soon winter would be over and spring would arrive again. It was a good time for finishing up things. She went back to the parlor window and looked out. Her garden was there. Snow was covering the dark ivy leaves, and she could see the white-rimmed bare limbs of the tops of the willow and mimosa trees above the wall. She should tell Christopher about the historical society agreeing to take the house.

At the hall tree she stopped and put on her heavy coat and tied a woolen scarf over her head. It was cold out and she didn't want to take a chill. As she went to the front door she put on one thick glove and on the porch she put on the other. Her legs were cold beneath her skirt, but she wore warm socks and leather shoes. She would only be outside a few minutes.

Holding carefully to the handrail, she went down the steps. It wouldn't do to fall, she told herself. She planned to talk to Christopher and be back in the house before Electra missed her.

The snow beneath her feet was crunchy, but not so deep as to come in over the tops of her shoes. As the snow fell silently all about her, she paused for a moment and caught some flakes on her gloves as she had when she was a child. She could remember the time she and Electra had examined snowflakes with their father's magnifying glass and how they had marveled over each one being so different from the rest. She was glad she and Electra had finally resolved their differences.

At her garden, she unlatched the gate and tugged, but the hinges were frozen and the gate failed to move. Putting all her strength behind her efforts, she pulled again, and it finally swung open. She left it ajar so she could avoid the same difficulty getting back out.

With no wind to speak of, the snowflakes were falling straight down and had covered the garden in an even whiteness. The sundial sitting amid a pool of white had a frosting of snow on its copper face. Clear icicles hung like a fringe all around it. The bare bridal wreath and forsythia branches huddled against the far wall, and the potting shed in the corner looked bleak and cold.

Amelia's knees were aching and her feet were reluctant to obey, but she walked over to the sundial and wiped its face clean. As there was no sun, she couldn't tell the time, but each of the raised numbers had a line of whiteness where the snow had already frozen in place.

"I guess I won't be back out here until next spring," she said in the quietness. "Not unless there's a spell of warm weather in between. Be glad your knees never went back on you, Christopher. It's no picnic, I can tell you."

She looked at the bare rosebushes and tried to recall which one bloomed in what color but gave it up. She could refresh her memory when they began budding out again.

"Bertha Cates's daughter was out. She's a Simpson now, I think. Anyway, Electra and I have willed Willowbrook to the local historical society. I knew you would be wondering, so I came out to tell you. I can't linger, though. It's cold enough out here to freeze the ears off a brass monkey, as Papa used to say."

She walked around the sundial and was about to go to the gate when a movement at the corner of her eye caught her attention. She turned her head and narrowed her eyes, trying to focus on the marble bench beneath the willow tree. She blinked two or three times, afraid her eyes were deceiving her, but the image remained. It was Christopher, sitting there smiling at her.

In amazement, her jaw dropped open, and at the same time she winced as a vise tightened inside her chest. As her left arm went numb, she pulled at the neck of her coat with her other hand. Then she fell.

After what might have been a moment or forever, Amelia blinked and sat up. Although it was still snowing, she no longer felt the cold. From somewhere nearby she smelled roses and wisteria. She looked back at the bench, and Christopher smiled again.

As she stared at him, he rose, came to her, and knelt beside her. His blue eyes sparkled and his hair was as bright as if sunlight were shining on it.

"Are you ready to come with me?" he said.

She wanted to say yes, but something held her back. "I'm afraid," she said at last.

"There's nothing to be afraid of. The worst is over. I'll be beside you all the way."

She opened her mouth to say she was old and that he must find her ugly, but even before she could speak, he laughed and shook his head as he took her hand.

"Look," he told her. Or at least that's what she heard, even though his lips didn't move.

Although reluctant to take her eyes off his face, she looked down at her hand and found it was supple and strong. Her skin was firm again, and her knuckles were not swollen.

She could only stare. Slowly she turned her hand palm up and flexed her fingers.

"Are you ready to come with me now?" he repeated.

"Where? Come with you where?"

"Anywhere you like. London, Paris, Istanbul. All the places you planned for us to go. All those and more."

The dreamlike state she was in was feeling more and more natural and she nodded. With all the lithe grace of her youth she stood, and as she did, she felt a gentle tugging, then a release. She gazed raptly up at Christopher's beloved face. Beyond him she saw the mimosa, wisteria, and honeysuckle blooming with a lushness she had never seen before, as if all the blossoms of all the past seasons were there before her. She felt his love envelop her, and her own love went out to him. Without a backward glance at the still form lying in the snow, they stepped into eternity.

Electra finished her letter to Saul and signed it in her strong, slanted handwriting. Taking a stamp from her dresser drawer, she licked it, then stuck it on the corner of the envelope.

There was a day full of things she needed to do. Drawers to clean out, personal letters to sort through. She didn't necessarily want the society to have her old correspondence. With fame came a certain responsibility. She didn't want every detail of her life to become public. Certainly not the parts that had included Bret Harley and Carter Symmons and others like them. Also she had had an inspiration for a dress while she wrote Saul, and she was eager to get it down on paper.

She went down to the entry hall and put Saul's letter on the table to be posted. As she was going to her drawing table in the back parlor, Helga stopped her.

"Miss Electra, I must talk with you." Helga held out Amelia's pearl necklace and earrings and the opal ring. "Miss Amelia gave these to me, and I don't know if I should be keeping them."

Electra's aged brow furrowed as she looked down at the jewels. She recognized them as the ones Amelia had described in her will that were to go to Helga. "Why did she give them to you now?"

"I do not know. Perhaps this is a mistake. Perhaps, I should put them back in her jewel box?"

Electra shook her head. "She meant for you to have them someday. I suppose she wanted the pleasure of giving them to you herself. Our attorney brought our wills out to us only this morning and these are the items of jewelry she had listed for you to inherit. There's no mistake." All the same, Electra felt a deep uneasiness. "Where is Amelia?"

"I am not knowing. I guess she is in the front parlor or in her room."

"Thank you," Electra absently replied. Her uneasiness was steadily building. She began searching for Amelia.

When she didn't find her in the parlor or in her bedroom she started a systematic search of all the rooms. Then with Helga's help she searched them again.

"Call Jerry's house," Electra said. "Maybe she went out there." She began pulling on her coat as she said it. "Wasn't her coat here earlier?"

"*Himmel*! She would not have gone outside in the snow!"

Electra pulled on her knit cap. "Call Jerry."

She heard Helga scurrying to the phone as she went out onto the porch. The snow was coming down in earnest now, and there was enough ice in it to make a hissing sound as it fell. Electra could tell at a glance that Amelia wasn't on the porch or in the yard. Then she looked at the walled garden and saw the gate standing open.

Her heart began to beat faster as she eased down the icy steps. Had Amelia gone out to the garden on a day like this? She couldn't remember if her coat had been on the hall tree earlier or not. The cold stung her skin and her body ached, but Electra didn't have a thought about turning back. With that gate open, she knew Amelia must be out there in the snow. Without another thought for her own safety, Electra hurried to the garden.

From just inside the gate, Electra saw Amelia's dark form lying in the snow beside the sundial. Already there were white drifts in the folds of Amelia's coat and scarf. As quickly as she could, Electra went to her sister and knelt beside her.

Amelia was dead. Electra knew it even before her cold-stiffened fingers failed to find a pulse. She pushed her hand under the scarf to search for a heartbeat in Amelia's throat. "Amelia? Amelia!" Her voice was harsh and stricken in the silence of the garden. Amelia lay with her eyes closed as peacefully as if she were sleeping, her lips curved up in the hint of a smile.

"He came for you," Electra murmured to the still form. "Christopher came for you, just as you knew he would." A numbness stole over her, but she remained huddled in the snow.

Within minutes Electra heard running footsteps, and she looked up to see Jerry bolt into the garden. When he saw them he halted.

In as calm a voice as she could manage, Electra said, "Help me get my sister back to the house."

Jerry drew Electra to her feet, then bent and picked up Amelia's still form. He had not taken the time to put on a cap, and as he stood there, snow began covering his thick hair and his eyes held tears not caused by the bitter cold. Carrying Amelia like a child, Jerry followed Electra back to the house.

CHAPTER 25

THE FUNERAL FOR AMELIA RADCLIFF JENKINS was simple, but the turnout was surprisingly large for a person so advanced in years. As Amelia had said, most of their contemporaries were dead or in nursing homes, but Amelia's friends obviously weren't limited to her peers. Saul had flown down from New York, and Electra put her hand in his as the preacher began the service. His strength was reassuring, and she felt ridiculously close to tears, knowing he had turned over his rehearsals to his assistant director in order to be with her during these harrowing days. He squeezed her hand comfortingly.

Electra didn't know the minister, but he had evidently known Amelia quite well. Electra hadn't realized her sister had attended church with any regularity, but Reverend Payne spoke of Amelia in a way that indicated she was well known to him and would be sorely missed.

The staff members from Willowbrook were there with their families, and Electra saw few dry eyes among them. Helga was sobbing softly. Electra didn't know any of the other mourners, but they all looked as if Amelia's death was a personal loss to them. She remembered again how Amelia always had been able to engender fierce loyalty from those around her. Electra had never understood what it was about her sister that affected people that way, but Amelia had made friends of all ages and from all walks of life.

Electra had chosen an oak coffin for Amelia and had asked that Amelia's curly maple box containing Christopher's letters be placed beneath Amelia's hand before the coffin was sealed. And at her insistence the coffin remained closed during the service, for she felt it was needlessly stressful on those left behind, if not barbaric, for the coffin to be opened so that people could have one last look. She would rather remember Amelia as she had been in life.

Electra thought her aversion to the rituals of death was likely the result of her being coerced by her parents into patting her dead grandmother's cheek and telling her goodbye. She knew her parents had meant well, but she had had nightmares about it for months afterward. Amelia had been too young to attend the funeral and had thus been spared the ordeal. Now Amelia lay in the same spot their grandmother had occupied, as well as both their parents in their turn. The idea brought no comfort to Electra.

She leaned nearer to Saul. "When it's my turn, I want to be cremated," she whispered.

A muscle tightened in Saul's jaw, but he nodded. Electra knew this was difficult for him, too. He hadn't seen Amelia often, but they had developed a close friendship. Electra felt a twinge of jealousy as she wondered if anyone would bother to come to her own funeral and if anyone besides Saul would mourn her passing.

The service ended and Saul put his hand on Electra's elbow to help her out of the pew. Electra held herself staunchly erect and refused to allow her tears to fall. She hated any public show of emotions, and although the other mourners might think her unfeeling, there was nothing she could do about it. With dignity she left the church and got into the limousine supplied by the funeral home.

Saul sat beside her and took her hand. "Are you okay?"

Electra nodded, not trusting her voice to speak. She tightly held his hand.

"It will soon be over," he told her.

Because of the bitter cold, the graveside service was short. Amelia was buried in the family graveyard beside her parents and beneath the double head-stone she had erected long ago for Christopher. In the following week a stone-cutter would inscribe the date of her death beside her birth date. Christopher wasn't there, of course, Electra found herself remembering. His body had never been found to ship home. At the time this had made Amelia distraught, but that was before she became convinced Christopher's spirit, or ghost or whatever, was in her garden.

Electra closed her eyes as Reverend Payne started the final prayer. Maybe Amelia had been right, Electra thought. Certainly that belief had brought her comfort. She still remembered how Amelia had been almost smiling when Electra found her, and her arm had been outstretched as if she were reaching for something. Christopher?

Finally it was all over and the last of the guests departed Willowbrook. As Helga and the two maids began to clear away the paper plates and leftover food, Electra and Saul went into the parlor.

"You look exhausted," Saul said.

"I feel it." Electra sat in her father's wing chair and

leaned her head back. "I don't think I've ever been this tired."

"It was so unexpected."

Electra opened her eyes and looked up at Christopher's photos on the mantel. She had considered having them placed in the coffin with Amelia, but had decided that would appear too morbid. "Evidently Amelia had had some premonition of dying. She signed her will that morning and gave Helga the jewelry she was to inherit. Of all the places she would have chosen to die, she would have picked the garden. I considered having her cremated and sprinkling her ashes there, but Helga was so upset by the suggestion that I went the traditional route."

"Funerals are for the living. You did the right thing."

Electra looked over at him. "You've always stood by me. Even when you've disagreed with me, you've never deserted me."

"I love you," Saul said quietly. "You've done the same for me."

"I've been thinking," Electra said. "I don't want to stay here at Willowbrook now that Amelia's gone. I'm considering returning to New York."

"I wondered how long it would take you to decide that."

"Don't be smug. I still love Willowbrook, but . . . well, it belongs to my past."

He smiled at her.

"I called Olivia Simpson at the historical society and asked if they would be interested in taking the estate now. She practically jumped at the offer. I asked only that my room be excluded so I can still spend weekends here from time to time. She agreed."

"I doubt you can get your apartment back. Do you want

me to find you one before you come up?"

Electra looked down at the floral pattern on the rug. "No, I have something else in mind."

"Oh?" Saul asked warily.

"I thought I might move in with you. You know, get married and all."

Saul stared at her.

"We aren't getting any younger, Saul. I for one am tired of being alone."

"You're sure? I don't want you changing your mind at the last minute."

"I've had twenty-six years to consider your proposal, and I've decided to accept." Her eyes met his and she smiled.

"You have the strangest sense of timing I've ever seen. Maybe you're just feeling sentimental because of Amelia."

"I had considered doing this before she died," Electra confessed. "And I'll bet wherever she is, Amelia is laughing. She always said I was too logical for my own good, and she was probably right."

"When can you move back?"

"There's no reason for me not to fly back with you when you leave. Helga can see to packing my things. Will you still have me?"

"Damn right." Saul reached out, and she placed her hand in his. "After all these years I'm surprised you have to ask."

Electra felt more at peace than she had in years.

When it was time to say good-bye to Willowbrook, Electra walked one last time through the house, savoring its scents and memories. She would be back, of course, but it wouldn't be the same.

After she had seen each room, she took a small paper

bag from her bedroom and, putting it in her coat pocket, went outside. She circled the house, then went to Amelia's garden. The snow had melted enough for her to open the gate and go inside. She looked around, wondering why Amelia had become so attached to this place. As a girl Amelia had shown no inclination toward having a green thumb.

Inside the sheltering walls, the snow still lay in patches the sunlight had not found. Electra carefully picked her way over the slippery bricks. The ground looked dead and frozen, and the trees and bushes were bare except for the old gardenias and a few plants Electra didn't recognize. She saw nothing here that she couldn't find in other gardens closer to the house.

She bent beneath the leafless willow boughs and sat on the marble bench. She had so rarely been in the garden that she had trouble remembering how it looked when the plants were flowering. But it had been special to Amelia.

The cold from the marble was seeping into her body, so Electra stood and walked back to the gate. Again she paused and gazed at the enclosure. Amelia had always been romantic, and the hidden garden, with its plants and bench and sundial, was certainly a romantic setting.

Electra stepped outside and closed the heavy wooden gate. After a hesitation she reached into her pocket and pulled out the paper bag. From inside it she drew out a heavy-duty lock. She threaded it through the latch so that the gate couldn't be opened and snapped the lock shut. For a long minute she gazed down at the key in her palm, then raised her arm and tossed the key over the wall.

The Catawba Mills Historical Preservation Society could

have all the rest, but the walled garden belonged to Amelia.

Electra walked back to the house and Saul with a light heart. She was ready and eager to return to New York and her new start on life.

Lynda Trent is actually the husband and wife team of Dan and Lynda Trent.

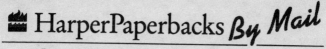

Y